Praise for Timothy S. Johnston

The War Beneath

"If you're looking for a techno-thriller combining I
Fleming, Tom Clancy and John Le Carré, 7
will satisfy . . . If you like action spy thrille
high tech in a science fiction setting this book
please. It's loads of fun. And fast-paced. Did I
paced? 'Cause it is." — Amazing Stories

"*The War Beneath* is a thrill ride from beginning to end, with several heart-stopping scenes that clearly illustrate the boundaries of underwater living and warfare . . . What I really enjoyed about the story, though, was the evolution of Mac, himself. The plot challenges his past, present and future and he has to decide not only who he is, but who he wants to be . . . " — SFcrowsnest

"... sit back, start reading and enjoy a deep sea dive into the future . . . One very riveting, intelligent read!" — 5 stars at Readers' Favorite

The Savage Deeps

"*The Savage Deeps* delivers on every level. The action is perilous, but not an exact repeat of what we've seen before. New technology abounds, all detailed with exhaustive research. Once again, Mac is the star of the production, a wonderfully complicated character written with delicacy. There is a point when you can push a character too far. Mac is nudged up against the edge and held there until you think he might break . . . The emotional impact of this book is just as compelling as in the first one."—SFcrowsnest

"*The Savage Deeps* is like a futuristic Das Boot with a lot of intense action and some interesting technology . . . I give *The Savage Deeps* a five star rating."—A-Thrill-A-Week

" . . . Johnston is an author skilled in bringing life to his characters through dialogue, engaging readers' emotions by their behaviors and thinking, and creating brilliant settings, all of which play out like scenes in a movie. Thinking of that, dare I suggest these two books are just ripe for becoming the next blockbuster movie? Food for thought!" — 5 stars at Readers' Favorite

Fatal Depth

"Timothy S. Johnston has the knack of getting the genre formula absolutely right in terms of balance. No one aspect hinders the others in any way. Plot, action, characterization, tech info, and originality are combined seamlessly into a tale that flows as rapidly as a river in flood. Some books are impossible to finish reading. This book is impossible to put down . . . " — Amazing Stories

"The excitement factor in *Fatal Depth* is no joke. You could almost compare it to a tsunami plow. The threads in the story culminate in an almighty push that will carry you all the way to the end in a dizzying rush. I read the second half of the book in one sitting . . . " — SFcrowsnest

"... heart-stopping action! Timothy S. Johnston is an incredible writer, word perfect, and so imaginatively creative one has to read his books to truly experience the cinematic aspects of his beloved underwater world. He builds tension with every chapter as his plot twists and turns throughout, and even the last page jolts us with an unexpected shock. Yet, somehow in the midst of all the dangerous excitement, his readers find themselves caught up in the emotional pasts and presents of his characters, but never at the loss of momentum or suspense. There's a reason Johnston was the winner of the **2018 Global Thriller Award**. Discover that reason for yourself when you read his entire *Rise of Oceania* series of books."
—5 Stars at Readers' Favorite

AN
ISLAND
OF
LIGHT

THE RISE OF OCEANIA

Fitzhenry & Whiteside

Published in Canada by Fitzhenry &
Whiteside
195 Allstate Parkway, Markham, ON
L3R 4T8

Published in the United States by
Fitzhenry & Whiteside
311 Washington Street, Brighton, MA
02135

Fitzhenry & Whiteside acknowledges
with thanks the Canada Council for
the Arts and the Ontario Arts Council
for their support of our publishing
program. We acknowledge the
financial support of the Government
of Canada through the Canada
Book Fund (CBF) for our publishing
activities.

ONTARIO ARTS COUNCIL
CONSEIL DES ARTS DE L'ONTARIO
an Ontario government agency
un organisme du gouvernement de l'Ontario

Canada Council   Conseil des arts
for the Arts   du Canada

Design by Ken Geniza
Interior schematics by Cheyney Steadman
Printed in Canada by Copywell

**Library and Archives Canada
Cataloguing in Publication**

Title: An island of light : the rise of
Oceania / Timothy S. Johnston.
Names: Johnston, Timothy S., 1970-
author.
Identifiers: Canadiana 20210361395 |
ISBN 9781554555819 (softcover)
Classification: LCC PS8619.O488 I85
2022 | DDC C813/.6—dc23

**Publisher Cataloging-in-Publication
Data (U.S.)**
Names: Johnston, Timothy S. 1970-,
author.
Title: Island of Light / by Timothy S.
Johnston.
Description: Markham, Ontario :
Fitzhenry & Whiteside, 2021. | Series:
Rise of Oceania. | Summary: "Murder,
a cover-up, an assassination attempt,
and the ultimate espionage ploy to
rescue Mayor Truman McClusky's
sister from agonizing torture by
the US Submarine Fleet in a heavily
guarded underwater prison. Mac has
to do it stealthily, but this time, war
with a rival nation is what he wants!"
-- Provided by publisher.
Identifiers: ISBN 978-1-55455-581-9
(paperback)
Subjects: LCSH: Submarines (Ships)
-- Fiction. | Espionage -- Fiction. |
Thrillers (Fiction). | Fantasy fiction.
| BISAC: FICTION / Science Fiction
/ Action & Adventure. | FICTION /
Thrillers / Military.
Classification: LCC PZ7.J646Is | DDC
813.6 – dc23

fitzhenry.ca

TIMOTHY S. JOHNSTON

AN
ISLAND
OF
LIGHT

THE RISE OF OCEANIA

Books by Timothy S. Johnston

The Rise of Oceania

THE WAR BENEATH
THE SAVAGE DEEPS
FATAL DEPTH
AN ISLAND OF LIGHT
THE SHADOW OF WAR (Forthcoming)
A BLANKET OF STEEL (Forthcoming)

The Tanner Sequence

THE FURNACE
THE FREEZER
THE VOID

Timeline of Events

2020
Despite the fact that global warming is the primary concern for the majority of the planet's population, still little is being done.

2055
Shipping begins to experience interruptions due to flooded docks and crane facilities. World markets fluctuate wildly.

2061
Rising ocean levels swamp Manhattan shore defences and disrupt Gulf Coast oil shipping; financial markets in North America become increasingly unstable due to flooding.

2062–2065
Encroaching water pounds major cities such as Mumbai, London, Miami, Jakarta, Tokyo, and Shanghai. The Marshall Islands, Tuvalu, and the Maldives disappear. Refugee problem escalates in Bangladesh; millions die.

2069
Shore defences everywhere are abandoned; massive numbers of people move inland. Inundated coastal cities become major disaster areas.

2071–2072
Market crash affects entire world; economic depression looms. Famine and desertification intensifies.

2073
Led by China, governments begin establishing settlements on continental shelves. The shallow water environment proves ideal for displaced populations, aquaculture, and as jump-off sites for mining ventures on the deep ocean abyssal plains.

2080
The number of people living on the ocean floor reaches 100,000.

2088

Flooding continues on land; the pressure to establish undersea colonies increases.

2090

Continental shelves are now home to twenty-three major cities and hundreds of deep-sea mining and research facilities. Resources harvested by the ocean inhabitants are now integral to national economies.

2093

Led by the American undersea cities of Trieste, Seascape, and Ballard, an independence movement begins.

2099

The CIA crushes the independence movement.

2128

Over ten million now populate the ocean floor in twenty-nine cities.

2129

Tensions between China and the United States, fueled by competition over The Iron Plains and a new Triestrian submarine propulsion system, skyrockets. The USSF occupies Trieste following The Second Battle of Trieste.

Winter 2130

Trieste Mayor Truman McClusky begins a new fight for Independence against the United States. With new deep-diving technology, he defeats French and US warsubs in battle in the Mid-Atlantic Ridge, killing Captain Franklin P. Heller.

Spring 2130

Russia launches dreadnought *Dragon*, a new terror in the oceans. She is 414 meters long, can travel 467 kph underwater, and possesses a new weapon: the Tsunami Plow. *Dragon* sinks many vessels and destroys the Australian underwater colony, Blue Downs. McClusky leads a raid to infiltrate and destroy the submarine.

June 2130

Present day.

"It is forbidden to kill; therefore

all murderers are punished unless

they kill in large numbers and to

the sound of trumpets."

—Voltaire

Prelude: The Murder

15 June 2130 AD

```
Location:          Latitude:      27° 34' 29" N
                   Longitude:     54° 56' 11" W
                   The Gulf of Mexico, Trieste City
                   Living Module B
Depth:             30 meters
Date:              15 June 2130
Time:              2200 hours
```

MEAGAN MCCLUSKY WAS ABOUT TO commit murder.

Premeditated murder.

It was a Thursday evening. Outside the module, the waters were warm and still. Inside the habitat, the sigh of the ventilation fans and pressure monitors created a steady *thrum* of white noise. There was the odd click of machinery meant to keep Trieste's inhabitants alive, a grinding of gears as bulkhead hatches slid open or shut somewhere on the same level, and the beeping of comms and the shuffling of feet on the deck nearby as her neighbors spoke with friends and colleagues, ended their day's activities, and conducted their bedtime routines.

It was enough to lull anyone to sleep at the end of a tough day.

Most anyone.

Meg's heart was pounding in her chest.

She could hear the blood coursing through her head; it was as if her ears were full of water, and each beat resonated loudly within her skull.

Her breathing was shallow and her muscles tense.

Her cabin was only four square meters. Two by two in size, with a bunk, a desk, and a drawer unit directly over her bed. It was miniscule, but that's how Triestrians lived. They rarely spent time sleeping; they were generally working hard to ensure that the colony thrived. Most were only in their bunks for a few hours a day.

But now Meg sat on the edge of her mattress and glanced around, wondering how she would kill a man in there quietly.

There was only one way, of course. The only reason for someone to enter a woman's cabin was for sex. Meg had heard enough of it during her time at Trieste. It was like living in a dorm at university. It was a single person's module, after all, with cabins packed tightly together, and it was impossible to suppress the noise of fucking completely. She often heard the moans of men and women echoing through the corridors of the module.

Her victim, Admiral Taurus T. Benning, had made his feelings obvious in the weeks prior. He always leered at Meg whenever they were together. His hungry eyes would drink her in as they moved upward from her thighs. They would linger on the curve of her hips and breasts before settling on her freckled face, blue eyes, and blonde hair. Then he'd cast his eyes downward again, back to her breasts before flicking again to her eyes.

And there was always that damned half-smile on his face as he did it, as if he knew what he was doing, and knew she was aware of it, but he didn't care. Why would he? He was one of the most powerful men in the Gulf and Caribbean regions.

Disgusting.

She didn't really give much thought to hiding the murder, covering it up, obscuring her motive. It was obvious to anyone who knew the situation.

She would just kill him and then worry about later.

She reached for the comm.

—••—

BENNING HAD A CABIN IN the city. He'd been staying there for a few days while healing from the recent injury during his mission to sink *Dragon*, the Russian dreadnought. He had sustained a gunshot wound to the leg, which the doctor had bandaged. It itched severely as his body repaired the damage; antibiotics were helping things along. He'd been lucky to survive the mission. He and seven others had infiltrated the massive warsub. They had made it to the reactor core, which they sabotaged, then engaged in a running gun battle with Russian crew through the ship while they figured a way out. The fact that the Russians had captured Benning during it all hadn't helped; thankfully, the Mayor of Trieste, Truman McClusky, had made it to the brig to rescue him and help him off the doomed vessel.

Now, five days after returning from the adventure, Benning lay in his narrow bunk, in Module C, staring at the bottom of the metal drawer just inches from his eyes.

His leg was aching.

He closed his eyes.

The comm beeped.

He glanced at the clock and swore. It was just after 2200 hours. His ship, *Devastator*, was still en route to the city from the battlefield in the South

Pacific, and they had been working on keeping the warsub seaworthy without him. They knew he was recovering from his injury. He doubted it was his XO.

"What do you want?" he grumbled.

"Hi."

It was a simple word, said without any emotion, but his eyes snapped fully open and in an instant, he was wide awake.

"Hello," he replied after a heartbeat.

—••—

MEG STARED AT THE COMM. *That was easy*, she thought. Men are so damn predictable. Always thinking with their cocks.

And in this case, it was going to get Benning killed.

Finally.

She'd tried to do it five days earlier, while on the Russian dreadnought, but hadn't been able to carry out her plan. It had been the perfect time and place. People would have assumed he'd died in the battle, drowned as the ship went down. But her twin brother, Truman McClusky, had stopped her.

He'd had second thoughts and knew that to kill an Admiral in the USSF would end up bringing the Fleet down on Trieste harder than ever. Cause another occupation perhaps.

He was probably right, and Meg gave in.

But each day that passed was harder than the one before. She couldn't stop thinking about Benning.

She couldn't continue with her own life at Trieste with Benning still there.

The conversation had been easy, if somewhat flat. She'd called Benning. He'd answered quickly enough—he hadn't been sleeping—and she'd invited him to her cabin. He'd paused, asked why, and she had stumbled through an excuse about needing to discuss recent events. She'd said she felt ashamed and needed to talk things through.

She knew he would come.

She looked down at her hands.

There was a long knife gripped between her sweaty fingers.

She exhaled harshly.

—••—

BENNING STARED AT THE COMM.

That was odd, he thought. But it did make sense. This woman had tried to kill him just a few days earlier. Maybe she was feeling some remorse. After all, he was the most powerful man in the region. Perhaps she was just realizing that.

He swung his legs off the bunk—grimacing as he did so—and threw on a light-colored shirt and loose-fitting pants. His uniform had not yet arrived, and he was wearing the only thing he had, provided by the clinic staff.

He checked his face in the mirror. As he did so, he thought about Meg McClusky. She was so damn beautiful. Maybe, just maybe, she was so remorseful she'd be willing to have sex with him.

Yes, he thought. He was the commanding officer of the entire United States Submarine Fleet in this region. If he used that against her, perhaps he could end up in her bed tonight. It would certainly help Trieste.

He'd make sure to tell her that.

He felt a pressure in his groin.

He slid open the partition and marched into the hall.

—••—

MEG HID THE KNIFE UNDER the pillow.

Then she stared at her bunk for a few seconds, hesitating. That was pretty damn obvious and cliché. She pulled it back out and put it in a drawer just above the bed. *That's better. Less obvious.*

Her heart was really pounding now. Her face was flushed. She wished she could splash some water on it, but the common restroom facilities were down the corridor.

She checked herself over, made sure her clothes accented her figure. Her shirt was tight. She looked good, but there were dark circles under her eyes.

Mac would point them out next time they saw each other.

The thought made her stomach drop.

Mac.

Her twin would not like what she was about to do. In fact, she was supposed to be with him at that exact moment; he was expecting her for drinks with the team at the pub. They'd survived the dangerous mission and were celebrating.

She shrugged the thought away.

It was 2230 hours.

—••—

BENNING APPROACHED HER CUBICLE. HE was limping, but he tried his best not to show it. He thrust his chest out and squared his shoulders.

The pressure was still there, in his groin. He'd been going over a rather incredible fantasy during his walk to the module.

5

He couldn't wait to see her.

He knocked on the partition.

It opened.

She was standing there, staring at him, in silence.

"Hello, Meg," he said in a soft voice.

She stepped aside.

He entered, and she closed the partition behind him.

———•••———

"WHY DO YOU WANT TO speak with me?" Benning asked. His voice was softer than normal, less forceful, and it took her aback for a second or two.

"To . . . apologize, I guess." Meg knew she had to seem contrite and demure. She had to get him to lower his guard, and had to get him into bed. Then she'd pretend to go to the drawer for a condom perhaps, and when he looked away, she'd make her move.

"You tried to kill me," he muttered. His voice was like gravel.

"I did."

"You were going to shoot me in the face."

"I was."

He was staring at her. The hardness so prevalent in his expression had returned, and she knew she had to get him to relax.

She sat on the bunk. The cabin was so small that he was standing directly before her. He shuffled slightly to the side and lowered himself into the metal chair before the desk. He turned it to face her.

She stared at the deck.

"You killed my father, Benning."

The man sighed. "We've been through this, Meg. On the warsub. It was thirty years ago. The CIA gave the USSF orders, and they told me to carry them out. Your dad was stirring up a hornet's nest here. We couldn't—"

"Don't lecture me!" Meg snapped. Then she paused and caught her breath. *Don't get emotional*, she thought. *Just get his guard down, then kill the fucker.* "I'm sorry," she said after a minute. He was just staring at her, waiting. "I know what happened. I've been dealing with it ever since. And I'm sorry that I let my emotions get out of hand."

"You were going to murder me in cold blood!" Now he was growing angry.

She held up her hand. "Don't, please. I can't take any more hatred or violence. I called you to apologize in person. I hate the person that I've become. I can't deal with it anymore. I just want to live in peace and see this underwater colony succeed." It was partly true, anyway.

Benning eyed her. "You want the USSF off your backs?"

"It would be nice."

"You want me and my ship away from here."

Meg shrugged.

He paused for a long minute and looked away. "Interesting. And what about what I did to your dad?"

"I have to just get over it. Mac was right. I need to forgive and forget. For Trieste's sake."

Benning nodded imperceptibly. Meg saw it from the corner of her eye. She knew what was going through the man's mind.

It made her snort inwardly. *Typical.*

—••—

BENNING SHIFTED IN HIS CHAIR as he stared at the bulkhead. Meagan McClusky was saying exactly what he needed to hear. A part of him realized that maybe she was playing him, using him.

But he didn't care. He'd just use her, too. Just get her into bed, get what he wanted, then he'd decide how much to give her. Maybe it would start up a pleasant partnership. Sex for Trieste.

Yes. His thoughts were dark. *Yes. I'll give Trieste more freedom. Stay away. But I'll come back once a week for a fuck.*

He turned back to her.

Now there was a smile on her face.

"The problem is this city and your brother. You are Americans. Trieste is an American colony. You can't have independence from America. That is why your dad died. We have to remain in the area to monitor you."

"But do you have to stay so close to us? It makes our citizens antsy."

Benning paused. She was stating her demands, but in a circuitous way. He had to draw it out of her. "What are you willing to do for Trieste?"

She glanced down at her bed.

That was all he needed.

He shifted to the bunk and sidled up next to her. She'd turned her eyes downward. Her freckles were so damn attractive, he thought. And her blue eyes . . .

And her breasts.

My god, her breasts.

He wanted to see her naked, and he was going to use his power over her.

"If I leave Trieste alone, will you be . . . *open* to me?" His question hung in the silence over them.

He waited.

"Yes, I will," she replied, her voice barely audible.

"And what about your dad?"

"I will never bring it up again."

"And my troops?"

"They can't stay here in the city."

Benning laughed. "That's a tall order! We are in the area. They need to unwind. To relax." He watched her closely. He was using this against her. He knew that she'd do anything to get him, his warsub, and his troops as far from Trieste as possible. "Besides," he continued, "the Russians are pressing. You know that. We have to patrol here from time to time. They're building three more dreadnoughts."

She blinked in surprise.

He had her, he knew.

Hook, line, and sinker.

She nodded and tilted her face to him.

He grabbed her head roughly in his hands and pulled her toward him.

He kissed her.

—••—

MEG ALMOST PUKED.

His hands were calloused and rough. His breath was disgusting. His skin was cold and his lips dry.

But she pretended to enjoy it. She breathed out slowly as they kissed. She flicked her tongue over his lips. She did everything she knew to do, and had to clamp down on her revulsion. The man was disgusting.

He had murdered her father.

He had locked him in a travel tube in the southeast quadrant of the city, back in 2099. He had shot him in the head, then flooded the tube just to make sure.

And now he was going to die.

Meg pushed Admiral Taurus T. Benning down on the bunk and straddled him. She lowered her face to his and continued the kiss.

It was almost time.

—••—

BENNING WAS THRILLED. IT HAD worked! And all he'd had to do was promise to stay away from Trieste, something he didn't really intend to do. After all, he'd grown aware of Truman McClusky's activities in recent weeks, and he knew that they'd prefer it if the USSF were not around. But all he wanted, at that moment, was to fuck this beautiful Triestrian woman. He would leave for a bit at a time, and then he'd return, ostensibly for some USSF order or something, and demand more sex. And if she didn't agree, he'd just ramp up their presence.

Easy.

She continued to kiss him, and he noted with satisfaction that she was pushing her hips downward now, rubbing against his erection. Dry humping him.

—••—

INSIDE, MEG WAS ON THE verge of screaming. Her skin crawled. This was the worst thing she'd experienced, but she was almost done.

She pulled away and glanced at the ceiling.

"The lights," she whispered.

He reached up and grabbed her breasts through her clothing. Roughly.

But she didn't resist. She forced a smile.

She got to her feet and turned the lights off.

—••—

BENNING PULLED OFF HIS SHIRT and flung it to the side. A string secured his pants at the waist; they were simple to pull off, so he just left them on. For now.

He couldn't see anything in the cabin anymore. The darkness was total.

He heard a drawer above his head open.

"What are you doing?" he hissed.

"I don't want to get pregnant," Meg replied.

Benning nodded. He would let her have this one concession, for now. But in the future, he would demand that they not use one. He'd give her some time to arrange an alternative.

The drawer closed and the bunk shifted as she lay down next to him.

"Take off your clothes," he grated.

There was a silence and she remained still, on the bunk.

Perhaps she wanted him to rip them off her, he thought.

So be it.

He grabbed her shirt and pulled it upward—

And there was a piercing, cold sensation in his chest.

He gasped.

—••—

MEG CLUTCHED THE KNIFE. SHE had practiced this earlier. She angled it upward, toward Benning's heart. She couldn't see—she was guessing where it was—and she pushed it savagely toward him. As she did, she couldn't prevent a cry of anger from escaping her lips.

There was little resistance as the knife sliced inward.

Benning grunted and instantly jerked backward, but the bunk was tiny and there was nowhere for him to go. She pushed harder and buried the weapon in bloody flesh. His back was pressed against the cold bulkhead. Then she pulled it out and did it again.

It slid in smoothly once more.

"You fucker," she hissed.

He attempted to cry out, but all that emerged was a gurgling, wet rasp.

She struck again and again. He was flailing now, trying to get away from her, but still she struck out in the darkness of the cubicle. He tried to slap the knife away, and she turned the sharp edge toward him and sliced into his skin. She felt the blade slide against the bone of his forearm. Then she struck his chest once more.

—••—

BENNING COULDN'T BELIEVE WHAT WAS happening. He thought she'd be open to his demands. He couldn't believe that she would actually risk her city by attacking him like this. He flailed against her as best he could, but the blade kept slicing his arms.

He was finding it difficult to breathe now.

The cabin was completely dark, and he was beginning to lose strength.

Dammit! he thought. *This is not happening!*

He swung with his right fist and connected with her face. At least, he thought it was her face. She grunted and fell back.

He pushed himself up. He felt gouts of hot blood spilling down his chest into his lap and around his buttocks on the mattress.

Then he felt the knife plunge into his chest once more.

He opened his mouth to scream, to call for help, but nothing came out.

It was so damn dark in there, he thought.

Why can't I breathe?

—••—

HE WAS GURGLING NOW. HE'D finally fallen back and wasn't resisting anymore.

She struck again and again, as hard as she could.

Then she aimed for his neck and stabbed there as well.

Finally, she stopped, her lungs heaving.

It was over.

She flicked the light back on and stared, horrified, at the scene before her. There was blood *everywhere*. It was on every surface. There were splatters on the bulkhead and the desk and the deck and the drawers. It was all over her arms and body. Benning was lying on the bunk, blood pooling around him, and there were open, gaping slices in his chest and torso. His jaw was slack, his eyes open and staring lifelessly, and his pants were wet with urine.

Meg continued to take in gasping breaths. She needed to calm herself. Already anyone outside may have heard, although someone passing in the hall may have misinterpreted the sounds as sex.

The thought of Taurus T. Benning lying in her bunk suddenly disgusted her. She grabbed his arm and pulled, sliding the corpse off her mattress and onto the deck.

Blood on the deck can be cleaned easier than from sheets.

Benning's leg remained on the bunk.

Then there was a sudden knock at the partition.

"Meg?" a voice called. "Are you there?"

Her heart caught in her throat. It was her brother, Truman. He'd been expecting to meet her . . . and she should have expected that he'd come to check on her.

Damn.

"Meg—I can hear you in there. Are you okay?"

"Don't open it, Tru! I'm—"

The partition slid aside, and her brother, the mayor of the underwater colony, stood framed in the opening. He was tall and broad and he filled the entire space.

His jaw dropped at the sight that met him. He scanned the interior without making a sound.

Meg rasped, "I'm sorry, Mac. I just couldn't get past what he did. I had to kill him."

TRIESTE

THE UNDERWATER CITY

LIVING MODULES

F E

D C

B A

COMMUNICATION MODULE

STORAGE MODULE

LOADING BAYS/
AQUACULTURE
VEHICLE MODULE

MECHANICAL/
REPAIR MODULE

BUSINESS /
COMMERCE
MODULE

AQUACULTURE
PROCESSING MODULE

DOCKING
MODULE

TRAVEL TUBES

RESEARCH MODULE

MINING INTERESTS MODULE
(Experimental)

NUCLEAR PLANT; 1100 MWe
(Buried)

DEPTH	*30 meters*
POPULATION	*215,000*
CITY SURROUND	*Fish and Kelp Farms*
LOCATION	*30 km West of Florida on the US Continental Shelf*

⊕ All modules contain moonpools, emergency hatches, and airlocks

⊕ Internal environment maintained at four atmospheric pressures (atms)

⊕ All modules and travel tubes are equipped with emergency watertight bulkhead hatches

0 m   200 m

Part One: Visitors

Two Weeks Later

30 June 2130 AD

Chapter One

THE BODY WAS ON MY mind.

I hadn't stopped thinking about it since that evening in Meg's cubicle.

The blood had been everywhere. She'd been like a woman possessed, and totally unlike the sister I knew and loved.

I had pushed her too far, I realized that now. The dream for independence, the fight against the USSF, the legacy of Dad's murder at the hands of the CIA thirty years ago . . . it was all too much for her to take.

And add to it the Russian destruction of Blue Downs two months before.

Meg had lived there for years, and she and I had watched the dreadnought destroy the city with its Tsunami Plow via a video broadcast from its Repair Module.

And now we were in the fight to create an independent nation on the seafloor, made up of the world's underwater colonies, right under the noses of the superpowers who settled the cities!

Maybe it was too much for me, too.

I definitely felt the stress of it all.

I was mayor of the city, and somehow had to keep it all a secret from the United States Submarine Fleet, the branch of US military who were always in the area, always leaving troops at Trieste who would harass our people, get drunk, cause damage, and start shit with good, law-abiding Triestrians.

I sighed.

But the real pressure on Meg had been Dad. He'd led the fight for independence in the early days of the colony, and once the CIA got wind of it, they'd killed him. It had shattered our family. Meg and I had been teenagers at the time—both fourteen years old—and our mother withdrew like a turtle into its shell. And with our father gone, our mother present but in name only, it was a horrible way to grow up during those final few years as we brushed the edges of adulthood.

Meg had fled to Blue Downs, the Australian underwater colony, where she had picked up the profession of aquanautic engineer, and I had finished university and then joined Trieste City Intelligence (TCI), the secret agency always fighting the superpowers and underwater cities to maintain advantages in technology and resource acquisition in the oceans.

But years later, Meg had returned with me to Trieste to continue Dad's struggle for independence.

And now the pressure had finally gotten to her. She'd needed to settle this one final score, atone for Dad's murder, and had ended up committing one herself.

I sighed again.

Johnny Chang, my deputy mayor, was sitting in the office with me. He was my former partner in TCI, and was now helping me run the city.

"You sound . . . preoccupied, Mac," he muttered as he eyed me.

I hadn't told him about the murder yet. "I guess."

"Too much work?" He gestured at the stack of papers and files in front of me.

"There's always too much."

"We could just set it aside. Go for a swim."

I glanced through the tiny viewport at the scene outside. The kelp farms were there, leafy vegetation swaying in the currents, seacars churning through our waters, bubbles rising serenely to the surface—which was only thirty meters above—fences of bubbles containing our stocks of fish, and the sun cutting through the water to the seafloor. It shimmered like diamonds in a floodlight.

His suggestion sounded excellent, actually. A swim always took my mind off things. I usually did a five kilometer loop around recognizable features outside. South to the big triangular rock, east to the old rusty anchor, north to the wrecked schooner, and so on. The route ended back at Trieste and was just over 5,000 meters. Many Triestrians had started to do it, and to begin the day by viewing the life surrounding us, touching the sandy seafloor, soaring through the kelp . . . it was marvellous.

I sighed again.

The body would still be in my thoughts, I knew. It wouldn't help.

Meg had shredded the man. The knife wounds had been all over his chest, forearms, and neck. I knew what our doctor would have said had she seen the corpse. Benning had fought back valiantly but hadn't had a chance.

I knew why she had done it—*I'd* wanted to do it, too!—but I thought I'd talked her out of it. The fact that she hadn't planned anything afterward was worrisome. No idea how to get rid of the body, nothing to clean the blood, no alibi . . .

It was frustrating.

I didn't feel any guilt for Benning's death. Meg's actions had actually lifted a weight from my chest.

But they had created another.

A very heavy one.

"Not today, Johnny," I finally managed.

He nodded. "Okay." He gestured at the paper before me. "Let's keep going over that, then. I am still not understanding it."

I glanced at the order. "I need a zircon mine."

"I see that. But the only deposit we know of is in The Iron Plains. You know that the US, China, and Russia are all arguing for rights to that area right now. And you want to just go there and plop a mining facility down right in the middle of it all? Ships are disappearing there! It'll—"

"I know, but zircon is essential."

"You still haven't told me why."

I glanced at my watch. "You'll know why very soon."

That made him blink. "But Mac, the location—"

"We have no choice. If that's the only location, then that's where the mine will be."

He rose and started to pace the tight confines of my office. We were in the central Commerce Module, at its highest deck, just outside of City Control. "First," he said as he ticked the items off on his fingers, "the countries who are contesting the area are not just going to sit back as Trieste starts a mining settlement in a place they believe belongs to them. Second, the depth is too great for a manned operation! It's at five kilometers, Mac!"

"We've got the new syntactic foam. Meg says it'll work at that depth." *That's why we stole it from the French*, I wanted to add.

"Third," he pressed, "it's too far from us. It's near the Philippines for Christ's sake! We're off the coast of Florida here. If our people need help, there's no one nearby."

"I know that. Trust me, I know."

"Four, I have no idea why you need it. It's not useful for us in any way."

"Water and air purification, mostly."

He stopped pacing and turned to me. "But we import items we need for that. We don't need zircon—"

"Let's just call Laura Sukovski, okay? Find out more." I couldn't hold it against Johnny. He was just doing his job as my deputy mayor.

Laura was in charge of the Mining Interests Division. Whenever I needed more of a certain mineral, I reached out to her.

She hated it.

Sure enough, when her face appeared on my comm, she scowled. "Mac. To what do I owe the pleasure?" She was in her office. Behind her, a featureless steel bulkhead. There were papers on her desk. And then her expression dropped. "You're not calling to increase quotas again, are you? Mac! That would crush—"

"I'm just calling to see about mining a zircon deposit."

She paused and leaned back. "But why do we need zircon?"

Next to me, I could feel Johnny laughing inwardly. Now it was my turn to scowl. "Look, I'm just curious how soon we can get working on it."

"Ah, come on, Mac!" she snapped. "You know the closest one is in The Iron Plains. You're really serious about this?"

"I am."

"It's dangerous! The Chinese, Russians, the—"

"I know all about it. How soon can you launch the mission?"

She stopped and stared at me. A long silence stretched out between us. "I guess in a few days. But don't give me any ridiculous deadlines. I can't handle that this time."

"We'll see," I muttered. I reached out to cut the signal, and—

"Hey, what's going on with all the questions?"

That took me aback. "What?"

"From the USSF."

I leaned forward. "Laura, what are you talking about?"

She narrowed her eyes as she studied me. "You didn't know? A woman from the USSF contacted me a few days ago. Asking me all sorts of things about you."

"What, exactly?"

"If you ever give me weird orders." She snorted. "Like this zircon one. Or that thorium one you gave me a few months back."

"And what did you say?"

She grew suddenly serious. "Mac, I lied, don't worry. I trust you implicitly. You're keeping us safe. But the questions were odd, that's all. They asked about Meg, too."

A shiver worked its way down my spine. "Continue."

"She was asking about your sister's behaviour lately. Her state of mind. As if I'd know."

I shifted in my chair. But it meant that if Laura had received a call, then others at Trieste probably had, too. "And she was from the Fleet?"

Laura frowned. "Well, she was in a warsub, I could see that. She wasn't wearing the uniform though, now that you mention it."

"Thanks, Laura. Keep me updated on the zircon mine."

I keyed off and stared at Johnny.

He met my eyes and remained silent, but I knew what he was thinking.

——••——

THE COMM BEEPED AND KRISTEN Canvel's voice echoed from the speaker. She was just outside my office, in City Control, and was in charge of the City Systems Control department. The position also meant she was my assistant. She was highly professional and efficient; she did her job well, never missing a deadline or messing up a procedure, though she didn't know anything about TCI or our quest for independence.

Very few knew about that.

"Mac," she said. "We have two contacts approaching the city."

I frowned. I wondered why she was telling me and not Grant Bell in Sea Traffic Control. "Go on."

"The first is a USSF attack sub. The computer has it listed as a *Matrix* Class warsub. USS *Blade*."

I glanced at Johnny. So, here it was. First Laura's cryptic comments and now this. The first signs of the USSF since Benning had . . . *disappeared*.

My guts slithered.

"And the second?" I asked in a quiet voice.

"A private seacar from the mainland. A man is asking to dock and then come up to see you."

"Name?"

"Max Hyland."

I nodded. So, here he was. Finally. "Thanks, Kristen. We'll deal with the USSF first. Keep Hyland separated from them for now. Maybe in a lounge somewhere. I'll find him when we're done with the warsub."

She clicked off and I noted Johnny staring at me.

"Is this about the zircon?" he asked.

"It is."

His face flattened. I knew he'd be happy to finally get some answers.

"And the USSF?"

"Probably about Benning."

Johnny frowned. "Weird that he suddenly got up and left the city."

"It is, isn't it." It wasn't a question, and Johnny snapped a look at me.

"You don't happen to know anything, do you?"

"If I did, I wouldn't say anything."

"Not even to your deputy mayor? Your former partner? Your best friend?"

"I wouldn't want to get you involved." Johnny knew what had almost happened on the Russian dreadnought. Knew that Meg had almost killed Admiral

Benning. But when Benning had gone missing from Trieste, no one had really given it much thought. We were all happy that he was gone, and Johnny hadn't pressed on it.

But now, I knew, he would.

Especially with *Blade* showing up.

I pushed myself to my feet. "We better get down to the umbilical. They'll be docking soon."

—••—

WARSUBS LIKE USS *BLADE* WERE too large to enter our Docking Module, rise through the moonpool, surface, and debark people like a seacar. Instead we had to extend an umbilical to one of her airlocks and sailors could march over to the underwater colony that way. Since we standardized all vessels, cities, and habitats at four atms, it made movement around the oceans far more efficient. No depressurization needed.

Blade was sixty meters long with a top speed of seventy kph. She could hit a max depth of 3,200 meters and had one large screw at its stern. There were fifty-two of that warsub class in the USSF. These facts I had memorized years earlier and filed them away due to my position as Director of TCI.

It wasn't the largest warsub in the USSF, so I wasn't too concerned about who might be arriving. Usually admirals and senior leadership in the US military sailed on board the largest, most deadly classes of subs: *Reapers*, *Doomsdays*, and *Terminators*, for instance.

Johnny and I stood waiting for the umbilical to mate with the warsub. Beside us, a technician was operating the controls and a whine echoed through the corridor as he extended the tube. At our feet, the deck vibrated. The view outside the deck-to-ceiling port was magnificent. Myriad fish swam about, investigating the large vessel outside. Scuba divers had also approached so they could get a close look at the vessel—no doubt they were pissed about more USSF presence at the city—and seacars flitted about, performing routine maintenance on the city and our farms. Kelp production continued on a daily basis—it was the reason for our existence on the shallow continental shelf, for we converted it into a variety of foodstuffs and shipped it out for further processing into methane for topside nations, though lately the United Sates had been taking most of it for a very reduced price, which angered me.

There were even some wildlife wranglers outside, wearing bright orange vests.

I wondered absently if someone had spotted a large shark in the region. We always had to be on the lookout for danger, especially as we had school classes outside on a daily basis, exploring the geography of our city and getting the kids accustomed to the life that we had carved for ourselves in this unique environment.

Global warming topside had ensured our continued existence here. The land nations were suffering. Cropland was dying, populations exploding . . . it was all falling apart up there, I thought absently. Bangladesh was gone, as were all low-lying island nations. Coastal cities were inundated where there were no walls to stop the floodwaters. Riots, governments falling to dictatorships and extremists, a lack of resources. Empty shelves in grocery stores.

The need for expansion in the oceans was pressing, and we were at the forefront of it all.

But there was a growing call from our citizens for independence.

I couldn't let the USSF know. That would spell disaster.

I swallowed.

Johnny was watching me from the corner of his eye. "So who is Max Hyland?" he muttered.

"A scientist. We'll meet him after this."

He nodded. "He's going to help us?"

"Yes." I left it at that.

Soon the umbilical had mated with the airlock, there was a *thunk* as the warsub's hatch ground aside and locked into place, and a group of figures emerged from the USSF vessel and marched toward us. We could only see their distorted shadows, and we waited patiently for our own hatch to slide open.

Outside, scuba divers watched the USSF sailors cross the umbilical.

It was almost comical.

They hung suspended just inches from the transparent material, bubbles soaring upward from their regulators, to see the figures within.

The hatch opened.

I gasped.

————••————

HER NAME WAS LUCILLE QUINTANA.

Admiral Lucille Quintana.

My earlier thought that a senior official would not be in a less-than-impressive USSF warsub had been incorrect. Quintana was the only Fleet Admiral in the United States, a member of the president's Joint Chiefs of Staff, and other than the president, she had more influence over military direction in the oceans than any other American.

She was a five-star admiral.

I'd seen her numerous times on the news, at the president's side, sitting around the table in the war-room, and so on.

And now she was here, at Trieste.

What the hell?

I glanced sideways at Johnny. He had paled and his jaw was slack.

I steeled myself and stepped forward. "Admiral Quintana. We didn't expect you. Welcome to Trieste."

She stopped before me and eyed me in silence. Her face was flat and emotionless. She wore the form-fitting blue uniform of the USSF, the customary symbolic dagger of scuba divers on her thigh, and her gray-streaked brunette hair was pulled back into a tight ponytail.

"So this is Truman McClusky," she finally muttered. Her voice was soft but pointed at the same time.

"I am."

"Your father led the independence movement against us many years ago."

It was a topic that made me uncomfortable—one of those things that wasn't spoken about in open conversation, especially with a fleet admiral in the USSF. Inwardly, I groaned. This was not the direction I wanted the conversation to take. I said, "He paid the price for his actions. I just want to see Trieste continue to contribute now."

Her lips peeled back into a thin smile, but I could tell it was far from genuine. "Good answer." She turned to Johnny. "And you are?"

"I'm the deputy mayor here. John."

She stared at him for a painful heartbeat. I had no doubt that she knew exactly who he was: a former traitor to Trieste. He had defected to a Chinese underwater city years earlier before I'd lured him back.

She turned to me. "You keep interesting company, McClusky."

I decided to ignore the comment. Instead, I glanced at the three people at her side. Two were obviously guards. Likely SEALs, highly trained and deadly in combat. They wore body armor and helmets. Their eyes were like lasers as they studied me.

No doubt they knew me by reputation.

The other was a slight woman, willowy even, with long, feathery blonde hair. She had piercing eyes and she was staring at me intently. "And you are?" I asked.

"I'm Agent-Investigator Eleanor Zyvinski."

"Investigator?" I frowned. "CIA?"

"Yes."

There was a long silence as we processed that information. I stared from one to another and back again. Finally, I said, "What are you investigating?"

Zyvinski answered without hesitating. "The disappearance of Admiral Taurus T. Benning. Last known location Trieste City, Module C. Now he's missing, and no one knows where he is." She paused and then, "We suspect foul play."

Chapter Two

HER STATEMENT HIT LIKE THUNDER. I struggled to keep my face emotionless, but inside I was shaking. Both women were staring at me intently, studying my reaction. Luckily, I had trained for many years with TCI to keep such reactions from showing.

Johnny, on the other hand, was shocked. I'd kept the secret for this exact reason. "He's not here anymore."

"We know that."

I said, "He left on his own two weeks ago."

"He did?" Zyvinski said. Her voice was like a reed, a hiss almost. "How do you know this?"

Johnny said, "He was in Trieste, recovering from the mission to the dreadnought. He'd been shot in the leg. Our doctor had treated him. I was with him on the mission. We both were." Johnny gestured at me.

"He fought with us side-by-side," I added. "We made it back here safely. Then, five days after arriving, he left."

"He just . . . left?"

I shrugged. "He didn't tell anyone. He didn't have to. He's an admiral in the USSF."

There was another long silence as the investigator and the admiral stared at us, then at each other.

"I guess we'll find out," Admiral Quintana said finally. "The investigator is here to find out where he is. She is extraordinarily proficient at her job. She'll uncover the truth."

There was another painful silence. Johnny looked confused and stunned. It was a perfect response: truthful and genuine. They would not suspect him.

I, on the other hand, was a different story. I had a guarded, calm expression on my face. No doubt they would be asking me questions. Soon.

"We will be staying on our ship," Zyvinski rasped. "I'll cross over to conduct interviews. I'll want to know where he was on his final day here, and what his routine had been for the five days in Trieste."

"I'll connect you with our security chief, Cliff Sim. He can help you with anything you need."

The two nodded, spun on their heels, and marched back through the hatch and into the umbilical, followed by the SEALs.

—••—

"WELL THAT WAS SHOCKING," JOHNNY muttered.

I grabbed his elbow and led him away. We moved through the travel tube back toward the Commerce Module. The tubes were three meters high with curving, transparent ceilings. The deck was a conveyor that carried us quickly from one module to another. Outside, the sun's rays pierced downward and fish darted about. Despite the beauty of the scene, my guts ached and my stomach was in my throat.

We were in serious trouble.

Meg and I were, at least.

Johnny was staring at me. "Mac, you don't know where Benning is, do you?"

"I might."

"What happ—"

"Not now. Your reaction was perfect and it was what I wanted."

He blinked. "It's why you kept me in the dark?"

"Yes."

"But where did—"

"I said *later*. For now, we have to go meet Max Hyland. And then I want you to get the zircon mine up and running."

"But what about *Blade*? She's here now. *They're* here. The CIA. And things are not going to be easy."

No, they're not, I wanted to say. But I held my tongue.

—••—

KRISTEN CANVEL HAD CALLED FOR an escort to direct Max Hyland to a lounge in the Commerce Module. The module was the largest in Trieste. Five stories up and four down into bedrock, it was nine stories in total with a large skylight at the top. Natural sunlight penetrated straight down, filtering into every shop and office and restaurant and bar in the city. The central area of the module was totally open from Decks One to Nine, and vines and plants covered the perimeter railing, intertwined among its metal spindles. It was a breathtaking scene.

Modules made up the underwater colony of Trieste. Travel tubes connected them so we could easily walk from one to another. The city was at thirty meters depth—or a hundred feet—which meant the outside pressure was at four atmospheres. For this reason, the interior environment was kept at the same pressure so our structures wouldn't implode. We even had moonpools in every module—open water at the lowest decks. Since the pressure inside perfectly balanced the outside, water didn't rush in and air didn't rush out. We could dive into the pools and swim outside without tanks. The salt made us buoyant, though; we'd rise quickly upward without weight belts.

And certain death awaited us at the surface: the bends.

Our tissues were saturated with gases at four atms. To travel to the surface safely meant a hundred hours of decompression.

We were trapped in the oceans, as were all other undersea inhabitants, as well as members of the world's various submarine fleets.

There were fifteen major modules in the city. Six of them were the living habitats for Triestrians; there were over 200,000 people there. All worked with the same goal in mind: to extract resources from the surrounding waters to ensure our usefulness to the United States, our colonizing nation. We fished, grew and harvested kelp, and drilled for minerals.

The increasing movement for independence always weighed me down, because I was the person in charge of our intelligence agency—TCI—and if the USSF found out, they'd arrest me for treason.

As Johnny and I marched toward the lounge and the meeting with our guest, I noticed he was darting glances in my direction, but he kept his lips pressed tightly together.

"What is it?" I asked eventually.

Johnny and I had been through a lot together. Former partners in TCI, then adversaries when he'd defected to the Chinese underwater colony, Sheng City, then friends when he'd ended up back in Trieste, working with me to achieve independence and gain allies in the underwater quest for *Oceania*, a network of cities to benefit each other instead of the topside nations. Now he was my deputy mayor.

He pulled to a halt just outside our destination. He leaned against the bulkhead and crossed his arms. Around us, Triestrians were going about their daily business: lugging scuba tanks to their work on the farms, running the stores and offices and restaurants of the Commerce Module, returning from work, anxious to catch a few hours' sleep before the next day, or getting some R & R on their breaks before their next shift.

We operated on a three-shift day, each made up of eight hours. Triestrians worked for eight hours, then got the next two shifts off. Generally, they used one for sleep, and the third they spent volunteering at another job elsewhere in the colony. There were many families and children living with us, so there was lots of work to do.

"What?" I asked again.

Johnny said, "We are in serious shit here." I pursed my lips but didn't respond. He stared at me. "Aren't you going to say something?"

"You mean about Quintana? She'll be here for a bit, then she'll leave."

His jaw dropped. "But they mean to take over Seascape. That's where the next USSF HQ is going to be. Everyone is talking about it."

He was correct. Since the Russian dreadnought had destroyed both the Atlantic and the Pacific headquarters for the USSF, senior administration needed to locate a new base of operations, and soon. I'd been hearing rumblings that it would be Seascape, and others had, too.

I said, "We'll deal with it when it happens."

"Do you have a plan?"

I shook my head.

"And now Quintana is *here*. At Trieste! And she's brought a CIA investigator with her! This Zyvinski person."

"I am aware, Johnny. Trust me."

He eyed me for a long, painful heartbeat. "You know where Benning is. It's going to cause serious trouble for us if you don't tell them."

"I'm aware of that, too. I didn't want this to happen."

"What did happen, exactly?"

I ground my teeth as I studied the man. I knew I could trust him implicitly, but I'd been hoping to keep this quiet for as long as possible. Forever, I had hoped. "He's dead," I whispered, glancing around to make sure no one could hear us.

Johnny's face dropped. He mouthed the word and then shook it off. "But I thought you'd decided not to kill—"

"I had."

He stared at me for a brief second before realization hit. "Holy shit." He looked away. "Meg did it. She wanted him dead. We all knew it."

I raised my finger. "No. Only those of us on the mission to the dreadnought knew it. Now I have to keep it contained. Somehow."

He remained silent as he mulled it over. "You need to speak to Cliff. Get him to help you."

Cliff Sim was in charge of our security at Trieste. He was former USSF, but now totally devoted to Trieste and our struggles in the ocean, both internal and external.

He was also a part of TCI.

"I'll speak with him as soon as this meeting is over."

Johnny glanced into the lounge. We could see a man sitting at a low table. It was the scientist, Max Hyland. "Is he involved in Benning's . . . disappearance?"

"No. He's here for another reason."

"Being?"

I forced a grin. "Come on, buddy. Let's go chat. I think you'll find it interesting."

And it would take my mind off Quintana and Zyvinski.

For a little bit, at least.

—••—

MAX HYLAND ROSE TO HIS feet as we entered. Kristen had emptied the lounge for our use, so it was only the three of us in there.

I locked the hatch behind us, though the expansive windows that allowed sunlight to filter in allowed anyone who passed by to see us speaking.

"Hello, doctor," I said. I shook his hand. "I'm Truman McClusky."

He was just under six feet with a square jaw and a charming smile. He had brown hair, dimples, and a five o'clock shadow. He was forty-three years old and held himself with an air of confidence. I liked him immediately.

"I appreciate you calling me," he said.

I introduced Johnny and we lowered ourselves into the chairs surrounding the table. Kristen had arranged some empty glasses and a pitcher of ice water. I poured the drinks and raised my glass. "Thanks for coming all this way."

He grinned. "I wouldn't have missed it! I've wanted to see the underwater colonies for decades. Never got around to it."

"How is it?"

"Incredible. The views outside are astonishing."

"Care to take a swim later?"

His smile grew broader. "I'd love to." There was a viewport in the lounge, and he gestured at it. "I can't wait." Then he turned back to me. "And to meet Truman McClusky in person . . . I just couldn't say no. I know all about you, your dad, your history at Trieste, and your dad's fight for independence."

I remained silent at that. I still found discussing my father a challenge.

Johnny was watching the exchange with interest. I knew he was dying of curiosity. "How can we help you?" he interjected.

A look of confusion spread across Hyland's features.

I said, "I invited the doctor to visit."

"Please, just call me Max. Or Hyland. 'Doctor' is too formal."

"Okay, Max."

Johnny was still staring at us. "So . . . " he prompted.

It made me chuckle. Johnny was still reeling from the USSF presence, and he was trying desperately to figure out what was going on here.

"When we got back from the mission to the dreadnought, I knew we needed more help," I said.

"Military help?"

"Yes. We've got a huge dilemma before us. We couldn't sink the dreadnought with conventional torpedoes."

Hyland leaned toward us. "Let me finish for you, Mac. The Russian warsub had devastated the US coast in Virginia and California. Someone had to destroy it. But how? The submarine was so huge and compartmentalized that it didn't matter how many holes you put in it, there would still be a core interior pressurized at four atms which would keep the ship afloat."

I nodded. "Go on."

"And even if the buoyancy grew to negative, if she had thruster power she could just use her control surfaces to maintain depth, or make it to the surface with ballast purged. Am I right?"

"So far."

"So you considered nukes. But that would cause other issues. Mainly, it could start a major nuclear conflict underwater—"

"And on land."

"—which you want to avoid, and smartly so." He grinned. "So you ended up sinking it by . . .?"

"I caused a meltdown in the fission core. The corium—"

His eyes widened. "Melted through the interior and destroyed compartmentalization." He shook his head. "Brilliant, but difficult."

"It was indeed."

His eyes narrowed as he studied me. "So you infiltrated the sub and managed to do that?"

"Yes."

"I think my way is easier." Then he laughed.

"Well, I have done my research, that's for sure."

"But most people see me as a crackpot now." He shrugged. "I've been blacklisted by every university. The academic journals won't publish me anymore."

"But others have confirmed your work, correct?"

He offered the hint of a smile. "Some groups have confirmed, but the work is so sensitive and the ramifications so huge that they can't publicly admit it. They don't want to be blacklisted, either."

Johnny had an expression of utter confusion on his face. "What work? And what do you mean, your way is easier?"

"The problem," Hyland continued, "is that you need a bomb big enough to take out a dreadnought, but one that can't be nuclear. It has to skirt the non-proliferation treaty so other nations won't get upset with you. It has to have enough force to penetrate multiple hulls and render a warsub of that size negatively buoyant without starting a war that'll leave the Earth irradiated. It also has to be an explosive that is small enough to be manageable, meaning something that can go in a briefcase—"

"A torpedo," I injected.

"Yes, a torpedo. Small, but with a massive punch. Like Bruce Lee."

Johnny said, "And you have such a thing?"

Hyland shrugged. "I was on track. I had published my findings. Then most others in the scientific community couldn't replicate my experiments. They compared it to cold fusion."

He was referring to an experiment published in 1989. Fusion was a nuclear process that took place at temperatures in excess of a hundred million degrees. In it, atoms of hydrogen fused to form helium and energy. It's how our reactors worked, and how our superfast SCAV drive worked, as well. But the crucial requirement is reaching that temperature. Back in the late '80s, scientists Martin Fleischmann and Stanley Pons claimed to have achieved the process at room temperatures. This would have transformed the world's economy, eliminated the burning of fossil fuels, and shifted our energy production to something clean and safe. In short, it might have stopped global warming and slowed the rising waters. Other scientists, however, were unable to replicate the experiments and called the science *pathological*, meaning it had tricked people into believing they'd achieved the desired results due to wishful thinking.

In reality, the scientists hadn't achieved cold fusion at all.

There were still researchers working on it, even after all these years, with no significant developments since those initial experiments in 1989. There had been an ongoing quest to create hydrinos by lowering hydrogen electrons below ground state, but that was also proving difficult. People involved in that quest believed they'd created dark matter.

Johnny said, "And scientists have compared your work to . . . to—"

"Cold fusion. Yes." He winced. "It ended my career. I still work on it, of course. In my house, in my lab. But I've lost all funding, but there are others in the community who still believe."

"Believe in what?"

Hyland blinked in confusion. "My bomb, of course. That it will work."

Johnny was processing this. "A bomb that generates a nuclear-scale explosion, but not a nuclear reaction."

"Exactly! And it won't give off any radiation byproducts, either—after the initial blast anyway—so no nation will come on the scene later and suspect that you used a nuke."

"And it's not a nuclear bomb?" he repeated.

"No. Definitely not."

Johnny glanced at me. "Why are you investigating this?"

I said, "Because two weeks ago I found out that Russia is working on three more dreadnoughts. They'll put to sea soon."

A look of shock exploded across his features. It was yet another crushing development. The Russians were very angry with us after what had happened. Hell, add them to the list, I thought. The French still wanted to kill me, the Chinese, and now the Russians did, as well.

My quest to form the underwater nation of Oceania had ensured a steady stream of enemies.

The superpowers hated me. And if some hadn't yet figured it out, they would soon.

"You're serious? How'd you find out?"

I almost said, *Because that's what Benning told Meg before she stabbed him to death*, but I didn't. I settled on, "I suspect. But there are other enemies out there, Johnny. You know that. We always have to be prepared, and we always need to stay ahead of the competition."

"Yes, I agree."

Of course he would. TCI had to make sure that Trieste stayed ahead of the pack. To make sure we continued to prosper and stay at the forefront of ocean exploration technology.

And ocean defence.

It's why we had acquired the supercavitating drive, the invention that allowed our subs to travel upwards of 500 kph underwater.

And the new syntactic foam, able to withstand greater pressures, so our vessels and deep exploration habitats could remain at greater depths than ever before.

And the Acoustic Pulse Drive, which allowed our subs to go deeper than any other vehicles in the oceans.

We had to continue pushing the limits of our technology. If we ever sat back, the other underwater colonies and superpowers would pass us in the quest to colonize the ocean floors, and that would render Trieste useless.

And put a swift halt to my fight for independence.

Johnny said to Hyland, "And what is this bomb you're trying to develop?"

"Well, if you'll let me stay, and if you'll fund my work, I'll continue on it here.

I'll live in Trieste. Gladly. But I can't promise anything yet."

"You mean you haven't succeeded?" Johnny said.

"No, no. Remember, the academic community blacklisted me! I have been unable to finish my work."

My deputy mayor turned to look at me, his mouth agape. I smiled at him.

"So there is no bomb?" he asked.

"Not yet. But I'm hoping there will be soon."

"And what's it called?" he asked again.

Doctor Max Hyland grinned. "It's called an Isomer Bomb."

Chapter Three

I ASKED KRISTEN CANVEL TO set Max Hyland up in a cabin and give him some space in our Research Module. I still had to discuss with him what he needed for his work, but for now I'd let him get settled before diving in a little deeper with his requirements. His grin was effusive—and in fact, *infectious*—and it thrilled me that he was going to stay and work with us.

Trieste seemed to have that effect on people. They came to help our struggle underwater, and despite the hardships—the cramped conditions, the lack of open living space, the lack of simple luxuries like a wide variety of food, the omnipresent danger from pressure and living in a saturation environment—they always seemed to love being underwater with us. I'd seen it with Katherine Wells, the inventor of our SCAV drive. I'd seen in with Manesh Lazlow, who had invented the Acoustic Pulse Drive, and with Renée Féroce, the former French captain who now lived with us and operated the Trieste City defence network surrounding the colony.

And now we'd added Max Hyland to the fold.

If he could finish his work on the Isomer Bomb.

The thought reminded me that I had to speak with Renée and the others, to inform them about the new threats from Russia and warn them about the USSF's presence.

Outside the lounge, following the meeting with Hyland, I mentioned this to Johnny. He agreed with me, and we set a time for a meeting.

Then I went to see the Chief Security Officer at Trieste, Cliff Sim.

—••—

HIS OFFICE WAS JUST DOWN the corridor from City Control, on the highest deck in the central Commerce Module. He was in his office, and he barely looked up as I entered and took a seat before him.

He was broad shouldered and muscular. His mannerisms were curt—abrupt even—and he was absolutely loyal to Trieste and me. He was a former military man—the USSF. He had left the service after the action in 2099 resulted in my father's assassination. He'd come to Trieste to work security, and now headed up the division.

It was a tough job, because whenever the USSF docked with us, their sailors would cross over and cause all sorts of trouble. Drinking, fighting, looting . . . the list went on and on. There had even been assaults, rapes, and murders. Cliff's job wasn't easy. I'd compounded his responsibilities when I'd brought him into TCI and had started sending him out on missions.

Cliff was absolutely dependable, and now I needed his help more than ever.

—••—

"WHY DIDN'T YOU SPEAK TO me earlier?" he said in a flat, toneless voice.

I snorted. "You mean you already knew?"

"Benning got up and disappeared one day. Of course I looked into it."

"Without me asking?"

"He was the senior USSF officer in the region. We'd just come back from the mission to destroy the dreadnought. He'd been shot and he was recovering here. And then one evening . . . gone. Of course I had to investigate."

I shifted in my chair. I studied the man while a painful silence hung over us. I noted that he'd used the past tense when referring to Benning. But Cliff still hadn't looked at me. "And what did you find?"

He put down the papers he'd been studying, leaned back, and finally settled his gaze on me. "Where's Meg, Boss?"

Inwardly, I groaned. So, he knew. I shrugged. "She's here. In Trieste. Working on sub repairs and maintenance, as usual."

"A USSF warsub has docked with us. USS *Blade*. *Matrix* Class."

"I met their envoy today."

"They're here to investigate Benning's disappearance?"

"They are."

"Interesting." He stared at the metal ceiling over our heads. "So they'll come and speak with me soon?"

"Without much question."

"And who's in charge?"

"Admiral Quintana and Investigator Zyvinski."

Cliff Sim's usual emotionless countenance cracked. He blinked and a look of utter shock exploded across his features. "You're serious?" he finally managed.

I sighed. "I am, Cliff. I spoke with both of them."

He shook his head. "This is . . . not a good development."

"No."

Another long and dark silence descended over us. I just watched him while the gears worked in his head. Quintana was the president's USSF representative. A member of the Joint Chiefs, no less! Finally he muttered, "Tell me what happened."

"I'm not sure you want to know too much, Cliff."

"I can guess. But if I can, surely *they* can, as well. After all, Meg made her intentions clear."

"I thought I had convinced her."

He stared at me, incredulous. "Mac, this kind of thing doesn't just *go away*. The man killed your father. Meg's been stewing about it for thirty years. Then she finally gets an opportunity for revenge. You talking to her for thirty seconds won't just magically change her mind."

I shrugged. "I thought it had. I thought I'd made an impact. It's not easy killing someone." My voice trailed off. I just couldn't believe what I'd gotten myself—

No, I reminded myself. Not what *I'd* gotten myself into. What *Meg* had gotten me into.

"You've killed a lot," Cliff continued. "So have I, in my time with the USSF and now with TCI. You're right, we carry a lot of weight because of it. But Meg carried a weight greater than the consequences."

"We should have followed up on it, you're right. Gotten her some counseling."

He eyed me. "And you?"

"What do you mean?"

"Do you need counseling? After the things you've been through? After the USSF warsubs you've sunk? Kat's death? Do you carry pain like Meg does?"

The question shook me. My throat tightened at Kat's name.

I rose to my feet and paced before the desk.

Cliff just watched.

Months earlier, I'd faced French and US warsubs in the Mid-Atlantic Ridge. Katherine Wells had died in the fighting. I'd sunk many vessels and killed hundreds of sailors, just to keep our research base there a secret. To hide our quest for independence and the rise of Oceania. Eventually the USSF found out, of course, but they had blamed Russia for the destruction. I had to bear the guilt for it, but by saving Benning's life on the Russian dreadnought, I thought I'd atoned for what I'd done. My guilt had eased, my conscience had cleared. I had been sleeping better. My nightmares had lessened, but had not disappeared.

But then I'd walked in on Meg that evening in her cubicle, and my world had fallen to pieces.

Again.

I turned back to Cliff. He had to know. Everything.

"Meg killed him," I whispered. "She stabbed him. In her cabin. There was blood everywhere."

His expression didn't change. "This was two weeks ago, roughly?"

"Yes."

He looked down and now he shook his head. "I'm your CSO, Mac. You should have told me. I could have helped."

"I didn't want to involve too many people. I wanted to shelter Meg."

"But there is likely a ton of evidence."

I snorted. "Probably."

He paused, then, "There is highly incriminating video."

A jolt shot through my body. My blood turned cold. "Of what?"

"It didn't take me long to figure out what happened. On the night he disappeared, Benning went to Meg's cubicle. Since he was staying in Module C, he had to leave his cabin and travel to hers. He walked along a corridor—limping due to his injury so it's clearly him—down a ladder to the main deck, through the travel tube to Module A and then to B, and then up to Meg's deck. Then into her cubicle." He hesitated. "He never walked out of there."

"And then what did you see?" My voice was a rasp.

"You showed up. You stepped inside the cubicle. The partition slid shut behind you." Cliff's voice was clinical now. He was just reciting the facts as he'd seen them. "You were in there for twenty-seven minutes. Talking or arguing probably. Then you left again to get some items from the laundry. A large cart. Some cleaning solution—"

"Bleach."

"—and towels."

"We had to move the corpse and clean Meg's room."

"And her bloody bedsheets?"

"Took those out, too."

"And her mattress?"

I stared at him and he nodded. "Then she'll need a new one." He made a note on a pad of paper. He continued, "Then you both emerged from her cubicle, pushing the cart. It was after 0200 hours. You took the cart down to the moonpool. Then you and Meg went for a swim, after you pushed the contents over and into the water."

I wanted to swear. If only Meg had thought more clearly about what she was doing. But she hadn't planned it out at all, other than the part where she killed

35

TIMOTHY S.
JOHNSTON

him. She didn't seem to care about the ramifications.

Or about involving me.

Cliff was right. She'd needed some counseling, and I'd abandoned her. I'd just left her alone, thinking that she would get better on her own.

But I'd been wrong.

And now we were in serious trouble.

"And where is the body, Mac?"

I sighed. "We took it outside. We'd bundled it all up with cords. The body was in her bedsheets. We swam it out to the Docking Module, and moved it to *SC-1*." That was my seacar. "Took it up through the moonpool there. We left in the vehicle and got rid of it."

"Where?'

I stared at the man. "I think the less you know about that the better, Cliff."

He frowned. "I think I've made it clear that you need to include your security chief in these considerations. Keeping me in the dark will only hurt."

"Better that you don't know," I repeated. "Meg is the one who needs help now."

"No. You're wrong. You helped her, so you're in trouble, too. You're an accessory, Mac."

"He killed our dad," I muttered. "I wanted to kill him, too."

"But you didn't. You kept yourself from doing it."

"Because I've killed so many others. I couldn't bring myself to." My voice was a harsh whisper now.

"Meg carried it out, and you helped hide it. You helped get rid of the evidence. You're just as guilty. And the USSF is here now."

"Maybe it doesn't matter."

He stared at me, not understanding. "The independence movement can't die with you. You have to stay and continue on the course. *Oceania*, Mac."

He did understand, after all. I took a deep breath. "You're right. I know you are. But I can't lose Meg. I can't let them have her."

"Then let me help." He sighed and stared up at the ceiling again. "They called me, you know. Days ago."

That startled me. I recalled what Laura Sukovski had told me. "Really? You didn't mention it."

"I was waiting to see if you'd tell me."

"What did they ask?"

"They asked about Benning. Where he was. I said I didn't know. I said that we don't keep tabs on USSF officers in our city. A total lie, of course, and I'm sure she knew it."

"Who?"

"Zyvinski."

"Ah. She's CIA."

Cliff's face was emotionless. "They don't fuck around. You know that. We can probably delay it a bit, but eventually they're going to figure it out. And when that happens, they're going to take us all. Meg, you, and me." He glanced away. "Does Johnny know anything?"

"I kept it quiet. He doesn't know much."

"Good decision there. So, it's just us three, then."

"I didn't want to involve you. They're going to take you now, too."

He grinned. "I'm sure you'll come up with something."

The hatch ground open.

I turned to glance at who had disturbed us.

It was Fleet Admiral Quintana and CIA Investigator Zyvinski.

Interlude:
Meagan McClusky

Location:	Latitude:	27° 34' 29" N
	Longitude:	54° 56' 11" W
	The Gulf of Mexico, Trieste City
	Repair Module
Date:	30 June 2130
Depth:	30 meters
Time:	1433 hours

MEAGAN WAS SITTING AT HER desk in the Repair Module offices. Outside, floating in the pool, were several seacars that her team had been working on. Most were in for minor repairs, like Jessica Ng's vehicle, which had suffered a short circuit in the control console. Smoke had drifted into the cabin during her most recent trip to Ballard, and she had smartly isolated the circuit, tripped the breaker, then brought the vessel in for maintenance. Jessica was a veteran of the colonization attempts and had not panicked at all.

There was another private seacar there, also in for routine maintenance on its battery system. Another vehicle had suffered a shattered screw blade, which they'd had to order in from the mainland, and there were three harvesting vehicles in from the kelp farms. Those ones were always breaking down because the work was rough and the harvesting strenuous, on both people and equipment.

Meg turned from the viewport and stared at her hands, crossed before her on the desk.

She had been having a hard time thinking about her work recently.

She couldn't get the body out of her mind.

Admiral Benning.

She didn't have any regrets about killing him. In fact, she'd *enjoyed* it. The act had removed a suffocating weight from her chest. She could breathe easier now. Thirty years of pain . . . nearly gone.

Her dad had led the independence movement from nearly the day he'd arrived in Trieste. The people had voted him mayor, and he'd openly spoken about independence from the United States. Truman, Meg, and their mother, Joanne, had often argued with him, pleading with him to be quiet and not talk so brazenly about it. But he'd ignored them all, and when the assassination finally came—Admiral Benning and the CIA's work—they had expected it.

But it hadn't made it easier.

Things in Trieste settled down after—there was no more open talk of independence, though it was still on peoples' minds—but George Shanks had taken over Trieste City Intelligence and continued operating the network of Trieste operatives in the world's oceans. The movement had pulled Truman into its fold soon after his graduation from university, though their father's legacy had likely played a huge role, as well. Meg had run away to Blue Downs by then, but when Shanks had started pushing for independence again, it had wrapped up Truman and Meg in a complicated and dangerous series of events. Frankly, Meg couldn't believe that she and Tru were still alive. Others had died during the fighting over the past eighteen months—most notably Katherine Wells and Agent Lau—but the one who should have died hadn't.

Taurus T. Benning.

So Meg made sure it happened, despite Truman's warnings.

But she'd been careless.

A massive understatement! She hadn't given any thought to what would happen once there was a dead body in her cabin.

And all the blood.

Luring him there had been easy.

The murder had been satisfying.

Pushing the knife into his heart had felt *good*.

This had shocked her. She wasn't prepared for the kind of satisfaction that had coursed through her body. His blood on her hands, her face, the deck.

The pain from all those years had seemed to melt away.

Or so she thought. There was still anger inside her about the past. About her dad and the breakup of the family. And on top of that inner pain that remained, there had been a body to deal with.

Her brother had done what he could. The only thing he could think of. Get the body out. Take it outside the city, swim it over to the ship. Then take it to the Trench and dump it. Sea life would take care of the rest.

She hoped.

But she knew it wasn't over yet. She knew people would come to ask questions.

Already she'd been hearing the tremors. Her coworker on the docks, Josh Miller, had mentioned that someone had called asking questions about her. It made her uneasy.

Then a USSF warsub had docked at Trieste earlier in the day. USS *Blade*.

She didn't know anything about who was on board, but any time the USSF showed up, trouble followed.

She assumed they were searching for Benning.

And she knew they'd be on to her pretty quickly, especially since they were already speaking with her coworkers.

But this time, she'd prepare.

She'd be ready when they came for her.

She looked down at the needle gun in her lap. There were five rounds in the chamber. Each was twenty centimeters long, stainless steel and deadly sharp. The barrel was square and as black as death.

The weapon operated better underwater, but it worked just fine in air, as well.

She wasn't going to go without a fight.

Part Two: Investigation

Chapter Four

THE TWO NAVY SEALS WERE with them. They took up position on either side of the hatch. Their eyes were hard, and they stared at me and Cliff. We sat there, silent, as the hatch closed with a thunk.

The locking mechanism ratcheted into place.

I stared at Quintana. "Hello, Admiral. How can I help you?"

Zyvinski stepped forward. "Funny that I find you here speaking with your security chief."

It made me hesitate. It wasn't a good way to start. "Why's that funny? I'm the mayor. He's in charge of security."

"What are you discussing?" Her tone was pointed. Her eyes made me uneasy. Her blonde hair framed her angular features and her confident posture betrayed her slight and willowy figure.

"A USSF warsub just docked at Trieste. In the past we have had enormous difficulties with Fleet sailors. They cause trouble here. We need to prepare."

She smirked. "And what troubles are you expecting?"

"They usually drink, cause problems. Our citizens worry."

"Strange that you should worry about USSF troops."

I frowned. "Why?"

"We're investigating the disappearance of a USSF officer. A senior officer. Somehow he went missing here, at your peaceful city. It should be *us* worrying about *you*, don't you think?"

I shook my head. "History has not shown that, actually."

"You mean all the attempts by Trieste to remove itself from the United States Submarine Fleet makes you worry about us? There's a murdered Admiral in the mix."

I sat up straighter. "What do you mean? There's been no murder here."

Her face flattened. "Then where is Admiral Benning? Point him out to me, please."

I noted that Quintana hadn't said a word. She was watching the exchange intently. Absorbing every detail.

I said, "If I knew that, you wouldn't be here." I sighed. "Look. Benning fought bravely with us. He helped us take down the Russian dreadnought. He got shot during it. He was here recovering, then he left. He didn't keep me informed of his whereabouts. He's not required to. I really don't know where he went."

Zyvinski remained silent and studied me for a long series of heartbeats.

I could feel my heart pounding.

Then she turned to Cliff. "And you, Mister Sim. Do you know where Admiral Benning might be?"

"I have no idea. We don't keep tabs on him, as Mayor McClusky just said. He's free to move around as he pleases."

"When was the last time you saw him?"

Cliff paused and glared at the CIA investigator. "You already asked me this during your video call last week."

Zyvinski snorted. "Come on, Sim. You know the method. You're in security, for Christ's sake. We ask repeatedly until stories change."

Cliff's eyes hardened, if that were at all possible. The lines in his face grew deeper. "My story is not going to change, and I'll not have you here disrespecting me. I'm the Chief Security Officer in this city."

Zyvinski's expression remained fixed. She just stared him down. "This isn't the Wild West. This isn't your town, *Sheriff*. Trieste belongs to *us*. To the United States Submarine Fleet. Someone knows something, maybe multiple people." She snapped a glance at me. "And we're here to discover the truth and prevent a cover-up."

"Why would anyone hurt Benning?" I said.

Quintana finally spoke. "The Admiral and I communicated just after your mission to the dreadnought, McClusky. Roughly two weeks ago."

"Did he fill you in on it? Together we infiltrated—"

"Yes, he did. It was quite an achievement."

"We worked as a team. We would not return here and then kill the man." My insides tightened as I said it. *Where the hell was Meg?* I swatted the errant thought away. The last thing we needed was for her to walk in right then.

"And yet someone did. Don't you find that odd?"

"I do, actually, but even stranger is your claim that someone here killed him."

Zyvinski said, "We know he's dead."

A dark silence descended over us.

—••—

"How do you know that?"

"Evidence." It was all she said. She just stared back at me.

The expression on my face was incredulous. Finally, "You're going to have to share some of it, so we can help the investigation. Cliff will offer whatever assistance you need."

She turned her piercing eyes back to my security chief. "Yes, why don't you offer your assistance now?"

"Anything you want," he replied.

"I'm still waiting."

Now it was his turn to look confused.

"Your story," she continued.

Cliff frowned for a minute and then understanding lit his features. "I understand. I'll tell you whatever you want. Again."

"So where did Benning go after he entered his cubicle on the evening of 15 June at 2100 hours?"

This was the evening Meg killed the man. Inside, I trembled. *They knew precisely when Benning had gone to his cabin.*

Prickles crawled up my scalp.

Cliff replied, "Security video shows that he entered his living space in Module C."

"And when did he leave?"

"We don't see him leaving until the next morning."

Zyvinski's expression changed for the first time. There was a look of shock on her features. "You still claim to see him on 16 June? On security video?"

"I do."

"And where did he go?"

"The Docking Module."

"For what purpose?"

"To leave."

There was another long, drawn-out silence. The CIA investigator clearly didn't believe this. "How do you know?"

"Because he left." Cliff stopped speaking and just stared at her.

Zyvinski continued to glare at him, then she looked to Quintana, then back to Cliff. "What ship did he board?"

"A private seacar. I'll trace the registry for you. You only just arrived; give me some time to put together a file for you."

"But we called you days ago. Why is nothing prepared for us?"

"I didn't realize you were coming. You asked me questions and I answered them."

"I'll say it again. An admiral is *missing* and we presume murder."

"You can say that as many times as you want, but I know it's not true. He is not missing. *He left.* He boarded a vessel and went somewhere else."

"Before his ship arrived? *Devastator* is still en route to Trieste. Why would he leave before—"

"You'll have to ask him that. Or his XO. Or his immediate supervisor."

Quintana grated, "*I am his immediate supervisor.* I know he meant to stay here."

There was another long silence as we all stared at each other. The two guards were eyeing me in particular. I could feel their anger cut through me. "Look," I said, "why don't we get Cliff to put together his file. This is getting us nowhere. All you really have is speculation and fantasy, and it all seems driven by fear."

"Of what, exactly?" Zyvinski snapped.

"Fear of Trieste. Of her people, of our intentions." I threw my arms up in the air. "I'm not sure what, exactly. Or why you dislike us." I hoped it was a good act. "But let's just give him some time."

"How much does he need?"

Cliff said, "I'll work up his movements and the registry on that seacar. I'll get it to you by tomorrow morning at the absolute latest."

Quintana exhaled. "You'll work it up?"

"Yes."

"Meaning, you'll *make* it up?"

Cliff rose to his feet. He was a towering specimen of a man, and if he meant to intimidate, it might have worked with normal people.

But these were not normal people.

These two could end our lives in an instant. The only reason they hadn't was most likely due to the fact that the citizens of Trieste would rise up violently if anything ever happened to me. Despite my misgivings at my dad's past, and his actions as a father, he remained a powerful force in the city. Triestrians *worshipped* him, and it had translated to me and Meg as a result. Often I found the adoration difficult to endure, but at times like this, I appreciated it.

The two SEALs, on the other hand, should the order come to kill me and Cliff, would have had their hands full. Despite their effectiveness as elite guards, I didn't think they would be able to carry out such orders.

Cliff and I were highly skilled. We went on missions on a regular basis. We'd killed, and just recently at that.

These SEALs were big and tough and looked mean, but they didn't have mission experience like we did. Their training was mostly rehearsed, I guessed. We achieved ours through real life and death. When you don't know what the person you're fighting with is going to do at any second, that's where reality bested training, every single time.

Everyone tensed as Cliff rose to his feet. The guards put themselves between him and the two women instantly.

"Cliff," I muttered.

"I'll not be spoken to like a common criminal," he grated between clenched teeth. "I said I'll investigate, and I will."

That, too, was a great act. I had to give it to him. He was convincing.

I said, "Why don't we meet here tomorrow morning? Oh nine hundred hours?"

Quintana and Zyvinski stared at Cliff for a long few seconds. Then they turned to me. "I'm interested to see what he discovers," the CIA investigator said. Her voice was soft yet menacing. "I want the surveillance video, too. In the meantime, we'll continue talking to potential witnesses."

And with that, they left.

———•••———

LONG AFTER THE HATCH CLOSED, I finally spoke. "Well done, Cliff."

"Do you think it was too much?"

I shrugged. "Perhaps. They know the truth, anyway. They're going to wade through whatever we give them and figure it all out. It won't take them too long."

"Probably."

Which gave us just eighteen hours to figure out what to do. To plan. And then once we gave them the fake details of Benning's *departure*—a euphemism if there ever was one—they'd confirm it was all a lie and then arrest us.

Likely Meg, Cliff, and me.

And we wouldn't have a hope in hell.

And the independence movement would die.

Chapter Five

My mood was grim. I knew what was on the horizon; it was an oppressive cloud hanging over us, a suffocating and toxic presence from which there was no escape.

I couldn't stop thinking about the two visitors and what they represented.

And what it meant for Meg.

Johnny had arranged a meeting for the entire team in my office. Cliff and I entered and it was like wading into a sea of people. The cabin was small to begin with, and there were too many people in there.

But it had to be done.

We had to inform them, and make sure we were all on the same page.

I'd instructed Kristen Canvel to mislead Quintana or Zyvinski—to send them to a different location—should they appear in City Control, and she responded with a curt nod. She was so professional she would never have asked me exactly what was going on. Surely she must have known what we were up to, but she had never questioned me or my motives.

One day I'd have to invite her to join TCI.

Inside the office, Johnny, my deputy mayor, was having a discussion with our two most senior members: Richard Lancombe and Jessica Ng. These two had worked with my father in the 2090s, fighting for independence against the USSF. They had disappeared after his death, only to reappear recently and pledge their support for me. They'd been with us during the recent battle in the Mid-Atlantic Ridge—where we had destroyed hundreds of USSF and FSF warsubs—and they had actually been with Katherine Wells in *SC-1* when she had died. They were currently in Trieste working on our defences; they had begun construction on a bunker underneath the Commerce Module that could house a large portion of Triestrians in times of imminent danger. They were going to do the same under each Living Module, as well, as soon as the primary bunker was complete.

Also in the office was Renée Féroce, the French captain who had tirelessly tried to kill me for firing on her warsub the previous year. After taking her prisoner and explaining my situation, she'd left the French Submarine Fleet and had joined us in Trieste. The French had assumed her dead, and since then, Renée had convinced the French undersea colony Cousteau to join our quest for Oceania. The tall and broad-shouldered woman had short dark hair, the bearing of a military officer, and a toned, athletic figure. She and I had a special connection, one that had started with adversity and had since grown to friendship, and perhaps more. She loved living in Trieste and had embraced it fully. I had put her in charge of the defence station in City Control—able to shoot torpedoes at incoming enemies and launch countermeasures—and she also spent her off time working the kelp fields and scuba diving. Her smile was radiant, and the lines at the corners of her eyes had grown in recent weeks.

I held my gaze on her for longer than normal as I greeted her; I couldn't help it. The others could most likely tell, and I was pretty sure that she'd noticed, too. She touched my arm when I walked past her and shot me a look that most men would recognize as being an invitation for more.

"See you later if you have time?" she whispered.

I nodded to her, but wasn't really sure if it would be possible.

Manesh Lazlow, the acoustician, was a frail, elderly man with spider-like fingers, white hair, sunken cheeks, and a zest for Triestrian life. He'd only recently come to live with us; he'd invented the Acoustic Pulse Drive, which allowed our vessels to descend to five kilometers and beyond—he predicted *eight kilometers*, but we hadn't yet tested his invention fully. It had given us sea superiority in battles against our enemy. Still, it had some major flaws, which the French had exploited in battle, and it was something Lazlow continued to work on.

And finally, also in the office with us, was my twin sister, Meg McClusky.

She was standing against the bulkhead, not speaking or interacting with any of the others. She fixed me with a look and kept her features blank. We were both forty-five. While I was beginning to look beaten and tired—the effects of a lifetime of espionage and training, including four months of imprisonment and torture—I couldn't deny that she was radiant and beautiful. With blonde hair, blue eyes and freckles, she was a mechanic who was a whiz with seacar construction and maintenance. We'd had to rely on her skills multiple times to get us out of dangerous situations. Men found her irresistible, but since we'd reconnected and she'd moved back to Trieste from Blue Downs, she'd devoted herself to the fight for independence and my struggle.

And, apparently, to killing Admiral Benning.

There were dark circles under her eyes from lack of sleep, but the bruising on her face was nearly gone.

I knew why she seemed withdrawn: she was embarrassed that her actions had resulted in the USSF presence.

Then I studied her for another brief moment, and I realized I was wrong. She didn't feel regret at all. She was worried that she'd put us and the city in danger, but she didn't regret killing Benning one bit.

I grunted to myself.

I'd misread Meg after our mission to destroy the dreadnought.

I wouldn't let that happen again.

It was cramped in the tight space, so people pressed themselves against the bulkheads. It grew silent.

"The USSF is back," I said in a soft voice.

—••—

"WHY ARE THEY HERE?" RENÉE asked in her thick accent.

"Admiral Benning has disappeared." I noticed Johnny staring at me; he knew the man was dead, and knew Meg had killed him, but didn't know anything else beyond those facts. "The USSF is looking for him."

Richard was frowning. "His injuries maybe?"

"No. It was just his leg. He was healing fine. We think he left on the sixteenth. Cliff is looking into it."

Cliff just nodded and said nothing. I hated lying to my team, but until the investigators had finished their questioning, I didn't want to put the others at risk.

They were all looking at each other now, wondering if anyone had any other details to share.

No one did.

"So who's looking?" Jessica Ng said.

I steeled myself for this. "Admiral Quintana is here."

The news cut through the group. Their jaws dropped and their eyes widened. They simply didn't know what to say.

"With her is a CIA investigator named Zyvinski. Watch out for her. She's . . ." I trailed off, not knowing what to say.

Cliff interjected, "They suspect the Admiral is dead. They'll try to pin it on someone here in Trieste." He hadn't looked at Meg yet, and she wasn't even watching him.

She was staring at me.

She was pale. The news had shocked her.

"I know this is daunting," I added. "But we'll get through it. Answer anything they ask you, but of course, nothing related to our ongoing plans or new defences."

Richard nodded.

"There's more news," I continued.

As one, they looked at me, curious, but remained silent.

I said, "We have another new visitor. His name is Doctor Max Hyland. He's doing some interesting research and I'll introduce you soon."

"What kind of research?" Lazlow asked in his reedy voice. He had folded himself into one of the three chairs there and was watching me with interest.

"He's working on a new bomb for us. Russia is going to put three more dreadnoughts to sea soon, and we need to be ready."

There was another stir as this news swept through the cabin.

"Three more?" Renée gasped. "But the first thing they'll do is attack Trieste."

"It's why we need this bomb. We need a faster way to deal with the threat."

"The Russians hate us."

"There are many people who hate us now, after all we've done. Which is why we're building defences and shelters. But this weapon is going to be something special."

"Nuclear?" Richard asked.

I filled them in on the particulars, and they nodded in appreciation.

"How'd you hear about this?" Renée asked me.

"After we returned from the Russian mission, I knew we needed better weapons. I did some research, discovered Hyland's story, and invited him here. He's just arrived."

"And how did you hear about the three new dreadnoughts?"

I stumbled slightly and hesitated. This was not something that I wanted to explain. Before I could say anything, Meg stepped forward.

She said in a soft voice: "I found out from Benning the night I killed him."

—••—

NOW THERE WAS AN ABSOLUTE *explosion* of shock through that cabin. I put my head in my hands. I wished she hadn't done that. Now they were all in danger.

She pressed on, "I killed him because he killed our father. We took his body out afterward and dumped it."

Now it was deathly silent in there.

Finally, Renée hissed, "You've brought the USSF down on our heads now, you know that, Meg. They won't leave until they discover the truth."

There was another smothering break as people continued to process this bombshell.

Richard said into the silence, "I don't blame you for doing it. I wanted to do it, too."

"And me," said Jessica.

"Me, too," said Cliff, "but it's put us in a tough position."

"One thing's for sure," I added. "It'll be over tomorrow."

"How do you know?" Johnny asked, confused.

"Because they're expecting Cliff to turn over the video of the evening in question. When he does, they'll arrest Meg and me and take us away."

"There's no way we can make something up?"

"We're trying, but they'll see through it." I sighed. It was next to impossible to escape this situation. I stared at Meg, and she simply returned my look, face blank once again.

—••—

"WHAT ELSE DO WE HAVE?" I said to break up the mood. "Renée?"

She pursed her lips. The news of the murder had rattled her, and she spent a few moments calming herself. Then, "The other two French cities are talking to us now."

That made me smile. "They've joined?"

Other smiles lit up the office. Whenever a city joined our struggle, it was stellar news.

"Not yet. But the SCAV drive we gave Cousteau is too great a prize to ignore. Conshelf Alpha and Beta both want it, too. And with the news that we defeated the Russian dreadnought, underwater citizens everywhere know that we're more powerful than they expected. They're on the verge of joining us, I'd say. But they haven't yet."

And because the French prized freedom and independence so greatly, I knew they would not remain under mainland control for long. This was fantastic news, indeed.

Johnny said, "The Chinese cities are also following suit."

I blinked. "They are? But so far only Sheng City has joined up with us." It was why Agent Lau had accompanied us on the dreadnought mission. He had died during it—shot by Russians on the vessel's bridge—but he'd been Sheng's representative, and proof that they were totally onside with us.

"The SCAV drive is too important." He gestured at Renée. "Just like the French. They see the coming struggles in the oceans. Only we have the drive right now, though the Americans will be putting warsubs to sea with it soon. The Chinese know they have to maintain the balance, so they need it, too."

I nodded. The SCAV drive propelled ships at nearly 500 kph underwater. It was the greatest innovation in undersea living since Cousteau's *aqualung*. And every superpower needed it for their colonization attempts. I'd used it to interest the Chinese and French undersea cities, and it had succeeded.

A huge part of me wanted to jump for joy. There were six Chinese colonies and three French. If we could convince the French cities, then including Trieste, Ballard, and Seascape—the other two American undersea cities—there would soon would be twelve of us working for the undersea dreams of Oceania.

"So who's next, then?" I asked no one in particular.

Meg's news had shocked people, but this had buoyed their spirits.

"Work is progressing on the bunker," Richard said. "It should be done in a few weeks. Then we'll start working on the ones under the Living Modules."

"Good job. Keep it up." We needed those for protection. Underwater colonies were extremely vulnerable to attack. The Russian destruction of Blue Downs a few weeks earlier was proof. A nearby explosion or even sabotage could take down a module without much difficulty. It's why I had buried our nuclear plant the previous year.

"The drones are nearly finished, too."

That startled me. "Already?"

He nodded. "Nothing new about them in terms of technology. The crew at The Ridge is working on making as many as possible for you."

They were our latest advance in undersea combat. I turned to Johnny. "Can you go to the Research Module and get Max Hyland set up? Make sure he has what he needs. Order anything he wants."

My deputy mayor nodded. "Got it. Then what?"

I offered a sly smile. "The zircon mine. We have to get it up and running."

He snorted but knew my mind was set. "Let me guess, for water and air purification."

"You got it."

The others seemed confused by this. Johnny said with a smirk, "All right. I'll do it."

I turned to my security officer. "Cliff, you get the material ready for the investigators tomorrow. Doctor the video, do whatever you have to do."

He was staring at me, his eyes somber. "I'll try my best."

I knew what he wanted to say. Fabricating lies would likely be obvious to the CIA, but we had to try.

No one else had anything to add. Meg was still staring at me, and I knew I had to speak with her. I said, "That's it, everybody. Be careful of the investigators. Just tell them you have no idea where Benning went. Tell them the last time you saw him. Be honest about it. Hopefully it will all be over by tomorrow."

As I said it, a shiver worked its way down my spine.

—••—

MEG WAS THE ONLY ONE left in my office. She remained standing by a bulkhead. Her gaze kept shifting away from me, then returning to study my expression.

I loved my sister. It was a deeper love than I'd ever had with any other family member. Maybe it was because she was all I had left. Mom was dead, the CIA had murdered Dad, and my girlfriend, Kat, had died earlier in the year in the battle against the FSF and the USSF in the Mid-Atlantic Ridge. Meg had sacrificed everything to come back to Trieste with me, to join in my fight for independence. Originally, she'd been against it . . .

Until she'd witnessed the SCAV drive in action. It was a massive leap forward in aquanautic engineering and submarine warfare. Other subs could only travel a maximum of eighty and they didn't stand a chance against us. And she knew I'd be leading the fight for independence in a much safer and more responsible manner than Dad had. He'd been reckless, and Meg still blamed him for the destruction of our family unit when we'd been teens.

He wasn't the only one she'd blamed.

Admiral Benning had been the other.

Meg sighed. "Thanks for lying for me, but I can't have you do that to our people. I had to tell them the truth."

"You've put them in danger now, too."

"Because they know I killed Benning?"

"When they lie to the investigators, it'll be obvious."

"Maybe. But they don't know where he is or any of the details."

I shook my head. "It wasn't smart, Meg." Nothing she had been doing lately was smart. The murder was reckless, but I knew a force more powerful than she'd been able to control had caused it. Hell, I'd barely been able to keep it in check. I'd wanted to kill the bastard, too.

"We should have done it on the Russian dreadnought," she said. "It would have been so much easier."

There was nothing I could say to that. Meg would have been happier. The USSF would have accepted that the Admiral had died destroying the Russian warsub. Hell, he would have been a hero.

That would have been much better than being a victim in an underwater colony.

It seemed that every time I eliminated a threat to the city, another one sprang up. I'd dealt with George Shanks, and then Captain Heller had appeared on the scene. I got rid of him, then Benning and the Russians. And now Quintana and Zyvinksi.

I exhaled. I wanted to just focus on politics, to bring more underwater cities on board with us. To form Oceania. But all these complications kept springing up.

The thought made me want to kick myself. Oceania was not going to be easy. The superpowers were not going to just sit back as they lost their colonies. This was a fight, and a deadly one at that.

People were going to die. It was inevitable.

"Tell me about this bomb," Meg said. "It sounds interesting."

It brought me back to the present. I sat behind my desk and Meg took the chair in front of it. I was sick of thinking about the investigation and what was going to happen in the morning. "It's called an Isomer Bomb. Massive explosion but in a small package. Non-nuclear." *Bruce Lee*, Hyland had called it. The one-inch punch.

"It's like a tactical nuke, then?"

"Yes, but without the lingering radiation. It'll get us around the non-proliferation treaties, and we'll be able to take down large subs without worrying about a nuclear confrontation."

"Good idea. But how'd you convince Hyland to come here?"

I told her the entire story. About how the academic community had blacklisted him. No journal would publish him. No university would let him continue his research.

She was nodding as I spoke. "It sounds perfect," she whispered. "What are the difficulties with it?"

I frowned. I wasn't a scientist, so I wasn't the best person to answer this. "We need to speak to him more, but as I understand it, the academic world believe it's a fantasy. Bad science."

"How does it work?"

I thought back to my reading on the subject. "It's a two-stage weapon. It needs an initial blast of X-rays to trigger the energy release. Something about certain elements and how there is energy stored within them. If you can trigger its release all at once instead of over a long period of several half-lives, the blast is *huge*. It's the trigger that's the tough part, getting the energy out."

She was staring at me, and then she cocked her head to the side. "Let me guess. The zircon mine?"

I grinned.

Chapter Six

"MAC, WE'VE GOT AN ISSUE here."

"What is it, Grant?"

I was in City Control, really just passing through on my way out of my office, which was located through a connecting hatch just under the massive map of the Gulf and Caribbean region that hung across one bulkhead. Colored dots and attached labels identified each ship with its name, bearing, and depth.

Grant Bell was in charge of Sea Traffic Control. He monitored all ocean-going traffic—on the surface and under it—not only in the immediate region, but in the Gulf and Caribbean, as well.

He said, his voice ominous, "I see numerous contacts heading for Seascape."

I stuttered to a stop and turned slowly to face him. "Say again."

He was sitting at his console, staring at the screens before him. Their light illuminated his face from below, creating a ghostly appearance. The look in his eyes was dark. "Mac, it seems as though the entire USSF in the region is headed for Seascape."

—••—

I MARCHED TO HIS CONSOLE and stared at the screen. Then I glanced at the map over our heads. He was right. There were *hundreds* of points of light, all headed for the same location.

"I've got thirty *Houstons* showing here," he muttered. "Twenty *Cyclones*, fifteen *Typhoons*, eleven *Matrixes*, and more. *Tritons, Neptunes, Tridents,* and *Reapers,* too. All in, I'm seeing 252 USSF contacts heading to Seascape, and those are just the warsubs. There are surface vessels, too."

Seascape was located south of Texas, on the continental shelf, just sixty-five kilometers from Freeport.

"Surely they can't mean to destroy it," Joey Zen whispered from my side.

I glanced at her. She was in charge of Pressure Control. "No, they don't."

"Then what are their intentions?"

Inside, I shuddered. I knew exactly what they were doing, but couldn't bring myself to vocalize it. A part of me wanted to just shove it aside and ignore it, and hope it wouldn't happen. But I knew it would. It's why Admiral Quintana was in Trieste. She'd been en route to Seascape, but had stopped here first to take care of this business.

I had been hearing rumblings about the USSF taking over Seascape for many months. Their mayor, Reggie Quinn, had also suggested it to me. Their tourists had dried up after the environmental devastation had really started taking a toll topside. Few could afford the luxury and expense of Seascape anymore. Now there was a better use for the colony.

Damn.

Kristen called out, "Call coming in for you, Mac."

"Who is it?" I asked, staring at the map and the USSF tracks. Grant had illuminated their courses, and they were all pointing toward a single spot on the map.

It looked like a bullseye.

"Grace Winton."

That startled me. She was the mayor of Ballard City, the undersea colony on the shelf south of Louisiana. I'd last heard from her just before the mission to destroy the dreadnought.

"I'll take it in my office," I mumbled, staring at the map. *This is not good*.

My greatest fear was coming to pass right before my eyes.

———••———

"Go ahead, Grace," I said.

"Truman, nice to hear your voice," Ballard's mayor said to me. Her face was on my vidscreen; she was African American, in her mid-forties, and she was part of my quest to achieve Oceania. She also operated an intelligence agency, and I had given her one of our superfast vehicles equipped with SCAV drive—a *Sword*. I'd last seen her in Ballard when I went to speak with her about joining our fight for independence. After she'd witnessed what our ships could do, she'd eagerly jumped in with us.

"Are you seeing this traffic?" I asked.

"It's why I'm calling. The USSF is descending on Seascape. There are surface freighters headed there, too. Construction crews, as well."

"To assemble docks on the surface as well as on the seafloor, no doubt."

"Docks, umbilicals, storage modules, and so on. They're taking over, Mac."

Breakwaters or sheltered bays usually protected naval bases—like at Norfolk or San Diego—but Seascape was underwater and therefore somewhat protected from the weather. At thirty meters down, it would still experience currents if there were high waves on the surface. The construction crews were likely there to build umbilicals and docks at different depths for a multitude of warsubs.

It made sense. They had lost both the Atlantic *and* the Pacific HQs during the conflict with Russia a month earlier. The United States was still dealing with the environmental disaster from the collapse of the walls holding back the oceans at both locations. They needed a new HQ, and they'd picked one in the Gulf, where it was close to both the Atlantic and the Pacific, through the Panama pass-through.

And close to their two volatile undersea colonies.

I stared at Grace's image in silence.

There was nothing more either of us could say.

—••—

AN HOUR LATER, I WAS still sitting at my desk, reviewing the events in my mind. I had a headache from it all. It was almost too much to take in. Meg's issues were the greatest, and I knew I had to find some way out from under the investigation and my imminent arrest the next morning, but this one was yet another source of tension.

I exhaled forcefully.

Nope, I thought. *Didn't help.*

I tried again.

Still nothing.

It was enough to make me laugh.

I knew we were in real trouble, and it wasn't the theoretical kind where something *might* happen if people in high-ranking positions made certain decisions. Or the kind of trouble where we'd made a tough decision and had to deal with the consequences later.

Admiral Quintana and the other Joint Chiefs had already made those decisions. Maybe even the president.

Now the damage was done.

These were the consequences for our actions in the Gulf.

The USSF was setting up shop just a few hours away. They'd be near Trieste *all the time* now—not just once in a while as a warsub passed nearby, or periodically as a particularly domineering captain stopped to demand more produce or more minerals, as Captain Franklin P. Heller had done.

I thought about Reggie Quinn, the mayor of Seascape, and how his tune had changed over the past few months. After the environmental disaster had really started to affect the surface. No more money was flooding into the city. No more people coming to live underwater for a week as they played in the underwater games park or went scuba diving with dolphins. He'd first kicked me out of his city for even suggesting independence. Then, just weeks later, he'd called me asking for help. Told me he was willing to fight the superpowers.

Then the Fleet had swooped in, set up shop, and had taken over.

I wondered idly where Reggie was at that moment. What he was doing. How he was dealing with the looming arrival of *over 200 warsubs*.

In the past, at Trieste, the arrival of just one could cause great consternation among our populace.

As *Blade* just had.

And the investigation . . .

Absently, I reached for the comm and contacted our doctor, in the clinic. Her voice floated to me and I said, "Hello Stacy, how are you?" She was an older woman with white hair, sometimes pulled back into a bun, with a curt and cold manner. She was highly professional, however, and a good doctor. She usually treated ailments that families often deal with—sick children, sores that wouldn't heal because they were always wet, and so on—but on occasion a serious workplace accident on the kelp fields or the mines ended up on her clinic table. I sometimes wondered how doctors dealt with such things—with people in enormous pain, or patients who were always ill, and with families who were always grieving—without letting it affect their personal lives. Then, I realized, it probably did. Maybe it was why Reynolds was so cold.

"I'm fine, Mac. You?"

"I have a problem I need help with."

There was a pause. She was completely quiet, and it made me smile inwardly. She was just sitting there, at her desk, not saying a thing, waiting for me to tell her the problem. The last one I'd hit her with had been because of injuries from our recent mission. And before that, a dead body a Triestrian had hauled in from outside, and a mystery about the time and cause of death. Turned out that Captain Heller had killed the man on board his warsub and dumped him outside.

A cold shiver worked its way through my body at the thought.

. . . *had killed him and dumped him outside* . . .

My guts tightened.

"What is it?" Reynolds said finally. "I've got patients, Mac."

"Yes, I know," I finally managed. "You're good at waiting for me."

There was another pause. "Dammit, I mean it literally. Not patience. *Patients*. There are people waiting for treatment here. What do you want?" Now her tone grew even colder.

"Oh, sorry." I took a breath, wondering how to ask her. "I need you to do something for me."

—••—

FIVE MINUTES LATER I'D MADE two more calls and had given each person at the other end instructions to meet me in the clinic to see Doctor Reynolds. It had been a confusing order, but I'd had to do it.

Accepting the inevitable was difficult, but sometimes we had no choice.

I'd also made a call to the mayor of Seascape, Reggie Quinn.

Within ten seconds of placing the call, he was on my comm. He face was haggard, the lines on his forehead tight. He was bald with a goatee, African American, and wore black-framed glasses.

He was in City Control, and his team of people behind him were hard at work. Some were tearing through the room, carrying charts and screens to show others, and many had nervous expressions. They knew the USSF was on their way.

It was why Quinn had accepted my call so quickly.

"So, it's happened," he said in a soft voice. He put his hands on his head and stared at me. "Mac, I don't know what to do."

I felt his pain. He was the mayor of a city that had lost its purpose. We mostly farmed kelp, though we also had fish pens. Ballard focused on fish.

Seascape was a tourist destination.

Until recently.

"I have a huge problem," I whispered, leaning in.

"You do? I think we—"

"There are USSF investigators here right now. One of them is CIA."

He frowned. "Why?"

"Admiral Benning is missing. They think someone here murdered him."

"I see . . ."

I stared at him, and an uncomfortable silence stretched out over us. He just watched me.

"I need your help," I said.

—••—

FIVE MINUTES AFTER THE CALL to Seascape I was still sitting at my desk, staring at the comm.

I didn't want to believe that what we'd spoken about might actually happen, but I had to prepare for the worst.

Then the comm beeped, and it sounded angry. I stared at it, now miserable. "What is it?" I finally asked.

—••—

KRISTEN'S MESSAGE WAS ENOUGH FOR me to locate Johnny and bring him with me. He had been in the Research Module, checking to see if Max Hyland had found the workspace arranged for him. It was a lab, modestly sized, but well equipped. Johnny needed to make a list of equipment that Hyland needed; he was going to order it immediately, but I'd grabbed Johnny before he could do it.

My deputy mayor was staring at me, confused.

"He's from *where?*" he asked.

We were marching to the same lounge where earlier in the day we'd met with Dr. Hyland. "I think he said he's from New Berlin."

"And he wanted to see you?"

"Yes. Kristen thought it was concerning enough to tell me immediately."

"Why's that?"

I pulled to a halt and stared at my deputy mayor. "Because he didn't ask for me at first."

"Who was he—"

"He was asking for George Shanks."

—••—

I APPROACHED THE MAN SLOWLY. I was watching his eyes, searching for subterfuge. He was in the lounge, standing before the couches and staring back at Johnny and me. His eyes flicked from one of us to the other. There was a simultaneous mix of confusion and worry on his face.

"Who are you?" I asked. Johnny was at my side. I'd locked the hatch.

"My name is Ricardo Ruiz. I work for George Shanks."

A jolt shot through my body. Shanks had headed up Trieste City Intelligence. I had left the agency in 2122 following a disagreement with the man over policy. He'd been torturing Chinese undersea city agents, and when Sheng City had captured me, they'd tortured me in kind. Eventually they'd released me in a prisoner exchange, and when I'd seen our own prisoners at the trade, beaten and weary and fragile—just shadows of the men and women they had once been—it had sickened me. I'd quit TCI and vowed to never work for Shanks again.

All that had changed when Katherine Wells had appeared in Trieste with her SCAV drive, and I rejoined the agency to protect the city and begin a new fight for independence. But there had been a seven-year break while I worked the kelp farms and tried my best to ignore ocean politics and stay away from TCI, and I had no idea what our agents had been doing during that time.

Or even who some of them were.

I was down to only a few operatives now, including myself, Johnny, and Cliff, and this man's presence confused me.

If he was telling the truth.

"You worked for him in what capacity?" I asked, still studying his face. He had olive skin, stubble on his chin, dark eyes, and a thin, wiry appearance. Shoulder-length hair pulled into a ponytail. He was Latino. He seemed quick and agile, and would likely be good in a fight, though he didn't have the bulk needed for facing deadly opponents in hand-to-hand combat.

Like those Navy SEALs currently marching around Trieste.

He glanced around. "Are you in charge here?"

I frowned. "What do you mean? I'm the city mayor."

"Shanks wasn't the mayor when I worked for him. Janice Flint was."

"So how did you work for Shanks?"

He hesitated. I knew what he wanted to say, but he was worried about spilling it to someone who didn't know about TCI. Finally he settled on, "He sent me on missions."

"Do you know who I am?"

"Truman McClusky. But I thought you were farming now."

I took a deep breath. It was as if he'd been away for a year and a half or more, and had no idea what had transpired in the intervening time. "I had been. Then I stopped."

He was staring at me. His focus was intense. Then he glanced at Johnny. "I know you, too. You defected to Sheng City."

Johnny frowned. "I did. But then I came back."

"So you both left, then came back to Trieste."

I said, "You could say that."

He considered this for a long moment, then swore. "I guess I have no choice, since Shanks is gone. At least I know who both of you are, even if you don't know me. I am an agent of Trieste City Intelligence. I've been on a mission. And now I'm back."

—••—

I SAID, "WHERE HAVE YOU been all this time?"

"New Berlin."

I considered that. He was saying that George Shanks had sent him on a mission before I'd returned to TCI, and before I'd assumed the position of Director. He had no idea that Shanks had left or that I was now in charge. If what he was saying was true, then Shanks must have recruited him during the period when I'd been farming kelp. "When did you start with TCI?"

"Mid-2026."

"Where did you live before that?"

"In Module B."

"And before that?"

"Nicaragua."

"Why did you come to Trieste?"

"To work. To colonize the oceans. The same as everyone else."

"And how did you meet Shanks?"

"He recruited me. I fit his profile, I guess."

"Describe it."

He squinted at me. He knew I was testing him. Then he shrugged. "Okay. I studied martial arts as a teenager and in my twenties. I won an international championship in karate. When I came here, I worked the fish farms. One day in the fields, I rescued a teenager who got into trouble. His tank ran out of air. He panicked. I swam out to get him and we buddy-breathed all the way back here. It really wasn't a big deal, but Shanks noticed me then. He studied my file and we had a few conversations. He realized that I'd make a good field agent, and he made me an offer."

It sounded like Shanks, all right. But that kind of information was probably easy to gain access to, especially if Ricardo was a member of the USSF.

I said, "Where did Shanks work out of?"

"The Communications Module."

"Where was his office?"

"Deck Three. It was a small cabin."

"What was his main goal?"

"To protect the city and—"

"Don't give me that bullshit answer! Tell me what he wanted for the city."

He paused and stared at me and Johnny. Then, "Independence, of course. That's what he was working toward, the whole time."

—••—

"WHAT WERE YOU DOING IN New Berlin? What was your mission?"

He sighed. "It's secret, McClusky. I can't tell you that."

"I'm the Director of TCI now."

Johnny gasped and grabbed my arm. "Mac, what are you doing? We don't know this guy. He could be a USSF spy!"

Johnny knew we could never tell a civilian what we were really doing underwater. I had just contradicted our greatest coda. It had horrified him.

I shook my head. "Possibly," I said, still staring at the newcomer, "but he knows more about Shanks than they do."

"Unless they knew more than we thought. They already proved that to us last year!" He was referring to the fact that Captain Heller had known TCI existed when we all thought the agency was utterly secret.

"They knew Shanks was in charge, you're right. But still . . . " I chewed a lip as I considered Johnny's warning. If what he was saying was true, and this man was a plant designed to catch me, then the USSF already knew that I was in charge of TCI, in which case it didn't matter. "Keep talking, Ricardo," I growled.

"Rico. Call me Rico."

"Go on."

He gestured at a chair. "Why don't we sit down? It's a long story."

—••—

HE'D BEEN IN THE GERMAN underwater colony, New Berlin, located in the Jade Bight on the North Sea. The city was one of the largest underwater colonies, also located at a depth of thirty meters, just off the coast of the city of Wilhemshaven, though large tides there famously caused issues with their moonpools. When the tides rose, the moonpool hatches had to close, or the module atmospheric pressures had to increase in order to compensate. This caused a debate in the early 2100s, as their citizens had to make a decision about what course of action to take. They decided, and wisely so, to close the moonpools during high tides. To alter the pressures would cause disruptions to travelers venturing to the city; it would make depressurization necessary for anyone who wanted to leave the city, and this was contrary to every undersea agreement standardizing our pressures at four atms.

Rico claimed to have been there to monitor the elections of 2128. He'd left just before I returned to the agency, so he had no idea what had transpired at Trieste. One of the candidates had openly promoted independence for the world's underwater colonies, so Shanks had sent him to monitor the elections and support the candidate.

I shook my head at that. In addition to increasing our grasp of resources and acquiring new technologies to aid in the colonization attempts, it seemed as though George Shanks had also not hesitated to manipulate foreign elections.

Rico had helped the campaign, and funnelled some funds into it. The candidate's name was Gunther Gerhardt, and he'd ended up winning the race. He was currently mayor of New Berlin.

"But where the hell have you been for the past year?" I asked. *And why don't you know what the hell has been going on?*

"Captured by the German Submarine Fleet. They figured out what I'd been doing. I left New Berlin after the election and was on my way back home to Trieste. They intercepted my seacar. I've been prisoner."

———•••———

"Go on," I whispered. I had to give it to him, his story was indeed compelling.

"I've been rotting in a cell, McClusky. The GSF were not happy that I'd influenced their colony's election."

"Do they know who you are?"

"They never got it out of me. I only ever spoke Spanish to them."

"They never saw you in New Berlin? Heard you speak English?"

"I kept a low profile."

"They could have asked questions there. It wouldn't have been hard."

"I helped Gerhardt privately. We worked together quietly. We couldn't let people know what I was doing."

"They don't know you're Triestrian?"

"No."

"And yet the GSF found out about you," Johnny said. "How?"

He exhaled. "I still don't know."

Johnny shot me a look. I knew what he was thinking.

"So how'd you get out?" I asked.

He looked down at himself. "I've lost a ton of weight. I'm not usually this skinny, but I did it deliberately. We'd been patrolling along the Northern European coast. The GSF warsubs don't usually stray far from home. They have a cluster of ships offshore, and frankly the German government is on alert right now."

"For what reason?"

He shrugged. "They're worried about losing New Berlin. They know the populace just elected Gerhardt. They're keeping close tabs on the city."

I grunted. It's exactly what the USSF was doing to us.

He continued, "One day I pretended to pass out from illness." He grinned. "I was faking, of course. I felt fine. But I escaped from the clinic and made it to an emergency escape hatch."

"What class of sub?"

"*Attentäter . . . Assassin* Class."

"How long is it?"

"Seventy-five meters."

"How many tubes?"

"Only six, but it has mines, as well." He was staring at me with a grin on his face. He continued without me asking: "Thirteen in the fleet. Twelve crew. Two screws. Max depth 3,000 meters. Max speed, sixty kph. It's their stealth war-sub, built for quiet." He cocked his head. "Come on, man. Are you still testing me?"

"Yes, of course I am."

"Did I pass?"

I frowned. He knew his stuff, that much was certain. As any TCI operative would know.

Or any USSF spy sent to infiltrate TCI.

"What happened then?"

"I got out the emergency escape tube. Almost died. We were over 200 meters down, but I couldn't stay on that sub any longer. I'd been isolated. Had no idea what had been happening. I'd been there nearly a year, McClusky! Shot myself out of the hatch and almost died of the bends."

I gasped. "You went to the surface?"

He nodded. "For a bit. Only thirty seconds or so." He shook his head and remained silent for a moment. "I actually saw the sun," he whispered. "Hadn't seen it for *years*. The open space above . . . it was indescribable, really. The ocean stretched on forever. The light was . . . it was extremely bright."

"You liked it?"

"No. Hated it. I love Trieste. I love living underwater."

"So why didn't you die?" Johnny asked.

"I'd grabbed a scuba tank before I climbed into the escape chute. I strapped it to my back and descended back to thirty meters."

It was a crazy story. Without being able to float on the surface—because his tissues would have been saturated at four atms—he'd had to stay underwater. But how did he get out of the situation?

He anticipated my question. "I knew we were near Cousteau City. I'd heard the GSF sailors talking. Some of them had been on leave and had visited the city. As soon as the sub disconnected from the colony, I started my act and ended up in their clinic. I escaped within thirty minutes of the ship leaving, so I knew I was close. I swam like hell in the direction I thought it would be." He shrugged. "I guessed correctly."

TIMOTHY S.
JOHNSTON

"And you swam to the city."

"Yes."

"Kilometers."

"Yes."

"On one tank of air, after floating to the surface and suffering the bends."

"Yes." He nodded with enthusiasm. "Once I got back under pressure, I was fine. I just had to get to safety, and fast. I knew I only had a couple of hours of air. But I made it."

I found his tenacity admirable. He sounded like a TCI agent. We didn't give up. We always fought until the bitter end.

"And who helped you at Cousteau?"

"Their security came out to get me. I'd been calling for help. I was out of air."

Johnny was staring at me again. This, at least, we could corroborate with the city. I knew Mayor Piette well.

"And now you're back, and you want to help TCI again."

"I am an agent, McClusky. Operative First Class. I'm back, whether George Shanks runs it or not. I'm not going anywhere. I love this city."

I stared at him for a long series of heartbeats.

Chapter Seven

AN HOUR LATER, I WAS marching back to City Control with Johnny at my side. Triestrians were moving all around us with purpose. Some were going to work, some to catch a few hours of sleep, and others were lugging scuba tanks on their backs, dripping wet and trailing puddles as they walked the corridors and travel tubes of the city. It was a common scene. Wet hair was more normal than dry, which was why most wore it so short.

"And the hits just keep on coming," Johnny said.

First the murder, then the USSF investigators, then the USSF takeover of Seascape, and now Rico Ruiz. "This one isn't so bad, though."

"You believe him?" Johnny said.

"I want to, but we have to check him out." I'd burned all of Shanks's files after The Battle, just minutes before the USSF occupied Trieste. I hadn't wanted them in enemy hands. No doubt if Rico was telling the truth, his name would have been in them.

But now we'd never know.

He said, "I'll get on it."

"Check his story. Did he have a cubicle back then? Did he work the fish farms? Really rescue a kid, win a karate championship? And so on."

"I'm on it. He could be another Robert Butte." He was referring to my former deputy mayor, who'd turned out to be a USSF spy.

"All the more reason to keep him close. It worked with Butte."

"True. Just don't let this 'Rico' get too close to our activities, Mac. We can't risk it."

I nodded. "I know. But his story does ring true."

Johnny paused, then he turned to me with a grin. "It's incredible, actually. And, it means one extremely important thing."

I smiled. "New Berlin."

Another city with a government very much in favor of independence. And now I'd be reaching out to their mayor—Gerhardt—to bring him into our sphere.

—••—

EVENING HAD COME TO TRIESTE.

Topside, the sun had dipped below the horizon, tripping on our exterior lights. Floodlights illuminated the modules of the underwater colony, and a multitude of fish swam closer to us to study the steel, glass, and anechoic tiles of our city. Swarms of different species soared through the beams of light. There was a blue floodlight at the top of the Commerce Module—the central module and largest in the colony—illuminating it in a glow that even filtered into the nine levels of the atrium. Since the module's ceiling was mostly transparent to allow sunlight in, it shone down into each deck of the large module, penetrating right to the lowest level. Blue light bathed the shops, restaurants, and bars of the entertainment district; it was like our own version of moonlight on the surface.

I stood in front of a large viewport and studied the scene outside, as was my nightly custom. This time I had picked a view on the east side of the city, so *Blade* was not in sight. I hated seeing USSF warsubs when they docked with us. They were a sign of oppression and control. They took our resources—what we'd extracted through hard work, blood, sweat, and tears, for sometimes Triestrians died while working outside—and gave us very little. I was sure we could arrange economic partnerships with other topside nations for our produce far more profitably than what the US was doing for us.

But we were a colony of the United States, and we all knew that they would never sit back and watch us leave their control.

I had to do this carefully, with as little bloodshed as possible.

The problem was, so much blood had already spilled. Crushed hulls, shattered screws, sunken warsubs, and drowned sailors represented it all.

Sailors who had likely screamed my name just before their heads dipped under the rising water inside their vessels.

I'd killed many people to achieve my dreams—to achieve my father's dreams—and sometimes I wondered if it was all worth it.

—••—

I KNEW THE INVESTIGATORS HAD been hard at work. They'd been tracking down people and questioning them about Admiral Benning's final days at Trieste. It was those last few hours that concerned me the most, and I wondered who would have information that could incriminate Meg and me.

When we'd carried the body down to the moonpool, it had been late at night. Since we operated three shifts at Trieste, normally that wouldn't make a difference—people were always working and would have been present in the corridors. A third of the city was always working at any time. Roughly 70,000 people.

In the past, we'd had people living near each other in the same modules and on the same decks who worked different shifts. This had become an item of contention soon after the city switched to a three-shift schedule. The halls were always busy with people coming and going, and it made sleeping difficult.

The solution had been simple. We now kept people on the same shift living close to each other. It kept the noise levels down and allowed people to get rest.

As a result, when Meg and I had dumped the body in the moonpool, we hadn't passed anyone in the corridors.

I'm sure that if they had seen their mayor and his sister rolling a laundry cart around, they would have noticed.

But there was video.

Hopefully Cliff could deal with that issue.

Then there was the fact that Meg and I had left in *SC-1* in the early morning hours. Where had we gone? For what purpose? I dreaded the questions that would surely come in the morning. There was no way I could hide my ship's departure. Even if we altered the sea traffic logs, the USSF sonar nets would have noticed.

I groaned. It seemed hopeless.

My thoughts drifted to Rico Ruiz, the agent who had shown up unannounced earlier. He had told an interesting story, one that I need to follow-up on. The reports of Germany's activities in the North Sea were largely innocent. They were looking for mineral resources, there were blooming kelp forests north of the Arctic Circle, and so on. They needed resources for their people. They had only the one ocean colony—New Berlin—but no news broadcast had shown anything about the election or mentioned a mayor sympathetic to the independence movement. Johnny was skeptical, and I reminded myself I always had to question motives, as well.

He might be a USSF spy, sent to squash our fight for independence.

I had to watch Rico closely.

In my cubicle, hours later and long after darkness had fallen over the city, I sat at my desk and called Cousteau City.

—••—

81

MAYOR PIETTE WAS ON MY screen with a smile on his face as he watched me. We exchanged pleasantries, discussed the recent battle with the Russian dreadnought, and then got down to business.

"What do you know of Ricardo Ruiz?"

A quizzical expression flitted across his features, but only for an instant. "A weird story, that one. He appeared out of nowhere, swimming like hell for us."

"He didn't have a seacar?"

"No. He claimed to have been out with friends and they left without him."

I frowned. "He was all alone?"

"Yes, and out of air. We had to send security on personal scooters out for him. He was minutes from death."

"Did he tell you where he was living?"

"He wouldn't say. He had no passport and no reason to be at Cousteau, so we sent him on his way." His expression changed to curiosity. "Why? Where is he now?"

"He's here, at Trieste."

"Interesting. We sent him on a sub to Central America. He claimed to be Nicaraguan."

"But living underwater?"

The French mayor shrugged. "You've got me. But that's why we shipped him out. The thought that he was a foreign agent bothered us. But he was malnourished, sick, and there were signs that he'd been beaten."

"Bruises?"

"Yes. Indeed. But far, far worse, too."

"Such as?"

"Evidence of a broken arm. Cuts, scrapes. Scars. Many, many scars, as if he'd been tortured. Some were fresh, some older."

I looked away and processed it. "Tell me one more thing, François—did a GSF warsub depart from Cousteau within the previous hour the day you found him?"

He blinked. "Give me a second on that one." He glanced away as he tapped on a keyboard. Then he looked back at me. "Yes, it did."

"What class?"

"*Attentäter*."

—••—

"THEY'VE BEEN BOTHERING US A lot lately, you know."

"The Germans?" I asked.

"Yes. They're doing something in the North Sea. They come to our cities sometimes to drop off their arrogant, trouble-making troops. Drives us crazy."

"Let me guess," I muttered. "They drink, cause shit, but they spend money, which makes it worthwhile for you."

"Yes, but the trouble they cause is starting to offset their economic value. Soon we'll tell the Germans to stay away. On top of it all, they've sunk some of our ships."

I swore. "French ships or Cousteauian?"

"Both. The bastards are escalating in the region. It's pissing off the other French colonies, too."

"Alpha and Beta?"

"Yes."

Interesting.

—••—

PIETTE SMILED JUST AS I was reaching to terminate the call. "How's Renée, by the way?"

"Renée?" I muttered, stalling.

"Yes. She's still there with you?"

I hesitated. Piette had told me weeks earlier that Renée was falling for me. She'd come with us on the mission to the dreadnought, but I hadn't seen her much other than during her training at Trieste. "She's happy. Working here. She's fit right in."

"Good." He was still smiling as I cut the call, and the screen shifted to blue. I knew what he'd been thinking, what he'd been wanting to ask. I didn't really want to answer those questions just then.

There was a knock at my partition. "Mac? Are you there?"

It was Renée.

Holy shit, I thought.

—••—

SHE ENTERED MY CUBICLE AND sat in the chair in front of the desk. There was very little room there, so I just sat on the bunk. The other Triestrians appreciated the fact that I lived in the same manner as they. I didn't occupy a massive suite somewhere. Didn't live extravagantly. I worked hard and never took my position for granted.

Renée Féroce was quite the sight. My heart pounded whenever I saw her. We'd had a tumultuous beginning—I had first met her face to face in combat—and she had vowed to kill me. I had turned her to our cause, however, and she'd defected from the FSF to join me at Trieste. She was fit from her work in the kelp fields, and she wore short sleeves that showed toned arms. Her dark hair was short and the crinkles in the corners of her eyes deepened as she smiled at me.

"Hello, Mac. How are you?"

"I've been better, I guess."

She frowned. "The investigation. It's why I'm here, actually."

A pressure seemed to lift from my chest. I didn't want to deal with this part of my life yet. Kat had died months earlier, but I wasn't ready for another relationship yet. Renée seemed to recognize this, and had given me space.

And yet here she was, in my cubicle.

And her eyes were locked to mine as she spoke.

I swallowed.

"Did they speak to you?" I asked, my voice a whisper.

"Yes. Zyvinski. She's a tough little thing. Zero emotion."

"She suspects someone murdered Benning here."

"She suspects correctly."

I snorted. "Yes. Meg. It's caused . . . complications."

"I wanted to talk about it."

"Meg? Or the murder?"

She looked away as she considered my question. "Both, I guess. And more. You, too."

"What do you mean?" I swallowed again.

She sighed. "We've been dancing around this for a while, haven't we?"

"What, exactly?" The hope that I could avoid this for a while longer evaporated suddenly. My heart pounded. The pressure on my chest resumed.

She scowled. "Come on, Mac. Don't play dumb. You convinced me to join up with you. For a year I wanted to kill you. Now I'm here."

"I thought you liked being here."

"I love it. But I left the FSF for this. I defected. I'm a traitor to them, dammit."

Was she now regretting her decision? I considered her words. I didn't want her to leave, and I did have feelings for her. It's why I had involved her in our movement and given her so much responsibility. "They think you're dead. Are you having second thoughts?"

"No, it's not that. But I'm—" She exhaled and looked away. "I'm just nervous about tomorrow, I guess. The investigation. What's coming."

"I'm sure they'll take me away."

"And leave the team all alone?" She pursed her lips. "I couldn't picture Trieste without you."

I sighed. "I hope the movement will continue."

A long silence fell over us. She kept glancing at me. Then she suddenly made a decision and moved next to me on the bed. She looked into my eyes, glanced down at my lips.

"Uh, Renée, I really like you."

"So? What's the problem then?"

"It's Kat."

She frowned. She knew what Kat had meant to me. "So you're going to push everyone away, is that it? Stay a recluse?"

"No, that's—"

"Not let anyone in, ever again? After everything we've been through?"

"I'm not—"

She was growing angry now. Her breathing had deepened.

She continued, "Don't you remember how I helped you? I gave you the coordinates to the French research facility. The syntactic foam!"

I sighed. "I know, Renée. I do like you, too."

Now she bolted to her feet. "So what's the problem then? You can't distance yourself from everyone because you've suffered tragedy. Sure, it's painful, but we all deal with it. We have to move on. It's why I'm here now, at Trieste. And I'm all alone, don't you know that?"

I wondered what I could tell her. If I could open up about the nightmares I'd been having about the many sailors I'd killed over the past eighteen months. Or about the hole that Kat's death had left in my heart.

In the end, I couldn't say it. I settled on, "I know these things, Renée."

"It's why I'm here!"

I frowned. "You just said that."

"I mean *here*. In your cubicle."

"Ah."

She paused and glanced around. Struggled to gain control of herself. Then she lowered herself to my bunk again. "Look. I know it hurts. But I'm not asking for a relationship. Not yet, anyway."

"You're not?" I hesitated. "What are you looking for, then?"

She glanced at my lips again, then stared into my eyes. Hers were brown and seemed very deep at that moment. I could lose myself in them, I thought absently.

"This might be our last night," she whispered.

"I'm trying not to think about that, actually."

She reached her arms around my neck and pulled me closer.

"Let's not think at all," she said.

Chapter Eight

RENÉE LEFT MY CABIN BEFORE it got too late. I wasn't sure if what we had done was a good thing or not—my thoughts were still drifting to my former love, Katherine Wells—but I had to admit that it was something that physically I may have needed. The stress had been killing me. After the dreadnought mission, we'd settled down to a pleasant routine, celebratory even, and had relaxed after months and months of efforts to keep the USSF off our backs, create new technologies to fight for independence from the superpowers of the world, and dance on a knife's edge of danger as we forged our lives in the world's oceans. But that period had only lasted for a few days. Meg had murdered Benning, and in a flash the tension and pressure had descended on me once more.

Had *crushed* me, more like it.

Dispose of the body.

Clean the cabin.

Fabricate evidence.

Deal with the guilt.

It was a cascading series of events I wished we didn't have to worry about, but my sister's life was on the line now, and I couldn't just turn my back.

And spending a few hours with Renée, giving in to something both of us had wanted for months now, had been nice.

Nice.

It made me snort. It had been more than nice. It had been a release that I hadn't experienced before.

I was sure that my neighbors had heard both of us crying out, and the thought made me smile. Perhaps it was cliché, but Renée didn't expect anything to come of it, wasn't demanding a relationship or a commitment, and wasn't expecting a ring in the morning. Inside I felt like a jerk, but she had really thrown herself at me.

Because tomorrow might be the day I die.

Her blunt and mature attitude had made me sit up and take stock of things. Yes, we both liked each other. Yes, sex would be nice. No, no relationship needed. *Hell, Mac—the USSF is going to kill you tomorrow! Let's just enjoy tonight.*

Blunt, to be sure, but probably true.

As the partition closed and I heard her footsteps padding down the metal grating of the corridor, I closed my eyes and wondered what the morning would bring.

—••—

I ONLY GOT A COUPLE of hours of sleep. I was at the security office meeting with Cliff at 0700; we only had two hours before Zyvinski would arrive, demanding proof that Benning had one day just up and left on his own.

Cliff hadn't slept at all. He'd been working all night since our meeting in my office the day before, and there simply hadn't been time.

It made me wince, because what had I been doing in the interim?

Fucking. Pure and simple.

But his eyes were not condescending and his attitude wasn't one of judgment. He was gruff and professional, if a bit tired, and what I got was classic Cliff Sim. This was a problem that he wanted to help me solve, and he was going to do whatever it took.

"Show me what you've got," I said.

He placed a series of photos on the desk before me. There were timestamps at the bottom right corner of each. "First, a video of Benning entering his cabin at 2106 hours on 15 June. According to the video, he didn't leave until the morning."

"How did you manage this?"

"Substituted video from a previous evening, doctored the date and time."

"Does he have the limp?"

"From two days earlier. It's worse, but at least you can see the leg bandaged."

"Good job. Next?"

Another set of photographs, also with time stamps. "These are from the next morning. You can see he exits his cubicle and goes to the Docking Module."

"How in the hell did you arrange these?"

He winced. "The video that shows him leaving is from the previous day. I spliced it with video of him going to the docking bay, but that happened before his injury. It's the best I could do, but if they pay close attention, they'll notice that his limp vanishes."

"Shit."

"Best I could do, Boss," he said. "There's no other way to show him going to board a vessel the next day."

"Especially since that was the story I cooked up for Zyvinksi."

"It is what it is." He shrugged his large shoulders. "Let's move on." He placed another set of photographs on the table. "This is us at the bar on 15 June. Late in the evening."

I frowned as I stared at the photos. Sure enough, it was the entire team—minus one—sharing stories and drinking together. Celebrating the destruction of the Russian warsub. I noticed Renée standing close to me, her hand on my thigh. I hadn't even noticed at the time. I'd been drunk, I guessed. "Meg's not here."

"No, she's not. There was no way to insert her image. It would have been too obvious."

I studied the timestamps. It had us drinking well into the night—into the next day, in fact. "You know, if they ask for access to our security server, they'll know all these are fake."

"Yes, I know. So we have to deny them permission should they ask."

And if they don't ask and just demand? With their SEALs helping? And Blade floating outside with torpedo tubes aimed right at us? What then?

I shuddered at the thought.

"I also have a video of you going straight to your cubicle after the bar. You stayed there all night."

A half smile spread across my face. "Good job, Cliff. What else are we overlooking?"

"The fact that you and Meg left in *SC-1* early in the morning." Cliff sat down and leaned back in his chair. "Boss. It's time for you to tell me the truth."

I studied the man. "I think I already have, Cliff."

"I know you have. But you haven't told me one important item. Where's Benning?"

I sighed. "Are you sure you want to know? They might interrogate you."

He remained silent and stared at me.

"Okay," I muttered. "We took him to the Puerto Rico Trench. Opened the moonpool. Wrapped the body in chain. Dumped him there." It was the deepest area of the Atlantic Ocean. "No one will ever find him."

It was over eight kilometers deep.

He eyed me. "It's a smart location, but also dangerous."

"We had to use the SCAV drive to get there and back in time. Someone will have heard."

"So what's your cover story?"

"Prospecting." It was the common excuse I used with the USSF, but it worked.

"So late at night?"

"We work three shifts. It's only late at night for one of the shifts."

"And why use the SCAV drive?"

"I have important things to do here. I can't spend two days going to one possible mine site."

"Why at such a deep location? That seems odd."

"It wasn't in the trench. The site was located on the other side of it."

"What mineral?"

"Aluminum."

"You have this in your log?"

"I do." I knew he was just testing me, and I let him do it.

He frowned. "It sounds good, but with just a little digging it'll all fall apart. They'll know your seacar paused over the trench at a depth of precisely thirty meters."

I could come up with something to explain that. And in the end, they wouldn't risk taking me away over something that was circumstantial only. Our citizens might rebel should Zyvinski decide to take me in.

I shrugged and just stared at the man.

He said only, "I understand," then he started collecting the photos and putting them back in their files. Accompanying them would be the videos.

I checked my watch.

Time was ticking down.

—••—

AT PRECISELY 0900 HOURS THE hatch slid aside and Zyvinski marched in. There was only one SEAL with her, and I wondered absently where the other was, and where Quintana was for that matter.

I should have guessed, but it didn't occur to me just then.

She showed no emotion. Her angular features and lined face, framed by her thinning blonde hair, betrayed the seriousness of her job. This person was all business. She was here to arrest people for murder, and nothing was going to stop her.

I just hoped our surnames would protect us.

"Give me your files," she said, her tone sharp.

Cliff watched her silently, but held out the folders, bound together by elastics.

"What do these show?" she asked.

My security chief explained Benning's movements on the night in question. He explained where I had been for most of the evening until my own trip to the

Docking Module and my prospecting trip to a potential aluminum deposit.

Zyvinski snorted at that, without even glancing at me. She was studying Cliff as he spoke.

He then explained that there was no record of where Benning had left, or what seacar he had taken. It was a military model and we didn't track those things.

"Bullshit," she said. "You track every sub that comes and goes."

"Our records show him leaving in a basic military seacar on the morning of 16 June. We don't have the registry recorded."

She snarled, "You told us you'd get the registry of the vessel he departed in."

"It's a military vessel. That's all we have. We don't record—"

"Bullshit," she repeated. She drew the word out, stretching it as she seemed to enunciate each letter. There was a pause as she glared at him. "Do you have the track for me from Seatraffic Control?"

"No. I didn't get that. I'll collect it for you today, though."

She snapped, "Don't bother. I already spoke to Grant Bell."

An icy cold wave swept over me. *Oh, shit.*

She continued, "There was no departure of any USSF seacar on the morning in question."

"I say there was," Cliff replied.

"There's no track recorded. But there is one of the mayor's personal seacar, designated *SC-1*."

No one spoke.

The silence was oppressive.

She continued, "I also know that on the night in question, Truman McClusky left the bar where this supposed celebration was taking place."

She was speaking of me as if I wasn't even there. "You can ask the employees—"

"Already did," she rasped, still not looking at me. She was glaring at Cliff. "The party broke up at midnight, not at 0200 hours as you state." She glanced at the photos. "Or as your photos show. And I know the mayor went to his sister's cubicle afterward, searching for her, not to his own bunk, as you say."

"Video evidence states otherwise," he said in a quiet voice. "You can't contradict it."

"Unless it's been doctored."

The lines in his face grew deeper. "That's a serious accusation."

"So is accusing someone here of murder," I said.

She continued, "The people working the docks claim Benning left in the morning."

Cliff blinked. "So they corroborate the truth."

Zyvinski shook her head. "No. Someone has coerced them. You, no doubt.

They say a military seacar left on the morning of 16 June with the Admiral piloting. But our own sonar nets showed nothing of the sort."

I glanced at Cliff. So, he'd had the foresight to speak to the workers there, and they were supporting our story.

The less I knew about this, the better, I thought.

"So you have eyewitness reports of what happened, and you still deny the truth?" Cliff said, his voice hard.

"We reject the lies."

Cliff looked away and took in a breath. He didn't know what else to say. Finally, "Are you here at Trieste to fabricate a murder?"

"We're here to arrest a murderer."

"Benning might show up tomorrow. Or next week. Maybe he's at Ballard. Or Seascape."

Zyvinski snorted. "Not likely there." Then she said no more.

I watched her, not speaking.

No one spoke.

Another period of silence fell over us as Zyvinski stared at the files in her lap. Ventilation fans droned. Eventually she said, "It would appear as though you have provided us with fabricated evidence."

"So this is a trumped-up investigation?" Cliff asked.

"Hardly. We have eyewitness reports. We know what happened. And when we dig through your video evidence, no doubt we'll discover it's been altered. The metadata will show it."

"So why don't you tell us what you think happened, then?"

The CIA investigator finally turned to face me, for the first time. "Simple. Your sister, Meagan McClusky, killed Admiral Benning in her cubicle."

I shook my head. "But the video shows he didn't go there. He left in the morning—"

"I know you are lying, and I know you've convinced people to create fake videos and lie for you."

"But why would they do that?"

"Because you're Truman McClusky. That's what Triestrians will do for you, and for your father."

"My father's dead. Killed by the CIA."

I shouldn't have said it, because now Zyvinski's lips peeled back and showed her brilliant white teeth. "And that would give you motive, wouldn't it?"

"To kill an Admiral in the USSF?"

"Yes. Especially if the person in question was the one who carried out the CIA's orders. The one who actually killed Frank McClusky."

I sighed. "You know so much, but the evidence doesn't support what you're claiming."

"I'm sure if we journey to the Puerto Rico Trench, we'll find out for sure."

"Find out what?"

She just stared at me, but she didn't answer. Instead she said, "I spent yesterday interviewing Triestrians and studying the USSF sonar logs of the area surrounding this colony. I know who left and when. I also know who *didn't* leave when you claim they did. I have spoken to people who were at the bar with your group on the evening in question. I've spoken to people in Habitat Module B who heard the killing take place."

"Say again?" I frowned, not understanding.

"Your sister killed him, McClusky."

I paused. Then, "A man twice her size? A trained soldier?"

"Because he killed your father, yes. The scuffle was obvious to people nearby."

"How do you know the noises weren't something else? From a different bunk?"

Her eyes narrowed. "Sex, you mean? Possible, but unlikely. There is too much other evidence. I'll dig into these videos, but for now, we are making arrests."

I stared at the SEAL in the room; his face was a mask of hate. "Who, exactly?" I asked. My blood was icy.

She turned to Cliff. "Your security chief is coming with us."

"And me?" I asked.

"Apparently you did not commit this crime. You probably covered it up, and our investigation will continue over the next few days. But for now, you're free to stay here and continue your work as mayor. But you will not leave Trieste, McClusky. You're under house arrest." Then her lips peeled apart into a thin smile. I could see her teeth. It was grotesque; her smile a contradiction to her expression. A vicious counterpoint.

I realized with a start that she wasn't done.

Admiral Quintana and the other SEAL were somewhere else at that precise moment.

She continued, "We are also taking your sister. She's coming with us."

Interlude:
Meagan McClusky

```
Location:      Latitude:    27° 34' 29" N
Longitude:     54° 56' 11" W
               The Gulf of Mexico, Trieste City
               Module B
Depth:         30 meters
Date:          1 July 2130
Time:          0955 hours
```

MEAGAN MCCLUSKY CHECKED THE TIME on her Personal Communication Device. It was just after 0900 hours. She knew what was most likely happening in Cliff's office, and she knew what would follow.

USSF troops would be at her cubicle any minute to take her in.

They knew she'd killed Benning.

They were coming for her.

She grabbed the needle gun from her drawer and belted the holster to her right thigh. The large weapon fit within perfectly. It was an acrylic material, meant for underwater use, and not leather as a surface one might be.

She left the snap open, so she could grab the weapon at a moment's notice.

The strap circled her leg in two places, and on the upper inside of her thigh it came close to the incision, which bothered her slightly.

She lowered the holster a bit and tested it again. The strap was now an inch from the stitches.

Still annoying, but better, at least.

She placed a few pillows in her bunk to simulate the appearance of a sleeping figure and covered it with a sheet. Then she stepped into the corridor and slid the partition shut behind her.

The cubicle directly across from hers was empty. The occupant worked the fish farms, maintaining the bubble fences and monitoring the stocks, and had already left for the day.

She positioned the desk chair so she could sit and monitor the hallway. With the partition open just a crack, she could see her own cubicle, only two meters away.

Perfect.

She settled down to wait, but within minutes the danger approached.

Sounds of booted feet marched on the steel grating outside.

She peered out the opening—it was just a sliver of space to see through, but the sight took her breath away.

USSF troops.

They wore the standard blue Fleet uniform. Each had the customary—and mostly ornamental—scuba dagger sheathed on their thighs.

There were four of them out there, she noted with worry.

And one SEAL.

Meg peered out farther, being careful not to knock the partition accidentally and cause movement, and saw a woman out there, as well.

A gasp caught in her throat.

Admiral Quintana.

The fucking Admiral of the United States Submarine Fleet was just a meter away, intent on arresting Meg and taking her in for questioning.

Or worse.

Meg slid the needle gun out of her holster, and held it before her.

Her heart was pounding.

Her breath quickened and she fought hard to control her breathing, as Mac had taught her. But he was a trained agent, an operative of TCI. She was a sub mechanic and not exactly used to this sort of thing.

There was a SEAL out there, for fuck's sake!

She took three more deep breaths—combat breathing, it was called—and slowly rose to her feet.

She didn't want to kill anyone.

Just injure, and then escape.

She'd run to the Docking Module. Jump in a seacar and try to get away. USS *Blade* would likely follow, fire a few torpedoes maybe.

It made her heart pound even more. There were no other options here, though. These were perhaps her last moments of freedom.

Outside, the troops had opened Meg's partition and were stepping into her cubicle.

She hurled the sliding divider aside and lunged forward.

—••—

THE TROOPS GLANCED BEHIND THEM. It had caught them off guard, because they'd assumed the work shift had already begun and there was no one there.

They'd been complacent, she thought.

She raised the needle gun—

And they cried out. As one, they lurched to the side, hoping to avoid the deadly stainless steel projectiles.

She had only five shots.

She had to make them count.

The first hit a sailor in his knee. The gun bucked in her hand as the gas cartridge propelled the narrow spear. He went down like a sack of rocks, gripping his wound, his agonized scream echoing off the bulkheads.

Meg turned to the next, also aiming at the leg, but making note that the SEAL standing next to Quintana had placed himself in front of the Admiral.

She fired again.

Another body hit the deck, accompanied by an arterial spray that painted the steel corridor walls.

Meg swallowed. Inside, in a deep place that she had smothered and was fighting to keep suppressed, she screamed in rage. She couldn't believe what she was doing.

Couldn't believe the person she'd become.

But she was in survival mode now. She had few options, and of the limited choices, this was the best of the worst.

She pushed herself to the side and took aim at the third sailor.

He was raising his own weapon now—a gun from a waist holster—and leveling it at her head.

She cursed under her breath.

She meant to injure only.

But these troops meant to *kill*.

Meg threw herself back into the cubicle she'd been hiding in. As she fell back, she fired again. The sailor fired at the same moment, and the round hit the bulkhead behind her. It rattled to the deck, the crack of the impact exploding in her ears.

Her needle shot toward the man faster than she could see. There was only a glint of light as it disappeared into his torso.

The look on his face said it all.

It was a mixture of fear and agony. He clutched the wound, instantly dropping his own weapon, and fell backward onto the bunk writhing in pain.

She turned to the next and saw only a blur.

—••—

IT WAS THE SEAL. HE'D approached from the side—difficult in the narrow corridor—but he'd crouched and crept along the bulkhead. As she began shifting her aim toward him, he leaped forward and struck out at her arm.

She screamed in rage and fired, but the needle soared down the hall, hit a bulkhead, and skittered across the deck, twisted and bent by the savage impact.

She only had one shot left.

Her assailant kicked her arm and it jerked to the side. Meg stepped back as the SEAL entered the cubicle. Then, with a cry, she stepped forward and gave him a kick of her own.

She'd hoped that by attacking suddenly, she might catch him off guard.

And it worked.

He tried to block her foot but was too late. Her heel hit the man's solar plexus, just below his rib cage, where it would knock the breath out of him.

And then she could fire her last shot.

But her heel hit solid steel.

He was wearing a vest.

Dammit!

She pulled her leg back and tried an elbow, but now he'd regained his advantage, based on size and aggression and the fact that she was now standing on just one foot.

Meg tried to catch her balance but the man knocked her leg to the side and she stumbled slightly. She brought her gun to bear—

And he slapped her arm away.

She pulled the trigger—

And the needle hit the bulkhead right next to him.

She swore in frustration.

The SEAL's lips peeled back into a disgusting smile. He knew he had her.

Meg had one last chance here, and then it would all be over.

She spun and lifted her elbow, hoping to hit his chin just below the helmet. She dropped the needle gun as she did so, and it hit the deck at her feet.

But the SEAL had seen it coming.

His training had taken over now, and Meg was too slow.

He blocked the elbow and grabbed her, twisting her arm and turning his hips as he did so. It wrenched Meg to the side, and she cried out in pain as her arm ended up behind her back. She was off balance and she fought to regain her footing, but the man just pushed her again until her face was pressed against bulkhead and he forced her upward.

Pain lanced through her body and she groaned loudly.

He was fucking going to break her arm!

"Stop," a voice said. It was Quintana.

"She just shot three USSF sailors," the SEAL grated between clenched teeth.

"And now she's ours. There will be time for this later. Cuff her."

The man's breath was hot on the back of Meg's neck, and it made her shiver. She could feel him growl as the admiral's ordered registered. Then he swore softly and jerked Meg around. He pulled a pair of handcuffs out and stared at her.

There was sweat on his forehead and it trickled down his cheek. "You shot at me."

"Too bad I missed," she rasped.

He slapped her and it snapped her head to the side. Blood filled her mouth, and she spit it out.

"Enough!" Admiral Quintana yelled.

Meg thought that just maybe she might have another chance, but the blow had dazed her. Her vision was blurry and she didn't even know if she was standing anymore. She might have been lying on the deck; her thoughts were a jumble.

The next thing she knew, the SEAL was pulling her down the corridor, and she was stumbling behind him, trying to keep up. Steel handcuffs clasped her hands in front of her, and he was pulling her by the wrists.

Behind, she could hear the groans of USSF sailors in pain.

She smiled.

—••—

THE USSF SEAL HAULED HER through the corridors of the city as Triestrians watched, horrified—some of them even cried out and demanded the USSF stop—until they'd finally crossed the umbilical into USS *Blade*. A part of her realized that she was now no longer in Trieste.

They had her.

She'd made a decision two weeks ago, and now she was paying the price.

Soon, Meg McClusky found herself in the bowels of the USSF warsub, sitting handcuffed to a steel table, staring at the CIA Investigator.

Zyvinski was icy cold and matched Meg's gaze with equal intensity. She'd entered the cabin and sat before her without making a noise. Meg had been looking down at the table, and when she'd looked up, there she was. Just staring back at her with that wispy blonde hair that framed the aging face. The deep lines and the pointed nose. It was as if she'd drifted in on the air currents, like a ghost.

It made Meg jump.

Zyvinksi said simply, "We know you killed Admiral Taurus T. Benning."

"I did not," Meg said simply. She licked her lip, which was still bleeding. There was a puddle of blood on the table before her.

Zyvinski's expression turned incredulous. "You just attacked USSF sailors. You shot them. If you're not guilty, why do such a thing?"

"They were going to arrest me."

But Zyvinski ignored her. She didn't even care. She'd already glanced down at her notes and said, "You were in your cubicle that evening. You never left. You called Benning and invited him over. There are records of this call. He left and made his way out Module C, through Module A, and into Module B and up to your deck. We have eyewitnesses who saw him. Once in your cubicle, you killed him, likely by drugging or a plain, simple stabbing."

Meg's stomach was in her throat, but she tried not to show it.

They know everything, she thought.

The investigator continued, "You were supposed to be at the bar celebrating, but you didn't show. People nearby heard the scuffle, heard you cry out as you killed him. Then, shortly after, your brother arrived to check on you. People heard him knocking at your partition."

She paused and looked up at Meg, but she didn't say anything.

Zyvinksi shrugged and continued. "You and your brother likely cleaned up the mess. Then somehow you removed the body."

"*Somehow?*"

"You took it to *SC-1*. You left in the seacar and dumped it in the Puerto Rico Trench. We have sonar records of your track. The timing meant you had to use the SCAV drive, which is very noisy."

"I was not on *SC-1* that evening. I was asleep."

She continued, "You had a black eye following the murder. Multiple people have mentioned it to us."

"I got it—"

"We found a mattress in the city refuse yesterday. Someone had removed it from your bunk. The Admiral's blood is on it."

"It's not mine, if that's what you're saying."

"We found a brand new mattress on your bunk," she said, without missing a beat. "Your brother also told us, on the day we arrived, that Benning left on his own on the morning of 16 June. But how would he know that Benning had been alone? Why would he say that?" She tilted her head and her lips parted. "He messed up there." She closed the folder on her lap. "And now you are under arrest for murder. We have also arrested Cliff Sim for altering surveillance data and obstructing the investigation."

So Cliff is here with me. She filed that away as important information.

Somewhere, on Blade, *USSF troops are likely interrogating or torturing him.*

"This is ridiculous," Meg said.

"Your crime was hasty and not well planned. You left clues everywhere. You couldn't get away with it, no matter how hard you tried."

Around them, the sound of the warsub's thruster ramped up. The deck vibrated. Commands over the ship's comm echoed in the passageways, muted and distorted and difficult to understand, but it was clear that they were departing Trieste.

"Tell me about your new warsubs," she said, shifting the subject.

"What?" Meg barely managed.

"Your deep-diving subs. They can hit a depth of at least five kilometers. Crush depth for most warsubs is four."

"I don't know what you're talking about."

Zyvinski's eyes narrowed. "I know this from the recent battle with the dreadnought. Admiral Benning also reported it to us. Is it why you killed him?"

"I still don't—"

"You killed him to keep knowledge of this new technology from us, correct? Or was it simply revenge because of your father."

"What technology?"

"The deep-diving tech!" she snapped. "I'm being clear here. Tell me how your Triestrian subs can descend so much deeper than any other sub!"

Meg paused and stared at the investigator. Zyvinski's arms were tight at her sides, her teeth clenched, and her face red. It was the most emotion Meg had seen from her yet.

And it scared her.

There was a *clang* as the umbilical separated from the colony.

Meagan McClusky had succeeded in killing Benning, but in the end the authorities had captured her.

And now, life as she had known it, was over.

Part Three: Plans

Four Weeks Later

3 August 2130

Chapter Nine

A MONTH HAD PASSED SINCE they'd taken Cliff Sim and Meagan.

The mood at Trieste was somber.

People had seen USSF troops hauling Meg away. A beating had cut her face and there was blood spilling from her mouth. It hadn't been smart of them to do such a thing. Firstly, she was a McClusky. The people here revered our father. Each February 23 they celebrated his life, the man he'd been, and what he'd done for the underwater colony.

The CIA had killed him because of it, and it had created harsh feelings toward the USSF in the region. They'd never been able to repair the damage afterward.

And then they'd beaten and arrested his daughter, dragged her kicking and screaming down the corridors and into the umbilical. *Blade* had detached shortly after, and the warsub had left, taking two citizens of the city to a fate worse than death.

The people didn't even know why. Didn't even know what Meg and Cliff had done to warrant such actions.

The inevitable conclusion was that they hadn't done anything at all.

Of course I knew better than to reveal the truth. I didn't mention Benning's murder or the disposing of the body. I just grunted and swore that I'd make things right.

They were clamoring for action, though—and *openly* at that—and I had to implore them to stop. Behaviour like that would always result in more USSF presence, something we desperately wanted to avoid. Whenever someone stopped me in a travel tube or in the Commerce Module or while standing at a port and just watching the teeming life outside, I knew what they were going to say. The exchanges always went something like so:

"Hey, Mac. We're gonna kick their asses for this, right?"

"Don't be so loud. You can't let anyone hear you say such things."

"I mean, we're going to declare independence soon and show them who's boss, right?"

"I said, please be quiet."

"Sorry. But when are we going to announce it?"

"Things take time. We can't rush it."

"They took Meg! We have to go get her back. How can I help? Those fucking USSF assholes."

"Quiet! Thinking that is one thing. Announcing it to the world is totally different!"

"Sorry. But really, I want to help you. I loved Frank McClusky. He wouldn't sit back at something like this."

"I'm not sitting back."

"So you're planning something? Good! How can I help?"

"I'll let you know. Please lower your voice . . . "

It happened multiple times each day, with varying levels of vehemence or passion. Some Triestrians wanted to actually go and fight the USSF, hand-to-hand if necessary. Others just wanted to go shoot torpedoes. Others wanted to announce independence and then prevent USSF warsubs from docking with us. Forbid USSF sailors to visit. Those requests just made me shake my head. We were too vulnerable still. All it would take is one explosive—even from the *inside*—and it would all crash down on our heads.

And they would do it, too.

They'd proven it in the past.

Each encounter usually ended with the citizen pleading with me to use our military. I would step away and ask them to stop. Besides, the Triestrian 'Navy' was made up of experimental submarines and seacars, crewed and piloted by volunteers, with new technologies that we barely understood, let alone operated effectively.

But, that being said, we had scored some tremendous victories, and as hard as I tried, word was indeed getting out.

Some Triestrians knew of the USSF and FSF warsubs sunk out in the Mid-Atlantic Ridge. Many believed it to be our handiwork—and it was—but I begged off and told them I didn't know anything about it.

Of course, there was usually a half-smile on my face and a twinkle in my eye, so even I wasn't trying very hard to keep it that secretive. The citizen I was speaking to would usually get the hint, figure it out, and depart our conversation with a corresponding wink and a smile.

It always brought my mind to Max Hyland. He was in our research labs, working on his bomb.

One day, Johnny and I went to visit him to learn of any progress. There was intense security at his lab, which was great, because all it would take would be a French or Russian operative to infiltrate Trieste and steal his work and we'd have to embark on another chase around the world to stop the secret from getting out. It's what had happened with Johnny and the SCAV drive a year and a half earlier.

Inside the lab, I looked around in wonder. Hyland had ordered equipment for his work and now it crammed every possible space. There were tubes and wires and holoscreens everywhere, but even though I was not a scientist, I could tell it was very different from Dr. Manesh Lazlow's lab. His was full of listening or audio devices—headphones and oscillators and acoustic generators and so on.

"I hope you got everything you asked for," I mumbled, staring at it all.

Hyland had a grin on his handsome, dimpled face. "Not all."

"Oh? What else should we order?"

"I need a synchrotron." He set down a clipboard and marched toward us. His face was tanned, his hair trimmed, and he looked fit. It made me frown. Lazlow had thrown himself into his work, barely emerging for food and showers. I'd had to force those things on him. But Hyland seemed . . . *normal?* And socially adept, too. Triestrians whom he'd met universally liked him and I'd often seen him in the entertainment district laughing, sharing a drink, or socializing with others. He had fit right in. He loved it here.

"How big are those?" I asked. "You don't have much space left in here."

"The largest has a circumference of forty-three kilometers."

I snapped a look at him, and that smile was still there. He'd been joking.

"How's the work going?" I said as I continued to study the lab. A sign across one entire bulkhead read: I BELIEVE IN ISOMERS.

He noticed Johnny and me looking at it.

"Fantastic, actually," he replied.

"What's an isomer?" Johnny asked.

"It's the basis of all my research. Nuclear isomers. I started with tantalum, but I needed something else, something with a little more kick."

"Pardon me?" I said.

"The foundation of my research is *isomeric.*"

"I read a bit about it, but didn't fully—"

"You see," he pressed on, "isomers have energy contained within their atomic structures. Most isomers decay rapidly, giving off gamma radiation, and are extremely unstable. But some isomers have a much longer decay rate. Thirty years, say, give or take. Those also give off radiation, but they are more useful to me. We call them 'nearly stable.'" He marched us over to a diagram on a bulkhead that listed numerous isomers, with a value next to each. "This is how much energy each isomer contains. You can see tantalum is pretty low on the list, but it's also more readily available, which is why I started with it."

"I see," I mumbled. Next to tantalum-180m was, *Binding Energy (MeV)*: 475.

"Within the atom there is energy stored. It's like a firecracker ready to go off. All it needs is a little help, and the theory is that you can release that energy all at once instead of during its long half lives of decay. It's called *isomeric triggering*. That's what I've been working on for all these years."

"It's why you got blacklisted?" I asked.

A dark cloud passed across his handsome features. "Yes. The academic community stopped publishing me. The University of Dallas pushed me out. I was a laughingstock topside. But not really."

I took note of the way he spoke the last.

He said, "Others believe in my work, even if mainstream academics don't."

"Why's that?" Johnny asked. He'd been pushing me to explain Hyland's presence, but I hadn't really been able to, other than what we'd discussed upon first meeting the man. It's why I had brought Johnny to the lab. I wanted to know more, too.

I wanted to know if this bomb was going to be able to help us or not.

The itching on my thigh had largely disappeared, but I absently rubbed the scar with my thumb. The stitches had come out a few weeks earlier.

Hyland continued, "You see, I started with tantalum. One of the isotopes is an isomer. There is energy stored there. I ran some early experiments where I could release its energy in a controlled manner. But there are other isomers which have *incredible* energy stored within their atomic bounds, and I shifted to those."

"What energy?"

"A condition found in some atoms where neutrons or protons exist in higher energy levels than the others. Bringing those particles—*nucleons*—back to ground state is what releases the energy."

"Sounds nuclear, a bit," Johnny mumbled.

Hyland rounded on him. "That's the trick—to release energy without the splitting or fusing of any atoms! *Induced Gamma Emission*, or IGE. That's why the Isomer Bomb is so revolutionary."

I said, "Others believe you, other than me?"

"Yes. You see, I switched to other isomers. I had students once, I was a professor, highly esteemed by my peers. One term my team conducted an interesting experiment. I got some isomer from a synchrotron in Switzerland. I put the smear—there wasn't much at all, just a few grams—on an upturned Styrofoam cup. We rigged up a dental X-ray machine to send a beam at the stuff. We'd purchased the machine from a dentist who'd just closed up his shop. We used an audio amplifier to modulate the beam a bit. I let it run for weeks and studied all the emissions from the isomer. Sure enough, the evidence was there!"

Silence met the statement. Johnny and I just stared at the man. "What evidence?" Johnny finally asked.

"The energy emission was greater than the input! We had succeeded in cracking the isomer and extracting some of the energy."

"Did it explode?"

"No, no. It was very subtle, but it proved that isomeric triggering is possible."

"So you published," I asked.

His expression dropped. "Yes. And that's when it all fell apart. Even though it passed peer review, others couldn't replicate my experiments." He clenched his fists at his sides. "But they were doing it wrong. They were either using the wrong energy level to crack the isomer or they weren't studying the released energy properly. They were blind to it. But they all jumped on me, declared it pathological science, and put me in the same category as cold fusion."

"But you said others believed you?"

A sly smile spread across his features. "Yes, indeed. You see, there were some experiments that validated my work. But they didn't publish. There are also all sorts of rumours out there, which is how you found me, I assume."

I frowned. "But if they validated—"

"Because we're talking about a new class of bomb here, McClusky."

"'Mac,' please."

"Mac. Okay—thanks. It's non-nuclear. Nuclear non-proliferation treaties don't touch it. Nations can test freely. It skirts all of the previous agreements."

"So it is a bomb," Johnny injected.

"Not yet. But once I accomplish the triggering dilemma—to extract all the energy at once instead of small amounts over time—it will be."

"How big?"

He shrugged. "It'd be like Hiroshima in a hand grenade."

"But non-nuclear."

"Yes. But there would be radiation, too. A gargantuan surge of gamma rays."

"What would they do?"

"Liquefy flesh. Detonate the bomb next to a warsub, and even if you don't crack its skin—which it likely would, anyway—it would liquefy anyone inside the steel and titanium hull."

Johnny peered at me, horrified. "But that sounds like a—"

"No, it's not," Hyland interrupted. "It's totally different. And if we get the triggering down perfect, there would not be any remaining radioactive particles left over, either. Just one massive explosion to take down whatever sub you wanted. The gamma rays disappear quickly."

I paused and studied the man. He seemed convinced, there was no doubt of it. And his lab looked professional enough. But inside I knew that I was taking a gamble on this man. I said, "Why are the experiments that backed up your initial work not common knowledge? Why haven't they published, too, to validate you?"

"And remove me from their blacklist?" he asked. He snorted. "Well, for one, the Defence Advanced Research Projects Agency got involved. Shovelled a bunch of money at their government-funded labs to prove my work."

Johnny gasped. "DARPA? But if they're involved, why don't others believe?"

"Because science is taught by people who have been taught by others who also don't believe it's possible, Mr. Chang. It's self-perpetuating. It's always that way for scientists on the edge. But once we've proven it, then it's taught in universities. Until then, we're crackpots."

I said, "So DARPA is funding it in the United States, too. But why, if no one believes?"

"Because of those few experiments which did initially corroborate my results. They proved that it was possible to release the energy. And when it became common knowledge in the scientific community that other countries were researching Isomer Bombs . . . "

"The United States didn't want to be left behind without one. They had to fund it, even though the scientific community didn't believe."

"Precisely."

"But not fund you."

His face twisted into an angry mask. "They only fund their government agencies. Not the people who actually did the ground-breaking work on it. But the DARPA people remember what happened with Enrico Fermi."

Neither of us responded, and Hyland sighed in resignation. "Fermi was conducting experiments on atomic fission in the late 1930s. He tried to convince Navy Admiral Stanford Hooper of the importance of such a bomb."

"It worked out okay for Fermi, then?" I said.

"No. Can you believe it? The US Navy turned him down. Hooper dismissed him, and as the story goes, someone on his staff used a racist slur. Called him a wop. But Fermi convinced others, and it all laid the groundwork for the atomic bomb. Ended WW2. No one wants to be Stanford Hooper again, Mac. No one wants to lose out on something of this importance."

Johnny was studying a series of charts displayed on holoscreens, but nothing made any sense to us, anyway. He said absently, "So you described an isomer as a firecracker. And you're just trying to figure out how to trigger it."

"How to get the energy out, yes."

"Energy that's just naturally in there."

"Stored in the atoms, yes."

"How much energy is in there?"

"That's the big question, isn't it. Well, I've already told you that a hand grenade-sized Isomer Bomb would be like a small nuclear explosion. But if you want a better comparison, here's one: Each molecule of TNT has one electron volt of energy. But in this bomb, each atom of the isomer has 2.5 million! There is 10,000 times the energy per gram as TNT."

Johnny and I both gasped. "You're saying this bomb is two and a half million times more powerful than an equal amount of dynamite?"

Hyland frowned at us, realizing—sadly, I assume—that we weren't scientists and weren't able to fully comprehend the energy that he was talking about. Instead he shrugged and said, "More or less, yes. The emissions would be as gamma rays, X-rays, and light."

A silence descended over us as we tried to process that.

"And how do you trigger it?" Johnny asked.

"With X-rays. You need a blast of them of the correct magnitude and frequency. That's the Primary. Then the Secondary blast occurs, and that's the big one. It releases the isomer's energy all at once. Remember the half life?"

"No."

"The half life is three decades. It takes thirty-one years for half its energy to dissipate via gamma rays. But we're going to release all of its energy in one instant."

Another silence fell over us. Then Johnny darted a glance at me in sudden realization. "The zircon mine?"

I smiled. "Not really."

"No?" His shoulders slumped. "But Mac, we sent people there weeks ago. The mine is in The Iron Plains, halfway to hell in the Pacific Ocean, with Chinese and Russian and US warsubs circling just above them, ready to destroy them if they're even found out, and they're trying to mine your zircon quietly, for Christ's sake! And now you tell me that it's not even zircon that we're after for this?"

Hyland grabbed Johnny and led him back to the list of isomers with the energy expenditures listed next to them. Tantalum was there, near the bottom of the list. Its binding energy was 475 MeV. His finger traced the isomers and it moved up, to the top of the list. There was the element that we needed:

hafnium-178m2. Next to it was, *Binding Energy (MeV)*: 885.

"That's it there," Hyland whispered. "That's the element I'm using. And wherever you find zircon, you'll find hafnium, but it's as rare as hell. But there's so much energy there, if we can trigger a gamma ray emission, the energy released will crack the hull of any warsub you aim your isomer torpedo at. Probably split the entire thing into kindling-sized pieces and melt it into slag."

For our next mission, I wanted to say.

Because now Meg and Cliff were on my mind, and first on my list of priorities was a rescue.

Chapter Ten

JOHNNY AND I LEFT HYLAND'S lab. The doctor was continuing his research using an X-ray machine—souped up and modified to crack energy from the hafnium—when Johnny stopped me in the corridor. Our feet had clanged on the steel grating as we'd walked, and now silence fell over us as he stared at me. "What's this bomb for?"

I blinked. "I think that's obvious."

"Meg found out that the Russians are about to launch three more dreadnoughts. When they do, they'll head straight for us. I know that's why you first reached out to Hyland after you learned it. But that's not our concern now, is it?"

I sighed. "We need to rescue Meg and Cliff. It might come in handy if Hyland finishes it in time."

"He's had years. He hasn't been able to. What makes you—"

"That's not true. He's been struggling. He didn't have a lab anymore, or a budget. The U of Dallas kicked him out. He didn't have a team. They'd black-listed him, right?"

Johnny frowned. "So you think with a good lab and some funding he can do this quickly?"

"That's my hope. We're on his side now. He has what he needs. It's just a matter of time."

"But if DARPA hasn't been able to do it yet—"

"Maybe they have. We don't know. But Hyland is the original mind behind this. If anyone can do it quickly, he can."

Johnny said, "Time is not on our side, Mac. Or on Meg's. Who knows what's happening to her—"

"Don't you think I know that!" I snapped. "She's my sister! They're torturing her over there. They know about our *Swords*, as well, and they'll be getting whatever info they can get from her. From Cliff, too!" I regretted my outburst immediately, and I backed off, breathing hard. "Sorry." I grabbed his shoulder. He was my best friend, and I didn't want to treat him poorly. "Really."

Johnny nodded. "Sorry I said it. Of course you're worried."

I leaned against the bulkhead and took a break to calm myself. "Cliff knows a lot, too. He's been on missions for TCI. But Meg knows about The Ridge! She's been there. If they suspect, and start asking her, she might give up the location."

We'd watched the track of USS *Blade* as the boat had powered away from Trieste to the west.

To Seascape.

I had suspected, of course. I knew the USSF had relocated their HQ there. Many of their subs were already headed there. Mayor Reggie Quinn had told me that Benning had wanted to use the city for his purposes, because the tourists had stopped going.

So I knew where Meg and Cliff were.

Generally speaking, of course. They were somewhere there, but when it came down to it, I'd have to know *precisely* which module the USSF was holding them in.

But what to do with Seascape was an even bigger issue.

And how to rescue them, without bringing the USSF down on our heads.

The trick was to get them out without revealing our identity.

Of course, Admiral Quintana and CIA Investigator Zyvinksi would know . . .

Which is why they'd have to die.

The Ridge was our secret research facility in the Mid-Atlantic Ridge. Our team there was working on our next generation of weapons to win this fight for Oceania: drones.

But Cliff and Meg knew about our Acoustic Pulse Drive, which allowed the *Swords* to descend so much farther than any other vessel. If the USSF discovered that we could possibly reach 8,000 meters, then it would likely be over.

They'd invade and take over, as they had at Seascape.

And at Trieste, it would have to be with violence.

The oceans were the future for humanity. Seventy percent of the world was underwater. There were untold resources here, and new technologies were going to help extract them.

The worse things got topside, the more violent the superpowers would get *down here*, I thought. We had to make sure we were more powerful than anyone else in order to protect ourselves.

I knew that we had to rescue our people, and the sooner the better. The thought of them torturing Meg was too much for me sometimes. Over the past few weeks I hadn't been sleeping well. Hadn't been eating. Others had noticed, but hadn't said much to me, other than asking how I was doing, but that was a question I couldn't really answer.

I had to solve this problem.

"Look," I said. "Hyland may not have his weapon done in time for this. But I have a plan. We're going to rescue them, but in a way that won't put a shred of suspicion on us. I'm under house arrest, don't forget! I can't leave."

He frowned. "You're going to stay while—"

"No. Of course I'm going to leave. But no one can find out."

And I had been mulling over a plan.

—··—

JOHNNY AND I WERE WALKING back to the Commerce Module when all hell broke loose.

We'd finished our conversation in the corridor outside of Hyland's lab, and I had to get back to my office to take care of some administrative details. I also wanted to speak with Rico Ruiz in more detail. He'd been living in Trieste now—working the kelp fields—and I hadn't used him for anything intelligence-related.

Johnny and I were the only people in the travel tube exiting the Research Module. We were silent now—I was still thinking things over, and Johnny was letting me—when a figure appeared ahead of us, on the other side of the hatch.

He wore a black hooded wetsuit, although he didn't have his tank or flippers. But he was wearing his mask.

That's odd, I thought.

Then I realized it was more than odd.

And with a tremor coursing through my body, I skidded to a halt. My TCI instincts instantly ratcheted into place.

The man was working the keypad next to the hatch, and an instant later it slid shut with a clang, leaving him on the other side.

He stared at us through the port for a second or two before spinning on his heel and marching away.

His mask was tinted; there was no way to make out his facial features.

There was a sound behind us now, and I jerked around to see that hatch closing, as well.

A figure in black was walking away.

We were trapped in the tube.

Outside, dark shadows swam toward us.

Black wetsuits.

Tinted masks.

Oh, shit.

This is how my father died.

I almost said it out loud.

They were approaching the glass. Reaching for it. There were four of them out there, two on each side.

I sprinted back to the hatch and slammed my palm on the RELEASE button. It wouldn't open. There was no one on the other side. The comm on the hatch controls wasn't functioning, either.

Fuck!

"Johnny," I muttered.

"I know," he replied. "We're going to have to fight our way out of this one."

I pulled out my PCD and signaled the first person I could think of: Renée Féroce.

She answered a few heartbeats later. "Mac, I'm so glad you—"

"Travel tube to Research Module. We're in trouble. Get someone here ASAP."

She didn't hesitate. "Got it. How many are there?"

"Four outside, two in. The two are likely on their way out right now, though."

"What's happening?"

"They're going to flood the tube, Renée. With Johnny and me in it."

She swore. "I'll get help. Hold your damn breath!" She clicked off.

I thought hurriedly. What was the closest moonpool? We'd have to swim for it. Buoyancy was going to be a real issue, though. The Gulf was extremely salty. Normally in emergencies people could tether to the exterior or grab handholds. That was not going to be possible in this case.

I banged on the hatch and willed someone to walk into view. A scientist or researcher. Hell, maybe even Hyland! No one was there. They were all hard at work, locked away in their labs researching. Lazlow didn't even come out for meals.

The scuba divers were touching the travel tube now. I ran over to them and looked upward. They ignored me. One had the figure of a woman. She had a device in her hand, and she placed it on the glass. It was the size of a hockey puck.

"Oh, shit. Get ready, Johnny."

"The problem is, if the hole is small, we'll drown."

He was right. We had to make sure the hole was big enough to swim through. We'd have only a few minutes of air.

We both started to take rapid and deep inhalations. Oxygenate our blood as much as possible. Increase our ability to last without air for as long as possible.

I looked around, frantic. There was a conveyor belt in the tube, but there was nothing to use there. Beside it, deck plates covered wiring, plumbing, air hoses, pressure sensors, and communication cables. I knelt to study the deck in more detail—

I turned to look at the scuba divers outside—

And the bomb went off.

It was a bright flash, but it was small. There was a sharp *crack!* and a jet of water shot downward and into the travel tube.

Blue lights started to strobe along the deck.

The blast and flooding had triggered the pressure alarms.

—••—

THE DECK PLATES WOULD COME up easily enough, and they had some weight to them.

I grabbed one and gave it a jerk. It was about five pounds and solid steel.

It would do.

Water was now around our ankles, and I stared up at the divers. They had backed off but were floating there, watching us. They had needle guns and knives on their thighs.

One of the men lifted his hand and waved at me. Then he tapped his watch. *You're running out of time . . .*

He was taunting me, the bastard.

I had to act fast. If the water got too high, there was no way this would work.

Johnny grabbed the other side of the deck plate and we stood directly under the stream of water. It was jetting down between us and spraying in all directions as it continued filling the tube.

"On three," he grunted.

We counted down and swung the steel grate upward. It connected with the transparent ceiling but barely did any damage. The water flooding in had slowed it too much.

"Try here," I said, repositioning just beside the stream. "When we're out, go for the one who just waved at me. Got him?"

Johnny nodded. We swung the deck plate up again, and it cracked the hole open. It was still too narrow to get through, but it was wider than it had been. We moved a foot away from it to strike again.

We were still breathing heavily, preparing to fight. "And when we get him, grab his tank and try for the Commerce Module," I gasped.

"It's too far."

"They all are. But it's our best shot."

The water was thundering in now. It was up to my waist and rising fast.

We'd probably have to kill the scuba divers in order to survive.

Steal one of the tanks and buddy-breathe while fighting the others.

And hope we could keep from floating to the surface.

It was our only chance of survival.

We hit the ceiling again and it spiderwebbed out like a chip on a car's windshield topside. It grew as we stared at it, stretching toward the downward stream of water.

We dropped the deck plate.

"Here we go," I muttered, gulping in more air.

"Do you have a weapon?"

"Nope."

He swore.

The hole suddenly opened wide and a final surge of water crashed in, tossing us madly about inside the travel tube.

It had now filled completely.

And there were at least four divers out there, armed, ready to kill us.

Chapter Eleven

THE FLASHING BLUE LIGHTS ILLUMINATED the water. The salt stung my eyes horribly as I forced them to stay open. I hauled myself through the hole, being careful not to cut myself on the sharp and jagged edges, and saw the figures ten meters away. They were hovering there, watching. They hadn't gone for their needle guns yet.

Stupid mistake.

They were expecting us to drown.

I hoped Renée's call would get someone to us soon. I was floating up and away from the tube, but I held onto it and my feet began to rise.

I shot a glance at the Commerce Module.

It seemed so far away.

We didn't have flippers. We'd never make it.

I pointed at the divers.

Johnny nodded.

We began swimming for them.

I couldn't see well—it was difficult to make *anything* out—and their masks were tinted, but I imagined their eyes widened at our boldness.

Then they drew their guns.

Behind us, the travel tube had completely filled with water. The flashing blue lights illuminated the entire thing, shining down the cylinder like a massive fluorescent bulb.

The ocean around us was blinking.

I pulled to a halt and wondered what to do. I wanted to scream. There was no solution. The divers were still several meters away. Their needles would tear us to bits. Johnny and I were fighting to stay level; we were constantly kicking to keep from rising.

I looked upward.

There was fresh air there. I could shoot up and breathe, as Rico had, see the sun, and then try to swim back down to thirty meters depth.

Bullshit.

We'd never make it back down. A hundred feet, without a weight belt. Without flippers.

And then one of the divers suddenly twisted and convulsed in agony. He spun to look behind him—

And Johnny and I saw our opportunity.

There were others approaching—they were still a ways off—but they were coming, and they'd just shot a wave of needles.

Trieste City Security.

—••—

JOHNNY AND I BOTH CONVERGED on the same diver. He was slightly shorter than the other men, but also more muscled. Johnny approached from one side, and I from the other. He was looking at the approaching enemy, most likely assuming Johnny and I were no longer a threat. We were drowning, anyway. We didn't have a chance in hell at surviving this, he probably thought.

I tore his mask off savagely. Johnny had simultaneously grabbed his regulator and ripped it from his mouth.

How do you like it? I thought, grim.

My heart was pounding now, and I knew I didn't have much time left. Around us the water had tinted with surges of red; a needle had sliced someone's artery. I reached down to the man's thigh and ripped the dagger from his holster. He was flailing now, panicked, for he had allowed our security to distract him. In one swift move I dug the knife into his neck and wrenched it downward.

Blood *gushed* into the water and swirled around us.

One down for sure, probably two.

I peered around me but couldn't make much out. I thought I saw two figures moving away to the south. They were swimming like hell. I pointed at them and, not knowing if our security could even see me, made a shooting gesture with my right hand.

Then I began searching for the regulator. I was desperate for a breath, my eyesight was growing dim, and a headache had begun pounding deep in my skull.

Then Johnny held it to my lips and I sucked it in eagerly. I took a deep breath and immediately my eyesight lightened.

107

I heard the sound of needle guns discharging.

—••—

ONE OF THE DIVERS HAD spun around and was racing back toward Johnny and me. The dagger was in his left hand, and the gun in his right.

I grunted inwardly. He'd decided that there was no hope, so he was making a last desperate attack, hoping security would not fire so close to me.

He was right. The storm of needles had stopped. He was trailing blood from his right thigh; the wound left a swirling trail behind him, red eddies mixing in the Gulf waters.

Salt with salt, I thought absently.

He fired.

Snap!

He'd aimed right for me. I had moved my body head-on to him, giving him the smallest target possible. Johnny had done the same. Dangerous, should a needle spear right into the top of my skull, but it was the only choice. We both held our hands toward him, fists clenched, to give us added protection. We called it *Supermanning*.

A sudden shooting pain shot down my scalp and I gasped. He'd hit me. Missed my hands, my arms, shoulders . . .

More blood clouded the water.

Johnny began swimming toward him; I followed an instant later. The needle had only grazed me, skimming my skull and disappearing into the ocean behind. I'd need stitches, but I was still alive.

Johnny wrapped him up in his arms and they began to struggle. The glint of the blade flashed. I gritted my teeth. I couldn't let him hurt Johnny, but I was growing short on air again. I reached out, desperate to lock him in a bear hug from behind . . .

He'd gotten the upper hand on Johnny somehow. Grappling underwater was far different than from on land. The orientation didn't matter. You could be upside down fighting for your life with someone oriented sideways. Like fighting in zero-gee. Now he was beside Johnny, his arm wrapped around his neck and shoulders, and he was squeezing with all his might. The muscles under his wetsuit bulged.

I reached a little farther—

Johnny's face was a mask of pain. He was struggling to escape, but the man was strong . . .

—and I tore the mask from the attacker's face and with my other hand ripped out his regulator. Then I wrapped up his knife hand and with both arms forced it toward his face.

His eyes were bulging.

He was struggling with two of us now.

The blade stabbed into his eye and his mouth opened to scream. Bubbles escaped and fluttered upward.

I pushed it in farther.

Still he struggled.

I pushed.

—••—

"THEY'RE GERMAN," RENÉE FÉROCE SAID. "Their equipment shows no markings, no flags, and there are no dog tags, but we've noticed this."

We were standing in a bare cabin with four bodies stretched out before us. It was the morgue, in the Commerce Module one level directly beneath the clinic. A metaphorical and symbolic location if ever there was one. Stacy Reynolds was there with us, looking at the bodies disapprovingly. She was a doctor and hated seeing death. But it was them or us, and I'm sure she understood that.

She had dressed my head wound—there had been fifteen stitches needed and the gash had produced a lot of blood.

The attackers hadn't expected our security to get there as quickly as they had. But we were well prepared, being Triestrians in the middle of a Cold War. We had trained hard for such an event—always pushing to suit up *fast* and get out into water as soon as possible—and it had paid off.

It had saved my life.

Renée was pointing at a tattoo on one of the bodies. It was on his biceps, and it said *Bis Zum Ende*. "It means, 'Until the End.'" There was a submarine behind it, with torpedoes lancing out and bubbles trailing the vessel.

I shook my head. "He's met his end, all right."

"There are two others. They got away."

The two from *inside* the city. The ones who had closed the hatches.

She continued, "But why are they after you? Why kill you?"

I stared at Renée. "I can think of one really good reason, although I'm not the one to blame."

Johnny said, "Rico Ruiz. If his story is true."

I said, "You still question it? After this?"

"This might be a good way to convince you. Especially if he's an operative."

"It would mean sacrificing four people—maybe six—to make you trust one." It was possible, but unlikely. "Are there any other marks on them?" I asked the doctor.

"No. They all have excellent physiques, including the female." She paused. "Each is in wonderful condition. I would say these are athletes."

"Agents," I ground out. "They're spies." I pointed at the one with the tattoo. "Except him."

"Why do you say that? He's just as muscular."

"Look at the tattoos. They're on his calves, his biceps, his pectorals, and neck." I grabbed the corpse, hefted it, and peered under it. "On his back, too. His shoulder."

"So?" Reynolds said.

"Spies don't have markings. Which means he may have been regular German Submarine Fleet. They all possibly came from the same sub."

I had already asked about this, and Grant Bell had informed me that there were no hostile subs in the region. But then again, one could have sailed in slowly. Silently.

"But why are they here?" Renée spat. Her face had twisted in rage.

It made me smile. She was a bit possessive over me, even though there was no arrangement between us.

———••———

FIVE MINUTES LATER, RICARDO RUIZ was standing in the morgue staring at the four naked corpses. His long hair framed his olive features, and his expression was hard. His gaze lingered on one of them. "Someone tore his neck open." He pursed his lips. "With his own knife, I'm guessing."

"Why do you say that?" Johnny asked.

Rico pointed at the heap of equipment below him. "There's no knife. Whoever did it still has it, or dropped it outside."

"Very good," I muttered.

"Your handiwork, I take it?" Rico asked me.

I nodded. I punched the comm and signaled for Kristen Canvel.

"Mac!" she yelled. "Are you—"

"Fine. But the travel tube to the Research Module is out of commission."

"Yeah, crews are on it."

"Can you notify the people in the module, please?"

"Already done."

"Thanks." I clicked off. Our new Triestrian, Max Hyland, was going to wonder just what the hell was going on. He was currently stranded in his lab. I turned to Rico. "They're German."

He sighed and continued to stare at the corpses. "I guessed that."

"How do you know?"

"Only that I escaped from a GSF vessel. Now they're here. They know I ma-nipulated an election at New Berlin. They're here to send a message."

"Message?" Reynolds said, confusion painted on her features. She had no idea about TCI or spies or even The Second Cold War going on in the oceans.

"*Don't interfere*," I grated.

Rico said, "I'm really sorry, Mac. They likely wanted to do this to Shanks or Flint, but they're not in charge anymore."

"So it falls to me," I muttered.

"Sadly, yes."

"I'm the target."

He didn't respond to that and just stared at me in silence. Then he said, "Let me go."

"Pardon?"

"Let me go after them."

"They're dead."

"No. I mean the warsub. It's nearby. It has to be. Let's go get them." He clenched his fists suddenly and lurched toward me. I held my ground, some-how knowing he wouldn't hurt me. The others in the cold chamber jerked forward at Rico's sudden movement, but I raised a hand to stop them.

"The things they did to me," he rasped. "I was there for a year, dammit. They tortured me. Humiliated me. I want to kill them for what they did." He was inches from my face now. His teeth gnashed. "What *he* did to me. I want to kill *him*. Let me go, Mac."

Chapter Twelve

I GRABBED RICO AND WE headed to the entertainment district. The pub was on the lowest level of the Commerce Module; I distantly remembered it as being the same place where Blake had approached to ask me to rejoin TCI. I'd nearly assaulted him, not recognizing the man, but it had brought me back to active service and I'd left shortly after on a hunt to capture Johnny Chang.

Actually, I'd wanted to kill Johnny—now my deputy mayor—but I'd had second thoughts.

Just after meeting Blake, I recalled with a hollow feeling in my gut, I'd ended up outside fighting agents from another country. I'd killed four of them out there.

And more had just died during a very similar experience.

Nations were paying a deadly price for this Cold War. Warsubs sunk and sailors drowned were common events now. But this was hand-to-hand combat . . . the deadliest kind. Back then, eighteen months ago, I'd fought with the Chinese operatives who'd killed Blake. Now we were facing Germany in combat under the waves, a nation that had been off my radar until now.

But Rico's story about the New Berlin election intrigued me. German news was likely censoring the situation, because it was not common knowledge.

And perhaps one of the reasons why they were trying to kill me.

But something they didn't know about me was that an attempt to kill was more of an invitation than a warning.

Rico and I settled into chairs in a dim corner of the tavern and ordered kelp beer. We both took a gulp and grimaced. It took some time to develop a taste for it.

I was still waiting for it to happen.

On the corner was a video screen and a news report was droning on. "Waves continue pounding shore defences around Wall Street, and Florida's Everglades are almost completely underwater. The Army Corps of Engineers are busy adding to the current US walls holding back rising ocean levels, and senior leadership is pointing to their inability to keep up. Congress has rushed a bill to vote meant to increase funding, and lawmakers have even proposed a national draft to bring new construction workers in to help. And ever sadder news to report—" the scene shifted to a view of dried and withered corn and wheat "—farmers are reporting yet another year of failed crops. Despite universal water restrictions and the new Irrigation First Laws, the temperatures are just too high for them. Cropland has migrated north into Canada, but the soil in regions not previously used for farming is in desperate need of fertilizing, and nearby lakes are experiencing massive eutrophication as a result." The images now showed lakes clogged with algae and dead fish, floating bellies-up. "Local cultures are protesting the measures to grow crops, for while the government is attempting to buoy one crop's harvest, they are killing others." An image of Trieste—stock footage, I could tell, for the nuclear plant was visible in the southwest quadrant of the city, since buried for protection—now appeared. "The one bright spot in the environmental devastation are the world's undersea colonies. Kelp harvests increase every year. Fish stocks are high, and in fact every conshelf colony in the world expands their fish farms yearly. However, the clamor for independence continues to ring out around the world's oceans as colonizing nations harass citizens and demand more produce, compounding an already tense situation." The image now showed the newscaster, a man in his early fifties. "There's no doubt that conditions on the surface continue to worsen. There's no end in sight, especially as the world's populations skyrocket. And with the recent inundation of Bangladesh, the disaster in East Asia is beyond imagination. Millions of refugees have flooded China and India. But the oceans remain a frontier of hope, and no doubt governments are going to continue colonizing, likely at a rate faster than ever before."

I groaned. The story was nothing new, but seeing the images was disheartening. Especially in East Asia.

Rico said, "It's been falling apart topside for decades, Mac."

I studied the man. He'd calmed down following his outburst in the morgue, and I'd been hoping that a drink in a quiet spot would get him to open up a bit. I'd largely ignored him after Meg's arrest—he'd been working in the fields and minding his own business. I'd asked security to monitor him, but he wasn't doing anything out of the ordinary. Meg and my own plans had preoccupied me, and Rico had sent me the odd message, asking me to 'put him back to work'—meaning sending him on a mission with TCI—but I'd held off.

Until now.

"We're lucky to be down here," I muttered, taking another gulp. I tore my eyes from the images on the screen and focused on Rico. He was staring at me, the lines in his forehead deeper than normal.

"Sorry about what happened, Mac."

I shrugged. "Part of the job."

"But it put Triestrians at risk. I don't want that."

"Tell me more about this German warsub."

"I'm not sure if it's the same one."

"You seemed convinced an hour ago."

He sighed. "I just want revenge. I didn't recognize any of them. They're not from the warsub that was holding me."

"Likely special forces called in from the GSF."

He nodded. "Which means they won't stop trying to kill me, Mac. Or you. Meddling with New Berlin is obviously something they want us to stop doing."

I considered that. Then, "Tell me about *him*."

Rico's face was blank.

I continued, "You asked me to let you kill *him*. What did you mean?"

He sighed and stared at his beer. "On the sub. He was the worst. He tortured me. But not even to get any information. He never asked any questions when I had a session with him. He was just . . . enjoying it, I guess. He liked to cause pain."

I shuddered. I'd been through it before. Four months of torture in Sheng City. I sympathized with Rico. "So tell me about him."

He shrugged. "He's a sadist. Broke my arm during one of the sessions. Liked to cut me with his knife. You know, the one sailors wear? He liked to pull it out and use it. Talked about 'death by a thousand cuts' quite a bit. Some days when I returned to my cell I was absolutely *covered* in my own blood. You couldn't even see where it was coming from."

I noted the scarring on the man's forearms and biceps. "And he was a member of their crew? Or from somewhere else?"

"He was crew. There was often grease under his nails and on his hands."

Even though the vast majority of subs in the oceans now were electric—our batteries could last for weeks on a charge and were vastly different from the chemical batteries of decades ago—engine screws and shafts still needed lubrication.

"And he ran the sessions sometimes?" I asked.

"Most of them. His teeth had rotted away. They were brown with black dead spots."

"And the session interrogators—what did they ask you?"

"Where I was from, what was my goal, why I'd interfered in New Berlin's election, and so on."

"What did you give up?"

He shrugged. "Nothing. It's why they continued to beat me. They assumed I was from one of the colonies in Latin America. I let them believe that."

"Had you talked you could have avoided it all." I studied his eyes as I said it.

He looked shocked at that. "But I care too much about Trieste. I didn't want to bring them down on us. But that's happened, anyway."

"Yes, it has," I murmured, looking away.

"What?"

"Just wondering how they figured out you're a Triestrian."

"I was thinking about that, too. Cousteau put me on a sub to Central America. When I arrived, I arranged passage to Ballard. Then got a cargo sub to take me to Trieste. I worked my way on both boats as part of the crew. Unpaid. There was no record of it."

I leaned back and considered it all. We were on our second drink, and we'd been sharing stories of our time in captivity and our torture. I understood the source of his anger, but now he felt embarrassed about letting it get to him, and openly begging to go out for vengeance. I told him not to worry about it. He would get his chance.

I was absolutely against torture. It was a part of my character that conflicted and confused me at times. I had nightmares about warsubs I'd sunk. I'd fired torpedoes at the FSF in the past. At the CSF, USSF, and RSF. I'd killed divers in underwater hand-to-hand combat. I'd drowned people, stabbed them, shot them, and broken necks. Hell, on the dreadnought I'd sabotaged the fission reactor and sent the boat to the bottom with all hands. The corium had even melted out and killed crewmen as they stumbled about the ship's dark corridors.

But even though I was open to killing to achieve Trieste's freedom, why was I so against the concept of torture?

Because I'd endured it, in Sheng City.

They'd done everything to me to get me to speak. To spill names. To give up TCI's secrets.

They'd cut me, beat me, electrocuted me. Denied me food, sleep, and water. Tormented me.

I'd never broken, but I'd wanted to, some days.

And through it all, I vowed I'd never do the same to anyone else.

We were all serving our cities. Serving our people. Ensuring our survival on the ocean floors.

And we were above torture.

Wherever I saw it, I knew I had to stop it.

I said, "What was his name?"

"*Heinrich*." He bit the name out. "I heard other crew call him that. I pretended not to notice."

His face was tight and he'd pulled his lips back unconsciously, showing his teeth. I studied his reaction. His breathing had increased, too.

"And he was an officer?" I continued. "Or a crewman?"

"Definitely not an officer."

"And you'd recognize him again if you saw him."

Rico's eyes narrowed to slits. "Absolutely."

I studied the man. "Are you sure you can remain objective here?" I was worried that if I did one day send him out on another mission, he would abandon it for his own priorities.

He shook himself out of it. "Yes, Mac. Don't worry about me. I won't betray Trieste."

"It's not Trieste I'm worried about."

"I would never put a mission at risk for my own needs."

"Other people might depend on you one day."

"I know."

"What was the name of the warsub?"

He shook his head. "I never found out. All I knew was the class—*Attentäter*. I often heard them talking about bugs or insects, so I think it was infested. Three different types. But I personally never saw anything."

"How's your German?"

"Okay." He shrugged. "Passable, but not perfect. I often spoke to Gerhardt in broken German and a mix of Spanish."

Gerhardt was the mayor of New Berlin. I sat back again and considered the situation. Meg and Cliff were prisoners at Seascape. The USSF was holding them. Maybe someone was torturing them. I wouldn't put it past Zyvinski. Meanwhile, the Germans were after me for a mission Shanks had ordered years ago. There was a way out of this—I knew there was—but I just had to put the final pieces together. To bring it all in a full circle so I could figure out this problem.

If I attempted a rescue, the USSF would come down hard on Trieste. Likely arrest me, too, despite the problems that would cause amongst the populace of the city. But if I didn't try, then Meg and Cliff were going to spend years in a prison. Eventually the USSF might even move them out of Seascape.

Meanwhile, New Berlin was vulnerable to us. If I could speak with the mayor, without anyone listening in, I might be able to bring them into our alliance.

To add another city would be a monumental achievement.

And the German Submarine Fleet was harassing the French colonies.

Meanwhile, Hyland was working on the Isomer Bomb. Hopefully he'd be able to perfect the trigger. Once we had a guaranteed source of hafnium that we could convert to HF-178m2, we would have a bomb capable of doing real damage to massive warsubs with a single torpedo strike.

No more infiltrating subs and sabotaging nuclear plants.

And crews at The Ridge were working on a new stealth tech to attack warsubs, from a distance, to keep us as protected and as safe as possible . . .

I put my hand on my thigh and felt the scar. Four weeks had passed and it had healed nicely.

In a flash I had it.

I knew what I had to do.

I pushed myself to my feet. "Rico, grab a bag."

"Bag? What—"

"You're coming on a mission."

"Where—"

"Not now. Meet me in the Docking Module in one hour." I stared at him. "We're going for revenge."

Chapter Thirteen

DARKNESS HAD FALLEN OVER THE city. Our security forces were on high alert and were patrolling the colony with a fervor, knowing that someone had just attempted to assassinate their mayor and had flooded a travel tube to do it.

History from thirty-one years earlier had almost repeated itself.

There were also armed guards at every moonpool, anticipating another attempt.

I found Johnny in City Control and told him to pack a bag—and weapons—and meet at *SC-1*. Then I called Renée.

"Mac," she said, breathless. She was outside, in scuba gear; I could hear it over the comm. Her voice sounded muffled and there was a chatter from other workers in her full face mask.

Kelp maybe? Harvesting? It grew fifty centimeters a day at our location; it was our most valuable crop.

She was swimming or—

Then it occurred to me, and it was like a flare going off in my skull.

She was chasing the other two Germans.

"There was a report of two divers far from the city. A seacar pilot called it in. Thought they needed help. We realized who they were, of course."

I should have ordered a more expansive search. Turned out City Security already had. Someone had stepped up in Cliff's absence.

"I ordered it," she said, panting. "I hope you're okay with that."

It made me smile. "Of course. Great job." *And here I was drinking while I should have been working.*

"Are you okay?" she said. "I was hoping we could talk after what happened."

"I'm okay. A needle grazed my scalp, that's all."

"That's not what I'm referring to."

"Oh." I frowned, then I realized. Our lovemaking, which had turned into a weekly routine. "Are you . . . okay about it?"

She chuckled. "I'm better than okay. I'm thrilled. I just wanted to see you again."

"You're going to get that chance, very soon."

"I'm a bit busy right now . . . but . . . " There was a long break as she continued swimming. "Just know that I can't wait to see you."

It made my heart pound. I was excited about seeing her, too. "As soon as the patrol is done, meet at *SC-1*. Bring your gear." It was an unspoken suggestion: *Bring your weapons.*

"Got it."

"One hour."

Then there was a startled gasp. "Wait a minute, Mac!"

"What is—"

"We've got something here." There were a series of calls over the comm and I distinctly heard the mention of '300 meters' and 'two contacts.' Then she blurted, "Needle guns! Get ready! Scooters, get up there!"

We had security forces on one-man vehicles called scooters that were like jet skis on the surface. They could collide with swimmers and cause a lot of damage, and they had a 'windscreen' at the front that could deflect needles.

"Red squad, take the left flank!" she yelled. "Blue squad, the right. Green will go straight at them!"

She was barking orders at our people now, coordinating the attack.

"Needles!" someone called.

"Stay down!"

"They're at fifty-three meters!"

"Go above them, take them from up there. Frankie, you go below. Descend to a hundred—"

"I don't think I have the right mix for that."

"Who does?"

"I've got it!"

They were taking the two from five different directions as they tried to swim away. I didn't envy the attackers; they were in serious trouble, unless they had friends nearby.

It made me wonder, so I switched channels and contacted Grant Bell in City Control.

"Go ahead, Mac."

"Security has found two people trying to escape."

"Yeah, I'm tracking them."

"They're going for something. Check that direction. See if their ship is nearby."

"I'm on it. I'll let you know if I find something."

I switched back to Renée and there was a cacophony of overlapping voices on the line.

They were engaged in a shootout, underwater, at fifty meters.

At nighttime.

"Be careful, Renée," I muttered, mostly to myself. Seeing her injured was the last thing in the world I needed right then.

"I can't locate them!"

"They've split up. Changing depths."

Smart move, I thought.

"The one going shallower is out of needles. He's down to his dagger."

"The other still has ammo. Be careful!"

I broke into their exchange, "This is Mac. Try to keep them alive if possible."

Another terse series followed:

"Shoot for the legs."

"They're Supermanning."

"Just keep them pinned down. We'll get them from the flank."

Pinned down. Funny.

"Got one! He's struggling. Hit him in the thigh . . . he's . . . *dammit!* He just dumped his tank and regulator! He's going—"

Shit. He'd rather die than come back to Trieste.

The remaining fight took another two minutes. The other attacker had also ditched his gear, and I was sure that both had died.

—••—

I'D BEEN WRONG.

One of the men had drowned. Security had lashed him to a scooter and powered back as fast as possible, but there'd been no hope.

He'd been under for too long.

The other one had also ditched his gear, but security had wisely waited for him to fall unconscious before getting a full mask on him, clearing it, then hoping he'd start breathing again.

He had.

And they dragged him back to the city, still unconscious.

He woke up in the clinic, where I was looming over him, watching for signs of life. We'd cuffed him to the table. He was naked and cold, shivering, and bloody. Several needles had hit his legs, and the doctor was stitching him up and checking to make sure his arteries were undamaged.

He saw me over him, and his face tightened.

But he remained quiet.

It was one of the men who'd sealed me in the travel tube to drown me. And now my people had saved him from trying to drown himself.

Irony at its most violent.

"Yes, it's me," I said. "You failed."

No response. He just glared.

His eyes were like burning embers.

"Your friends are all dead. You're the only one who made it."

"Bullshit," he finally growled. His diction was almost perfect—mostly American—but there was a hint of an accent.

German.

I said, "They're below us right now, in the morgue. A woman, too."

"I don't believe—"

"They're all special forces, like you. No markings. No identifying features. No dog tags. Except one, that is." I described the man and his tattoos, and our prisoner's eyes widened slightly. I said, "So now you believe me."

"Fuck you."

"No. You're the one who's fucked, because you attacked us with the intention of killing the city's mayor. But we left you alive."

"You won't get anything out of—"

"We'll see. Or maybe I don't care what you have to say."

He frowned at that, but remained silent.

I continued, "Maybe I don't give two fucks about your story. The only thing I care about is killing or hurting anyone who comes to mess with a Triestrian."

"So get on with it, then," he finally muttered.

"Oh, I will." I gestured to the two guards who were in the clinic with us. "Move him to my seacar. Drug him. Chain him up there."

It had quite the effect. In a second he was straining at his restraints, veins in his neck bulging. The doctor was watching the entire exchange, not fully sure of what was going on.

"I won't go with you!" he screamed.

"You don't have a choice. I'm going to keep you in my seacar chained like a dog. Keep you alive. For a bit, anyway. Then I'm going to peel you apart and feed you to the sharks, a bit at a time."

The doctor was about to say something—to object—but I cut her off with a gesture. Then I turned to the guards. "Go ahead. Get him to *SC-1*."

I pulled Stacy Reynolds into her office, and once the hatch sighed shut, she exploded. Her usual severe and cold demeanor dissolved right in front of me. "How dare you, McClusky! There's no way—"

"I'm not going to hurt him, don't worry."

She stopped suddenly and blinked. "But—"

"It's just strategy. I'm scaring him. After what I've been through, I wouldn't wish it on anyone else. He was just doing a job. I'll keep him safe." *For a bit, anyway,* I wanted to add. *Before I sink their sub and kill them all.* But I didn't say that.

"You won't kill him?"

I knew she was a doctor and had vowed to save lives. "I just want to know where his ship is." I had tactfully avoided the question. "Then try my best to get him back home."

"But why were you saying those things?"

"Just to let him know that they can't push me around. If I presented any less severe an attitude, they'd just keep attacking, Stacy."

"So it's an act?"

I shrugged. "Kind of. But I don't torture people. Don't worry."

She'd stopped breathing hard and no longer clenched her fists at her sides. "I really have no idea what's going on. This is all so shocking."

"It is. Another country has attacked us. I have to make sure it doesn't happen again. We can't have more Triestrians in danger."

She sighed and stared at me. More creases traced her face than normal, but eventually she nodded. "I understand."

I turned and marched from her office. "Please help security get him out of here."

"And the bodies in the morgue?"

I skidded to a stop and turned back to her. "What do we normally do with unidentified remains?"

She pursed her lips. "Doesn't happen often, but we cremate and disperse the ashes outside."

I turned and continued on my way out. "Burn them."

—••—

FRANCOIS PIETTE WAS ON THE comm again. I was in my office and things were moving quickly. I knew what I had to do, and there wasn't much time.

"Hello, Mac!" he said. "Nice to hear from you—"

"I have some news. I'm going to be coming by to see you soon."

His eyes grew wide. "When, exactly?"

"A few days. I'm going to the Mid-Atlantic Ridge first. Then north to Cousteau. Can you arrange a meeting with the other mayors?"

"Of Alpha and Beta? Of course. I think they'd love to meet you, finally."

"Good." I calculated the time versus my seacar's velocity. "We'll be there in . . .

in three days. Give or take. I think the mayors will like what I have to say."

He nodded. "See you then."

—••—

AN HOUR LATER WE HAD collected in the living area of my seacar, *SC-1*, also called *SCAV-1*. Johnny, Renée, Rico, and me. I pursed my lips, wondering if I should include Lazlow, Richard Lancombe, or Jessica Ng. Or even Max Hyland. They were all working on projects for Trieste at that moment and I didn't want to pull them away.

Especially Hyland.

We'd deposited a series of duffle bags on the deck against the bulkhead. Within were needle guns, pistols, grenades, and knives. Workers had already stocked *SC-1* with food, water, and torpedoes. Charged the batteries.

We were ready for the mission.

I glanced at the top hatch, and Johnny pulled it down and cranked it tight.

In the living area, on the deck next to the couch, our prisoner lay, drugged, sleeping, his wrists and ankles cuffed, and now in hospital scrubs. The others stared at him for a few heartbeats, wondering who he was, before realization kicked in.

"We're bringing him with us?" Johnny breathed.

"Renée helped catch him outside. He might be useful."

The French captain stared at him. "You didn't kill him."

"No."

Then Rico kneeled over him, staring at his unconscious features. "I don't recognize this one, either."

"They're not from the same warsub, then."

"But that doesn't mean there isn't one out here, somewhere."

I had given Grant Bell orders to search for it, but he'd been unsuccessful. "Keep an eye on him back here. Make sure he's in submission at all times."

"Got it. When will he wake up?"

"A couple of hours."

"What . . . Mac, what are we doing with him?"

"Using him for leverage."

"So, no torture I take it?"

"No torture."

He nodded, a flood of relief evident on his features. I knew he wanted revenge for what had happened, but apparently he'd directed his anger at the people responsible, and not their entire fleet.

Or, like me, he wanted to avoid torture because he'd been through it.

Johnny and I took our places in the pilot chairs and, using the ballast controls in the central console, made the seacar's buoyancy negative.

We silently slipped below the surface.

I slowly powered the seacar out of the Docking Module and turned us to the east. Trieste's lights angled downward from the city, illuminating scores of fish and plankton in the warm waters. Lights from other seacars flashed like fireflies in the night, and I noticed groups of Triestrians out for an evening swim.

There was a halo of light around the city—*an island of light*—and it was a truly remarkable scene.

Like a beacon of hope, I thought, but to ocean colonizers only. The topsiders didn't see us that way. To them we were merely a source of resources. A tool to exploit the seas. The GSF were mainland security for Germany. They saw us in the same way.

I increased power to eighty percent and we soared past the colony and out into the dark, nighttime waters of the Gulf of Mexico. Johnny stared at me. "Where are we going, Mac?"

I had been formulating the plan for many weeks. I knew now what we had to do. The final piece had clicked into place. "The Ridge," I said in a soft voice.

He nodded, glancing down at our course. "Speed?"

"SCAV drive."

He blinked. "Really? That'll attract attention."

I thought of Meg in Seascape, possibly enduring torture. "We don't have time. It's already been too long."

He considered that, then said, "You're right." He plotted a course on the computer—I watched him plug in the waypoints on the console between us—and glanced at me for confirmation. He had us going northeast to the Mid-Atlantic Ridge, at which point we would descend into the Rift and head due south for 500 kilometers until we hit our base.

I nodded, then opened the panel for the SCAV drive. I pushed the button and the fusion drive powered up.

Immediately behind the control cabin were two bunks on either side, recessed into the bulkheads. Behind those, the lavatory. Then the carpeted living space, which contained a couch and a few chairs, a galley, an airlock, and the hatch to engineering where there were batteries, ballast valves, environmental equipment, and other necessary controls for the seacar.

And behind that, on the other side of a recessed hatch, was the fusion compartment.

There, in the reactor core, temperatures hit over a hundred million degrees through radio waves and an intense magnetic field that folded the plasma onto itself. Hydrogen atoms fused to form helium, releasing intense heat energy.

We used the heat to flash-boil seawater to steam, and ejected this out the rear thruster nozzle.

It pushed *SCAV-1* into the water at high speeds, and the nose of the seacar created a low pressure zone that generated an air bubble from cavitation.

Eventually the air bubble stretched back and encompassed the entire vessel, reducing friction to almost nothing.

Supercavitation.

The Soviets had first invented it for underwater missiles in the 1970s. Katherine Wells, using a small fusion reactor in this seacar, had adapted it for use in crewed vessels, and seawater provided an unlimited source of fuel.

SCAV-1 could hit 450 kilometers per hour.

Behind us, in the living area, I could hear Rico's amazement. He'd never experienced the SCAV drive before. "This is incredible," he breathed. The force of acceleration had thrown him into a couch, and then he rose to his feet and, leaning forward, struggled to march up the narrow corridor, past the bunks to the control cabin. Now he stood behind me, gripping the chair, his knuckles white on the leather.

"It's what we're using to convince other colonies to join us."

"Have you had success?"

"Plenty." I told him which cities had already joined, and his eyes widened. "Incredible."

Every vessel in our passive range could hear us—there was no hiding this drive from anybody—but it had revolutionized travel and warfare in the oceans.

And we were the first to have it.

We were rounding the tip of Florida, *screaming* through the water, and I piloted using the yoke. It was similar to an airplane's. It operated our control surfaces—bow and stern diving planes—and the foot pedals operated the vertical control surface to steer us port or starboard. It really was like piloting a plane, especially because we were cocooned in a bubble of air. Johnny was scanning the passive sonar screen. We couldn't hear much from surrounding traffic because of the noise we were generating, but suddenly he tensed. "Mac, a vessel just hit us with an active sonar pulse."

Someone had pinged us, which was odd. They could already hear us, so why ping us, unless they wanted to know more about our vessel? The size, make, and so on.

"Maybe they're just curious about who we—"

"Mac, it's a warsub. It hadn't shown on the screen before."

I hesitated. "USSF?"

"German," he whispered.

Chapter Fourteen

It was a *Mörder Class* warsub.

Killer Class.

One hundred meters long. Top speed seventy-five kph. Eight torpedo tubes with mines and a crew of twenty-four.

There were twenty of them in the GSF, and here was one, in the Gulf of Mexico, just outside of Trieste.

Surprise, surprise.

And now they had pinged us.

They knew who we were, I had no doubt.

I snapped a look over my shoulder; our prisoner was still unconscious, but the acceleration of SCAV drive had stretched him out. His legs were limp but angled aftward, toward engineering, while his arms were over his head and locked to a pipe welded to the bulkhead.

I exhaled. There was only one thing I could do here, but destroying a German warsub just off the coast of Florida would not be smart. It could start a war topside. I didn't mind fighting this Cold War, but I wanted to do it secretly. Stealthily. Shift the blame to others. Stay off people's radars.

But they knew we'd come from Trieste.

So we'd give them a taste of our capabilities.

Sting them. Teach them a lesson.

Stay away, or else.

I cut the SCAV drive and brought our conventional thrusters online. We slowed, the bubble receding past the canopy over our heads. "Hold on," I said. The sudden friction with water slammed us forward against the safety straps. I gripped the yoke tightly as our forward momentum hit zero in an instant and the straps tightened severely on my shoulders.

"Whoa," Rico said, still standing behind me.

"It's what makes the SCAV drive work."

"What's that?"

"The bubble reduces friction with water." Now that water surrounded us once again, our top speed was significantly lower. *SC-1's* max was seventy kph. I studied the sonar screen and located the blip that marked the *Mörder* Class warsub. It was thirteen kilometers away at a bearing of 153 degrees.

"What are your intentions?" Rico said.

"This isn't the warsub that held you. But it is the one that attacked Trieste." No doubt the special forces troops had left their own scooters nearby and had been attempting to swim to them and would have eventually boarded this vessel to make their escape.

"You going to destroy it?"

I glanced back at his features. I could tell that he wanted me to. "That's not the vessel that held you, Rico," I repeated softly.

"Does it matter?" he bit out. His expression was tight, and his gaze was fixed on the image in the VID.

Johnny was staring at me. "Mac?"

I shook my head. "No. Not here. Not now. But . . . " Something had occurred to me. It might be useful to us. I glanced at the sonar again. There were surface vessels around—normal shipping and fishing boats—but no other warsubs. "I need this boat to stay here. In the Gulf."

"They'll follow us into the Atlantic, though."

"Yes."

"Which means . . . you want to damage it."

"I want to put it on the bottom."

Johnny swore. "Mac, that's a GSF warsub. They'll shoot back."

I frowned. Torpedoes had a top speed of eighty. Our SCAV exceeded that, no problem. We could avoid their weapons easily.

Unless they had SCAV torpedoes, which could travel at speeds of around a thousand kph. A number of nations already did. The USSF, FSF, and CSF had all demonstrated them to us—up close and personal—over the past year and a half.

It was a chance we'd have to take.

I swung our nose toward the GSF vessel and pushed the throttle to full, bringing our speed to seventy. I checked the depth at the warsub's location: only 220 meters. It was still over the shelf.

Perfect.

We drew nearer to the boat. Finally, what I'd been waiting for happened. The comm beeped.

"Attention, incoming Triestrian vessel," a male voice spoke. "You are on an intercept with a warsub of the GSF. State your intentions."

On our screen, the sonar displayed the vessel's ID:

```
Registry: GSF Dunkler Winter (Dark Winter)
             Mörder Class SSN
          Depth: 207 meters
          Speed: 75 kph
```

Our computer had the specific acoustic signatures of most of the world's submarines. It had identified this one easily. They were not running quietly anymore.

They were at flank speed.

"My intentions are none of your business. Yours, on the other hand, are clear. You attacked citizens of Trieste."

There was a pause. Then, "We did no such thing. Change your course or we'll be forced to fire on you."

"We are an American seacar just off the coast of the United States. Don't threaten us. What are you doing in this region?"

"We are in international waters."

"Barely. You're over the shelf."

"We are more than 200 nautical miles from your nation. And who are you to—"

"Your troops just tried to kill the mayor of Trieste City."

Another long silence stretched out. I stared at the sonar as we approached. We were still over a thousand meters away. I cut the mic and said to Johnny, "Prepare a torpedo. Homing on their screws."

He nodded and pressed the buttons on the weapon's panel, programming it. I keyed the mic back on.

"Six of your special forces just attacked our mayor. We've been looking for a nearby GSF warsub. You fit the bill. I think you dropped off the troops, and now you're running. Your mission was a total failure. Your superiors will not be happy, especially after we sink you."

"You'll do no such thing!" The voice was angry now, the accent thicker. "I am captain of this vessel. If you draw closer, I'll fire at you. Veer off now!"

I activated the SCAV drive and shoved the throttle forward. At our stern, steam started shooting from the thruster nozzle and began pushing us ahead faster.

I cut the conventional screws.

Johnny was staring at me again.

I muted the mic and said, "I want them to fire on me."

He shook his head and looked away. "You have a death wish, Mac."

I smiled. "No. I have a plan."

Our speed was increasing now, though we hadn't reached supercavitation yet. And then it happened.

"Torpedo in the water!" Johnny cried. "Heading straight for us. Eight hundred meters. Speed sixty kph and climbing."

I held my breath, hoping it was simply a conventional torpedo . . .

"Speed at eighty and holding!"

I exhaled. Perfect. We could handle this.

I continued to accelerate. Soon we were at 200 kph and I backed off on the fusion power. No doubt the GSF crew were staring at their screens in horror, now understanding our intentions. I turned away from the torpedo, keeping it at a safe distance, and swung around *Dark Winter.*

"You see now, don't you?" I muttered into the mic. "You won't stand a chance against us."

"You are threatening a German state vessel!"

"You're the one who just fired a torpedo. Your troops tried to kill our mayor."

"We did nothing of the—"

"Bullshit." I hauled back on the throttle, lowering our speed. We were *behind* the warsub now, pointing right at its single massive screw. The computer aided me in seeing the vessel by projecting its image on the canopy over my head. It was the VID system.

And I nodded at Johnny. He pressed the large red button marked FIRE and a torpedo shot from *SC-1*'s bow.

Straight for the massive screw.

SC-1 shuddered as we ejected the missile, and the vibration coursed through the yoke into my fingers.

It felt good.

The warsub began blowing ballast—an explosion of bubbles cascaded toward the surface from the vessel—and launched several countermeasures, meant to distract and confuse our weapon.

But we were too close.

Our weapon accelerated . . .

And then it erupted.

—••—

THE EXPLOSION SENT A FLASH of white across our sonar screen, and on the canopy it appeared as a blazing supernova of light. The release of energy flash-boiled tons of water to steam, and a flower of bubbles shoved the boat's aft end upward. In an instant the explosion warped the vessel's screws into twisted scrap. The warsub shuddered as the explosion vibrated the steel hull and rattled its crew inside.

Then water pounded back into the empty cavity the explosion had created, further pounding the hull.

Johnny glanced at the sonar. "Detecting transients inside. Pressure alarms. We punctured the hull."

Before us, the vessel began sinking. She'd lost neutral buoyancy, and her screws were useless. The depth was relatively shallow here.

I knew she wouldn't be going anywhere.

The sonar sounded an alarm, and I glanced at it, suddenly concerned.

Torpedo in the water.

It was the one they'd shot; it had swung around and was heading for us again.

Then the ship fired another.

A new alarm blared.

I pushed the SCAV drive to full and pointed us eastward, away from the foundering vessel. We tore through the ocean now, heading around the tip of Florida and deep into the Atlantic Ocean, toward the Mid-Atlantic Ridge and the rift that cut through the center of the ocean from north to south.

The German captain came back on the line. "How dare you fire at my vessel! This is an act of war!"

"You committed the first hostilities at Trieste. You also fired first. Try explaining that to your superiors." Then I cut the mic.

His warsub would lie, damaged, on the shelf for some time as they made repairs.

For days, probably.

My plan was moving quickly now.

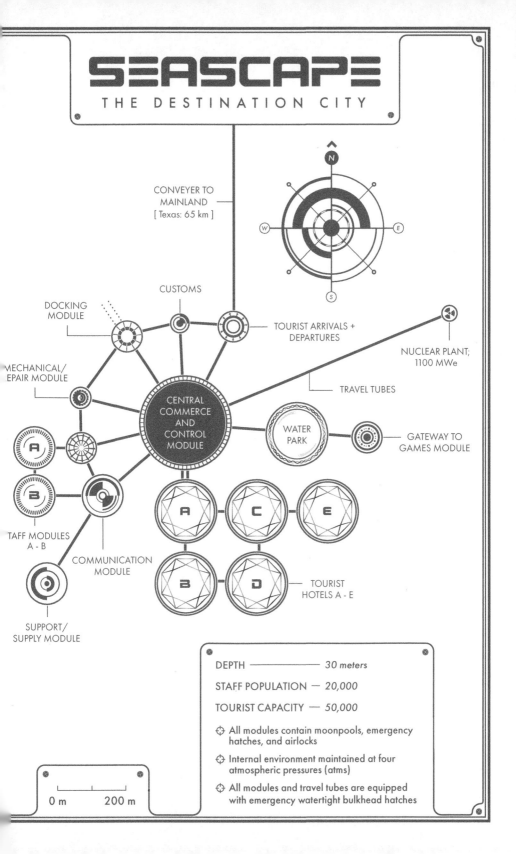

SEASCAPE
THE DESTINATION CITY

CONVEYER TO
MAINLAND
[Texas: 65 km]

N

W   E

S

CUSTOMS

DOCKING
MODULE

TOURIST ARRIVALS +
DEPARTURES

MECHANICAL/
REPAIR MODULE

NUCLEAR PLANT;
1100 MWe

TRAVEL TUBES

CENTRAL
COMMERCE
AND
CONTROL
MODULE

WATER
PARK

GATEWAY TO
GAMES MODULE

A

B

STAFF MODULES
A - B

COMMUNICATION
MODULE

A   C   E

B   D

TOURIST
HOTELS A - E

SUPPORT/
SUPPLY MODULE

DEPTH ——————— 30 meters

STAFF POPULATION — 20,000

TOURIST CAPACITY — 50,000

⊕ All modules contain moonpools, emergency
hatches, and airlocks

⊕ Internal environment maintained at four
atmospheric pressures (atms)

⊕ All modules and travel tubes are equipped
with emergency watertight bulkhead hatches

0 m   200 m

Interlude:
Meagan McClusky

```
Location:        Latitude:    28° 41' 24" N
                 Longitude:   94° 54' 5" W
                 The Gulf of Mexico, Seascape City,
                 USSF HQ
Depth:           30 meters
Date:            3 August 2130
Time:            Unknown
```

THE LIGHTS WERE DIM. THE cabin was humid and warm and it smelled like sweat. It was a small area, roughly three by three meters, but, she reminded herself daily, it was larger than her cubicle back at Trieste. There was no bunk or desk here, though—just a metal toilet in the corner and a single sheet lying in a matted clump on the deck which she'd been using as a pillow. It was too hot in there for a blanket, anyway. She was no longer wearing the clothes she'd had in Trieste—her captors had removed those long ago—and she was now in a loose-fitting jumper, mottled with blood stains, wrinkled, and torn in some places from guards moving her from her cell to the interrogation chamber and back again.

Knots tangled her greasy hair. There were bruises on her arms and legs, cuts on her torso, and her fingernails were black. Blood had clotted the spaces under her nails; Zyvinski had smashed each with a hammer one day, grilling her for information about the Acoustic Pulse Drive.

Meagan had made mental notes of the questions. They focused on Trieste's technology and their superior abilities underwater. Where the SCAV drive had come from, who had invented the APD, where did the inventors live in Trieste, the location of the labs in the Research Module, and so on. So far Meg had remained quiet about everything—*almost* everything, that is—but her resistance was faltering. She was growing weaker. One day she'd give in. Promises of a shower, a bed, a cool cabin, eight hours of uninterrupted sleep, and a good meal—kelp salad, grilled fish with ceviche conch, kelp tea—would be enough to break her if this lasted one more month.

She touched the scar on her inner thigh. *Soon*, she thought. There would be a way out of this, and then it would be time.

She knew they were in Seascape. When they grabbed her from the cell and hauled her down the corridor, they usually first put a black hood over her head so she couldn't see anything. Once, however, the hood was only partially on, and she got glimpses of the corridors and tubes of this place.

And it was *wonderful*.

She'd never been in Seascape City, but now she knew why the tourists had loved it. The bulkheads were largely transparent. The ceilings as well. In some places the decks were, too, with seawater underneath. Marine life was teeming around the structures, and below was coral in all directions, stretching into the distance.

She'd spoken with Truman many times about this place. The tourists had come from the states, but when the environmental disaster had really hit, they had stopped coming. Mac had pleaded with Reggie, the mayor, to join the quest for independence and fight the USSF, but the mayor had turned him down at first.

Then the tourists disappeared.

And with it, Seascape's purpose. Within weeks the USSF was there, building umbilical docks for a multitude of warsubs, sailors had occupied the hotel facilities, the noise and rattle of construction pierced every cabin, tube, and corridor of the colony, and Meg knew that this was an issue that would consume Mac until he could figure out a solution.

He did not want the USSF HQ so close to Trieste. Already their presence in the Gulf was a concern for his team—and for all Triestrians—but more importantly, their presence was dangerous to his quest for independence. Mac was busy building new ships for their Navy and investigating new technologies to exploit and colonize the oceans faster than the superpowers, and having the US military so near was a danger.

She knew something would happen soon, but she didn't know when.

Cliff was also in Seascape with her.

She'd heard the guards beating him, one day, while others were dragging her through the corridors. They'd been yelling at him, demanding to know about the APD, but he'd remained totally silent. She could hear the wet slaps and thuds of fists pounding his face.

She'd wanted to throw up.

But at the same time, a thrill of joy had filled her.

Cliff was nearby.

He was still at Seascape with her. The USSF had taken them both from Trieste at the same time, on board the same warsub, and he was still here.

They had a chance.

—••—

ZYVINSKI SOMETIMES RAN THE SESSIONS. She would ask the questions—sometimes in a whisper, her hot breath in Meg's ear and on her neck, and sometimes screaming, her lips an inch from her face and spittle spraying across Meg's nose, lips, and eyes—and would strike out when Meg didn't answer. Sometimes she used an open hand. Sometimes a fist.

Sometimes a rubber club.

A baton.

There was a taser some days, too. They had tased Meg more times than she could remember. She didn't mind it because you couldn't actually speak during it. Zyvinski hadn't figured that out yet, but Meg derived a sense of satisfaction from it.

Sick, but true.

Admiral Quintana was also in the area. Meg sometimes heard her outside her cell, her commands ringing down the corridors and sailors running to obey. Meg was sure the sailors hated having her at Seascape, but it would only grow worse. There were hundreds of boats there now, and the captains and officers of each would be around daily.

A session with Zyvinski often went like so:

"Tell me, where did you build your vessels?" She would bring in a cushioned chair and lounge comfortably in the small chamber, her legs thrown across the chair's arm, picking at her nails, studying them, sometimes filing them. Once she'd stabbed Meg with the nail file, but that was at the conclusion of a long session in which Zyvinski had got nothing after hours of questions.

"Vessels?" Meg feigned confusion.

"Yes, your *Swords*. Come on, Meagan. You know what I'm referring to."

"What about them?"

"Where do you build them? Is it a civilian contractor topside? It's not at Trieste; we destroyed the facility in The Battle last year."

"I don't know anything about them."

"The little seacars that make up your Navy."

"I still don't know what you're asking."

A sigh. "You piloted one before. You know their capabilities."

Meg frowned. "No, I don't."

"They can go deep. We saw it happen during the fight with the dreadnought."

"Maybe they're not ours. How would I know?"

Zyvinski's face twisted. "*Really*. That's bullshit. We knew they were responding to McClusky's orders from the Russian warsub."

"That doesn't mean they belong to us. You think Trieste possesses superior technology to the USSF?"

Her face lit. "*Superior?* How do you know this, unless you knew their capabilities?"

"You keep asking about them. You keep mentioning that they descended to over 5,000 meters in the battle."

"We saw it happen. Admiral Benning even reported it to us later."

Meg shrugged, but it was difficult with her hands bound behind her back. "I have no idea what he saw, or what you recorded, but they're not Triestrian."

"Just like the SCAV drive, is that it?"

"No, that's ours, which you know about. You took it from us in the Second Battle of Trieste last year when you arrested Shanks and Mayor Flint."

The CIA Investigator remained silent for a long, painful minute. She just stared, her eyes black and her face emotionless once again. "I will make your experience here miserable, McClusky."

"It already is."

"It'll be worse."

"Okay."

"You killed Admiral Benning."

"He murdered my father. I really had no choice."

"You screwed up. You killed a senior official in the USSF. Did you think we'd just stay away?"

Meg looked away. "I didn't really think about it, actually. I just did it."

"Did your brother know about it?"

"No."

"Who helped you get rid of the body, then?"

"I did it myself."

"In his seacar."

"Yes."

"Bullshit."

"I don't care what you believe."

"We'll arrest him, too, then, and bring him here for questioning."

"If you could you would have already done it."

"What?"

Meg smiled. "He's not here, so you can't do it."

"We can do anything."

"You say you could, but you didn't. You're too scared to anger Triestrians."

"We took you and nothing happened."

"We'll see."

Zyvinski bolted to her feet. "Are you *threatening* us?"

"Not at all. But Triestrians are likely very angry with you. You don't want that."

"And why not? They're insignificant compared to the Fleet."

"Really? It's been thirty years and you're still having problems with us.

Killing my father didn't help, it just made things worse. Killing me will have the same impact. Imprisoning me will likely be worse."

Zyvinski snorted but looked away. Meg knew she'd hit home. If they killed her she'd be a martyr. If they kept her hidden away somewhere, she'd be a source of friction and a rallying-cry for Triestrians.

They'd made a mistake taking her.

But then again, Meg had made a mistake by killing Benning. She knew that.

Mac had been right.

"Let's get back to the *Swords*."

Meg sighed. "I don't know about the technology."

"Which one?"

"The one you keep asking me about. I can't answer."

"I'll pull your fingernails out this time."

"It's all the same. I don't like the pain, but if I don't know the answer, I can't make it up."

"Who invented it?"

"Invented what?'

"The deep-diving tech. It uses sound waves."

"For what?" Meg screwed up her face.

Zyvinski growled under her breath, and it made Meg satisfied. "To go deeper, somehow," the Investigator said finally.

"If you say so."

"Did you invent the tech at Trieste, or somewhere else?"

She was trying to dig out information about The Ridge now, Meg knew. It was Mac's secret facility in The Mid-Atlantic Ridge, but Meg had denied every question about it so far. "I still don't know what you're talking about."

Zyvinski picked up the rubber baton.

Inside, Meg shuddered.

The beating lasted an hour, during which there were no more questions.

———••———

ONE DAY THE HATCH GROUND open and a man stood framed in the opening. He was black, bald, and had a goatee. He wore glasses. Meg gasped, for she recognized him from news broadcasts about this city. It was Reggie Quinn, the mayor. Truman had met him on a couple of occasions, while trying to convince him to join their movement.

Meg propped herself up on an elbow and watched him, curious.

He shot a look down the corridor and stepped inside.

The hatch shut behind him.

"Are you here to ask me questions?" Meg said. "To beat me?"

He winced. "I'm sorry you're going through this. I'm not one of them."

"But you're on the USSF's side."

"No, I'm not."

"That's what Mac told me."

Reggie paused and looked around. His nose wrinkled at the smell. His gaze finally settled on her, and a look of guilt flooded his features. Her arms were bruised, both eyes black, and there were smears of blood still on her face. "I'm so sorry," he said again. "I didn't want this to happen."

"You didn't want the USSF to take over? Didn't want to lose your city?"

He paused. "I didn't want to accept . . . the truth, I guess. That your brother was right."

Meg laughed—difficult because of multiple cuts on her lips—and sat leaning against the bulkhead. She pulled her knees up to hug them. She stared at the colony's mayor. Then, she realized, he wasn't mayor anymore, and there was no colony. It was now a USSF base.

"What are you going to do about it?" Meg whispered.

He stared at her. "I'm not going to break you out, if that's what you're asking."

"It is, kind of."

"That would be useless, because they'd catch me and then I'd be dead. There's no stopping something like that. No people who would rise up, angry, if they murdered me." He remained standing and leaned against the hatch. "But I might be able to help. To make it look like you managed it yourself . . . "

Meg sat up straighter. Here it was, a first sign of good fortune. After four weeks of hell. "Where's Cliff?"

"He's just down the hall. Three hatches. He's not doing as well as you."

She stared at her black fingernails. She didn't think she'd been doing 'well,' but the interrogators were likely beating him with more vigor because he was so much bigger and stronger. "That's . . . terrible," she whispered.

"I spoke to Mac, weeks ago," he continued. His voice was quiet now.

"And?"

"He expected this. He said he had a plan, but he wouldn't tell me what it was. But he told me to be ready."

"Sounds about right."

He blinked. "What do you mean?"

"That Truman would keep you in the dark."

He frowned and looked away. "He was right all along, you know. He predicted this all happening. Not the Russian dreadnought and the attack on the coasts, mind you, but he knew the environmental devastation on the surface was coming. He knew it'd affect our tourism."

Meg nodded. "He does seem to guess correctly about these things. Just like our dad."

"He figured you'd end up here."

"What's happening to the city?"

"They're building a massive docking structure with a series of umbilicals for warsubs. Dredging the area south of us so the bigger ones can approach safely. Troops are in the hotels, though they call them 'barracks' now."

"And the water park?" It was a glass dome to the east of the central module, famous in the States for its wave pool, waterslides, and water rides, all contained in a glass bubble of air underneath the ocean.

"Empty," he replied. "There's no use for it anymore, but I'm sure they'll convert it to repair docks or something of the sort."

Meg sighed. "This is not going to get better for Seascape. It's only going to grow worse." She watched him as she said it.

"I know." His voice was quiet.

"Quintana is here. She will likely make this her permanent—"

"She already has. She took my office."

Meg snorted. "Figures. You're lucky you're still here. Why are you, I wonder?"

"They kept me and my staff. We know the city well."

"Ah. But when they've learned all the ins and outs, you'll be gone."

"Likely." Then he stepped forward and kneeled before Meg. "Which is why I want to help sooner rather than later. What can I do?"

Meg stared into his eyes. He seemed genuine, she had to give him that.

But, Meg's gut cried out that it could very well be a ploy.

By Zyvinski.

Meg knew not to give anything away, so she just shrugged. "I don't know. You could talk to Cliff. See if he has an idea."

"I will. What else?"

"You could tell me when there are fewer guards out in the hall. You could give me the access code for the hatches. You could give me a schematic of the city and tell me where I am right now."

He listened to it all, intently. "I'll try my best."

Meg watched him for a series of heartbeats. "Are you committed to helping Mac?"

"I already told him I was."

She looked away. So, this might be the only way, then. "Do you know what he's planning?"

"No."

"Neither do I."

"But when something happens, I can let you know. To arrange your break when he's nearby maybe."

It was something, at least. Meg nodded. "And Cliff?"

"I'll tell him, too. And I'll figure out when there are fewer guards." He hesitated. "But I don't think I can get any weapons."

"Not even a small knife or blade?"

"No. The guards search me."

Meg's face split into a wide grin; her first genuine smile in weeks. "Don't worry, then—I'll take care of it."

Part Four: The Assault

The Ridge

Latitude:	28° 05′ 13″ S
Longitude:	17° 23′ 58″ W
Depth:	3,782 meters

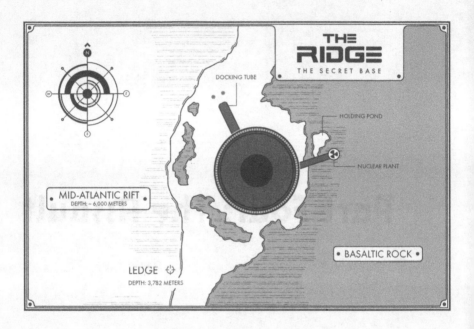

Chapter Fifteen

THE RIDGE WAS OUR MANUFACTURING facility. We'd built it over a year earlier. Workers had started construction immediately after the USSF occupied Trieste and arrested Shanks and Mayor Flint, and I'd ended up as the new mayor and Director of Trieste City Intelligence. I'd sent workers to the base immediately following The Battle—people the USSF had assumed dead. Once there, they'd begun work on our fast little seacars, called *Swords*, and during that time, Kat and Meg had recruited Doctor Manesh Lazlow, an acoustician, to put his theories to work and develop his life's dream: the Acoustic Pulse Drive. Using soundwaves, it pulsed rhythmically and drove the ocean back on itself for a brief period. A vessel could move forward into the 'low pressure tunnel' before the acoustic generator's next pulse, pushing the ocean back once again.

It was a magnificent invention, and equipped with it, as well as the SCAV drive, our *Swords* had defeated a force of a hundred USSF warsubs and double that number of FSF vessels.

The Ridge had proven itself a thousand times over. To have a location that was secret from the superpowers of the world, and one where we could invest our energies into creating technologies to further colonize and fight in the oceans, made our mission far easier. We weren't worried about the USSF showing up to destroy it, although the Russians had attacked the facility a few months earlier after the traitor Robert Butte had directed them to the base.

We'd built The Ridge to be a manufacturing base, and we had constructed the dome to maintain silence in the dark depths of the Rift. It was double-hulled with vacuum between layers to trap errant noises. We'd placed the power plant deep inside a cliff behind the facility, and the workers stayed for months at a time before we swapped out the crews. There was no way to communicate with the facility itself, for we had wanted to cut down on the chance that someone nearby might intercept transmissions.

The broken hulls of many dead USSF and FSF warsubs were twenty kilometers to the south, but they were located in the pit of the Mid-Atlantic Ridge at a depth of six kilometers. FSF warsubs were still in the area as they investigated the disaster, so my people were on high alert, but so far no one had suspected our location, and we were going to keep it that way.

SC-1 powered through the Rift southward, piercing the rising warm waters. Magma churned below, creating new crust as the world's tectonic plates spread slowly in opposite directions. The turbulence was the same as on any flight over heated land, but the seacar cut through it so quickly that it was only a minor inconvenience. Renée, Johnny, and I had all experienced this before, but it was new for Rico, and excitement painted his face.

For so many years vessels in the Earth's waters had traveled at incredibly slow speeds. During WWII, for instance, submarines cruised mostly on water at a speed of under forty kph. They submerged when in danger or attacking, where their speeds were much slower: under twenty kph. In the nuclear age, submarine design changed to being mostly underwater vessels and therefore adopted the 'cigar-shape' hull for greater stability when submerged. These boats traveled much faster: the US *Los Angeles* Class had a top speed of nearly sixty-five kph. And in the colonization age, we'd hit the upper limit of travel underwater due to incredible friction of steel against water: eighty kph.

But now our SCAV drive had obliterated that limit, shoving a crewed vessel through the ocean at 450 kph, as though driven by a hammer. Our *Swords* could go 460. Rico just couldn't believe it. He'd stared out the viewport for long minutes, transfixed by the shimmering bubble and the distorted view of seawater beyond. He spent hours in the fusion chamber in the seacar's aft compartment, and placed his hand on the intake pipes that carried water to the furnace where it was flash-boiled to steam. The noise was thunderous in that chamber, but he'd weathered it with a grin on his face as he studied the myriad pipes, controls, valves, and buttons. And in the center, the fusion reactor: a sphere studded with pipes and injection rods. Within that metal device, contained in a high energy magnetic field, temperatures hit millions of degrees Kelvin and hydrogen atoms fused to become helium and heat.

Our prisoner had woken during our trek southward through the Rift.

His face showed confusion at first, then he saw me and his jaw tightened.

I rose from the pilot's seat and stepped back into the living area of the seacar.

But he looked away as I approached, for the vibration and rumble through the vehicle were different from any submarine he'd ever experienced. He glanced around again, studying his surroundings. He pulled himself up, leaned against the bulkhead, and peered out a viewport. "Where are we?"

"What's your name?"

He pressed his lips together and stared at me.

"We could have let you die outside the city. We saved you."

"So you could torture me."

"I'm not going to torture you. I abhor it."

"But you said—"

"I told you I was going to feed you to the sharks."

"Sounds like torture to me."

I shrugged. "Maybe. But maybe I was just trying to get the name of your vessel out of you. But we found them, so it doesn't matter anymore."

"I don't believe you."

"What's your name?" I asked again.

He stared at me, then his eyes flicked around the interior of the seacar.

"Come on," I said. "Just your name. Otherwise I have to make one up for you."

He sighed. "You can call me Franz."

"Good. Thanks."

"You were trying to scare me earlier. I understand. But what type of vessel is this?"

I chewed the inside of my cheek, wondering if it mattered. This man had tried to kill me. I was going to use him to help break Meg out of Seascape, and it would likely kill him in the process. Then I shrugged inwardly. "It's our SCAV drive. Trieste has it. Other nations are developing it, or already have it, as we speak."

His eyes widened. "Of course I've heard of it . . . " he whispered. "How fast are we going?"

"Over 400 kilometers per hour."

His jaw dropped.

Rico appeared at my side. We were standing over the prisoner, looming above him, and Rico's arms were now tight at his sides.

"Easy," I hissed at him.

Rico ignored me. "You followed me to Trieste. To kill."

"I told you already, I'm not speaking."

I said, "It doesn't matter, because we already know about you. While you were sleeping we destroyed your warsub on our way out of the Gulf."

"I don't believe you."

"It was *Dark Winter*. We located it, and we destroyed it."

He laughed, and it was a short and sharp bark. "The warsub you mention is a *Mörder* Class attack boat. There's no way—"

"After experiencing our current velocity, do you really believe what you're about to say?" I said.

That stopped him. He stared around again, soaking in every detail. "This seacar is too small."

"We're fast and we have torpedoes. SCAV torpedoes, as well. Your vessel didn't stand a chance."

"There are men and women on that ship. I can't believe you'd kill—"

"You came to kill me. Now I'm going to make Germany pay."

His face grew slack, and he turned his eyes back to me. "I . . . I don't think you know what you're doing."

Rico lifted his arm and displayed the network of scars tracing across his sinewy muscles. "Look what your friends did to me," he rasped through clenched teeth. "Tortured me for a year. Now I'm going to get my revenge. And you're a part of it."

"Bullshit. Go ahead and kill me. But you won't be able to kill any other Germans."

"Is that so." I snorted. "You know I'm growing tired of surprising people."

"What does that mean?"

"People keep underestimating Trieste. But when you came to infiltrate our city and kill her citizens, you declared war on us." It was a vast overstatement, because it was the same thing I'd done countless times to many other undersea nations. It was part of the intelligence game, and the ocean colonies had been a part of it for many, many decades now. I pressed on, "I'm going to find some more German subs, and I'm going to sink them."

"And what am I doing here?"

I just stared at him and didn't speak.

I turned and marched back to the control cabin.

—••—

RENÉE HAD WATCHED THE ENTIRE exchange and moved toward the pilot chairs with me. She touched my arm and said, "What are you going to do with him?" I understood her concern. Months ago I had done something similar with her, and she had eventually left the FSF to join our cause.

I glanced back at her. "I've got a plan for him. I'm using him."

Her voice was barely audible. "Will he die?"

"Probably, but I don't really know."

She stared at me in silence, her eyes somber but accepting. She had been a captain in the military, and could accept the reality of the situation. She swallowed but remained focused on me. "I see. Did you notice how Rico reacted to the man?"

"I did, actually."

"Was it an act?"

"I was acting. I'm not sure about Rico though."

I turned and looked back at the living area. Rico was sitting on a couch, staring at Franz.

His eyes were like embers.

We forged through the Rift, an insect a thousand meters deep, insignificant compared to the massive diverging mountains tearing the ocean crust to pieces. We screamed through the dark waters toward our secret base. The wake behind us disrupted the natural currents of the geologic feature—the largest mountain range on the planet—tossing marine life aside as we plowed ahead. We made more noise than any other sub in the oceans, but we were deep now, in the rift between mountains, which would block our presence.

On board, we were silent.

—••—

THE RIDGE WAS A DOME set on a ledge at a depth of roughly 3,700 meters. It was so deep that conventional subs could barely reach it—many could not—and beyond the ledge was an abyss that plunged downward for another 2,300 meters. It was a sheer cliff leading to hell. Geologic forces had broken and shattered the crust. Bubbling magma and 'black smokers' released an unrelenting stream of ash and soot into the water, mottling the floor and clouding the waters.

I powered *SC-1* into the Docking Tube, through a large airlock hatch, and depressurized the exterior environment to four atms. The inner lock ground open and I maneuvered the seacar into the docking pool and shifted our buoyancy to positive.

We broke the surface and, as the water flowed off the canopy, I noted a familiar figure standing on the metal mesh dock within, watching.

Jackson Train.

A smile split my features.

He was a sight for sore eyes.

—••—

TEN MINUTES LATER, AFTER HANDSHAKES and hugs, we ended up on the upper level of the main dome in a small lounge with curving bulkheads and a concave ceiling. His eyes had widened when he'd noticed Renée emerge from *SC-1*—the last time he'd seen her, she'd been a prisoner at this facility, though moving about freely—and now she was a citizen of Trieste and actively fighting with us for independence.

I'd put Jack in charge of the facility immediately following The Battle. His mission had been to not only to construct the base from scratch, but to get an assembly line up and running, building our small submarine fighter seacars, *Swords*.

A Russian incursion had damaged the facility days afterward, but Jackson had led the repair efforts and now the facility was up and running once again, churning out our little *Swords*.

He was a fantastic leader, his workers loved him, and he kept the facility operating with incredible efficiency. He was a bear of a man—overweight—and had a jovial, fun-loving air about him.

"What brings you to The Ridge?" he asked me as we lowered ourselves into couches.

We'd left our German prisoner, Franz, in *SC-1*.

"How are the drones coming along?"

Jackson blinked. "Fine. We've been working on their programming. They're easy enough to build—simple remote ROVs that we've adapted to our own uses—and we have some already finished."

Renée said, "Remotely Operated Vehicles?"

I glanced at her. "Yeah. Umbilicals usually attach them to the control panel. These ones don't need them; we'll be able to control them wirelessly from *SC-1*."

"But what for?"

I turned to Jackson and waited for him to explain. He said, "They are very small—each less than a cubic meter—and are neutrally buoyant. They have thrusters that gimble, so they're highly maneuverable. Not very fast, though, so you'll have to get them close to be effective."

An expression of confusion met him. Renée said, "But they're for exploring wrecks, right?"

I shrugged. "Traditionally, yes, but we're not exactly traditional, are we?"

—••—

WE'D RELOCATED TO THE HOLDING Pond behind the cliff, back where the fusion reactor generated power for the base and the assembly machinery. On the surface of the dark water were small floating vehicles—our drones. Pipes and small tanks attached to their exterior hulls, and the gimballing thrusters jutted out from the stern of each.

Usually they had 'arms' or tools to do basic tasks like grabbing an object from the ocean floor, twisting a bit of debris aside, grasping a cable and bringing it back to the surface, and so on. These drones had no such things. There was a larger tank on their bows, painted bright red, and two protrusions on either side of it. Each ended with a flat piece of black rubber with a spring just behind it.

There were over thirty of the drones there, just drifting in the pool.

I smiled. "You've built a lot of them!"

"Just doing our job," Jack said with a matching grin.

"But Mac," Renée said. "I still don't understand."

Johnny was smiling, too. He knew exactly what they were, because he'd been part of the team that designed them. "I wasn't sure you could build them so fast."

Jackson snarled, "What's so hard? We just bought pre-existing ROVs and retrofitted them. Easy!"

"We're going to take some," I muttered, "along with a method to control them."

Jack said, "It's easy. It'll tie into your panel in the pilot room, or we can put a fixture in the living space of your seacar."

"The co-pilot's panel, please," I said with a gesture at Johnny. "He can operate them."

Johnny's grin grew wider.

Renée had watched the whole thing with an upraised eyebrow. Then she studied the nearest drone. She knelt next to it, reached out, and pulled it closer. She turned it in the water, bringing the bow into view.

Water rippled around it, splashing on the edge of the mesh dock.

She studied the red tank . . .

There was a painted symbol there.

She peered closer . . .

Then her expression exploded into shock and surprise. *"Merde Sainte!"*

Chapter Sixteen

WE DECIDED TO SPEND ONE night at the base before continuing northward.

So we had a party.

It was difficult, knowing that the USSF had Meg and Cliff, but the workers at The Ridge were thrilled to see us and I didn't want to let them down by taking their hard work, paying little attention to them, and then steaming away an hour later.

They put on a banquet for us. Sushi, kelp beer, swordfish steaks, and some sort of pastry for dessert, which piqued my curiosity because flour was just not a possibility underwater. We had a variety made from powdered kelp, but as with all other seaweed-related foods, it was quite salty and newcomers often complained of it tasting fishy.

I was unsure where this pastry had come from, but one of the male workers grinned at me between drinks and drawled, "It's ground fish bone!"

I grimaced but shoved it happily into my mouth.

We drank long into the night.

We danced and sang and toasted again and again and again. We spoke of the battles against the CSF, the USSF, the FSF and, of course, the RSF. Our songs were rowdy and accompanied by people slamming their steel cups on the table to provide rhythm. Beer splashed everywhere. The mess stunk of it for days later, I discovered long after we'd gone. The songs spoke of battles and adventures and the undersea quest for peace and freedom. They were all original, written by the base's workers and crew. They were always looking for entertainment in their off hours. There wasn't much else to do.

> Give us an ocean
> And wide expanses
> With spaces to fill

For life and adventure
For life and adventure
And enemies to kill!

The singers really drew out the second last line, screaming it, syllable by syllable, tilting their heads back and closing their eyes as they bellowed. And then they pounded out that last line, drumming their fists on their thighs. Then there was Jackson's favorite:

Our Swords are the class
With the SCAV for the win
Better turn back now, Cap'n
Cuz we're gonna kick your ass!

Renée kept glancing at me during dinner. She laughed and sang with the rest, and it couldn't have been easy for her. She knew most of these people—they had once held her captive—and now she was sitting amongst them, breaking bread, drinking, and having a grand old time.

But she'd proven herself to me a thousand times over, and I couldn't help but watch her, too.

And even when I wasn't looking, I was aware of her.

Her short dark hair, dark eyes, and toned muscles were alluring, but that's not what I liked most about her. Her determination and dedication to the undersea world attracted me the most. Strange as it may have seemed, her quest to kill me had fascinated and excited me. I had hurt her career, and she had vowed to punish me. We had first met in hand-to-hand combat, and had almost killed one another.

She moved next to me after we'd finished eating, and I noticed her hand resting on my thigh.

I smiled at her, and she smiled back.

I had first told her about my father in this very facility. I'd told her about Benning, how he'd killed Dad, and how I'd vowed to kill the man because of it.

And yet, I hadn't done it. I hadn't been able.

I'd been suffering too much guilt because of the warsubs I'd sunk. I hadn't been sleeping well because of it.

So I'd spared the man.

I rose to my feet, the party in full swing around me, music blaring and people dancing. Rico in particular was enjoying it. There was a huge smile on his face, and multiple women had surrounded him, all with drinks in hand and similar looks on their faces. They were dancing and singing and it looked as though he didn't have a care in the world.

I knew better.

I knew that drink and women and parties never erased trauma. They only masked it, temporarily, and the real emotions continued to bubble below, churning, preparing to erupt.

But Rico was happy now, and he was extremely likable.

I noticed Johnny watching him from the corner of his eye, though. He still had his suspicions.

Then I turned back to Renée and reached out to her.

She grinned and took my hand.

—••—

"WHAT'S THIS?" SHE ASKED, TRACING her fingers along the new scar. It was on my upper thigh, on the inside of my leg.

I glanced at it. She was bright; she knew it was too old to have been from the scuba fight outside of the travel tube only the day before.

We were in the upper level of the dome, in a bunk surrounded by curtains. It's how the workers lived; there were no individual crew cabins. Just a large open space sectioned by heavy, black drapes. We had grabbed what seemed like an unused bunk, fell into it breathlessly, and made love long into the night. The sounds of the party echoed around us, and a part of me worried about attracting attention. Then again, the *Sword* assembly line, when it was running at full speed with every worker on a task, was far louder. The base's double-hulled construction worked well.

Now Renée was lying next to me, naked, looking at the scars on my body from my years with TCI.

I said, "Insurance. It's uncomfortable."

"That's cryptic."

"It is."

There was a long break while she lie there, her eyes open, staring at me. "Why are you so driven to do this?"

"Independence?"

"Yes. Fighting the superpowers. People tried to kill you yesterday. Warsubs try to sink you. Everywhere you go, seems like. And you don't mind."

"I mind. I just . . . *accept* it, I guess."

"But why?"

I stared at her. "Are you questioning my sanity?"

She laughed. "Not at all. But I'm wondering about your motives."

I sighed. "You know about my dad. He gave his life for it."

Her eyes widened. "You don't mean—"

"No, not that I'm anxious to die. But he felt that this was important for all undersea colonists. He felt it was best for the human race, too. And I agree with him. Look what's going on topside."

"The riots. Flooding."

"The death. Yes. They're growing desperate. We are a source of resources. Frank McClusky knew that, too. But he wanted to make sure our colonizing nations properly compensated us. Treated us as equals. I agree with him now."

"But not at first?"

"Not when I was younger. I agreed with his philosophy, but not his methods. But now that we are technologically superior . . ."

"Now that you actually have a chance at it."

"Yeah. We have families living with us. I don't want to put children in harm's way for a hopeless cause."

She nodded and looked at the domed ceiling. "I see." A pause, and then, "And what about the people you've killed?"

I grew tense. "What does that mean? You think it's easy to sink a warsub?"

"There are sailors on them. How do you feel about it?"

"I'm struggling with it. But if they're trying to kill me, then what choice do I have?"

"It's one way to look at it."

"What's the other way?"

She shrugged. "That they're innocent crew, just doing their jobs."

"They joined the submarine fleets of whatever country that attacks us. They harass our citizens when they're on leave. They're not innocent."

"I used to be a captain in the FSF. You fired on my warsub."

"To protect myself. You were going to arrest me. Did you forget?"

She could sense my growing anger, and patted my chest with her hand. "I don't mean to annoy you. I'm just digging into what makes a McClusky work. Please don't get upset."

I remained silent.

She pushed her head into my neck; her hair tickled my cheek.

"It's a sensitive issue, just at the moment," I muttered.

"Why's that?"

"I feel guilty. I'm having . . ."

"Go on."

"Nightmares, sometimes. Of sailors drowning. Calling my name in rage."

She hesitated. "Your goals are noble. I don't think you should doubt them."

"You're questioning how I've killed people. I'm telling you, it's not easy."

"I know that."

"But for the greater good."

"For the people in the colonies?"

"Yes. Not just Triestrians—for *all* people underwater."

I closed my eyes as a wave of pressure surged through me. How many had I killed? How many had died trying to kill me? What dangers had I brought to Trieste? And now Meg was in serious trouble. Our dad's quest had sucked her into his path, as well, and she had committed a murder.

Our father was a stain on our lives, like a black hole that consumed everything and everyone around it, and he was long dead. But his dreams and desires hovered over everything we did. The people of Trieste revered him. They saw *me* as *him* on most days. They assumed I wanted the same things he did. They saw me as some kind of saviour, which really annoyed me. I didn't want their adoration. It's why February 23—the day they celebrated Frank McClusky's life—was so difficult for me.

Eventually, next to me, Renée's eyes closed and her breathing grew regular and deep.

But I couldn't sleep.

—••—

THE NEXT MORNING WE BOARDED *SC-1* and prepared to depart The Ridge. We had loaded eighteen drones into the seacar—bringing them up via the moonpool—and stored them in engineering. Each was relatively small, but together they occupied a lot of space, and it made that cabin especially cramped. We bolted some to the deck to keep them from sliding around, and stacked others on top.

Franz was sitting on the couch, watching us with hooded eyes. We'd left him chained to a pipe in the vessel, with a bucket to use for his excrement. I dumped it in the toilet and brought the pail back. Then I prepared a meal for him—a ration pack, heated—and he hungrily ate it, without looking at me again.

I thought back to my conversation with Renée. Here was a prisoner who had tried to kill me. Would she approve if I murdered him?

Franz had just been doing a job. I knew that. His superiors had taken him to the Gulf, pointed him in my direction, and gave the order.

But I didn't think he was so forgiving of me. I'd killed his team—or gave the order—and he wouldn't forget.

—••—

JOHNNY LOOKED TIRED BUT HAPPY as he sat in the right-hand seat in the control cabin. He'd had a good evening. Rico as well. Drinking and dancing and who knows what else. But it had been a needed respite, and the crew at The Ridge had also enjoyed our visit.

I powered the vessel into the docking tube, we hit 370 atms of pressure, and I steered us to the north and my eventual destination.

I increased power and used the diving planes to go shallower; all it took was a tug of the yoke toward me, and we angled upward. The conventional screws pushed us at fifty kph, and we soared up toward my target depth of 2,000 meters.

I didn't want to touch the SCAV drive until we were well away from the base.

A while later the sonar lit up and Johnny snapped his gaze to it.

"Mac," he whispered. "Contact."

I hauled back on the throttle, lowering power to only ten percent. We were several kilometers from The Ridge now, but still too close for comfort.

"How many?"

"I've got three obvious contacts. All in the Rift. Distance ranges from four to seventeen kilometers away. There might be more, too."

Our passive sonar had detected them. The computer was always listening for nearby contacts, and its sensitivity was thirty kilometers. These contacts were quiet. "What's their speed?"

"They're moving slowly, along the cliff's edge."

"Make?"

Johnny hesitated, then turned to me. "They're German vessels, Mac. *Jäger* Class."

—••—

THEY WERE SMALL, FAST, AND well armed, but that class of vessel could only descend to 2,240 meters. Our base was 1,500 meters deeper, so I wasn't worried about them finding it, but a hot pit of fear flooded my gut.

How did they know we'd be there?

The French had lost many warsubs nearby, so I expected their presence at the Mid-Atlantic Ridge. But German warsubs?

I frowned, replaying recent events in my mind. Everything that had happened with Germany. Rico's escape from a GSF warsub, and then a German attack at Trieste.

And now here they were in the Rift, dangerously close to our secret base.

There was only one way they could have known these things.

I swore.

—••—

Renée appeared at my shoulder. "What is it?" she hissed.

"They're planting listening devices here."

Her face dissolved into shock. "How do you know?"

"Look at the spacing of the vessels. They're not exactly searching for us. They're against the rock wall of the canyon." Two massive mountain ranges stretching north-south in the middle of the Atlantic made up the Mid-Atlantic Ridge. The gap between the two—the Rift—was twenty kilometers across. Here were three subs, all on the east side of the Rift, hugging the mountains. "They're placing listening devices up and down the canyon."

"Maybe they're just searching using passive sonar."

"The vessels can't go that deep. *Attentäter* Class can go deeper. I don't think they would have sent *Jägers* if they were actively searching."

"Which means they know about us here."

"Yes." I stared at the sonar, wondering if there were more contacts. The conversation with Renée still rang in my head.

I couldn't let the GSF discover our location in the Rift. Their sensors might eventually pick us up and lead them right to my people.

But it would mean more killing.

Inside, my guts twisted. It felt like a knife in there, turning slowly.

"Shit."

Johnny whispered, "We don't really have a choice. We can't let them set up a listening network here, this close to the base."

"But if we sink them . . . "

"We're far from the nearest comm junction. They won't be able to transmit a message. They'll just . . . *disappear*."

"The GSF will send more boats. Finish the job."

"Then we'll have to start *Sword* patrols. Sink whoever comes near."

"It'll be pretty obvious the base is here, then."

Johnny frowned. "But they already know, Mac." He gestured at the canopy; the VID displayed the nearest GSF warsub on it in brilliant white against a dark blue background. "They're *here*. We can't let them place a bunch of sensors this close to the base."

Inside, I knew he was right. I also knew the GSF would keep sending warsubs until they found our facility. We would just have to deal with each as they came, and I'd warn Jackson Train about it next time we connected.

I sighed. "Prepare a homer, Johnny. You're right. We have to sink them."

—••—

THE TORPEDO WAS ARMED AND ready in our tubes. As soon as we opened the shutter, I suspected the closest warsub would hear and turn to fight. We were well within the passive listening range, although I didn't know the German military capabilities in that much detail.

"Open tube and fire."

Johnny pressed the button and the seacar shuddered. I pushed the throttle to full and followed our weapon toward its target. On the VID, the torpedo's screws churned the water, bubbles rose to the surface, and it closed on the first GSF warsub.

Our sonar displayed the torpedo in yellow. A friendly weapon. *SC-1* was at the very center, in green, and the GSF subs were red.

Johnny stared at the sonar, reading messages. "They're reacting. Alarms are going off on board. They've opened their own tubes."

"Get ready," I muttered.

And then our alarm blared. I jumped in my chair, even though I'd expected it.

Johnny snapped, "Torpedo in the water. Headed straight for us."

"Prepare countermeasures." I wasn't too worried. We had the Acoustic Pulse Drive, which meant we could descend below five kilometers, a depth that would crush their torpedoes.

He pressed the button, then frowned. "Nothing's happening."

The alarm was still sounding, and I snapped it off with a touch. "Try again."

"Nothing."

I pushed the throttle forward and steered away from the incoming torpedo. Our weapon was heading directly for the first GSF warsub; no doubt crew on the other two vessels were now studying their screens to see what was going on, and they'd be joining the fight imminently.

The alarm started again, blaring with even greater intensity.

I swore.

"The GSF torpedo is at a hundred kph and accelerating, Mac!"

It was a SCAV missile.

And they could go upwards of 1,000 kph.

Chapter Seventeen

"GET THE APD READY. WE'LL have to go deep."

I shoved the throttle to max and angled the nose nearly straight down. I heard startled gasps behind me, but I ignored them. They knew we were in trouble.

"How's our torpedo doing?" I muttered.

"The first *Jäger* is maneuvering," Johnny replied. "Launching countermeasures."

I grunted, studying our depth. We had passed 3,000 meters and were plunging into the depths. At four kilometers, we'd turn on the APD and its sound waves would displace the surrounding high pressures, and allow us to penetrate deeper into the Rift.

But their torpedo was closing fast.

"Mac," Johnny snapped. "The APD is down. Showing a red light. The generator is not functioning."

My insides went cold. A shockwave rocketed through my body.

The APD was down, too!?

There was only one other option. I punched the fusion reactor button and activated the SCAV drive. I slammed the throttle forward and willed the thrust to take over.

Get us moving!

The incoming missile was *screaming* through the water toward us now. It closed the distance remarkably fast. The *Jäger* Class boat had been 3,000 meters away; the torpedo was now at 1,030 kph and almost on us.

We were right next to an immense mountain range that plunged downward to a depth of 6,000 meters. It was nearly a sheer cliff, with protrusions, ledges, jagged fractures, and shallow caves. There were plenty of places to hide, should it come to that, but the German torpedo had locked onto us and we had to deal with it first.

"Renée!" I yelled. "Find out why our countermeasures and APD aren't working! It must be a breaker somewhere."

For both systems to be out simultaneously, I figured it'd be the same issue.

"On it," she said, disappearing aftward to engineering.

The fusion reactor was generating steam now and it was shooting from the stern nozzle. I gripped the yoke tightly in my hands and leveled us off at 4,000 meters. It was our listed crush depth; going any farther was just too dangerous. I pulled up on the yoke and we began ascending rapidly. I studied the VID to see where the *Jäger* was . . .

And I steered straight for it.

The warsub was trying to avoid our torpedo now, and had ejected its own countermeasures.

I would try to use the GSF deterrents against their own weapon.

SC-1 shot straight for the churning mass of bubbles.

Beside, a sheer cliff.

Below, a plunge to a depth that would crush us.

And the SCAV missile was right on our tail.

—••—

I BEGAN ZIGZAGGING THE SEACAR, tilting us to port and starboard and back again, getting the weapon on our tail to follow suit. We were in SCAV drive now, surrounded by a bubble of air. Our speed was 450 kph. Each turn slowed us slightly, but it did the same to the torpedo. The acceleration pushed us back into our chairs. The strategy had slowed it, but only marginally. It still had us outclassed by a wide margin.

I stared at the bubbling cloud just before us.

And we soared into it.

The countermeasures were emitting sound as well as cavitating to release bubbles. We heard them clearly through the hull as *SC-1* arrowed through them.

Then they were behind us.

I slammed the throttle to zero—cutting all noise—and held my breath.

Behind us, an immense explosion.

SC-1 shuddered massively and lights winked red on the control consoles. Alarms began to shrill but we shut them off quickly with the touch of a button. I stared at the readouts, trying to figure out where the damage had occurred.

No pressure alarm, though—no angry flashing blue lights.

I studied the VID, searching for a ledge, someplace to set down.

And then a *thud* echoed in the cabin.

A quick look at the sonar confirmed my suspicions. We'd hit the German *Jäger*. But it wasn't sinking.

The screws sputtered but continued normal operation.

I increased speed with conventional screws, keeping SCAV off for now, searching for a place to set down.

Finally, I saw it. At 2,340 meters, a small ledge jutted out from the mountain next to us. I pointed and Johnny nodded.

"Got it," he whispered.

We angled toward it, and I lowered our speed. Quiet was best here. No need to give away our position . . .

Our depth was increasing faster than I'd expected, and I noted that our ballast tanks were filling. I pushed the controls to positive, but nothing happened.

Aw, shit.

Damage to the ballast system. We couldn't make positive buoyancy.

I hoped the GSF warsub was dealing with its own issues at that moment, and couldn't worry about tracking exactly what we were doing. I tilted the nose down and altered power slightly. Then I extended our landing skids, and the whine reverberated through the pedals and into my feet. Shifting bearing, I positioned *SC-1* over the tiny ledge. There was barely enough room for us, but I figured it would be a good hiding spot, a place where they wouldn't expect us. I made sure our bow pointed out, into the Rift, and let our negative buoyancy carry us downward.

We touched the rock and the seacar shuddered at the impact.

The light from the red emergency indicators illuminated our faces, and our expressions were grim.

I stared into the expanse before us. The cliff was at our stern, and I could see it stretching into the distance on either side for as far as the VID projected it. The GSF *Jäger* was before us, neutrally buoyant, moving across our bow. Bubbles rose slowly to the surface from its hull; she was flooding.

There were two other subs out there, and they'd gone silent.

"SCAV torpedo," I hissed.

Johnny nodded and pressed the weapons control panel between us. "Ready."

"Fire."

A missile shot from our seacar and arced straight for the warsub. It was an easy shot; the vessel was making too much noise as it flooded, and sailors on board were likely scrambling to effect repairs.

My gut wrenched as I watched the death unfold on the VID.

The torpedo accelerated rapidly, bubbles screaming upward from its jet as it quickly tore through the water/steel friction barrier and the SCAV bubble surrounding it eliminated drag nearly entirely.

The *Jäger* turned, ejected more countermeasures—

But there was no hope. We'd been too close, and they had sailed right into our crosshairs.

The weapon exploded into a cloud of orange and red and white, and a rumble echoed through *SC-1*. The warsub's hull wrinkled just a bit at midship—

And then in an instant the blast pressure found the weakness and pushed, relentless, against steel.

The hull twisted inward and the boat crumpled as if a giant's hand had crunched it like a toy. A single, large bubble floated to the surface, followed by refuse and a cloud of oil.

The hull spun slowly as it descended into the canyon and toward the churning seafloor far, far below.

I swallowed.

—••—

DISTANT REVERBERATIONS CUT THE WATER and vibrated our hull as interior compartments imploded and the dead warsub plunged downward. Bubbles continued to stream toward the surface as the watertight bulkhead cracked in engineering and banks of batteries reacted to flooding; the result was a deadly mix of hydrogen and sulphuric acid churning the waters as it outgassed. Crushed bodies swirled with the wreckage, some trapped within, as they made the violent descent with their dead warsub.

I turned my attention to the sonar; there were still two other boats out there, and the captains knew our general location.

Johnny shook his head. "They're running silent now," he whispered.

I got shakily to my feet and marched back through the living area, across the closed moonpool hatch, past the airlock, and into engineering. Renée was there, peering at the electronics panel that held backups to the controls in the pilot's cabin up front. "Find anything?"

She looked up at me. "Not a thing. The APD and countermeasure connections to the power supply are fine. Could be a programming issue . . . I really don't know. I'm not an engineer."

Meg would normally have been the person to repair the seacar after a confrontation. She was a sub engineer, after all.

"Maybe the problem is in the forward compartment. I'll check."

"Mac—"

I stared at her. Creases lined her forehead and her body was tense. "You've been through this a thousand times, just like—"

"I know, but it doesn't make it easier. But the fact is, for both those controls to fail at the same time . . . it's *odd*."

"I was thinking the same thing." The APD could always get us out of a sticky situation, by just going *deep* and avoiding torpedoes and mines. And countermeasures were absolutely crucial when involved in a torpedo battle. "It's possible . . ."

"What?"

My mind was churning. I was thinking back to Trieste, and what had transpired over the past few days. The assassination attempt. The fight with the German special forces troops outside the city. "Back in Trieste. When they tried to kill me and Johnny."

"The German special forces?"

"Yes. We just assumed they infiltrated and came straight to the travel tube to take us out. But what if they didn't?"

She swore. "We didn't even check the video feed."

"Maybe Cliff would have, if he were with us. But we caught the guys so we didn't think much about it. Hell, how'd they even know this was my seacar?"

And if they'd planned on killing me in the travel tube, why sabotage my seacar?

Unless they'd planned on taking out my entire team.

Richard, Jessica, Renée, Lazlow, Hyland.

Cliff and Meg.

That thought sent shockwaves through me.

What if the Germans were trying to kill all of us, and not just me?

After all, Johnny had been with me in the tube.

It meant the others were still in danger, back at Trieste.

"I have to warn them," I hissed.

———•••———

WE HEADED BACK TO THE control cabin—past Franz, who just stared at us, his face a dark cloud—to check on the control systems. We slid the pilot chairs back as far as they'd go, and Johnny got on his back with his face under the console. He opened the panel and started searching the controls.

"Pass me a flashlight," he muttered.

Renée did, and we stood there, staring at his legs as he wormed his way around the wiring and computer control panels.

Finally, "Here's the problem with the countermeasures."

"What?"

"Someone's cut the wires."

"Are you sure? Perhaps when dropping out of SCAV . . . ?"

"No. They're cut. I can see where they enter the computer control box. They've been snipped with a tool."

I turned and stared at Franz.

His eyes were ice cold.

I moved toward him, angry, coiled like an angry animal waiting to strike. "I have been kind to you," I grated.

"You're holding me prisoner."

"You tried to kill me back at Trieste."

He shrugged. "I was carrying out my orders."

"Did your orders involve sabotaging my ship?"

He clamped his mouth shut; he just stared at me.

The sonar alarm sounded and Renée said, "*Contact*. Approaching from the north. Moving slowly about two kilometers away. Just a hundred meters above us."

Damn. We were sitting on a ledge, and along with our other issues, we now had no ballast control.

"I'm fixing the wires." Johnny's voice echoed from under the control console. "Shouldn't be too hard."

Someone had sabotaged the system to prevent us from a last-ditch effort to save ourselves from incoming torpedoes.

"What else did you do to this seacar?" I growled.

Franz shook his head. "I don't know what you're talking about."

"Yes, you do. You were one of the people who shut the hatch to the travel tube, locked out the comm, and prevented me from opening it. You have computer and electronics expertise. You were the one who snuck aboard this seacar and sabotaged it."

Still no response.

"If we go down, you do, too."

"That's the job, McClusky. Or did you forget?"

I exhaled and turned away. "No. I didn't. But I thought you might have a sense of self-preservation."

"I serve my country. You serve yourself."

"I serve all undersea dwellers. We're fighting the powers that repress us, that use us. Surely you can understand that."

"I understand that my superiors sent me to do a job."

"You don't think for yourself, then, is that it?"

"Of course I do."

"You don't have a brain of your own. You are a robot. Yes?"

"Not at all."

"So they asked you to trap me in a travel tube and drown me. You were okay with that?"

He stared at me. "You've done the same thing. You're a part of Trieste City Intelligence. Surely they've sent you out on the same type of mission."

I faltered. "Yes . . ."

"And you've done it, because those were your orders. You've killed people. Sabotaged equipment. Stolen new tech."

"I quit when faced with something I found abhorrent. But if it serves the greater good—"

"Meaning the people of your city. Well, I'm serving the people of my *country*. Something you don't have, obviously."

"I have a country. I have a nation. It's called Oceania."

He snorted. "It doesn't exist."

"It will. Openly. And you'll want to join, one day."

"Why?"

"Because you live underwater."

"In a GSF warsub. Not in a colony."

"But you understand what it means to be underwater. You know what the oceans represent for humanity. It's our future. We have to develop them peacefully, not under someone's thumb. We can't extract resources without considering the consequences. The oceans are all we have left, Franz."

In the control cabin, Johnny said, "I've found the APD control issue."

I turned toward him. "And?"

"It's toast. Unless we have a backup control system for the acoustic generator."

I sighed. "Lazlow might have had one." But we'd left him back at Trieste, in his lab. "What about the ballast?"

"That's an exterior issue. Not a control one."

I swore under my breath. I didn't want to go outside to fix it.

Renée was still watching the sonar. "They're approaching, Mac. We need to prepare."

"Got it." I turned back to Franz. "You many be allegiant to Germany, but Germany is on the edge. Just like every topside nation."

"What does that mean?"

"The environmental disaster is underway up there. The crash is coming, unless it's started already. The global crash. Economies, food supplies, health care, *everything*. We're the solution. The *only* solution."

"You're preventing the solution. Your colonizing nations need the resources."

"For how long? Unless extraction is sustainable, things down here will only last so long. We want to self-govern, to bring sustainability to the oceans, and to be a part of the market economy so everyone can prosper."

He frowned, staring at me. "You're dreaming if you think you can achieve that."

"That's my goal. My question to you is this—" I shoved my face next to his. "Why would your government want to stop that?"

He hesitated.

"Mac," Renée said. "They're almost here."

Franz said, "They don't want you interfering with our underwater colony. With New Berlin."

"I didn't."

"Someone did. *He* did." He pointed at Rico, who had been watching the entire exchange in silence.

I glanced at the agent. "Yes, he did. To offer people of the undersea world self-realization. I agree with it. And we're going to achieve it one day, Franz. And the rest of the world will view you and your Fleet as oppressors. As slave owners. And they'll be happy when we destroy you."

And with that, I left him sitting there to stew about it.

—••—

I BROUGHT THE CONTROLS ONLINE. There were still red lights everywhere, but the only ones critical to us were the ballast tanks and the APD.

We'd just have to avoid using them.

At least we had countermeasures back.

"Good job, Johnny," I whispered.

"How are we going to do this?"

I pursed my lips. There was a contact on the sonar screen; the VID displayed it, as well. Another Jäger, closing from the north. It was 813 meters away, just slightly above us now. Surely they had heard the other warsub implode and sink, following impacts with two torpedoes.

"We'll have to maintain our depth with pure speed and the control surfaces." I had learned in the past that *SC-1* could not maintain depth with flooded tanks and conventional thrusters only. However, with the SCAV drive, we would be able to. And we'd have to get past these two warsubs, and then make it to a repair dock somewhere. I continued, "We'll use—"

And then we heard a loud *Bang!* rattle the hull.

Then another.

And another.

It caught me off guard, and I jerked my head around to find out what it was.

Implosion, perhaps? Had the intense water pressures finally caught up to—

There was a scuffle behind us; Rico had thrown himself at Franz, and they were locked in a struggle.

Franz.

He had slammed something metal on the bulkhead, to draw the GSF's attention.

The *Jäger* on our screens turned directly toward us.

The sonar screamed.

Torpedo in the water.

Chapter Eighteen

"Subdue him!" I yelled at Rico.

There were multiple torpedoes now heading toward us, showing as angry red lines on our sonar screen, and white missiles churning toward us on the computer-generated canopy screen.

I slammed the SCAV drive to full, while we were still sitting on the ledge. I couldn't raise us off the rock, because water had completely flooded our ballast tanks, and there was no way to clear them.

The fusion reactor roared to life behind us.

Superhot gas began thrusting from our stern nozzle, pulverizing the rock wall behind us. Sand and gravel and large rocks flowered around us, soaring out over the ledge, and plummeted into the depths before us.

Steam bubbles roiled up the cliff toward the surface.

SC-1 started to move forward, grinding along the rock ledge.

It was a cacophony of overlapping, thunderous noise.

It was like a magnet drawing in the homing torpedoes; computers in the nose cone of each listened for every abnormal sound in the surrounding ocean.

Our bow cleared the ledge, and we hung suspended over a six-kilometer canyon.

A canyon that would crush us should our control surfaces not be enough to keep us level.

My heart caught in my throat.

And then we were off the ledge and *SC-1* lurched out into open water.

We plummeted downward.

I held my breath as I watched our depth gauge.

But our velocity was increasing slowly, and I pulled the yoke toward me, tilting the control surfaces—the diving planes—to keep us angled upward. Soon our speed was over a hundred kph and climbing, and we were maintaining our depth.

I exhaled.

The GSF warsub was close.

Damn close.

Turning toward it, I continued to accelerate.

There were three torpedoes on our tail and I snarled, "Countermeasures!"

Johnny dropped them right beside the GSF warsub, which began blowing ballast and turning to run.

But the three torpedoes closed—

And at least one exploded.

All three went up in a ball of energy and vaporized a massive volume of seawater. The yoke jerked in my hands, and I realized that if we lost the SCAV, it was all over for us.

But the explosion subsided, and I watched, with a pit of remorse burning in my gut, as yet another warsub headed to the bottom.

I turned away.

Johnny was staring at it, though, and he recited the depths until finally he grimaced. "Crush depth," he whispered.

The sound of an imploding sub echoed around us. Then another series of smaller implosions as interior compartments followed suit.

People were dying.

I glanced behind me. Rico had hogtied Franz. There was a gag in his mouth, too.

"There's one more out there," Johnny muttered.

I lowered our speed; I didn't want to enter supercavitation just yet. But we were making a tremendous amount of noise.

"Any sign of it?" I asked.

Johnny frowned, then shook his head. "I'm not sure where—"

The sonar screamed.

"Mac, torpedo in the water! Headed straight for us, bearing 273, distance 343 meters and closing fast! It's a SCAV tor—"

I turned us away from the weapon. Dammit. They had snuck up on us and fired at point-blank range, with a missile that could accelerate to a thousand kph. I shoved the throttle forward and watched the bubbles churn at our blunt bow. The envelope of air slowly built around *SC-1* . . .

"We'll have to do the same thing. Lead the torpedo right back at him. Dump some countermeasures on top of him."

"Got it."

"Prepare a homer just in case."

I banked us to the port now, and the g-forces pressed us to the right as I made the turn. The sonar was still screaming, and Johnny cut the noise with a touch of his finger. I located the GSF vessel—yet another *Jäger*—and I circled toward it.

It had already started dropping countermeasures and was trying to make an escape.

But we were just too fast for it.

SC-1 soared above it, and Johnny dropped the targets, luring the weapon in.

Another tremendous explosion lit the canyon.

The blast ripped through the waters and our seacar shuddered as the GSF warsub took the brunt of the impact.

We fired one more torpedo to finish the job.

Behind us, on the deck, tied and subdued, rage filled Franz's eyes; his face was a mask of anger.

He would never forgive me, and my efforts to convince him of our struggle would never succeed.

I realized that now.

He would rather die than help us.

———•••———

I MADE OUR DEPTH A thousand meters and we churned northward, between the mountain ranges and still in the canyon, at 450 kph. The battle had battered us, but we'd survived.

"Where are we going, Mac?" Rico asked.

I set the autopilot and turned to the others. "Cousteau," I said. "I called and asked Francois to meet, along with the mayors of the other French cities. The meeting will be tomorrow." I checked my watch. The French colony was more than 10,000 kilometers distant. At our current speed, we'd be there in just over twenty-two hours. I'd decided to stay in the Rift until the other side of the equator, then we'd jump over the mountain range and stay more shallow in case our SCAV drive failed and we had to bottom the seacar.

"What are we going to do there?" Renée asked, curious.

"The first step in my plan to rescue Meg and Cliff."

The others blinked in shock. Renée's jaw dropped. "And it involves three French colonies?"

I nodded. "We have to continue bringing colonies into our sphere. Into Oceania. It's crucial."

"And they'll help rescue your sister?" Rico asked.

I pursed my lips. "Not really. But kind of."

It was a cryptic response, but I didn't want to say more because I was sure that Franz was listening.

SC-1 forged north through the dark waters of the Atlantic Ocean, and toward the French colony.

Renée, Johnny, Rico, and I ate dinner together, finding time to share stories of our adventure in the Mid-Atlantic Ridge and our stay at The Ridge, while Franz watched silently, now sitting on the couch, but with his wrists and ankles bound.

Renée and I made eye contact frequently, and before long we'd relocated to one of the narrow bunks recessed into the bulkhead just behind the control cabin, and we made love as the vessel forged through the water, its ballast tanks full, toward yet another confrontation.

—••—

COUSTEAU WAS LOCATED JUST OFF the coast of France, at a depth of thirty meters in the English channel. Francois Piette was waiting for me, and we pulled into the Docking Module, our SCAV drive making a tremendous racket, the steam exhaust churning the water and forcing it to splash over the docks. We caught everyone's attention, and they stared in fascination at this new method of underwater propulsion as we docked. The module was a large, cavernous expanse, and there were seacars moored to docks all throughout the chamber. People were standing on their vessels or walking on the docks, watching. We were unable to float because of our flooded tanks, so we had to exit from the airlock and swim the few meters to the surface. A minor inconvenience, but necessary, and within a minute we were on the mesh docks of Cousteau City, dripping wet, but hugging Piette and exchanging greetings. He glanced at Renée, then back again, with a tremendous smile on his face. He was happy to see us both together, and his eyes twinkled at the recognition of what was developing between us.

I wasn't too sure of what was happening myself—for me it was a sexual relationship, but nice to be with a companion again—because I still missed Katherine Wells, killed in the fighting with the FSF a few months earlier. I had been clear with Renée about it, because I didn't want to lead her on, and she seemed fine with the arrangement.

Piette said he'd have crews fix our ballast tanks, and he led us away to find dry clothes and a place to rest before our meeting in just a few hours with the other colony mayors. He already had the *Sword* technology, complete with the SCAV drive and the APD deep diving system, but they were not yet proficient enough to fix the acoustic generator. We had to wait until back in Trieste for Lazlow to get it working again.

He also removed Franz to a proper cell for the time being, so he could shower and rest without being restrained. It was the humanitarian thing to do.

I watched security take him through the airlock, swim to the dock with him, then hoist him up and lead him away for the rest of the day. He shot a look back at me, his expression hard. He had no idea why he was with us, or what he was doing, and I wanted to keep it that way.

Piette was also watching him leave. "Why is there a German spy with you?"

"It's not by his choice."

"I know he's your prisoner, but what's the point?"

I watched Franz round a corner with the guards, then I turned to the mayor. "He's part of my plan to rescue Meg and Cliff."

"And where are they?"

"The USSF took them. They're prisoners at Seascape."

"What are they doing there? That's a tourist—"

"Not anymore. It's the USSF's new HQ."

His face exploded into shock. "Oh, *mon dieu.*"

"Yes, you can say that again."

Piette shook his head in wonder. Then he turned to my companions and shook Rico's hand. "Interesting seeing you back here. I thought we sent you on a transport to Latin America."

"You did. But I found my way home and now I'm with Mac."

"You could have told me that you were Triestrian. We have a special arrangement."

"So I gather. But I've been away for quite a while, dealing with the Germans in New Berlin."

The mayor blinked. "Which is probably why the Germans are involved. I see." He then turned to Renée and gave her a tremendous hug. "So happy to see you back here. And I'm happy that you and Mac are . . . are spending time together."

"Yes, it's good to be back." She was blushing and I grabbed her by the arm. "I'm keeping her busy in Trieste. She's in charge of our defences."

Around us, people were walking along the docks, moving to their seacars for departure to some other colony, or arriving to enter the city. A pervasive sound of water splashing against hulls echoed in the chamber, along with the overlapping murmur of Cousteauians speaking in French.

Cousteau was an underwater city much like any other. Located just off the coast of her colonizing nation, it focussed on extracting resources for use topside. Cousteau's primary concern was fish and minerals, although they had been experiencing the same issues we had—increasing demands for exports by France, less remuneration for said resources, and abuse and harassment by FSF troops on leave from their warsubs. They experienced this from other countries, as well, especially Germany, as Piette had informed me earlier.

Piette led us through the Docking Module and into the Commerce Module, the central dome where Cousteauians conducted business, recreation, and entertainment. It was spacious and light; the ceiling was transparent and the sun was at its zenith. We walked up three flights of stairs and into a conference room. There was a large wooden table in the center and a number of chairs around it.

"The other mayors are already in the city. I'll call them when you're ready."

I nodded. "Thanks." I took a deep breath and then exhaled.

"Nervous?"

"Yes. A bit. This is an important meeting."

"They're nearly there, Mac. They want the SCAV drive, as well as the APD."

"I'll give it to them."

He grinned. "I think it'll be enough. But they're scared of the FSF clamping down on them."

It was a normal fear. "I also need something else from them, and I'm not sure how they'll respond." I left it at that, and asked for a private comm to contact Trieste while he was bringing the mayors to the meeting.

He directed me to a corner of the cabin and, after contacting his communications person in City Control, had a secure and private connection to Trieste in a few minutes.

Rico and Renée were on the other side of the cabin, waiting for me to finish. They were sitting at the large conference table.

A second later Richard Lancombe's face appeared on the screen, and his eyes widened. "Mac! How are you? I wasn't expecting this call."

"How are things there?"

"Fine. No issues."

"USSF?"

"No warsubs docked here. No troops. No interference."

I leaned forward. "Listen, I discovered something recently on my trip to the . . . *location*."

His face flattened. He recognized what I was saying. "Go ahead."

"Someone knows what we're doing, where we're going. Another nation."

He stayed silent and just stared at me. There was no response.

I continued, "Someone knows more about our activities than they should."

Finally, "I think I understand."

"Be careful whom you speak with. Someone has compromised our communications." I didn't want to come out and state my precise concern, or it would tip off the Germans.

"Acknowledged. I'll be careful."

"Inform the others."

"Got it."

"There's more. We discovered that someone sabotaged SC-1. They'd been in the Docking Module. They might be after the entire team, not just me and Johnny. All of you are at risk."

He face hardened. "Okay," he said finally with a nod. "We'll ramp up security."

"Check the video surveillance on the day of the German attack. I'll see you soon. Take care of Jessica." And with that, I clicked off.

I turned back to the others. "Are you ready?"

Chapter Nineteen

PIETTE ARRIVED MINUTES LATER, LEADING the other two mayors.

They were both women. Conshelf Alpha's mayor was in her fifties. She had dark hair with gray highlights. Her name was Vivienne Pelletier. She had a commanding presence, held herself tall and proud, and had a square jaw with a lined face.

Conshelf Beta's mayor was much younger: late twenty-something, wearing a dark power suit, and also with a formidable presence. She presented a persona of grand intelligence. Her name was Isabelle Gagne.

The expressions on their faces were noncommittal and serious. There were no smiles other than a simple courteous minimal stretching of the lips upon shaking hands; it was as nondescript a meeting as you could get.

I swallowed.

Piette made small talk while the two mayors watched me closely. Their eyes never strayed. They were studying every aspect of my body language. Without much question, they were evaluating my sincerity.

Francois Piette was saying, "... and this brings us to the reason behind this meeting." He gestured to me. "Mac here would like to speak to the three of us."

I cleared my throat. "I want to say thanks for coming to Cousteau for this. I have been in charge of Trieste now since The Battle in the Gulf. The USSF took our former mayor into custody—"

"Janice Flint," Vivienne said. "She was a total bitch, if you don't mind me saying."

I immediately liked Vivienne. "I agree. They also took George Shanks. He was the Director of TCI."

"TCI?" Isabelle asked. Her eyes narrowed.

"Our intelligence agency. I'm the Director now."

A deadly silence fell over us. To admit that such a thing existed was nearly unheard of. As far as the USSF knew, the agency had died with Shanks.

The three French mayors looked at each other. Piette said, "I am also confessing before you two that there is an intelligence agency here at Cousteau. We are upset with the way the FSF treats us. We've often spoken of it, us three."

"Yes," Isabelle said. She swore to herself. "Their troops treat our city as their property. They assault our citizens. Steal from us. Beat, harass, or mug our people. Can you believe that? It's uncivilized."

Vivienne Pelletier was nodding. "We experience the same."

"And France takes our produce and fish without paying market price," Piette growled. "They demand more and more, and pay less and less."

"It's the same with us," I said, "which is why we're going off on our own. We have developed new technologies to help us in the fight."

A silence settled over us. The mayors glanced at each other.

Vivienne said, "We know about your SCAV drive. Of course we've all heard of it, and Francois actually demonstrated one of your vessels—a *Sword*, I believe—and it, how do you Americans say—*blew us away*."

I grinned. "The inventor would be pleased. She died in a battle, however, with the FSF a few months ago." As I said it, a weight settled over me, and my grin evaporated. I couldn't meet Renée's eyes.

"You've fought the French?" Isabelle looked shocked. "How did you do?"

"We sunk a hundred USSF warsubs and double that number of FSF boats."

The only sound was the ventilation fans circulating the air. The people in that cabin grew dead silent.

"How is that possible?" Vivienne asked.

"The APD. We can descend below everyone else, and fire up at them."

"What classes? Little boats, or large—"

"*Reaper, Trident, Neptune, Typhoon, Houston,* and more on the USSF side. *Liberty, Requin, de Gaulle, Verdun,* and more on the French."

Their jaws hit the deck.

Piette said, "I've seen the Acoustic Pulse Drive in action myself, versus the Russian dreadnought some weeks ago. The vehicles are superior in every way to any other submarine fleet in the oceans today."

It stunned the mayors. They kept glancing at each other, and I felt that they may have already had conversations about independence.

"We've heard rumours about missing FSF warsubs," Vivienne said. "We weren't sure if it were true or not."

"It happened. In the Mid-Atlantic Ridge. I know it's a big decision," I said, "but independence is possible and very real. Already a number of cities have joined us. We are pledging a military alliance with one another."

"Meaning?"

"If anyone attacks you, the others will step in. It's also an economic alliance. We sell to each other. We sell to topside nations—*any* nation, not just our colonizers—and we charge fair market value. And no more harassment by visiting sailors."

Vivienne sighed and leaned back. "It sounds wonderful. But it is dangerous."

"*Highly* dangerous," Isabelle said.

"All things in life are dangerous," Rico spoke up, "but for the benefit of our citizens who live underwater, we have to look to the future. To Oceania."

We all turned to look at Rico, who until then had been a bystander. He continued, "I was at New Berlin a year ago. Helping the mayor."

"Gunther Gerhardt? He hasn't communicated much since his election."

I nodded. "Because the GSF has occupied them. They're angry with him."

"Why?"

"Because he speaks of independence openly. It's why he was elected."

"And is it because he's joined with you?"

I shook my head. "I haven't spoken to him yet. But I'm going to. And this brings me to the Germans."

"What about them?" Vivienne had practically snarled. Her distaste was obvious. "Their troops cause the most trouble for us whenever they visit."

"Tell me about it," Piette said.

"Well," I said, folding my arms on the table. "I've recently discovered that they've been spying on all of us."

—••—

"PLEASE EXPAND ON THAT, MR. McClusky," Vivienne said. Her expression was poisonous.

I took a breath and stared at Piette. "Before we left Trieste, I contacted you about Rico here. He had recently escaped from a German warsub that had just departed your city."

"*Attentäter* Class. Yes, I remember."

"GSF special forces attacked Johnny and me shortly after. They tried to drown us in a travel tube. The prisoner we have was one of them."

He frowned. "You're saying they were listening . . . ?"

"Later I contacted you to let you know that we were going to our base in the Mid-Atlantic Ridge. Guess which nation found us there? They were searching for us. Planting listening devices."

He nodded slowly. "So they've hacked our comm lines. Somewhere in the Atlantic." He glanced at the other two mayors. "They're listening in to our communications with other cities."

I continued, "And if they're listening to you, they're likely listening to Alpha and Beta, as well."

Vivienne and Isabelle looked stunned.

In fact, they had gone white.

"What's wrong?" I asked.

Isabelle replied, "We routinely speak with one another. Sometimes it's about . . . about the GSF problem."

"I sank three of their warsubs yesterday. *Jägers*. I also bottomed a *Mörder* Class boat outside of Trieste three days ago."

She raised her eyebrows. "Your technology seems . . . impressive."

"And I will give it to you willingly. If you join *Oceania*. We haven't declared independence, and won't until we're all ready."

They remained totally silent. Then Piette said, "Tell them what other cities are with you."

"Ballard, Cousteau, Sheng City, New Kowloon, Lau Tsi, Hanzhou, Taikon, and New Shanghai. We also have Seascape, though the USSF have taken over there. We also think, although we're not sure yet, that New Berlin will join."

"You have every Chinese colony?"

I grinned. "The more repressive a country is, the more likely their colonies will leave. History shows us that."

"Yes, I am aware," Isabella replied, drawing out the words in her French accent. She hesitated, and then, "You're giving me a lot to think about."

"That's the point of my visit." I indicated Johnny. "This is my deputy mayor. He's been to the Chinese cities. He's negotiated with them."

Johnny said, "The promise of this technology is what convinced them. They're unhappy with the Chinese Submarine Fleet, as well. They don't like the control from mainland. They're ready to declare independence."

She shook her head. "*Merde*," she whispered. "When do you need an answer?"

"The sooner the better," I said, "but whenever you feel comfortable."

They pursed their lips and stared at me.

I said, "There's more."

Piette snorted. "You've hit them with quite a bit already, Mac."

"The USSF arrested my sister and my Chief Security Officer. I am on a mission right now."

"As part of TCI?" Isabelle asked. Her lips showed the hint of a smile. Finally, I thought.

"Yes. It's a rescue mission."

"But I don't understand. How do you plan to rescue your sister this far north? Where is she?"

"Seascape."

"So what are you doing—"

I exhaled and glanced at Johnny, Rico, and Renée. I hadn't told them, either.

"I plan on using the GSF for it," I said finally.

As one, they blinked. Furrows appeared on their foreheads. "But—"

"You see, I'm going to attack a GSF warsub up here, in the North Sea."

"You are?" Rico blurted. The look on his face was incredulous.

"We're going to damage the vessel. Then infiltrate it. Then we're going to commandeer it."

"Which one?" Rico asked.

I hesitated, and then, "Hopefully an *Attentäter* Class vessel."

"An—"

It stunned him and he could barely process what I was saying.

I nodded. "And we're going to pilot it south, to the Gulf of Mexico."

Piette injected, "But what for, Mac? Why do this?"

I turned to him. "Simple, Francois. Because I'm going to use the sub to rescue my sister and CSO. I'm going to attack Seascape with it, and frame Germany in the process. I'm going to pull them into this, even more than they're already involved."

"But Mac, the GSF will go ballistic!" Johnny said. "You want to frame them for attacking USSF HQ?"

"And more. The GSF has already attacked me. They think we're passive. They think they can get away with taking jabs at me. I'm going to show them that if they want to play with the big boys and mess around with the world's undersea colonies, then they're going to get hit. I'm going to steal their warsub and start a war with it. They're going to find themselves facing off against a very hostile USSF. In the process, I'm going to save my people, destroy the USSF HQ at Seascape, and I'm going to pull Conshelf Alpha, Conshelf Beta, *and* New Berlin into our alliance to form Oceania.

"I'm going to leave immediately to find and commandeer the GSF warsub." I turned to Vivienne and Isabelle. "Now, do you still want to wait on this, or would you like to join up with me now and get revenge on the GSF?"

Interlude:
Meagan McClusky

```
Location:        Latitude:    28° 41' 24" N
Longitude:       94° 54' 5" W
                 The Gulf of Mexico, Seascape City,
                 USSF HQ
Depth:           30 meters
Date:            5 August 2130
Time:            Unknown
```

MEAGAN WAS SITTING IN THE cold metal chair, struggling to keep her legs from falling asleep. Black, rubber straps secured her—at wrists, thighs, and ankles. The guards didn't care about her comfort. Their purpose was to make her *un*comfortable, to make her want to say the things she had to say in order to improve her situation. A move to a cell with a bed, blankets, and a pillow, perhaps. Better yet, some decent food.

And a place without a taser and wooden clubs.

Her face was battered and bruised. Her legs were always sore. Dark black splotches mottled her thighs and calves. When a large, nebulous bruise began to disappear and turn yellowish at its edges, another bruise soon appeared, overlapping and disguising the signs of passing time as her body struggled to repair the damage.

Her nose seemed to always be bleeding from the many strikes. Sometimes from a fist, sometimes a club.

Her left cheek had hurt since a punch the second day of her arrival, and it had never stopped radiating agony. She suspected a broken bone—perhaps the orbital—but she couldn't tell for sure. The pain arced out from the area, stretching across her entire face.

CIA Investigator Zyvinski always sat across from her in the cushioned chair. She would ask questions in a lazy, droning voice, knowing there would not be an answer, and sit back and flip through a magazine or book as guards beat Meagan. Or she would file and paint her nails, staring at them for hours, as the questions and beatings raged. Sometimes she performed the beatings personally.

And the questions were always the same.

"Tell me about your deep-diving technology. Who invented it?"

"I don't know what you're talking about," Meg would gasp.

"How does it work?"

"What?"

"Where is the scientist who created it? In what module does he live?"

"Where?"

"In Trieste. Who created this new technology for you?"

"I don't know."

"What about your SCAV drive?"

"You have that already," Meagan said, frowning. It hurt her face. "Why do you care about that?"

"Because we want to know. Did you create that with the intention of starting a war?"

It would go on for hours. A series of questions, followed by a beating. Then more questions, then a beating. Then the guards would drag Meagan to her cell, where she would curl up in a corner with her dirty blanket, and just as her eyes closed and she drifted off to sleep—

—the door would burst open, and guards would haul her to her feet and drag her back to the interrogation cabin.

It was endless.

One day the questioning took a different tact, though Meg pretended not to notice or care.

Zyvinski was scraping at a thumbnail. "Your security chief, Cliff Sim, tells me you traveled to a secret location several weeks ago where pilots were testing the deep-diving tech."

"I don't know what you're talking about." It was the first mention of Cliff since they'd arrived. They didn't admit to his presence, although Reggie Quinn had told Meg that he was indeed there, and Meg had heard the beatings taking place.

"Cliff helped you murder Admiral Benning."

"No, he didn't. I did it on my own."

"He covered it up for you."

"Not that I know of. I stabbed Benning because he was a murderer."

"So you murdered a murderer, and that makes it okay?"

"He killed my father."

"And Cliff helped you. Did he also stab Benning?"

"No. It was just me. I stabbed him in the chest many times, then the neck."

"Why the neck?"

"To make sure he couldn't breathe. To cut his arteries so he'd bleed out."

"And Cliff helped carry the body away."

"No. That was me."

"How is that possible? He was a heavy man."

Meagan sighed. "I put the body in a laundry cart. I've said this before."

Zyvinski looked up and frowned. "But Cliff told us that he helped you."

"I doubt that."

"But why?"

"Because it's not true."

"He also told us that you went to the secret base."

"What secret base?" Meg's insides twisted. *They can't know about The Ridge!*

"Where you test your new weapons. Where you build *Swords*."

"I have no idea what you're referring to."

"It doesn't matter, because Cliff told us everything. He's been quite . . . *accommodating*."

"Thanks to the beatings, no doubt."

Zyvinski just shrugged and went back to her nails.

Meagan hesitated, then, "You're just a coward. Shielded by your guards. Getting pleasure out of these beatings. But you're nothing."

"I'm learning a lot, though," she drawled, picking at a cuticle. "I know all about your deep-diving tech now."

"Then why do you keep asking me about it? I don't know anything."

Her face grew harder. "To confirm what Cliff is telling us about it."

"Bullshit. You're fishing. It's so fucking obvious."

"Harsh language, dear. That won't help."

"Neither will your tricks and lies. I've admitted to killing Benning for what he did to my family. I don't know about these other things."

"Cliff also told us that Katherine Wells died in a battle earlier this year. What can you tell us about that?"

Meagan froze and her heart nearly exploded. She tried not to react. "Who?"

"Kat Wells. She invented the SCAV drive."

"I wouldn't know."

"Who was the battle with? Cliff told us a lot about it."

He wasn't even there, you bitch. "I don't know him well. I have no idea about any of that stuff."

"Were you fighting the French? We've heard the FSF is searching for missing warsubs in the Mid-Atlantic Ridge. Right in the Rift."

"You'll have to ask them."

"Your *Swords* defeated them there, right?"

"No idea."

"That's what Cliff is saying."

"Maybe he's saying what you want to hear because you keep beating him."

Zyvinski shrugged. "Or maybe he's telling us the truth. He's sleeping in a warm bed now, did you know that?"

She didn't respond. She just stared at the willowy woman across the table. After a few moments, Zyvinski gestured to Meg, without even looking, and the two guards on either side of her began to hit her thighs with the clubs.

Meg screamed.

—••—

SHE KNEW SHE NEEDED SOMETHING sharp. Something that could easily cut through flesh. There was nothing in her cell that could help. It was empty, cold, clinical. There was a toilet in a corner, and she had a blanket, but that was it. She'd dug around the edges of the toilet—had even put her hands *inside it* to hunt for something like a screw or a nail—but there was nothing. Her nails were black with blood under them, they were bruised and swollen, and her manual dexterity had grown worse in recent days. Even if she found something sharp, she didn't know if she could cut with it.

Then one day she stumbled across something.

She'd feigned unconsciousness after a beating, and the guards had half carried, half dragged her back to her cell. Meagan had been leaning against one of them and opened her swollen eyes to see the man's belt and holster only inches from her face. There was a clip there, meant to attach a key ring perhaps, with nothing on it.

She moved her hand slowly to it . . .

Hoping like hell they didn't notice that she was awake.

And she touched the cold metal. It was like a thick paperclip with a blunt end.

But the blunt end might just work. She could jab it into flesh and wrench it across the skin.

It would draw blood, she was sure.

Hopefully enough blood to work.

She twisted it slightly and it came off the guard's belt. Then she palmed it. The corridor swung crazily in her vision as they carried her back to her cell and threw her in.

She hit the deck hard, but didn't move. Her left fist gripped the metal clasp, and she kept it under her body, unmoving.

The hatch slammed shut and Meg waited there for a long stretch of time, knowing that they could peer through the eyehole at her.

Then, after an hour, she dragged herself to the corner and her blanket, and wrapped herself up.

She peered at the clasp under the blanket.

A feeling of utter joy filled her.

Strange, that such a minor success could bring so much happiness.

She rubbed her thumb across the end of the clasp.

It scraped her if she pushed too hard.

Yes.

She had something that would work.

—••—

SHE HID THE CLASP BEHIND the toilet. There was no other place to put it. She didn't have access to the water tank . . . just the bowl where she sat to relieve herself. She pushed the end of the metal piece as far behind as she could reach, poking it under the toilet, to hide it from the guards.

And she waited to hear from Reggie Quinn.

She needed to know when she could make her attempt.

But she didn't know how many more days she could last.

She had gone past tired, through complete exhaustion, and into a state of tormented existence.

She only had a few days left in her.

—••—

REGGIE QUINN CAME TO VISIT. The hatch opened and there he was, speaking to a guard about Seascape and the fact that the officers had selected the best hotel rooms available in the city—formally available only to the most wealthy tourists—and that the USSF had relegated crewmen and sailors to the staff quarters on the city's west end. His face was hard, but he was friendly to the guard, and then he gestured at Meg and mumbled a few words.

The guard nodded and motioned Reggie in.

The former mayor's expression dissolved into a series of sympathetic waves when he cast his eyes on her. He kept his face turned toward her, so the guard didn't see.

The hatch closed behind him.

Then he knelt beside her and stared at her exposed legs, at the mottled black, red, and yellow welts and bruises, at the lacerations on her forearms, and at the scars forming at old injuries, now painted with new bruising. He studied her face, his expression grim.

"Oh my god," he growled. "They're slowly beating you to death."

Meagan shifted on the deck and tried to prop herself against the bulkhead with the blanket; old splotches of crimson covered it. A groan escaped her lips;

her legs were on fire.

It hurt to move anything now.

Even changing her facial expression caused her pain.

"So it would seem," she muttered.

"How much longer can you keep this up?"

"Not long."

"Cliff looks the same. Maybe a bit worse. I think he might have a broken leg."

That wasn't good, she thought. *We need to be able to move when it was time.* She said, "Can he stand?"

"Yes, I think so, but he's limping badly. They're tying him to the ceiling and beating him with clubs. He hasn't slept more than a few hours in weeks. He might die from lack of sleep." He hesitated and then glanced back at the hatch. "I think if we're going to do this, it has to be *soon*, Meg. Neither of you is going to be able to get out of here."

"I was thinking the same thing."

"Then how about—"

"No. We can't yet."

He stared at her, horrified. "But they could kill you any day. Your heart might just give out. Why—"

"We have to wait for Mac."

He stopped abruptly and frowned. "But—"

"You said that he had a plan. You said that you didn't want to break me out."

"No, I can't. But I can help."

"Have you spoken to Cliff?"

"Yes. I got in there to see him. He seems to think there's a plan, too, although he wouldn't say anything. But Mac has disappeared; he's not answering calls to Trieste."

Because he's probably not there, Meg thought. *He's probably broken his house arrest, and when Quintana and the USSF find out, that might be enough to arrest him.*

Shit.

"Do you know the best time to make a break?"

"Late night. When the officers are asleep. There are fewer guards outside. Only two in this corridor."

"Late night . . . "

"What?"

"I can't tell what time it is."

"I'll try to figure out a signal for you so you'll know."

"Are you worried the USSF will do this to you?"

"Do what?"

Meg gestured around her, at her sparse surroundings. "*This*. Imprisonment. Torture."

He didn't respond, but Meg knew what was churning through his mind. She sighed. "What else can you do?"

"Perhaps suppress an alarm, should one sound. Arrange a route that has fewer guards."

"Where are we right now?"

"In a module near the staff quarters. It's not marked on the tourist schematics. We use it for training, for storage, for staff functions, and more." He shrugged. "Multi-functional."

"Does it have a moonpool?" Her voice was hoarse, barely a croak.

"Yes." And then his face lit for the first time. "We used it once for a staff exercise, a team-building activity. A scavenger hunt, trying to swim outside without tanks to find things and bring them back. Only the best swimmers did well, because they could hold their breath—"

His face had split into a wide grin and he was looking away, remembering. Then he choked off the sentence and stared at the deck.

It was all over, now.

His expression had turned dark and he couldn't meet Meg's eyes.

There was nothing for him here anymore.

"We have to be ready to go when it starts," she said.

He frowned. "When *what* starts?"

She tried to shrug, but it hurt too much. "Mac's plan, whatever it is."

"I told you, I can't break you out of here."

She watched him. His eyes showed fear, and his face had flushed. "Why not?"

"I just . . . I just can't. Don't ask me that."

"I thought you were ready to help Mac, because of what's happened here."

"I am. Just don't put me in a position where I could end up . . . end up—"

"Like me." She sighed. She understood, but his fears confused her. Surely Reggie could see that his life in Seascape would never be the same, couldn't he? "But you'll keep an eye on things, and when Mac shows up, you'll . . . *arrange* things for us, right?"

"I'll try my best, yes."

It better be good, she thought. "I can't last much longer. I hope it's soon."

The comment hung in the silence between them.

Part Five: Conquer and Command

Chapter Twenty

THE MEETING WITH THE THREE French mayors had absolutely stunned everyone in that cabin, including my own people. I'd kept them in the dark, not really explaining how I was going to do it, or even offering my reasoning behind our recent activities. All they had known was my ultimate goal: to rescue our people from USSF HQ.

But now they knew.

And the plan *horrified* them.

They didn't think we could do it. Last time we'd infiltrated a warsub, it had taken weeks of preparation *and the support* of the USSF. We'd had uniforms, training, and research backing us up. A team of people outside the dreadnought as well as in.

But this time, we had none of that. No task force coordinating a fleet of attack boats. No uniforms, no knowledge of German or the GSF.

But there was something vastly different about this mission.

We weren't going to infiltrate a sub, blend in to sabotage it, then escape.

No. We were going in guns blazing, and we were going to take control of the command center to pilot the vessel southward.

To lead a phantom German attack against the USSF, and hopefully start a war between the two countries.

The two French mayors agreed to join with us in an economic and military partnership. After the news of the German spying, they'd barely needed a push to convince them. They were French, after all, and respected freedom above all else. They knew the path before them was dangerous, but they'd pledged, on the spot, to join Oceania.

We'd grinned like children, celebrating for a brief moment, before promising to work out the details later.

Then I'd asked for a favor.

I turned to Piette. "I want you to wait for a few hours, until Vivienne and Isabelle are back at their cities. Then contact them via comm."

"And say what?" The request clearly perplexed him.

"Tell them that I was in your city before leaving to New Berlin. Warn the mayors that I might stop at their cities first. Tell them I was talking about independence, and you're concerned about it." I turned to the mayors of Conshelf Alpha and Beta. "And you two can act angry and annoyed at this news. Pretend that you don't want anything to do with me."

Piette gasped. "But Mac, that's exactly what we want to keep hidden from the world's superpowers."

"Unless the information is useful, Francois. And this is very, very useful to me."

—••—

FIVE MINUTES LATER, MY PEOPLE and I had left the meeting chamber. The feeling of joy was hard to suppress, but we tried hard to keep our faces from showing excitement.

"It's why you sank the *Mörder* Class boat south of Florida, right?" Johnny asked. We were marching back to *SC-1*, weaving our way among the French undersea colonists. Some of them recognized me, and waved as I passed.

I tried as best as I could to acknowledge them all, though I realized that I was supposed to be under house arrest in Trieste.

Inwardly, I shrugged. I didn't care anymore.

"Yes," I replied. "It provides context for a possible GSF attack on Seascape."

"Because someone attacked *Dark Winter* off the coast of the US. Then a GSF warsub attacks Seascape . . . "

"A totally reasonable series of events, wouldn't you say?"

It surprised Rico, but he was also thrilled. "Are you doing this for me, Mac?" he asked.

I frowned and glanced at him. "What do you mean?"

"You're giving me a chance at revenge for what I went through."

I stared at the deck now as we walked. It was steel grating, exactly like at Trieste. I thought about how Johnny and I had ripped a deck plate up and used it to crack the travel tube so we could swim out to fight for our lives.

My thoughts drifted to the four months of torture I'd endured at the hands of the Chinese after they'd caught me. That had been eight years ago, in 2122. Following my release, I'd left TCI and gone to work on the kelp farms for seven years, removing myself from all political intrigue, espionage, and spycraft. I'd wanted to just *exist*. To just work underwater and help

Trieste that way.

But that torture had never left my mind. The wounds still lingered, and the worst ones were not physical.

"I'm . . . I'm not sure," I finally whispered to Rico. "Who knows what boat we'll end up taking. But it's not about revenge for you."

"Then what's it about?"

"Revenge can consume you," I muttered. I knew about that all too well.

As did my sister.

"It won't solve the real problem," I continued, but I don't think he heard me. He said, "Your plan is . . . *audacious*."

"Thanks."

"But if we do find the right ship . . ." His voice trailed off, and I noticed that he'd clenched his fists at his sides. "Then, thank you."

I didn't respond. I just thought of Meg, and what she was likely enduring at that exact moment.

"It's crazy," Johnny muttered, but there was a half-grin on his face.

Renée also still looked gobsmacked by the revelation. She said, "You've been leading us all up to this, just to get our people back."

"And deflect attention from us."

"To the Germans."

"Yes."

"And possibly convince New Berlin to join us."

"Yes, that's right."

She exhaled. "*Incredible*."

We rounded a corner and entered the travel tube to the Docking Module. The tube was similar to ours, with a transparent ceiling. Above, the sea was murkier than the waters of the Gulf. Sand and muck swirled about the city's exterior.

I couldn't see any life.

I swallowed.

Johnny said, "Where to now?"

"New Berlin."

"The GSF will likely arrest us, Mac."

"Why's that?" I feigned confusion.

"Because they've occupied the city. They refuse to allow talk of independence. And then Frank McClusky's son shows up?" He shook his head. "They'll know immediately what's going on."

I smiled and snapped a look at him. "Yes, they will, won't they?"

PIETTE'S SECURITY TEAM BROUGHT OUR GSF prisoner, Franz, back to *SC-1* shortly after. Repair crews had fixed our ballast valves, and the seacar was floating once again. The voyage there had been grueling—battling with German warsubs in the Rift—but we were only a portion of the way through this mission.

There was a lot still left to do.

Johnny and I slid into the pilots' chairs—me on the left, him on the right—and, making the ballast negative, I brought us out of the pool, into the docking tube, and out into the English Channel.

And toward New Berlin.

Hopefully, Piette would soon signal the other French mayors, and plant the seed.

—••—

A FEW HOURS OUT, AND traveling northward in conventional drive only, Johnny gasped. He'd been on the comm, checking his messages at Trieste, taking care of administrative issues.

"What is it?" I asked, keeping my eyes on the instruments.

"Our zircon mine, in The Iron Plains."

That was the new extraction facility we'd set up. I'd asked Johnny to handle it over five weeks earlier. It was a dangerous location, with the other superpowers all laying claim to the massive area of ocean floor that contained trillions of tons of iron nodules—gravel-sized sediment precipitated from thermal vents in the geologically active region. We merely had to scoop it from the floor for processing. There was no drilling necessary. The area was immense and would satisfy the world's need for iron for a century—especially needed because of our drive into the oceans, and the superpowers' drive into space. And it was all there, just lying on the seafloor for the taking.

We'd snuck in and settled a mining colony there to dig for zircon, right under their noses.

But what I really needed was meant for Dr. Max Hyland's project.

Hafnium.

It occurred naturally within deposits of zircon.

"What about it?" I repeated. Johnny hadn't answered.

"It's gone silent, Mac."

"Say again?" A sense of dread filled me. We had numerous Triestrians there, extracting the mineral at a dangerous depth, in a deadly location, surrounded by hostile powers . . . and all because I'd asked for it.

"No communications."

"When was the last?"

"Two days ago."

I swore. Our people had gone there willingly, despite the dangers involved. They did it because they'd trusted me. "Any warnings beforehand?"

"They did say that there were some patrols in the area, overhead."

"Country?"

"China. They'd had to suspend activities until they left."

"But they left?"

"I don't know. They stopped transmitting."

"Shit." It meant the mainland CSF boats may have located and destroyed them.

It wouldn't have been hard. The depth was immense. The base was using our new syntactic foam, stronger than what we'd used in the past, to resist the violent pressures, but the slightest flaw would spell disaster for people depending on watertight domes and bulkheads. "This isn't good," I muttered. I didn't want to lose more Triestrians, but on top of it, we needed the hafnium.

I would have to notify the doctor.

Johnny read my mind. "Want me to contact Max?"

"No, it's too dangerous right now. We'll have to connect with him when we're back there." I swore again. Things were already in motion, and we couldn't stop now.

"Listen, Mac." His voice had dropped lower and he glanced behind him. "Are you sure about Rico?"

It startled me and I hesitated. "You're still having doubts?"

"A few. It seems convenient, that's all."

"For him to show up out of the blue."

"Yes."

I paused again and mulled it over. "We'll keep our eyes on him. Make sure he doesn't do anything. But I'm pretty sure."

"Why'd you bring him?"

The truth was, I wasn't entirely sure. I felt it was perhaps because of the torture he'd endured. I related to it. He needed to be able to put it behind him, as I had. I'd dealt with something similar, had fought with it for years after and, following the experience with the Chinese theft of the SCAV drive and my conflict with China, had finally put the incident behind me, and in fact had made peace with the Chinese cities. They were now a part of Oceania. But Rico had had no such resolution. The events on the German warsub were still very much on his mind.

But revenge did not provide peace.

I stared back into the living area, and watched him. He was sitting on the couch, staring at Franz, our prisoner. Neither was speaking.

—••—

EVENING SOON DESCENDED OVER US. We were traveling at a depth of only thirty meters, which was in the *euphotic zone*, meaning light from the surface could penetrate. Since the ocean currents there were moving northward in the upper layers, that's where we wanted to be so we weren't fighting the water's natural movements, especially because we were using our conventional screws at a speed of seventy kph. It was also safer, in case we needed to exit the moonpool in an emergency. We could only use the moonpool if the interior pressure matched the exterior—four atms—hence the thirty-meter depth.

The sun dipped below the horizon, and darkness fell quickly.

We grabbed food from the galley and decided to eat together in the living area. I left the autopilot on, powering *SC-1* northward through the channel. We had passed through the Straight of Dover, and were now off the coast of Belgium and officially in the cold waters of the North Sea.

Franz was glaring at me now, and I tried my best to ignore him. I wasn't too sure what he had heard, but he was bright, and he knew where we had just visited.

He growled, "Cousteau. Now we go north."

"Yes," I replied, pulling together our meal.

"What for?"

I stopped and considered for a moment if it mattered. It didn't. "We're going to find your friends."

He blinked. "My friends?"

"Other Germans. Preferably a warsub."

"Which one?"

I shrugged.

His face went blank, and his eyes remained fixed to me. "You can't be serious."

"I am. And eventually you're going to help me."

"Bullshit."

"I'm going to use you to carry out my plans."

He snorted. "Are you going to torture me for that?"

"No. There's no need." My insides went cold. There was the talk of torture again. I wanted to avoid it at whatever cost.

And yet I couldn't help but understand that in my psyche—the one Trieste and my father had forged while I was becoming a man—I had no trouble killing sailors, sinking boats, torpedoing Fleet submarines around the world, if it was all in the name of freedom and independence. Why was that? Why could I order a torpedo to kill a crew, and yet torturing someone was so abhorrent to me?

Because I'd been through it.

And because those sailors on those warsubs knew what they were doing. They were serving on GSF and CSF and FSF vessels, and had signed up for this willingly.

Because those troops entered our cities and harassed our people.

So they deserved death, but not torture? Is that it?

My insides shook. Even I couldn't explain it. It sounded ridiculous.

And yet, the drive to fight for Oceania dictated my life now. My father had filled my head with it when I was a child. Bedtime stories revolved around the underwater colonies of the world. When Meg and I had been toddlers, he spoke about what it was like to be underwater, to live underwater, and the evils of the world's superpowers.

It's *all* he talked about.

And then he brought us to Trieste and we fell in love with the city, with living underwater. We went on swims around the colony, soaking in the marine life and watching our scuba bubbles drift lazily to the surface as they passed through sunlight cutting downward from above. We stood below transparent travel tube bulkheads, staring at seacars approaching and departing at night, studying the seascape around us, marveling at the beauty and amazed we were part of the colonization efforts.

Going for midnight swims . . .

The list went on.

He quickly became mayor and also brought the disparate groups clamoring for independence together into one whole.

He openly spoke about it, begged for it, pleaded with the USSF for it.

Threatened the USSF with it.

And the writing was on the wall, for they killed him soon after to protect their flow of resources from their fledgling ocean colonies.

Now I stared at Franz, wondering exactly how far I was going to go with this.

Why exactly had I brought him? To punish him for trying to kill me and Johnny?

To teach him a lesson?

To show him what life underwater really should be?

I sighed as I placed the dinner before him.

AN ISLAND
OF LIGHT

—••—

THE REST OF US ATE together, and we let Franz consume his rations in silence. He was loosely bound so he could move his arms, and when he needed to relieve himself, one of us would escort him.

The others also wondered why he was there, but all I could say was that he was going to help our plans.

Inside, in a place I couldn't admit existed, I knew what would happen to him, but I couldn't vocalize it, for it would have spoken of the monster that I truly was.

—••—

JOHNNY, RICO, RENÉE, AND I were eating together. We also had some wine, which we had kept from opening for days now, but that first evening out from Cousteau we'd decided to crack the bottle and toast with it. They were still processing my plan, but it had begun to sink in, and they had accepted it as our new path. At least it gave them a direction. Rico and Johnny were struggling to figure out how we were going to do it, and Renée just shook her head whenever our eyes met. I think she believed that I was out of my mind, but she knew not to question me in front of the others. Besides, she understood me well enough to know that my plans were never completely crazy . . . there was always some foresight or thought behind them.

There was some logic there.

Even with this one.

The *Mörder* Class vessel lying at the bottom of the Gulf, for instance. The boat was still there, I had no doubt, because we had only pummelled the stern sections. The screws needed replacing. The hull needed to be welded shut and water pumped from flooded sections. Perhaps there was damage to the engines.

But the others recognized that it was an important piece of the plan.

"How'd you know *Dark Winter* would be there?" Johnny asked.

I shrugged. "I knew a GSF warsub had dropped the kill squad near Trieste. I knew it was there. I used our SCAV drive to attract their attention."

"Which it did. They pinged us."

"Yes."

"But what if they hadn't? What would you have done?"

"Then we wouldn't have had a German warsub lying out there to draw the USSF's attention later. I gestured to Franz. "But we have him, don't forget."

Renée said, "Attacking a GSF warsub so close to Germany won't be easy.

We are in a very small vessel here."

"We are technologically more advanced. You know that."

"We don't have the APD."

"But we are faster."

"Their SCAV torpedoes go a thousand kph."

I just stared at her and didn't speak.

"So," she said, "we'll cross that bridge when we come to it?"

"Something like that."

Rico said between bites of his meal, "They will call for help when they realize we're winning, Mac. If word gets out, more warsubs will join the fight."

"That might be a good thing, actually."

"Why? How many warsubs can we take?" He looked around the living area. "There are only four of us here. We can only pilot one—"

"But a fleet of warsubs on our tail might look good, don't you think?" I flashed him a smile. My eyes twinkled, I was sure of it.

He frowned, then looked away. "I get it. A group of GSF subs sailing toward Seascape will look like an attack, but really they'll be chasing us."

I shrugged.

"Won't work," Johnny said. "They'll be communicating with the USSF on the way down there."

"Maybe it'll be a trick. Because really it's an attack force."

"I understand where you're going with this, but I think the USSF will see right through it."

"I'm not so sure."

Renée said, "But Mac, surely you don't want to try to steal an entire boat while a fleet of other subs bears down on us."

I exhaled. She was right. "I've been thinking about it. Once we locate a candidate GSF warsub, I was hoping to destroy the nearest junction." Every twenty kilometers, along the fiber optic undersea network, junctions accepted incoming calls and fed them through the oceans to their ultimate destinations. If we could destroy the nearest one, the warsub's calls would go unanswered.

Unless there were others nearby, who could hear their communications directly.

Johnny eyed me. "So you want to find a GSF warsub that's all alone in the North Sea, disable any nearby comm junctions, then attack, infiltrate, and take it over without damaging it *too* much, and hope they're not able to call for help. Then sail south to the Gulf to attack Seascape."

I glanced at the three of them and then gave them a slow nod. "That's about it."

Johnny's face was hard. "Mac, I'm usually totally on side with your plans. You have a knack for doing the unexpected. But there are only four of us, and one of us has to pilot *SC-1* back. Maybe you didn't fully think this through."

"We'll be okay."

"But how?" Confusion painted his features now. "How will we find a GSF warsub out here? How will we take it over without destroying it?" He threw his arms up. "Explain it to us."

I stared at him. He was my closest friend in the world. He'd been my partner in TCI for many, many years. We'd had a momentous falling out years before when he had defected to Sheng City and had actually conducted some of the torture sessions when they'd captured me. But we had mended fences and he was back in Trieste, and I fully trusted him. That being said, I had hoped he'd have more faith in me.

"Johnny," I said. "We don't have to find a GSF warsub."

"No?"

"They're going to find us. The French mayors, remember?" I gestured around us. "It's why we're not traveling in SCAV drive right now. They're going to attack us before we reach New Berlin."

"Should we be worried?" Rico asked.

"A bit, perhaps. But give them some time to locate us first. By late tomorrow maybe. Then we have to be on our toes." I raised a glass. "But tonight, we can enjoy."

"I still don't know how you plan on doing this," Johnny muttered.

"You forgot something crucial, Johnny."

"What?"

I shot a look toward the hatch that led to engineering. "You forgot about our drones."

Chapter Twenty-One

THAT EVENING WE IGNORED THE elephant in the cabin—talk of infiltrating and commandeering a GSF warsub—and just enjoyed each other's company. Rico had a pleasant and gentle manner about him, and we were warming to his personality each day spent together. He spoke about some of the missions he'd been on in the past, and Johnny and I would interject and add to his story with our own knowledge about whatever undersea colony he was telling us about. He was totally on-side with my plan; he realized that he was on the precipice of getting revenge for what had happened to him during the past year. It wasn't exactly what I wanted for him; I hoped to give him a chance to confront his pain and get past it, as I had.

I didn't know if we'd be able to find the warsub that had held him, but there was a chance it might happen.

Renée and I sat next to one another on the couch as the evening progressed, and she kept touching me as we spoke. Her hand was on my arm, on my thigh, my shoulder. The signals were clear and obvious, and I didn't mind at all. I truly enjoyed her company, and our lovemaking was wonderful and intense. Thoughts of Kat still percolated into my thoughts on occasion, but a part of me knew that I would never forget her, that she would always be with me. I would always love her. Hell, the very seacar we were in had belonged to her. Katherine Wells had invented it and the SCAV drive, and her presence was all around us. Still, I was lonely, and Renée filled an important part of my life.

Even during the seven years I'd been away from TCI, while farming kelp, there had been women in my life. Lovers. Not romantic interests, for I had never allowed myself to open up to anyone after my experience in Sheng City, but a physical release with a willing partner was an important part of my healing.

But then Kat had come along . . .

And the FSF had killed her during the battle in the Rift a few months earlier.

Renée was an interesting addition to our movement. She had been trying to kill me, had *hunted* me, more or less, and I had taken her captive and turned her to our ultimate goal of independence for the underwater colonies.

And now we were having a physical relationship.

We spent that evening, the first following our departure from Cousteau, sailing northward along the coast of Europe at a depth of thirty meters, speaking about our pasts and our lives at Trieste and our hopes for the future.

Late into the evening, the lights turned low, Renée and I climbed into the bunk to end the evening together.

My mind was in turmoil, though, because I couldn't stop thinking about Meg and Cliff and what they were going through in Seascape. I was on a mission to rescue Meg, but I was free and having fun, drinking wine and celebrating with friends, and she was in a cell somewhere, enduring horrible agony.

Renée noticed the scar on my thigh again; she had first seen it at The Ridge following our lovemaking at the party the base's crew had put on for us. She frowned as she traced a finger along it. "This again," she murmured. "You said something about insurance last time I noticed?"

"I got it five weeks ago, give or take."

Her forehead creased. "But that would be around the time—"

"Yes. It was."

Then we started to kiss again, and she forgot all about it.

But I hadn't.

—••—

RENÉE WAS LYING ON THE bunk next to me, her head on my arm, her gaze fixed on the ceiling only inches from our noses. She turned to me and smiled. Her eyes crinkled.

"That was nice," she murmured.

"Yes. Amazing."

Then her eyes drooped, and I sensed sadness in her face.

"What is it?"

She sighed. "This. Everything. Sometimes it gets to me. Last year I had a mission. It drove me. Controlled me. Now everything is so . . . *different*, I guess."

"Last year you were with the FSF. Now you're Triestrian." I frowned. "Are you saying you're not happy?"

"No, not at all. I love living underwater in the colony. But I gave up everything, Mac, for your dream. Here I am. But I am . . . "

"What?"

"Alone. I have no family in Trieste." Her voice had grown quiet.

"You didn't on your warsub, either. You were out at sea all the time. Never home. Life hasn't really changed, has it?"

"No, you're right. I know you're right. But sometimes I wonder if there should be more."

Inside, my heart sank. I wondered where this was coming from. "You don't like this?"

"I love it. I enjoy your company. But your heart isn't fully with me, is it?"

I didn't know what to say. I settled on a weak, "My heart?" But I was just stalling, and she knew.

"This is just physical. But I want more."

"I see."

"And you can't give that to me."

"Not just yet. I'm still reeling, Renée. Please just give me time."

She nodded and just stared at the ceiling again. Then eventually her eyes closed, and she fell asleep.

I wasn't so lucky.

I was awake for hours after.

———••———

THE NEXT DAY WE WERE forging through the North Sea off the coast of the Netherlands, and we were nearly at German waters. New Berlin was located in an inlet west of Denmark called Jade Bight; we were very close to it.

I knew something had to happen soon.

Johnny and I were in the pilot chairs and staring at a navigation chart projected on the canopy over us by the VID system. There were a series of islands just off the coast called the East Frisian Islands. Borkum, Juist, Norderney, Baltrum, Langeoog, Spiekeroog, and Wangerooge. There used to be a narrow stretch of water between them and mainland Europe—ranging from a few kilometers to ten—but rising ocean levels had increased the distance between the islands and the mainland. Still, it would be a good place for an ambush, and we were keeping our eyes out.

The passive sonar was searching each nearby vessel—on the surface and under it—for signs that it was a GSF contact, and I was prepared to hit the SCAV drive at a moment's notice to escape in case I sensed a trap.

I knew they were coming for us . . . but I was hoping they would invest a minimal number of vessels to take one tiny seacar like SC-1.

———••———

I DECIDED TO MAKE A very dangerous call. No more waiting. Things were coming to a head in the North Sea, and soon I wouldn't have the chance.

Punching the comm controls, I signaled Trieste City. Johnny was staring at the destination code, and he blinked. "What . . . " he trailed off. Then he just snorted and leaned back. "I guess you know what you're doing. But you realize the GSF is likely monitoring all communications?"

"Yes, but I don't think it matters. It's the USSF I'm worried about here."

He frowned again, but didn't say more.

A second later, Kristen in Trieste City Control came on the line. "Hello?" Her voice was a whisper, barely audible.

It made me chuckle. "It's okay, Kristen. You know who it is."

"Yes, but the USSF ordered you to stay here. I don't want them to know that you've left."

"Are there any troops there?"

"Not at the moment. That I know of, anyway."

"Good point." I exhaled. "I need you to connect me with Seascape. Can you do that?"

"Of course. I'll have to transfer you to Communications Control."

"But I need the call to look like it's coming from Trieste, and not a transfer."

There was a pause. Then, "Shouldn't be an issue. Hold on. Zira's on duty right now. I'll talk to her."

The comm went silent for a moment, and Johnny glanced at me. "Smart. Make the USSF think you're still there."

"If it works."

"It should."

"Unless they've hacked these comm lines, too."

That comment hung over us; Johnny had no response.

A new voice came on the line: Zira Miller, one of the three in charge of the city's communications. "Mac, hi. Kristen told me your request. It's not a problem. Who do you want to call?"

— •• —

A MINUTE LATER, REGGIE QUINN, former Seascape mayor, was on the line.

My heart pounded; my stomach was in my throat. I needed to know if Meg was okay, but I had to assume that the USSF had bugged Reggie's office or they were listening to his comm lines. But surely the USSF knew that I'd be concerned about Meg, and a call from me was normal.

I made sure the scene behind me was featureless bulkhead. "Reggie," I started. "How is Meg?"

He chewed his lower lip and didn't respond immediately. He looked down.

I groaned. "That bad?"

"Yeah. She's not good at all. Neither is Cliff, Mac. But all they need to do is tell the USSF what they want to know."

I knew he was just saying it in case they were listening to him. "She doesn't know anything. I'm not sure what they're asking. It's still about the Admiral's disappearance?"

"His murder. And more, I'm sure."

I frowned. "What else?"

"Who knows?"

I paused and stared at him. "What's happening with you?" Then I noticed his surroundings. "It's not your office. Where are you?"

"They've relocated me."

"Who's in your office?" Then it hit me. "Admiral Quintana?"

"You got it."

"She really has taken over."

"Did you have any doubts?"

"No." I sighed. "I need you to help Meg."

"I visit her on occasion, just to check up on her."

I stared at him, trying to telepathically send him a signal. I knew he'd just have to wait for things to start, but I hoped he was smart and he'd figure it out. "Make sure she's comfortable."

"I'll try."

"Cliff, too."

He nodded, but with a resigned expression. The USSF must really be punishing the two of them. And Reggie seemed despondent, but I knew it was an act. He'd be watching the USSF routines and patterns. He'd know the best time to act, but he'd wait until I made my move, as well.

"Well," I said in an exasperated tone, "I'll just sit here at Trieste and wait, I guess. I need to know they're going to be okay."

"She shouldn't have killed the Admiral."

"I'm not sure why they're saying that."

"They have a lot of evidence, Mac."

"All circumstantial."

"Her black eye. The scuffle in the cabin. The motive." He folded his arms on the desk. "They know she did it."

"I don't. I don't even know the Admiral is dead. He could still be out there, traveling somewhere." I cringed at the comment, but I had to keep the act up.

He stared at me, then shook his head. "Mac. They know she did it, and Cliff helped cover it up. She's admitted it." He paused, continuing to hold his gaze on me. "They don't have a lot of time."

His comment hit me hard and I hesitated as I soaked it in.

They don't have a lot of time.

They were going to kill her there.

Damn. We had to get this plan moving faster.

—••—

IN THE AFTERNOON, OUR TENSION continued to escalate. The currents were strong and they tossed *SC-1* with immense force. The screws turned with great power, pushing us forward through the cold, dense, and murky waters, but we could feel the waves shifting the vessel port and starboard as we drove toward the last turn that would lead us into Jade Bight.

I stared at the sonar.

"The GSF have to be close," I muttered.

"Unless they're not actually paying much attention."

"I'm sure they are. If what Rico says is true, then they are monitoring New Berlin closely. And we know they've been listening in to the comms to and from Cousteau. It's how they knew we'd be in the Mid-Atlantic Ridge."

"True," he whispered. "And yet, they're not here."

We were just off the coast of Germany, rounding the point and navigating slowly into the Bight. But there were no GSF boats.

"Does this make sense to you?" I asked.

Johnny was staring at the same thing I was. "No warsubs. Not even on the surface."

"And we're only five kilometers from the coast right now."

I pulled the throttle back and our forward momentum slowed immediately. I punched the station-keeping control, and leaned back to stare at the map. We were more shallow now—only twenty meters—and the surface waves were buffeting us.

"We could risk an active pulse."

Johnny glanced at me. "That would tell everyone in the area where we are."

"That's what we want."

"We don't want to attract every sub, though, Mac. We only want one."

"True."

And then the sonar beeped. I jerked my eyes to it and stared. There was a point of light close to us that hadn't been there before.

"It's a GSF warsub," Johnny whispered.

"Class?"

"*Elite.* It was running silent. Just floating there. It's eleven kilometers to the northeast."

And stopping our progress had attracted their attention.

No doubt they had been looking for us, too.

More lights began to spring up all around, all at varying distances from us.

I grunted. "Looks like they're making their move." Each warsub was now headed directly for us, steaming at full speed.

"I wonder if they know we sank *Dark Winter*?" Rico asked from my back.

I couldn't respond. I was staring at the screen, studying my options.

I was searching for *Attentäter* Class boats nearby. There were three in the immediate area. Our sonar had picked up their signals now, and had displayed them on the screen: *Adler, Wolf*, and *Falke*.

"Interesting," I said. I pointed at their location. These ones are all to the west. They're trying to cut off our escape route." They'd let us in, and now they were going to try to keep us from getting out.

I stared at the map for a long series of heartbeats. Then I switched on the comm and signaled New Berlin.

"What are you—"

"Part of the plan," I replied.

The comm squawked. "Seacar, *wie können wir helfen?*"

"This is Truman McClusky of Trieste in seacar *SC-1*. I'd like to speak to Mayor Gerhardt, please."

There was a long pause. I knew what was happening. GSF officials were watching over that very station, monitoring communications to and from the city; after all, they had occupied the colony and were watching everything that was going on. The USSF had done it to us before; I understood how an occupation worked.

Eventually, "We read you, *SC-1*. I will connect you now." They had switched effortlessly to English for our benefit.

A few seconds later the comm beeped again and a new voice floated to us. "*Das ist Gunther,*" he said.

"Hello, Mr. Mayor," I replied. "It's Truman McClusky of Trieste City."

A long pause followed. No doubt he knew exactly who I was and why I was there. "Greetings," he said finally in a thick German accent.

"I'm on my way to your colony. I should arrive in a few hours."

"Okay . . . "

I could tell he couldn't speak openly.

I cleared my throat, "I'm here to present you with a deal."

"A deal?"

"An opportunity."

He cleared his throat. There was a long break. "I'm not sure we can—"

"I want to speak with you about declaring your independence from the German Submarine Fleet."

It was like a bomb going off.

There was an immediate scuffle on the other end of the line, while Gerhardt seemed to be struggling with someone. A hard voice snapped in the background, "*Sie werden diese Übertragung jetzt schneiden!*"

And then the line cut out.

I turned to Johnny. "Damn. That was sudden." They had troops *in the mayor's office watching everything he did.*

But that wasn't all. A few minutes later, active pulses began hitting *SC-1* from multiple directions, telling the GSF exactly where we were located, our course, and speed.

"Let's send our own pulse now," I said.

Johnny complied and our screen lit with hundreds of contacts.

On the surface, under the water, near us, and directly in our path to New Berlin.

There were GSF vessels *everywhere.*

"Oh, shit."

—••—

THEY HAD ALL ALTERED COURSE and velocity in the last few seconds; all were now steaming toward our location, most at flank speed. The exception were the contacts near New Berlin, which were moving, but much slower. They were staying near the colony to protect it in case we escaped their net.

Approaching their colony was the last thing I wanted to do, however.

I studied the list of warsub classes and names popping up on our sonars.

There were more *Elites*, more *Jägers*, *Mörders*, and more *Attentäters*, as well.

I peered at those *Assassin* Class vessels.

Attentäter.

One of them might be the one . . .

Nothing stood out to me.

The computer displayed their names with callout labels next to each contact.

Teutonic, Soldat, Dornenspinne, Herrschaft, Krieger, Schwarze Witwe, Vulkan, Wolfspinne, and *Schwarzer Berg.*

It then translated the names, as it had *Dark Winter.*

Teutonic.

Soldier.

Thorn Spider.

Domination.

Warrior.
Black Widow.
Volcano.
Wolf Spider.
Black Mountain.

I studied the names. Teutonic was a German tribe, or something pertaining to the Germans. *Herrschaft* could be interpreted in a number of ways . . . *Domination* was one, *Ruler* might be another.

"Mac," Johnny mumbled at my side. "They're coming. What should we do?"

"One minute . . ." I continued to study the list, hoping something would pop out to me.

There were two *Assassin* Class boats named after geologic features—mountains—and two after fighters of some sort: *Soldier* and *Warrior*.

Then there was a cluster of three warsubs northward, blocking the passage between islands, all named after deadly spiders.

Odd, to name a submarine after a spider, I thought.

Then again, they were poisonous, deadly, and stealthy. You rarely saw them coming. They generally snuck up on people, startling them when they were least expecting. It's one of the reasons people hated spiders.

You'd think underwater colonists wouldn't know much about them, but spiders did find their way into the cities, inadvertently brought in by transports. They didn't live long, though; there wasn't a food supply to sustain them.

Something had begun tickling at my conscious brain. Something about those names . . .

Spiders.

Something Rico had mentioned to me about the GSF.

Or about the warsub that had held him captive.

Mountains, warriors, and spiders.

Weird.

"Mac, we have to *move*. Now."

"One minute."

He knew it was an *Assassin* Class boat. He had all the specs down. Seventy-five meters. Twelve crew. Two screws.

A submariner could generally tell how many screws a sub had based on the vibrations in the hull. They rotated in different directions to balance each other out. Sometimes during a quick turn or maneuver one would switch to reverse to increase the speed of the turn. You got used to the vibrations, and he'd been on the warsub for a year.

He knew the number of crew.

He knew some of their names.

He knew every vibration, every rattle. It was normal after living on a vessel underwater.

He'd listened to the crew speaking with one another for a year.

He'd heard private conversations—when they weren't torturing him for information.

He knew that the boat was—

I froze in place, my hands gripping the yoke.

Johnny was staring at me, wondering what the hell I was doing.

Oh my god.

That's it!

I swung the seacar to the north and slammed my palm on the fusion drive control. The control blinked yellow: INTAKE IN PROCESS.

Behind us, the reactor throttled up and vibrated the hull.

"What is it?" Johnny asked.

"I think I know the boat."

"What? I don't—"

"I might know which one held Rico."

Chapter Twenty-Two

THE TWO ISLANDS NORTH OF us were rocky outcroppings with a large expanse of water between them. One was Minsener Oog and the other was Mellum. They were 7,500 meters apart, and the three vessels had taken positions equally distant in the space.

Wolf Spider.

Black Widow.

Thorn Spider.

The three spiders.

At SCAV drive, I knew we'd blow right through them without much difficulty.

I just had to worry about their SCAV torpedoes.

We couldn't lose power here . . .

If that happened, we'd never see Trieste again.

Our speed was building, the fusion drive boiling water to steam for thrust, the vibration rapidly cascading to a rumble, and the yoke was shaking in my hands. At our bow, the blunt protrusion created a low pressure zone and gases were boiling out from the water, forming the large bubble that stretched back to envelop the seacar.

Supercavitation.

Friction was lessening, and as the bubble built, the vibrations began to subside.

The yoke became easier to control.

Movement grew smoother.

Our dive planes and horizontal surfaces—the supports connecting the thruster pods to the hull—behaved exactly like airplane control surfaces.

Now we were flying, underwater.

Acceleration continued, and we cut easily through the water now.

I made my depth a hundred meters as we soared northward.

"Rico!" I called. "Get up here!"

He was at my back in a flash. "What is—" Then he noticed the three warsubs on the VID over our heads. "Oh, shit," he said. "You're heading straight for them."

I pointed. "All *Attentäter* Class."

He paled. "Yes, you're—"

"All blocking the same channel. All trying to keep us from escaping. All working together."

"Yes, I see, but—"

"Rico. *Look at the names.*"

He stared for a moment more before his jaw dropped. He swore again. "Three spiders."

"You said that the warsub you were on was—"

"Infested. Yes." Now he was nodding. "*Three* different types!"

"You heard them talking about it many times."

"I did." His breathing was shallow and now his face was hard as he stared at the names.

I held the yoke steady, but we were nearing them. I needed a direction . . . *and soon.*

Our comm beeped.

"Rico, which were you on?"

"Let me think for a minute."

Johnny had watched the entire exchange. Now he swore. "It would likely be the one you didn't hear as much."

Alarms were blaring from the sonar.

Warning and proximity alerts.

Torpedo shutters opening.

"Why do you say that?"

"The crew would mention the other ships more frequently. They might not refer to their own sub as often."

I nodded. He was right.

We were closing on them quickly.

We'd spoken about it on the journey from Cousteau. We had a tentative plan . . . something that we thought might work, but it was going to be tricky . . .

"*Black Widow,*" Rico blurted. "I think that's the one."

I located it on the VID. It was the one farthest to the west.

I turned us slightly to starboard.

Now all we had to do was take out the other two warsubs, then infiltrate the one remaining.

No problem.

My guts churned.

—··—

OUR SPEED WAS 400 KPH and we closed the distance rapidly. The comm continued calling for attention, and the alarms were sounding. I snapped those off with a quick press of my thumb.

"Prepare weapons," I said. "SCAV torpedoes."

I swallowed. We only had four torpedoes remaining.

The alarm *blared.*

Torpedo in the water.

—··—

WE WERE LESS THAN 3,000 meters away. I'd picked the boat closest to Mellum, the island to the east. It was no more than three kilometers across. The water was shallow there—less than a hundred meters now, and our wake churned sediment from the seafloor. Our drive was piercing through the channel waters and calling to all GSF warsubs in the area to close on us and open fire.

We only had a few minutes to deal with these vessels.

I angled around the torpedo, giving it a wide berth. It might be programmed to detonate at closest approach, so as soon as we began to increase the distance between us, it would explode, possibly damaging our propulsion or cracking the hull. We had to be careful.

It was growing even shallower.

We blew past the torpedo and turned behind the warsub. It was *Thorn Spider,* and I knew that the weapon would be turning now to come about and reacquire.

Or they'd—

"*Torpedo in the water!*" Johnny shouted. "*Number two!*"

"Shit." I slowed our velocity and studied the readout. We had ten seconds before we had to maneuver. "Fire torpedo. Homing on their screws."

"Got it." He fired and *SC-1* shuddered at the launch.

"Fuck you!" Franz yelled from behind us, startling me.

I glanced back as I hammered the throttle to full. "Make sure he's in submission!" I yelled at Rico.

"Done!"

Our torpedo shot out and rapidly built speed until a bubble surrounded the SCAV weapon. It *screamed* toward the warsub.

The explosion was tremendous. The yoke rattled in my hands and, without waiting, I banked to starboard and put some distance between us. There were two torpedoes there, circling, searching for us.

Johnny was watching the sonar. "Screws have stopped. Alarms are sounding. The warsub is dead in the water."

I exhaled. One more to go.

—••—

WE WERE CLOSING ON THE next GSF sub. It was *Wolf Spider*, and they weren't waiting for us to get close.

Our sonar blared once, twice, then three times.

Three torpedoes in the water.

And these accelerated faster than I thought possible.

They were SCAV weapons, headed straight for us.

And there were two conventional torpedoes, still behind us.

"Countermeasures," I growled as I turned us to the north. The waters were even more shallow, and *SC-1* left a steaming mass of churning bubbles that I'm sure aircraft could see.

"Done." Johnny pressed the LAUNCH button three times and the devices dropped from our underbelly and stayed in place, neutrally buoyant, churning the water and calling to the weapons.

My guts twitched. These torpedoes more than doubled our speed.

If this didn't work—

I yelled behind me, "Get a drone ready! Prepare to open the moonpool hatch!"

Renée shouted, "On it!"

I watched the sonar. The three missiles were approaching from the south. We were moving northward and had put some distance between us and the countermeasures—a white, glowing, and frothing mass on the VID system.

I hauled back on the throttle and waited. We slammed out of SCAV drive and the straps kept me from hitting the yoke. Then I realized that Renée and Rico were back there, walking around. "Sorry!"

Renée swore but I could hear her lugging a drone toward the living area.

The ballast controls were located between the two pilot chairs, and I made our depth thirty meters.

Behind me, there was a whine as the moonpool hatch retracted.

The SCAV torpedoes were slicing toward us.

They passed through the countermeasures—

There was a massive blast as all three went at once. It buffeted *SC-1* and water sloshed up the moonpool and into the living area. Emergency pumps kicked into action and flushed the water from the cabin. But it had surged around Franz's face, who was lying on the deck, and he struggled to keep his head above the salty water.

There was another splash as Renée pushed a drone into the moonpool.

"And another," I said, keeping my voice down now.

She nodded and disappeared into engineering. Johnny powered the controls that Jackson Train had installed on the co-pilot's station when we'd visited The Ridge.

"Here we go," Johnny muttered.

We had spent months working on the concept and Jackson had put our ideas into action.

Now we were going to see if they worked.

Renée put the second drone in the water and it sunk out of sight. Johnny maneuvered it away from us, we closed the moonpool hatch, and I made our ballast negative.

We drifted down.

"All quiet now," I hissed. The torpedo blast and countermeasure disruption had faded, but the immense explosion had been between us and *Thorn Spider*, so I knew the disturbance had shielded our actions.

But there were still two conventional torpedoes out there. I could hear their distant screws.

The drones were small and quiet, and Johnny could move them about slowly.

SC-1 settled on the bottom.

I turned to Rico, who stood behind me. "It's important that Franz can't make a sound."

"I've gagged him."

"Go back and sit on him."

Rico's eyes hardened, and he nodded. "I won't let him give our position away. Don't worry."

Franz had done it before; I didn't want a repeat of the incident.

On Johnny's control panel, he commanded both drones to the south.

Toward the GSF warsub.

Chapter Twenty-Three

THE *ATTENTÄTER* CLASS VESSEL CLOSED on us. It was *Wolf Spider*. On the VID system over our heads, the computer projected it in white. It was a moderately sized warsub with six torpedo tubes; four vicious shutters were visible at the boat's bow. There were also hatches in its belly to release mines. That made me grit my teeth, for we were so shallow, a mine would crush us like a tin can. I hoped we blended in with the bathymetry of the ocean floor.

The drones were hugging the bottom and moving away from us at a painfully slow pace. We needed them to be quiet, so we dared not increase speed. Their thrusters gimballed at Johnny's touch, and his eyes flicked to the sonar and back to the drone control panel as he manipulated them.

"Go for the screws," I hissed.

He nodded.

The warsub closed. It was moving at ten kph. Our sonar system detected its passive signal and projected it on our screens.

Then it disappeared.

Shit.

—••—

THEY'D GONE SILENT. TOO QUIET for us to detect.

"Johnny?"

"I have their last location. Switching to visual." He stared at the tiny VID screen. The water was murky, but the drones were close now.

A silence unlike any other stretched out.

It loomed over us like a thundercloud.

We had to put this vessel out of action so we could focus on infiltrating *Black Widow*.

—••—

Minutes passed. We sat, barely moving, staring at the screens. Their glow illuminated our faces. The lights in the cabin were off. Rico was sitting on Franz's back to prevent him from moving. Franz had tried to kick the deck, but Renée had removed his shoes and tied his ankles with bungee cord.

The drones were stationary now. Johnny held them still as he peered at the VID screen.

Then a black shape appeared.

The warsub was passing overhead.

Wolf Spider.

Slowly.

So slowly.

Johnny exhaled and manipulated the controls. The drones rose from the bottom, toward the boat's underbelly.

Franz was screaming through his gag.

Johnny pressed the red DETONATE button.

Nothing happened.

He tried again.

Still nothing.

—••—

"Go for impact," I rasped. The drones had two protrusions on either side of the bow. Each a blunt, spring-loaded trigger.

On the red tank at the bow—the explosive.

It was a remote bomb, but we hadn't activated the trigger properly. We had to go for an impact.

"If I go faster they'll hear," Johnny said.

"Do it. They can't get away in—"

And he rammed the throttle forward and aimed at the hull just before the screws.

The warsub suddenly accelerated, and it appeared on our sonar again.

The VID lit and the vessel glowed white—

It was insanely close. The explosion might—

And the drones collided with the hull. The spring protrusions compressed, triggering the explosive.

It was smaller than a torpedo, but there were two there and a simultaneous explosion just at the engineering cabin, possibly at the screws' shafts and the stern torpedo shutters, ripped out.

It flared on the VID.

A rumble shook the seacar.

And the GSF warsub stopped moving.

Then bubbles blossomed from its bow, and two more torpedoes lanced out.

They soared directly overhead, the whine of their screws making the hair on the back of my neck stand on end.

The warsub was dead in the water, but they still had weapons, and were intent on killing us.

—••—

I BROUGHT US BACK UP to thirty meters and we dropped two more drones from our moonpool. Renée studied the warning label first this time, then she muttered something under her breath.

The torpedoes were not SCAVs; apparently, the German captain was concerned about them turning about and coming right back at him. We were close, and they knew it. They didn't want to destroy themselves in a SCAV-fueled explosion in this shallow water.

But they hadn't anticipated our drone technology. We could hide somewhere, completely silent, and attack with our remote bombs from multiple directions.

Johnny smiled tightly. He was enjoying this.

He brought the next drones toward the warsub, active and emitting noise now as crews dealt with the damage on board. Alarms were sounding, compartments flooding, and there was a hammer and clang of steel tools as crews tried to contain the flooding.

A touch of a button should detonate these drones. Renée had located the activation button on the devices—she hadn't toggled it on with the first two—and Johnny piloted the ROVs right up to the bow torpedo shutters and—

The explosion warped the hatches inward.

They wouldn't open again.

Wolf Spider was dead in the water with no weapons capability.

I turned my attention now to *Black Widow*.

This would be tricky. We couldn't damage her; she had to remain seaworthy. There were twelve crew on board whom we had to subdue, and they had access to handguns. And once we did commandeer the boat, we had to hope like hell that the rest of the GSF didn't suspect us. If they found out, we had to make sure not to exhaust her weapons fighting our way out from the North Sea, because we needed them for Seascape.

But we had been planning this since leaving Cousteau, and we had the glimmer of an idea.

There were still conventional torpedoes churning through the waters. I wanted to track those weapons northward, to put some distance between us and the two spiders now out of commission.

I set course away from Minsener Oog and Mellum. The torpedo tracks were loud and clear on the sonar; they appeared as red lines on the screen. They were behind us and steady on our tail. Our speed was seventy—our max—but the weapons were doing eighty and approaching fast.

The whine of their screws increased in intensity.

Johnny's eyes showed worry as he stared at the screen.

"It's okay," I said. I punched the SCAV button and the fusion reactor roared to life. Soon we were ejecting steam, and our velocity increased. The bubble began to form around the hull, and the rattling in my hands died. Our speed closed on 200 kph, and I held the throttle back, not putting too much space between us and the weapons.

I needed them.

Black Widow was still on our screens, as well, at a distance of seven kilometers, and she had angled her course toward the north to try and cut us off. Impossible, of course, because of our speed, but I was indeed going to let them catch up.

I just had to make them think they had caught us against our will.

We were in an open area, far enough away from the islands and the disabled spiders, that we had some breathing room to act.

Johnny pointed at the map, and I noted the location of the nearest comm junction.

I slowed our speed and we fell from SCAV. "Hold on," I said over the rumble of the engine. The bubble collapsed and the hull hit the water with tremendous force as friction took hold once again. We slammed against the straps and I groaned; bruises were blossoming across my chest where the two shoulder straps crossed.

I kept our screws off for now, and ordered two more countermeasures released.

Johnny complied.

They were behind us, churning in the cold water, spinning, cavitating, generating bubbles and noise, hovering in place and neutrally buoyant.

I increased power to one screw only, keeping the other off.

"Adjusting trim," Johnny muttered. He touched the ballast controls between the chairs—the fine ones that adjusted the tilt of the seacar sideways or lengthwise.

In the old days of submarine travel, in the Twentieth and Twenty-First Centuries, one crewman was dedicated to controlling the ballast of a sub and keeping her level. It was a thankless task, and endless, for even the crew moving about the ship changed her center of gravity and affected the pitch of the boat.

At mealtime, for instance, twenty men and women might move from the bow to the stern to collect their dinners from the galley. This would change the vessel's orientation in the water, so the person operating the ballast tanks had to trim the vehicle, and pump an equal amount of ballast from the stern to the bow to exactly balance the number of people moving aftward.

If it didn't happen, then the sub's nose would tilt upward, the stern down, and the sub would drive shallower unintentionally.

Or vice versa, and the boat could plunge downward.

The trim tanks existed to keep the vessel level. Nowadays, it was all strictly computer controlled, so we didn't have to worry.

But now Johnny adjusted some knobs on the ballast control panel, and he pumped some water from the port side to the starboard.

Our starboard thruster pod dipped to the seafloor.

"Not too much," I whispered. "We need to be able to move around in here, but appear—"

"As though their torpedoes damaged us. Got it." He held it at a twenty-three degree tilt.

Meanwhile our single screw was still the only one turning, and I struggled to keep us on a steady course.

Behind us, the torpedoes were closing on the countermeasures—

And then they triggered.

The detonation rattled the hull and everything shook. Plates in the galley, equipment in engineering, anything on the deck. It all vibrated.

We'd left stuff out for this exact reason—to create as much noise as possible.

Both torpedoes had exploded and vaporized or displaced a large volume of water. Water flooded back into the empty cavity, and a second shock wave slammed *SC-1*.

I sighed and took my hands from the SCAV controls. Had one of the torpedoes survived, I would have had to get us out of there.

But it had worked.

I cut the one remaining screw and we drifted to a stop.

Our depth was eighty-three meters.

We were dead in the water.

And *Black Widow* was closing.

—••—

WE RELEASED ANOTHER DRONE—THIS ONE from the airlock—and Johnny stayed in the pilots' cabin, manipulating the remote controls and studying his screens. We remained listing at the twenty-three degree angle, and he was leaning against the starboard hull, trying not to inadvertently touch any other toggles, buttons, or the screw throttles.

We'd left Franz tied up. He glared at me from over the gag; lines creased his forehead and his face was a mask of pure rage.

I stumbled aftward, stepping over the prisoner, toward the airlock.

Renée and Rico were there, pulling tanks from the compartment and laying out scuba gear on the tilting deck.

My wetsuit was hanging from the hook.

We were going outside as *Black Widow* bore down on us.

Chapter Twenty-Four

RENÉE, RICO, AND I STEPPED into the narrow airlock and checked our regulators and masks. We tested the tanks with a few quick breaths. Johnny, from the control cabin, began increasing pressure to match the outside depth, and we had to force air into our ear canals and sinus cavities to prevent it from becoming too painful. We didn't want to rupture our ear drums.

My heart pounded.

Rico seemed intense. Nervous.

"You okay?" I said.

He blinked. "Just . . . anxious, I guess."

"You know the mission. That's all that matters. We need to get on that vessel without them getting a signal out."

"Got it." He looked away and stared at the hatch.

I frowned and turned to Renée. She flashed me a grin. "I've gone far deeper before, Mac. No worries here."

"When you tried to kill me earlier this year." She had attacked in a pitch-black canyon after damaging *SC-1* off the east coast of the United States. We'd fought her troops in hand-to-hand combat, and had taken her prisoner on board *SC-1* after. "Do you remember decompressing in this airlock?"

She snorted, but kept her voice down. "Three of us in here for hours. Could barely sit down."

"And all you wanted was to tear my head off."

"Still do, some days."

"You know that's not true."

She shrugged. "You convinced me to join you. But that didn't stop my anger."

"I thought you were happy to leave the FSF?"

"I was. But you're . . . maddening sometimes."

I frowned at that.

Johnny broke over the comm. "*Black Widow* is a few thousand meters away still, but they're making good speed. You only have a few minutes out there."

"And the comm junction?"

"The drone is nearly there."

"Are you ready to flood the airlock?"

"Yes. Are you suited up?"

Nods all around. Renée didn't meet my eyes. I touched her arm. "Hey. Are you okay?"

She turned to me and smiled. "I'm sorry. We can chat later."

"Can you do this?"

She looked startled. "Of course I can. I'm ready. Let's go." Then she looked away.

I frowned. Damn. I knew not to minimize her feelings, but it really wasn't the time for this. I pulled myself back to our current dilemma and said to Johnny, "We're ready to go."

The airlock began to flood.

—••—

OUTSIDE IT WAS DARK, BUT not pitch black. The sun was up topside, and some rays were piercing the murky waters of the North Sea, but we were deep enough that water and sediment had filtered out much of the light. There was maybe twenty percent left.

Our seacar was listing heavily to starboard. All engine activity dead. In a few minutes, Johnny would begin to flood the ballast tanks slowly and begin a lazy descent.

It was an old trick—one of the oldest—but we hoped it would confuse the GSF warsub long enough for us to sneak on board.

We had bags of weapons strung across our abdomens. I had a needle gun on my right thigh and a dagger on the left.

The distant sound of screws penetrated my face mask. I could hear my own breathing, as well as Rico's and Renée's, and we huddled beside *SC-1*, waiting.

Waiting.

Johnny's voice whispered in our ears. "Five hundred meters. Their torpedo doors are open. I'm ready to detonate."

The comm junction was near us, and Johnny had taken a drone down and had positioned it just beside. He would trigger it when the shit hit the fan.

And cut off all communication.

Black Widow could likely regain comms quickly by patching into another nearby junction, but by then I hoped it would all be over.

AN ISLAND
OF LIGHT

—••—

THE WATER WAS COLD. IT sliced along the side of the mask, into my cheeks and forehead. My limbs tingled. My fingers were going numb. I flexed my hand repeatedly, trying to improve circulation.

The others were doing the same.

The whine of the boat's screws increased.

And then a dark shape settled over us.

The warsub was seventy-five meters long. Not huge, but sizeable. There was so much automation now on vessels in the oceans that large crews were unnecessary. But still, there were twelve sailors there whom we had to subdue—*somehow.*

But first, we had to get on board.

Johnny began speaking over the comm. "The tanks are flooding . . . the engines are down . . . we're out of torpedoes . . . I'm telling you, *we don't stand a chance!* We need to signal surrender."

I was sure the acoustics officer was picking it up in *Black Widow.*

SC-1 began to descend. We were holding onto a rung, and the seacar pulled us down with it.

It wasn't quick, but it was noticeable. The warsub would also have to descend to maintain distance, and their command crew would detect that our seacar was flooding.

"We're going *down!*" Johnny snarled. "I can't keep it positive anymore."

He droned on. I wondered if their comms person would recognize that it was a rather one-sided conversation.

He wasn't speaking to anybody.

Rico, Renée, and I let go of the seacar and stayed neutrally buoyant. Our vehicle begin to move downward, away from us. Bubbles were drifting from her and soaring upward, toward the water's surface so far away.

We remained suspended in the North Sea as *SC-1* disappeared from sight.

I shivered.

We seemed so alone.

Above us, the dark shape loomed.

For a second I thought they weren't going to follow. Perhaps they'd just stay up there and fire torpedoes.

If that happened . . .

If they did indeed fire, Johnny had orders to immediately power up the SCAV and escape.

Leaving us there.

He'd have to come back for us, if we were still alive.

But they didn't fire. They were descending, keeping pace.

A thrill raced through me, and I forgot about the cold.

The ship was coming toward us, right overhead. It was going to collide with us, in fact, and we'd have to grab a hold of something.

It blocked all sunlight now—

GSF ATTENTÄTER
[BLACK WIDOW]

BOW VIEW

PLAN VIEW

— TORPEDO TUBES

— BOW DIVE PLANES

STERN VIEW

— THRUSTER POD

— HORIZONTAL CONTROL SURFACE

— SCREWS

VERTICAL STABILIZER

STARBOARD VIEW

| 0 m | 10 m | 20 m | 30 m | 40 m | 50 m | 60 m | 70 m |

CLASS ————	SSN Attack Warsub, "The Assassin"		NUMBER OF CREW —	Twelve
			TUBES ————	6 (4 bow, 2 aft)
NUMBER IN FLEET ———	Thirteen		LENGTH ————	75 meters
MAX SPEED/VELOCITY —	60 kph		OTHER ————	Mines, countermeasures
CRUSH DEPTH ————	3,000 meters			

—the hull slammed down on us.

I grunted and tried to keep breathing steadily. Rushing water pounded my ears. There was a surging, *thrumming* sound all around.

The three of us rebounding in different directions.

We should have thought to tether ourselves together, dammit!

I scrambled across the hull, searching, trying to find a protrusion. A hatch. A rung. A ballast valve . . . anything.

But there was nothing.

I was cartwheeling across the steel, my vision spinning. I stretched my arms out, but couldn't even connect with the warsub anymore. It had pushed me away—

And then it stopped, neutrally buoyant once more.

I gasped, orienting myself in the water, staring at the hull a few meters from me.

Johnny was saying, "I've got the flooding under control! I think we've stopped sinking . . . "

I grinned behind my regulator. He had to keep the act up. We couldn't descend much farther, for our mix was only good for a certain range. Otherwise the pressure would build and our bodies would absorb too much nitrogen.

Nitrogen narcosis.

Rapture of the Deep.

Already I was beginning to feel lightheaded, but I had to brush it off.

I peered around, searching for the others as I kicked toward *Black Widow*. I found a handhold, snapped a cable to it, and spun to search for them. Two dark shapes approached, kicking madly. I waved and they pivoted toward me. Now we tethered together, and stared at the hull next to us.

We needed an airlock.

—••—

IT DIDN'T TAKE LONG TO find one. During the search, the German comms officer contacted Johnny and demanded his complete surrender for attacks against the GSF. "An act of war!" he ground out.

Johnny feigned indifference, complaining that his seacar was going to sink anyway, and it didn't matter.

Keep stalling, Johnny, I willed.

Because once inside, we had to decompress.

And hope their command crew didn't notice that someone had activated an airlock.

The hatch slid aside, and we pulled ourselves in. As it started to close and begin the decompression process, I clicked my comm's transmit button three times.

The hatch shut, cutting off our view of the warsub's shadow falling across *SC-1*.

—••—

THE WATER DRAINED AND WE pulled our masks off, sucking in deep breaths of canned air. There was an odd odor with it, before I realized: it was *crew*. The smell of twelve people living together. Their food. Their daily activities. The work they did. The vessel contained every single odor, especially when it never surfaced to purge air. It couldn't, because it always had to maintain four atms.

There was a story I knew from the early days of the space race: *Gemini 7*. The mission, with a crew of two, had remained in orbit for a punishing fourteen days. Finally, at splashdown in the Pacific, three 'frogmen' awaited the hatch to crack open. Two of the three vomited from the smell; the odor generated by the two crewmen had overwhelmed the recovery swimmers.

I pushed it from my mind and studied my surroundings.

"The screws are starting," Rico said. His eyes were now hard, his voice emotionless. He was in *Mission Mode*.

He was right. The bulkheads were vibrating. "Johnny is powering up the SCAV. He knows we're on board. He's putting some distance between *SC-1* and this warsub."

And soon he would detonate the drone, destroying the comm junction.

I stared at the airlock panel; decompression would last another twenty minutes. We hadn't been out too long, and according to the dive charts I'd studied before coming over, we had to go from eight or nine atms to four. We'd been out for about thirty minutes at that pressure, so it was an easy matter to push the correct buttons on the airlock panel. Rico had been in New Berlin for some time, and could operate the controls without any difficulty.

My thoughts turned to Johnny.

He had to pilot the seacar by himself, avoid *Black Widow*, and operate the drone simultaneously. He couldn't keep it up for long, so we had to get this done. And soon.

Black Widow launched two torpedoes. We could hear the shudder echo through the deck plates, the blast of high pressure air pushing them out, and the whine of the screws.

We banked and turned. The engines—battery-powered in this vessel— churned faster, then slower, then back up to top speed. Johnny was leading them on a merry chase, I thought.

I knew what he was doing: taking us out toward empty ocean, toward the next comm junction, so he could remotely destroy that one, too.

Soon the airlock chimed.

Decompression complete.

We checked the weapons to make sure they were ready.

Safeties off.

Here we go.

Interlude:
Meagan McClusky

Location:	Latitude: 28° 41' 24" N
Longitude:	94° 54' 5" W
	The Gulf of Mexico, Seascape City, USSF HQ
Depth:	30 meters
Date:	10 August 2130
Time:	Unknown

DAYS HAD PASSED SINCE MEAGAN had last seen Reggie Quinn, the former mayor of Seascape.

The torture sessions had continued; too many to count.

She couldn't sleep for longer than a minute or two at a time.

When she did nod off, Zyvinski would slap her face or splash water on her to shock her back to consciousness.

Once they'd even used vinegar on her legs.

That had been excruciating.

They'd tied her to the chair, as was customary, but her chin was on her chest and she'd closed her eyes. She just couldn't take the questions anymore.

The same ones, over and over and over.

"Where is the Acoustic Pulse Drive right now? Who invented it? Where is the inventor? Where is your secret base? How are your seacars able to descend to five kilometers?"

So she'd gone to sleep, right in front of the CIA Investigator.

And a short moment later she'd felt a splash of cold liquid across her cut, bruised, and scarred legs.

A gasp worked its way up her throat.

Her eyes snapped open and she screamed until her lungs were empty and ragged.

She squirmed uncontrollably in the chair, trying something, *anything*, to get the liquid off.

Again and again she emptied her lungs, rasping cries thrust outward, hoping against hope that it would make the pain go away.

But it didn't help.

Waves of agony coursed across her legs and radiated upward into her body.

Zyvinksi just watched with a half smile on her face. She studied the reaction, filing it away for later use. Then she nodded and grinned broadly. "I've never tried that before. I think it worked well. I think I'll do it again. Maybe next session? What do you say?"

"Fuck you," Meg rasped.

"How original." Zyvinksi sat down across the table, and brushed wispy strands of blonde hair back from her face. "Tell me—"

"I already have. I admitted to murdering the Admiral. My brother doesn't know."

"But Mac tried to hide it. He lied about it. He tampered with evidence. Or at least he ordered his Chief of Security, Cliff Sim, to do so."

Meagan exhaled several times, willing the pain to go away. Her legs were still burning as if the guards had thrown gasoline and lit it. She said in a weak voice, "Cliff Sim?"

"Yes. He came here with you. Remember?"

"Sort of." Her voice was a croak.

"He's dead now."

Zyvinksi had said it in such a matter-of-fact way that it caught Meg off guard. Her eyes widened and she stared at the CIA Investigator. "Bullshit."

"He died from his wounds yesterday. He couldn't keep going any longer. We gave him what he wanted."

"Which was?"

She shrugged. "Release. He couldn't tell us anymore." She glanced up at Meg then back to her nails. She was filing them again. "He gave us everything we needed. Your base, the APD, the scientist who created it, and so on. We know all about it."

Meg's mind was whirling. She was in a haze of exhaustion, needing sleep and food and rest. It was a fog of uncertainty, and she couldn't quite focus on what Zyvinski was saying. The pain made her reel in agony, and the lack of sleep clouded her judgment. "What did you say?"

"You heard me."

"Cliff? He's still here?"

"No, bitch." Her eyes hardened and her face screwed up. "I told you, he's dead. We killed him. Finally."

"I don't believe you."

The other shrugged. "I don't care what you believe. He's gone. Now we just have you, but we have everything he told us, as well."

"He didn't say anything, because he doesn't know anything."

"He's a part of your efforts over in Trieste. He knows a lot."

Meg struggled to see through the haze surrounding her. Fought her way to the surface, to will the pain away, to get to air so she could catch a breath. In her mind she was underwater, swimming hard upward, just trying to break that surface.

To make it to safety.

She started to laugh.

Zyvinksi stared at her. "What is so funny? You're hardly in a position to laugh."

Meg laughed harder. It shook her body. The pain was still there, but now she was gasping to catch her breath as the laughter took hold.

"Shut up," Zyvinksi snarled. "Why are you laughing?"

"Because you used present tense, you cunt. He's still alive."

Zyvinski froze as she glared at Meagan McClusky. Her eyes shifted away as she reviewed what she had said.

Meg spoke between gasps as she continued to laugh. "I know he's alive now, and you're not very good at your job!"

Zyvinksi bolted to her feet, her chair flying backward. "You better think hard before you speak. I am going to punish you for that."

"You'll always be a loser. You can't even make up a story and keep to it for five seconds. You're pathetic."

Zyvinski leaned on the table and glared. Then she glanced at the guards.

—••—

THEY THREW MEAGAN BACK IN her cell and slammed the hatch behind her. She ended up on the deck, in the middle of the chamber, lying on her back and trying to ease the pain in her legs. They were aflame. Cuts and bruises mottled her thighs. At one point in her life, what seemed like years ago now, men had found her attractive. She'd always caught them looking at her. Then when she'd notice, they'd glance away.

They'd study her figure. Admire her freckles and blonde hair. Stare at her blue eyes. They'd soak up her toned legs, drinking her in from her calves upward. Sometimes it disgusted her, but sometimes, she had to admit, she enjoyed it.

She got the most attention when she wore a wetsuit or shorts when swimming. She'd walk from her cubicle to the moonpool, leaving a trail of men staring at her.

Of course, part of it was because she was a McClusky. Her dad had created this legacy for her and Mac. Triestrians idolized her. For years she had hated it, but recently she had learned to embrace it. Things were easier now.

She snorted when she realized what she was thinking.

Things were easier now?

When she dressed up to go meet Mac or the team at a restaurant or tavern in the entertainment district of the Commerce Module she got a lot of attention, too.

But not now, she thought.

Her legs were a disaster. They were swollen from the beatings. The cuts would turn to scars, and they would be permanent. She hoped an infection didn't set in. That would end her life before she had a chance to escape this place.

Meg struggled to the bulkhead and hoisted herself up so she could lean against it.

She searched her thigh, looking for the scar.

There it was.

Just one of many now.

Meg looked at the toilet.

Where was that clasp again?

She dragged herself to it and reached behind the steel bowl. She had hidden it there somewhere, she thought. Or had that been a dream? Was it something she'd thought about but hadn't actually done?

Had it been a fantasy?

It must have been.

For there wasn't anything there now.

Choking gasps worked their way up Meg's throat. She had dreamed it. She started to cry, but no tears came.

She'd cried them all out already.

The clasp had never even been there.

Or, she thought, her chest heaving as she struggled to cry, it had really happened and the guard had found and confiscated it.

Cliff, are you really dead? she thought. He was the only thing keeping her going now. She didn't know if Mac were coming anytime soon. Reggie Quinn had told her that he wouldn't break her out.

But Cliff was alive.

He was still there, in Seascape.

Meagan had just proved it to Zyvinski.

It's why Zyvinski had been so angry.

Then Meagan's fingers brushed something.

The clasp.

There it was.

Still there.

It hadn't been a dream after all.

She backed up against the bulkhead again and fingered the clasp.

She held it between her thumb and finger and stared at its end.

There was a jagged point on it now.

Of course! She'd been scraping it on the deck, filing it down.

To make it sharper.

How could she have forgotten?

She glanced down and found the marks on the steel. There. She'd been scraping it there.

Meagan held the sharp point close to her face, so she could see it better.

Yes, it was sharp. It would cut.

And soon she'd be able to use it.

Part Six: Rogue

Chapter Twenty-Five

RENÉE, RICO, AND I STEPPED into the corridor. Red light bathed it in crimson fire. It was narrow, lined with pipes and ducts and exposed wiring. There were electrical junction boxes and panels and valves everywhere. All labeling was German, and I studied it silently. Nothing of importance that could stop the ship from attacking *SC-1* stood out to me, so I gestured down the hall, toward the bow.

Toward the control center.

The gun was in my hand, my finger tight on the trigger.

It fired with bursts of compressed air.

Beside me, Rico's face was tight. He wasn't saying a word; he was in combat mode. All of his actions were exactly as TCI taught. His movements, hand signals, gestures. Textbook, the way we instructed, right down to the way he held his weapon and cleared cabins as we traveled.

I had no doubt about him anymore, though I knew Johnny still harbored a lingering fear.

This man was definitely TCI, and he had indeed worked for George Shanks.

The first two cabins were clear.

No GSF sailors.

They were all on high alert, in battle, and manning stations.

At least two would be in the torpedo rooms at the bow. Many vessels had automated weapon loading and firing now, but there would still be crew there to bring in new torpedoes when the auto loaders were empty.

Others would be in the engine room, monitoring the screws, the ballast, the batteries, and so on.

Others would be waiting in case of damage. This would be the damage control team, ready to seal compartments and repair anything that a detonation or concussion might damage.

And the rest would be in control, directing the warsub.

There were only twelve people on board this vessel, and we had to subdue them all.

"Communications first," I whispered. "We can't let them get a call out."

"But Johnny destroyed the junction, right?" Renée said.

"Yes, but the operator, when he realizes, will start searching for another. They can also communicate with nearby GSF boats. We have to stop that."

Rico hadn't responded to me. Hadn't even looked at me. He was studying everything around him.

"Is this the boat?" I asked.

Nothing.

I asked again, but still he didn't respond. He was looking at the ceiling.

The smell on board was intense. It was a mix of body odor and food and grease and tools.

If you lived underwater in a warsub, you never forgot the smell. In the old days it would be predominantly diesel, but nowadays our vessels never surfaced to burn fossil fuels. We always stayed below the waves. Batteries ran things—*high-powered* batteries that could drive the screws as fast as engines from years past—or nuclear reactors if the ship was large enough. Fusion reactors. Fission was a thing of the past for most nations . . . or so we'd thought. The Russians were bucking the trend, but that was due to their technological backwater mentality.

Turning from Rico, I thrust these thoughts aside, to focus on the GSF warsub.

We approached another cabin to clear it.

Renée and I triggered the hatch, then we entered, weapons first, sweeping the area before us to make sure no one was there to surprise us later.

The warsub continued to pitch as it maneuvered. Distant concussions reverberated on the deck and bulkheads.

Another torpedo fired.

We turned back to the corridor, and I gasped.

Rico was gone.

—••—

"WHERE THE HELL DID HE go?" Renée hissed.

My stomach fell.

A prickle worked its way up my scalp.

No no no.

This was wrong. He was not one of them. Not USSF, or GSF, or from some other nation intent on sabotaging our plans.

He was TCI. I knew he was. I felt it in my gut. He'd worked for George Shanks. *Hadn't he?*

Could Johnny have been right? Could Rico have been lying this whole time?

"We have to move," I rasped. "We don't have much time."

"What's he doing? Turning us over?"

I hesitated. "I don't think—"

"What else could he be doing?" Renée's face was tight; neck tendons bulged.

"We can't worry about it now. We have to move." I touched her shoulder. "Please. Let's just continue. Then we'll find him."

Her eyes were piercing, but after a heartbeat, she nodded.

We moved through the corridor quickly now, cabin after cabin, clearing each. We hadn't stumbled upon anybody, until the fifth one toward the bow.

There were two GSF sailors in it, monitoring equipment.

It was the sonar station, and I knew that once we subdued them, the captain would soon find out there were intruders on board. He'd be needing steady reports from these men, and when they stopped responding, it would be game over for us, and a shootout on board would quickly commence.

Renée and I stepped behind the two men.

It was over in seconds.

—••—

THE SONAR PANELS WERE SIMILAR to other undersea vessels, though all labels and readouts were, of course, in German. I could tell from the colored symbols where Johnny and SC-1 were, where there were torpedoes in the water, and what bearing we were on.

We were heading north; Johnny was leading us away from the other GSF boats.

Renée and I quickly moved forward, toward the captain and communications. Then we'd need engineering.

They'd made a mistake stopping so close to our seacar, and waiting. They'd let intruders board and no one had been studying the exterior hatch warnings.

That was the problem with silent running . . . no audible alarms. Perhaps we had actually triggered something, but it likely had been just a blinking light that someone had missed, never expecting this.

Always do the unexpected, I thought. It often worked.

We continued on, toward the bow.

—••—

SOON WE WERE AT THE command center. I glanced at Renée. Her eyes were hard. She met my gaze and nodded.

I tightened my grip on the weapon and checked the ammo.

My hands were sweating.

Wearing a wetsuit inside the warsub was uncomfortable. The air conditioning units were off to cut back on noise.

I thrust my discomfort aside.

We stepped in.

—••—

THERE WAS A DISCUSSION GOING on at a station on the port side. One woman stood over a female sailor sitting at her station. They were peering at a readout and speaking in low, mumbled tones.

A male crewman sat at a console on the starboard side, intent on his equipment, pushing buttons and adjusting controls. He wore a headset and mic.

Red spotlights illuminated the area, and they cast long shadows across the deck, twisting over cables and tubes and pipes.

At the far end of the chamber, a screen displayed the location of every nearby vessel, the bottom terrain, and the weapons currently churning through the water in the immediate area.

It was the German equivalent of our VID system.

Before it, a woman sat in a chair, her hands on a yoke. That was the pilot; she was chasing SC-1 on the image before her. I recognized my seacar instantly. The two thruster pods on either side, the vertical tail surface, the blunt bow.

I performed a quick calculation: we'd come across two crew already. There were four in this cabin.

Which left six others elsewhere on the ship, unless there were more sailors than we'd expected.

The conversation at the port station grew louder.

The woman standing was clearly the warsub's captain. She was speaking in an angry rasp.

They had probably just realized that the sonar room was not responding.

The crewman on the starboard station was likely in charge of the comms, and I pointed in his direction. Renée nodded and crept toward him.

I moved toward the captain.

My safety was off.

My hands were tight on the gun.

In my peripheral I could see Renée advancing.

We had to time it right.

And then the captain abruptly stopped speaking and stood upright.

She turned toward me.

She'd sensed my presence, knew something was wrong.

"Guten Tag," I said.

All eyes shot toward me, except for the boat's pilot.

—••—

"*WER BIST DU?*" THE CAPTAIN ground out. Her eyes were hard and she moved her hand to the crewwoman's shoulder.

I knew she was trying to signal her to do something . . . call for assistance, or send a Mayday, perhaps.

I ground out, "Do not make a move or I will fucking shoot you in the face."

I wanted to instill upon them a very real fear, so I was blunt and to the point.

Her hand stopped moving.

The crew sitting at their stations was motionless. They could tell how serious I was.

"You will get on the deck. All of you. Or we start shooting."

"But—"

"Don't fuck with me," I snapped. "It would be easier for me to just kill you all and deal with the others, but I am giving you this one chance. Take it, or die. Get on the deck, on your knees, facing me. Cross your ankles behind you."

"You won't get away with this," she said. Her expression was icy. She had switched to English effortlessly.

"I think I will." I motioned with the gun.

We had to do this quickly. We had no idea what Rico was doing. He wasn't here, in the control cabin, so we had to neutralize these people and find him.

The captain was staring at me.

I aimed at her face.

There was a momentous silence between us . . .

Time seemed to just *stop*.

Everyone else was just staring at me.

And then she sighed and stepped forward.

She didn't want to die.

The others followed her lead and kneeled on the deck. I also made them interlace their fingers behind their heads.

Renée moved to the forward station, grabbed the pilot, and shoved her toward me. Then she sat down and, studying the controls for a few moments, grabbed the throttle and pulled it toward zero. Around us, the vibrations slowed.

The *thrum* of turning propulsors died.

We came to a stop.

The captain snarled. Her gaze hadn't left my face.

I ignored her. "Make our buoyancy neutral, Renée. Dead in the water for now."

"Got it."

"Who's nearby?"

She studied the projection before her, manipulated it to peer around in 360 degrees. "I see *SC-1* and two torpedoes. Johnny has the SCAV activated and is staying ahead of the weapons."

I glanced around, searching for the fire control station. It didn't take long. It was the station on the port. The captain had been studying the readouts only a minute earlier. "Over there," I said to Renée. "Find the weapon controls."

She stood from the pilot's chair and moved to the port control station. In a second she had the correct panel. She eyed me.

"Destroy the torpedoes."

She located the self-destruct button and pressed it.

Distant concussions shook the vessel.

They echoed in the cabin; the torpedoes had been hundreds of meters away, so had not caused us—or Johnny—any damage.

I exhaled.

We had done it.

—••—

THERE WERE STILL SIX PEOPLE to worry about, though.

And Rico, wherever he was.

I had an idea, but wasn't entirely sure yet.

We had to find him.

I ushered the four command crew into one of the cabins we'd already cleared. They were muttering angrily—in German—but I convinced them to stop talking by showing my weapon.

Or, perhaps it was the look in my eye.

My gaze was hard.

My finger tight on the trigger.

I wasn't messing around.

I was on a mission, and I was going to see it through to completion.

My sister's life was on the line, and Seascape was my target now.

In a minute we held them captive in the cabin. Renée watched them as I dragged in the other two from the sonar room. They were unconscious. We carried zip ties with us, and I went to work restraining them. Then, one by one, we did the others. The captain was first. She was swearing now, clearly enraged, but I ignored her.

Within two minutes there were six of them on the deck, tied and lying like fish in our harvesting center in Trieste.

"Stay here," I said, getting to my feet. "Watch them."

"Where are you—"

"I have to find Rico. Figure out what the hell is going on."

Renée said, "Do you think he's turned? Or was he with the USSF all along?"

My mind was whirling. I didn't have an answer for her. "Just wait here. I'll signal before I approach."

"And if they make noise?"

"Kill them." I said it loudly so they'd know we weren't messing around.

Chapter Twenty-Six

THE WARSUB WAS QUIET. THE engines were off, we were drifting at neutral buoyancy, our prisoners were subdued with Renée overseeing them, and there were no alarms or commands over the comm system.

The other GSF sailors on the boat must have suspected something was going on, but intruders during a battle was likely the last thing on their mind. They probably assumed a mechanical error of some sort.

Except that Rico was somewhere, at that moment, and he might have tipped them off.

There were two directions I could try: forward, toward the bow torpedo compartment, or aftward, past the airlock through which we'd entered, and back to engineering.

An idea occurred to me, and I chose engineering.

I shot one last look at Renée, whose face was hard and commanding, and nodded. She winked and I gave her a half smile.

Whatever issues existed between us at that moment we had put aside until this was all over.

I marched through the narrow, cable- and pipe-lined corridor toward engineering. I didn't pay much attention to the cabins we'd already cleared, but once I arrived at the airlock, my common sense took over and I reverted back to mission-ready awareness.

I raised the gun, took a deep breath, and paused.

Then another deep breath.

Then another.

Combat breathing, Mac. Get ready.

Rico, where the hell are you?

I steeled myself.

I stalked forward.

The red lights were still blazing from the ceiling. Each was ten meters or so apart, so in between were large areas of darkness. These lights were visual indicators of silent running, and we'd left them on.

The next three cabins were empty.

Then a ladder going down.

A smell of grease wafted up from the level below.

Grease.

It was under his fingernails. On his hands and forearms.

I shoved the thought aside and marched down the ladder. It was narrow and steep. We'd ditched our flippers in the airlock, and all I had on my feet were the built-in wetsuit grips that extended halfway down my feet to the toes. They were silent and provided traction with the metal deck.

The level below was even darker. There were more pipes on the ceiling and bulkheads. More wires. Air ducts.

Civilian seacars and vessels hid the mechanics behind bulkheads or under deck plating. In Trieste we did that, too. But this was utilitarian—a weapon of war.

The smell of engine grease was stronger now.

His name was Heinrich.

I swept the area in front of me with the weapon, searching for the remaining GSF crew.

There was a gasp and a thud in front.

I stopped, staring at the shadows before me. The hatch into the engine room was open. I could hear breathing.

Another thud.

A wet slap.

I marched forward, holding my breath.

There, on the deck between the two large engines—one on each side of the sub, one for each screw—Rico was on his knees. His face was bleeding. His gaze was on the deck.

There was a man standing over him.

A very big man.

He was in a tank top and his muscles were obvious. There were tattoos on his biceps. Sweat covered him. He had lines on his face, a square jaw, hair shaved to stubble, and a whiskered face.

Behind him, I noted another ladder leading back to the warsub's main deck.

He glanced at me and grinned.

His fists were clenched.

There was grease on his hands and arms.

It was under his fingernails.

I leveled my gun at him. "You must be Heinrich," I grated.

"I'm sorry, Mac," Rico muttered.

I ignored him. "Step back from him, or you're dead."

He didn't do anything. He just kept smiling.

"I mean it." I aimed just over his head and pulled the trigger. The puff of air was barely noticeable, but the ricochet of the bullet on the bulkhead behind him was loud. The round bounced against steel, around the cabin, and skittered across the deck at our feet. "Move, or die," I ground out.

"I don't think so." He had a thick German accent.

"I'm sorry," Rico muttered again. "I left you and Renée."

"It's okay." I stared at his face. He had dissolved into tears.

I'd wanted to give Rico this opportunity, to help put the experience behind him. To recover from the torture. To confront the man who had done this to him.

But I hadn't expected Rico to abandon us mid-mission.

"It's over now," I said.

And a whistling noise caught my attention. I turned, shocked—

A steel wrench caught me on the temple and I staggered to my knees, stunned.

A voice from behind me said, "Yes, it is."

I blacked out.

—••—

MY HEAD WAS POUNDING. THE side of my skull ached and dried blood crusted my hair. My body was in agony; there were now bruises on my limbs and abdomen. They had sliced my wetsuit off and tied me to a procedures table in the warsub's clinic.

My eyesight was blurry and I couldn't make much out. The ceiling, medical instruments in a cabinet on the bulkhead, and on the deck by the hatch, a scale. There were blood pressure cuffs hanging from hooks, and tongue depressors on another shelf.

On a tray next to me were a series of sharp, polished, stainless-steel tools, all laid out in a row.

That doesn't look good.

And beside me, Rico Ruiz.

The TCI agent who'd gone rogue during the mission and had thrown my plans to hell.

Straps also restrained him to a table. He was naked and bleeding from various contusions and welts. I blinked when I saw him; scars covered his body. It was grotesque how much damage they'd inflicted on him before.

He was unconscious, his head rolling to the side, facing me. Bloody saliva dribbled down his chin and onto the table.

I wondered where Renée was. We'd left her in the cabin just aft of the bridge with six other GSF sailors—including the captain—restrained.

I swore softly to myself. This couldn't happen.

I couldn't see things end this way.

Johnny was out there in *SC-1*, waiting for us to commandeer this vessel.

Now, it was over.

They were going to torture us, kill us, and then dump our bodies somewhere. We'd fired on GSF warsubs, after all. Crewmen may have died.

I leaned my head back and just focused on breathing. The pounding in my skull was so severe that I felt I might black out again.

Beside me, Rico moaned. I hoped there were no broken bones or permanent injuries. We needed Rico, despite what he'd done.

He moaned again.

I turned to look at him.

His eyes were open, and he was staring at me.

"Mac," he said, barely audible.

"I'm here."

His voice was raspy. "I'm sorry."

"Why'd you do it?"

"I—I—" he trailed off, then took a deep breath. "I just couldn't think. As soon as we entered the warsub I recognized it immediately. The smell was the same. The lighting, the corridors. The sounds. This is the boat."

"It's a GSF sub. I'm sure they're all similar." But even as I said it, I knew how false it sounded. An undersea citizen knows the vehicles he's been on. Especially after a year with nothing to do but study your surroundings, listen to the noises, feel the vibrations, smell the ship odors. It was inevitable.

Yes, this was it.

And Heinrich's presence was proof.

"He's going to kill us," I whispered. "You escaped from him. Now you're back."

"Likely." His voice was hollow.

"I wonder where Renée is."

"We're moving, so she's been captured."

There had been six of them remaining, and just Renée left from our team. They would have overpowered her easily. I hoped Johnny was studying this warsub, keeping it in his crosshairs. He was our only hope now.

I had wanted to steal the sub and sail south, toward Trieste and Seascape. It was a 10,000-kilometer journey, through the English Channel, across the

Atlantic, into the Gulf and to the Texas coast. Seven days at sixty kph. Meg would have had to hold out for another week. It would have been difficult, but possible. We were going to use the lone GSF warsub as a tool to attack USSF HQ and start a war with Germany, rescue Meg and Cliff in the process, and pull New Berlin into Oceania at the same time. It was a daring plan, but now it had all fallen apart.

The GSF was going to kill us.

—••—

I MULLED MY OPTIONS OVER. There weren't many. The restraints were tight; my fingers were numb and I couldn't move my legs. My vision was blurry. My throat was dry and I needed water.

The one drawback of my initial plan was that it had just been one sub involved. We were going to take *Black Widow* across the ocean and attack Seascape. The sunken ship *Dark Winter* was still just off the coast of Florida; I'd done that to create a fictional "motive" for the GSF attack. If the Germans felt the Americans had attacked one of their warsubs, then a counterattack at USSF HQ was the likely response.

I sighed.

But it was all over now.

Unless . . .

There was something I could do, I realized.

I closed my eyes. There was still a way to make this happen, after all, but I'd have to be careful.

And I'd have to endure a bit of torture.

But not as much as Rico.

—••—

TIME PASSED. I CLOSED MY eyes for a spell—I wasn't sure how long—but when I opened them my head felt mildly better. There was a man staring at me, and a woman standing next to him.

I recognized her instantly. It was the warsub's captain, whom I'd restrained earlier.

The man was Heinrich.

I looked at the Triestrian restrained beside me. He was awake, his eyes narrowed, and he was glaring at the German sailor.

"Looks like the welcoming party," I muttered.

"It's worse than that," the captain snapped. "You don't have long to live,

McClusky. You attack GSF subs, board our vessel, assault our crew, and invade our waters. What did you think would happen?"

I tried to shrug but it didn't work. "I guess I'd end up killing you all and stealing your boat."

"So that was your intent? For what exactly?"

"Revenge."

She glanced at Rico, then back to me. Her brow furrowed.

"Ask the big guy." I gestured at him with my eyes.

She glanced at Heinrich. "You mean because this spy was with us for so long while we attempted to figure out who he was?"

"Likely."

She nodded and crossed her arms. "We caught this man in a German colony attempting to interfere with elections and bring independence to the city. When we found out, we—"

"Tortured him for one year."

She offered a tight grin. "If you say so, though I have no knowledge of that."

Heinrich was staring at me, his eyes icy and his expression hard.

I said, "Your moronic halfwit apprentice there—*Igor*—left his mark on my friend. We came to set things right."

"You failed. And now you're ours."

Chapter Twenty-Seven

I STARED AT THE TWO of them looming over us. The GSF captain and Heinrich, the henchman. I said, "It doesn't matter. Nothing matters now, I guess."

She stared at me, shifting her feet and mulling over the situation. "You sent a signal to New Berlin. You made your intentions clear, only hours ago."

I nodded. "Yes, I intend to bring the city into our sphere."

She laughed. "You think you can bring a German colony into the United States?"

"I said, *into our sphere*. Meaning Trieste."

She blinked. "But you're American."

"An American colony, yes. But Trieste acts on her own. I'm the mayor, and I'm bringing your colony, New Berlin, into Oceania. I suspect they'll join up and declare independence from Germany when all this is over."

She was staring at me, likely trying to figure out if this were a joke or not.

"But why?" she eventually managed. "Why would an undersea colony—and the mayor, no less!—make such a foolhardy attempt?"

"Because a GSF warsub dropped a kill squad near Trieste. They tried to assassinate me. Almost succeeded."

"Ridiculous. I don't think—"

"Oh, I know it's true."

"How?"

"Because I killed them all. Then I found the boat that had dropped them off and I sank it, just off the coast of Florida."

Her face went white. "Sank it . . . ?"

"With a supercavitating torpedo. It was easy. Your technology is inferior now, in the oceans. You may have SCAV torpedoes that can travel a thousand kph underwater, but my seacar has SCAV drive, as well. You've seen it in action. You're no match for us."

"What was the name of—"

"*Dark Winter.* I'm sad to say that she's on the bottom, hull cracked open, all hands lost. And the kill squad is gone, too. I dumped them out a moonpool." I grinned at her. "After inspecting the bodies for evidence, of course. Their country of origin was obvious."

"Bullshit."

"One of them was still alive for a while. Franz. We got what we could out of him, then dumped him, as well."

She took a step toward me. "How dare you? GSF sailors? An entire warsub? And then warsubs here, in the North Sea, as well?"

"If you hit someone, get ready to be hit back, bitch."

She stuttered to a stop and just stared at me. She couldn't quite process what was going on.

Rico was watching me, his forehead wrinkled. "Mac, what the hell are you doing?"

"What?"

"Why are you telling her we're Triestrian?"

"She knows already, Rico. We advertised it when I called New Berlin's mayor. But I want them to know that we have the power to kick their asses should they ever bother us again."

"Bullshit," she repeated.

"Oh, I think I've proven it to you. I boarded your warsub *during a battle.* With my one tiny seacar, I put *Wolf Spider* and *Thorn Spider* out of commission. Maybe there were some deaths there, too. Who knows?"

"What happened to our communications?"

"I have no idea."

"And you say you sunk *Dark Winter*, a *Mörder* Class vessel?"

I snorted. "She's not very bright, Rico. You say she captured you?"

"Yeah. Embarrassing, right?"

"For sure."

She watched the exchange, her eyes hard. "You will regret coming back here, McClusky."

"I was never here in the first place. But your attack on my city was an invitation. So here I am."

She stared at me for a long, pregnant pause. Then she moved to the comm on the bulkhead and pressed the call button. A mumbled voice responded. The captain said, "Where is the other one?" She had spoken in English, presumably so I could hear the conversation.

"In the lounge aft of the control cabin."

"Ask her where she's from. Why she's here."

"She's not responsive. She is refusing to say much other than to insult us. She has a French accent, though."

The captain stared at me. "French?"

"She's with us."

"Right."

"Her name is Renée. She's formally of the French Submarine Fleet, but she joined Trieste."

She frowned. "To assist with your war of independence, is that correct?"

"Sure."

The captain hesitated, staring at me. Then she glanced at Heinrich. He wasn't speaking; he just glared at me and Rico. Then the captain spoke into the comm again, in German. I tried my best to understand: "Contact GSF HQ. Ask them for *Dark Winter*'s location. Find out if they've heard from her in the past few days."

"Ma'am?"

"*Dark Winter*. The warsub. I want to know where she is. Got it?"

"Yes, ma'am."

"And set course for Trieste."

My heart was thudding now. I tried not to react. I hoped Rico was also not giving anything away.

"What do you—"

She snarled, "I said take us southward, to the Gulf of Mexico and the American colony, Trieste. Do you understand?"

"Yes."

"Make our speed sixty kph."

"Yes. But ma'am, communications are still down. I can't contact HQ yet."

"Then set course and keep trying. Eventually we'll get through and inform them." She punched the comm and turned back to me. Rage painted her face.

I said, "What are your intentions?"

"To see if you are telling the truth."

"Your country tried to kill me. I simply reacted in kind."

"By sinking a GSF warsub? You think that equals—"

"Yes. Your special forces flooded a travel tube with me in it. Then they tried to sneak away like it was no big deal. I had to kill them."

Her face was a mask of rage. "*Had to?*"

I shrugged. "Sure. I had to make sure the GSF would not bother us again."

She laughed now, and it was a short, sharp bark. "Well, I'm going to show you that we will indeed *bother you again*. You are the one who started this, McClusky. Interfering with New Berlin. It's why we picked up your man here, although we weren't sure where he was from."

"Well, I guess now you know, but it's not going to do you any good."

"Why do you say that?"

"Because we're going to blow you out of the water if you get close to Trieste."

A look of utter disbelief crossed her features. "You're threatening me? You're naked, unarmed, have no hope in hell of surviving this trip back to Trieste, and you're about to suffer enormously." She glanced at Heinrich. He stared back at her. "I think you're in for a painful crossing, McClusky. I don't think you'll be alive when we attack Trieste, but if you are, you'll see the city collapse under the detonations of our torpedoes." Then she grinned. "I hope you have a nice day." And with that, she spun on her heel and marched out.

—••—

I TURNED TO LOOK AT Rico, lying on the table next to me. Heinrich had stepped out of the clinic, and Rico was just staring at a bulkhead.

"Rico," I whispered.

No response.

"Hey. Get your shit together."

He turned slowly to face me. "What the hell have you done?"

"You're the one who gave us up."

"Not intentionally."

"You weren't thinking. You left your team. You abandoned us. But I've salvaged it."

He snorted. "Good job. Now we're in for—"

"A few days. That's all. Can you last?"

He exhaled and looked away. "I don't know. I really don't."

"I need to get away. To a cabin or a cell. Then I can make a break for it."

He stared at me for a moment, then burst out laughing. "You're ridiculous, Mac. You think you can get out of this?"

"I do. Now pull your shit together. Survive for just a little while. I have to ask you for this so we can get out."

"For what?"

"Get him to focus on you. Get him to put me aside for a while. Then I'll be able—"

"You want me to insult the man?"

I spoke through clenched teeth: "Do whatever it takes."

"So he'll torture me more." His eyes were frantic. Wild. "Mac, I endured it for months already. I thought I'd gotten away from—"

"This is your fucking fault. *You left us.* Now man up and do this. I can get us out, do you hear me?"

"I—I—"

"Listen. I know what you went through before. I understand. It's going to take a while to heal and get over."

"Ha. We're not going to survive this, Mac."

"I promise you we are."

"How?"

I shot a glance at the hatch, praying that Heinrich was not listening. "Just trust me. I'm your boss, don't forget."

"It doesn't much matter now, does it?"

"Of course it does. Oceania depends on us, for fuck's sake! We can't die here. Can't give up. The other colonies are counting on us to bring all the undersea cities into the alliance. The independence movement is here, on this warsub. If we die, it dies with us."

"You?"

"Yes. And you. And Renée."

He shook his head. "No. You're wrong. There are others, in other cities, like New Berlin. The movement will continue."

I sighed. "Sure, but not with the momentum we have. We already have eleven cities! Eleven, out of twenty-nine!" Seascape had been the twelfth, but we'd lost it to the USSF. "And right under the superpowers' noses! You have to trust me on this, Rico. Get him to forget about me. Get him to put me in a cell."

"While he tortures the shit out of me. Literally."

"For Trieste, and for Oceania. Yes. You're TCI, Rico. You fucked up today, but you can make this right."

My guts were twisting. Blood pressure through the roof, I was certain. I couldn't believe what I was asking of him, but I had no choice. Rico had already been through hell, and I was pleading with him to endure more of it, with no end in sight.

He was staring at me, his eyes bulging. He'd clenched his fists and was sweating profusely. I was shivering from the cold, but he clearly couldn't feel it.

Other forces had taken control of him.

I just stared into his eyes, waiting.

A flood of thoughts was cascading through him. Waves of pain and anguish passed across his face. He'd been through so much already . . .

I hoped his love for the city and for underwater life could take over. His allegiance to Trieste.

He sighed and his body seemed to uncoil. He nodded imperceptibly. "I hope you know what you're doing, Mac."

"I do. Trust me, I do."

He exhaled. "I just couldn't think straight." He swore and glanced around him, at the clinic and the tools laid out all around. "No wonder. Look where the hell we are."

This is not going to be easy, I thought.

But I'd been through it before, in Sheng City, for four months. They'd electrocuted me. Attached the electrodes to my scrotum. They'd cut me. Burned me. Beat me. I'd lost teeth. They'd concussed me.

And I'd made it. I'd compartmentalized the pain and just tried to ignore it. We taught it now, in TCI, but I didn't know if Rico had been through the training. But he had survived a year of it before, and I was sure he could handle just a few more days.

"We just need a bit of time," I whispered.

The hatch ground open.

Heinrich was standing there, filling the entire frame, and there was a grin on his face. He held a box of tools; a variety of clubs and blunt instruments was sticking out of it.

I swore.

Chapter Twenty-Eight

THE PAIN MADE ME PASS out.

And Heinrich enjoyed every minute of it.

He was a sadist. There was no doubt of it. He wasn't doing it because his captain had ordered it, or because the GSF needed information, or because their lives depended on it. He was doing it because he got a thrill from seeing someone in pain.

Heinrich enjoyed cutting to draw blood, then pouring a chemical solution of some sort into the wound. It was agonizing. He put needles under my fingernails. He threatened to pull my fingernails out; he'd brandish the long pliers in front of my face with a sick grin on his face. His teeth were malformed and rotten, and as I groaned and struggled not to scream and give him the satisfaction, I eventually saw those teeth even with my eyes shut tight.

He used electricity, as well.

When I saw the electrodes come out of his box, I winced. It made his smile grow broader.

"*Hast du es schon mal erlebt?*" he said.

"I have no idea what you're saying."

"*Gefällt es dir?*"

"Fuck you."

"*Sehr gut.*"

And he connected the wires directly into the boat's electrical system through a switch board of some sort, and clamped the electrodes to my nipples.

Oh, shit.

Already my body was on fire from the welts and chemicals he'd inflicted on me, but this was worse.

It shot through my flesh like angry flashes of red hot liquid, coating every piece of me from head to toe. It also jolted my central nervous system, lancing through my spine, brain stem, and brain. It lit up every nerve in my body, reaching every appendage and electrifying each cell.

My back arched uncontrollably.

I had to scream. I couldn't hold it in any longer.

It was piercing, and beside me, Rico watched in horror.

Heinrich just smiled, crooked teeth glinting in the clinic's light. The brown bits of rot didn't shine; they were dead spots.

I wondered why I was thinking about his teeth while the electricity consumed me—

FUUUUCK!!!!

And then he'd let up. He'd let me catch my breath, which I did in huge, ragged, heaving gulps.

Sweat pooled on the steel table. I could feel the puddles at my sides.

It only made the electricity worse.

"Rico," I wheezed. "Try to hold on for as long as you can."

"I should be saying that to you."

Heinrich hadn't started on Rico yet. He was having too much fun with me.

—••—

I BLACKED OUT FROM THE combination of electricity and chemical.

When I came to, Heinrich was waterboarding Rico. The TCI agent was gurgling and gasping and struggling for air. Then the water stopped, the rag came off his face, and he turned sideways and vomited profusely. Then he took massive gasps of air—

—and the rag went right back over his face and the water started again.

In the Twenty-First Century there had been debates about whether waterboarding was torture. Soldiers who had tried—just to see what it was like—admitted to only lasting seconds. Now Rico was enduring it, and I was sure my turn was coming.

Heinrich enjoyed speaking with Rico as he worked. I didn't catch much of what they were saying, but Rico seemed capable of communicating with the man in a broken German/Spanish/French mix. Heinrich kept smiling as he poured on the pain.

The clinic was a small cabin with stainless steel fixtures, bulkheads, and cabinets containing instruments. Our screams rattled the interior. The sound of tools hitting the steel table as Heinrich worked, our legs crashing up and down, our groans and cries of anguish, and the buzz of electricity as he cranked up the power echoed all around. I was sure the rest of the crew could hear it, as well, and probably Renée, too.

I hoped to hell they weren't doing this to her.

It was the last thing I needed.

I might have broken, had they brought her into that chamber.

—••—

THE FIRST SESSION LASTED A few hours.

Heinrich grew tired.

He left us tied to the tables, and he departed, leaving the hatch to the corridor open so other crewmen could come taunt and spit on us, which happened a few times.

I had to relieve myself onto the table. The urine pooled around my buttocks. There was a drain at the bottom that slowly carried the liquid away, but it only dripped into a bucket fixed underneath. The smell in there was horrid, especially after the torture. There was the metallic odor of blood, mixed with the corrosive chemical used on our wounds, sweat, the normal smells of the boat, ozone from the electricity, and now urine.

Each person who entered the room wrinkled their nose at the stench.

I closed my eyes, groaning against the pain. My wrists were bound and attached to the table above my head, and the position stretched my shoulders to their limit. My body was aching.

Waves of agony coursed through me, and aftershocks from the electricity rippled up and down my nervous system, shooting random jolts through my body. At times a limb would twitch uncontrollably, waking me from a leaden and grotesque slumber.

I saw those teeth.

I wanted to knock them out.

I slept.

—••—

THE NEXT SESSION WAS WORSE.

I was losing track of time already. I had no idea if it was the same day or the next.

I think it was the next, because Heinrich had slept and was wearing a different shirt, though still sweaty and covered in grease.

Six days to go, I thought. Then we'd be in the Gulf.

Heinrich was having fun. He had hooked us both up to the ship's electrical system, and could alternate between us. A goofy, joyous look crossed his features as he studied our writhing before him.

But the smell in the cabin was beginning to bother him, too. He started wearing a mask over his mouth and nose.

It was growing overwhelming, and I knew it was only a matter of time now. They would either move us to a cabin to clean up the clinic, or they would just kill us.

— •• —

DAYS PASSED. THE SESSIONS DRAGGED on. They were horrible.

Words can't explain what endless pain is like.

When there's no end in sight, there's no escape, and you can't move to avoid it.

You just learn to . . . *accept* it, I guess, and try to shut your mind off to it.

Screaming helped. And swearing. And falling unconscious was good, too, because sometimes time passed and I never knew how much.

The Chinese had done the same to me in Sheng City, one of their underwater colonies. I'd been on a mission there, with Johnny, and he'd given me up and turned me over to the authorities there. Torture sessions lasted hours, day after miserable day, and I eventually lost all track of time. Sometimes I thought years had passed. Sometimes, weeks. When they told me the truth it had surprised me. Not because it had seemed longer or shorter, but just because I hadn't known.

Now, on *Black Widow*, I lost all track of time again.

The sessions ground on.

They gave me water, but no food.

Which meant they wanted me alive for longer than a few days, but I knew what the end result would be if I couldn't get myself out of this.

— •• —

RICO COULD BARELY SPEAK. HIS head was lolling to the side, his mouth hanging open, and he was wheezing. We were all alone, presumably Heinrich had left for the evening—he seemed to be the only one running sessions with us—and we had some time to speak to one another.

"Rico."

"What?"

"You're still alive?"

"Barely. You?"

It made me chortle. "I'm here. I can't believe you withstood this for a year."

"It wasn't this bad. Sessions weren't so long. They weren't trying to kill me, I guess. This time, I think they are."

"It's possible." The electricity alone could stop our hearts and end it all.

"I think they'll move us soon. There are other crew who need this room, I'm guessing."

I grunted. It was a good point. The doctor, for instance, if there was one on *Black Widow*, must be upset we'd taken over his workspace. And if any crew needed attention, they needed a spot to address it.

Studying my surroundings, I searched for something sharp. Anything. I'd have to somehow grab and palm it, because I was still naked. No place to hide anything.

Unless . . .

I shuddered. That would be a challenge, in our current situation.

At least the warsub's course and speed had been steady. The vibrations in the hull and deck were constant, the sound of the engines unwavering.

We were forging through the Atlantic toward my ultimate destination, so we had that going for us.

The crew didn't know they were doing exactly what I wanted, but in order to carry out my plan, I still needed to commandeer the vessel.

I wondered if Johnny could help. Surely he knew what was going on. We hadn't tried to contact him, so he probably suspected capture. *Black Widow* was moving at sixty kph, and *SC-1* must have powered out of passive and active sonar range, otherwise the GSF warsub would have continued searching for her.

Perhaps Johnny had gone back to Trieste, in SCAV drive, to warn them of our return.

Maybe they meant to rescue me, after the crossing.

That would be nice, but unnecessary.

I planned to be out before then.

Days had now passed, and time was running out.

On the tray beside me were a series of scalpels. Heinrich had used them to cut flesh and then pour chemical in. He'd done it up and down both my thighs, on my chest, abdomen, and even on my penis. I had sworn profusely at him, but he just looked at me, sometimes hovering over me, with a lopsided, malevolent grin.

I'd never wanted to kill someone more.

I could try to grab a scalpel, but it was too long. They'd notice. I needed something sharp, but much smaller. A nail file was also too long. I wouldn't be able to palm it successfully, or hide it from Heinrich and the crew.

I continued to search, and my gaze finally fell on the counter against the bulkhead near the hatch to the corridor.

A razor blade . . . small enough to fit in a palm, with two sharp edges. My eyes lingered on it as I spoke to Rico.

Yes, it would work.

Rico was drifting off, and I left him to his pained slumber. He was moaning under his breath, his body slightly twisted from the pain and no longer lying flat on the table. I studied him a bit longer . . . his shoulder might have dislocated during the convulsions.

———••———

THE NEXT DAY, HEINRICH ENTERED and immediately flew into a screaming diatribe. He'd screwed his face up in anger and was gesturing madly at us.

"What the fuck can I do about it?" I yelled back. "You've chained us up here! There are no toilets, no showers—"

Within a minute other crewmembers showed up and, gagging on the smell—one actually vomited on the deck—they unhooked my restraints.

I could barely move my arms. They were over my head, lashed together, and I slowly tried to bring them down to cross in front of my chest. There were still ties on my wrists, but this was the best I was going to get.

They unstrapped my legs from the table and gestured for me to stand.

"I don't think I can," I groaned.

"Tu es oder stirb!"

Do it or die.

I swore. "I'll try." I sat up, my back soaking and covered in sores—I'd been lying in a pool of sweat and urine—and painfully swung my legs over the table's edge. Rico was doing the same.

"Water?" I asked. "Water?" We hadn't had a drink in days. My head was pounding.

Someone thrust a bottle in my hands and I sucked at it. The cool liquid was refreshing and a surge of confidence spread through me. Although pain lanced through my body and my limbs were on fire and my hands and feet sluggish, it made me feel alive again.

Glancing at Rico, I saw that he was also drinking.

Then he pulled the bottle from his lips and launched into an angry rant at the guards, and particularly at Heinrich. Each guard had his eyes on Rico . . .

And I made my move.

I lurched to my feet, immediately fell to the side, and crashed into the cabinet beside the hatch. Glass shattered and shards speared into my flesh. I arched my back and screamed and slid along the counter. I howled in pain as my legs collapsed under me and trays with tools flew across the chamber. I came to rest on the deck, bleeding and cursing.

The guards grabbed me under the armpits, swearing as they did so, and heaved me out into the hallway.

They dragged me down the deck, my feet trailing behind me, toward a cabin.

They threw me into the chamber and slammed the hatch behind me.

They hadn't noticed the razor blade hidden in my right hand.

Chapter Twenty-Nine

THE CABIN WAS SMALL EVEN by warsub standards. There was no bunk within, just a blanket thrown in a corner. The bulkheads were bare steel, the deck plates welded together and immobile. There was a stainless steel toilet, but no sink.

I studied each corner, making sure there were no cameras watching me.

Then I glanced down at my hands. Still tied.

The impact with the cabinet and Rico's screaming had distracted them. These sailors were soft, not prepared for people like us. They were not prison guards. They'd ended up in this situation against their will, and other than Heinrich, didn't know what to look for or how to deal with us.

And now I had a cutting tool.

There were no places to hide it, other than behind the toilet.

—••—

I MANAGED TO SLEEP FOR a few hours before the hatch ground open and the captain stepped in. She'd brought a chair with her and set it in a corner.

The hatch closed, and she stared at me.

"You're not scared of me?" I asked, pulling myself into a seated position against the bulkhead. I was naked and made no effort to cover myself. Her eyes scanned my body, pausing on the oozing cuts, and lingered on my penis.

"Yes, he cut me there," I said.

"I trust it hurt."

"Very much, yes." I studied her. "Motive to kill you, perhaps?"

"You're restrained."

"I could still do it. Strangle the life out of you."

"The guards would be in here like a shot. Or, I'd just kill you myself." She indicated the knife strapped to her left thigh.

"Maybe I'd rather die than endure any more of Heinrich."

She blinked. "You know his name?"

"Rico. He was here for a year. He knows the crew, more or less."

"Ah. Of course." She nodded. "I'm still trying to figure out why he came back."

"I told you. Revenge."

"You could have just sunk us, if your claim of technological superiority is correct." She paused and studied me, her eyes narrowed. "There's more here than that."

"Perhaps the need to get back at Heinrich was just too great."

"But you have no hope now. You'll die here, at his hands."

"That's a definite possibility." I sighed. "We didn't exactly intend to get caught, you know."

"And now you have, and you're here."

I grimaced. "Sadly. But what do you want?"

"You're wondering why I want to speak with you? You invade my boat, assault my crew, and ask that?"

"I thought you just wanted to torture and kill us."

"I want to know the truth about *Dark Winter*."

I watched her expression. "So you believe me now."

She only raised an eyebrow.

"I told you they dropped a squad to kill me. Instead I killed them, then sunk the boat they came from."

She frowned and stared at me for a long series of painful heartbeats. "Why can't we communicate via comm with GSF HQ?"

"Pardon?" That took me by surprise.

"What have you done? Our comm system seems to work fine. We've contacted neighboring vessels, and five of them are accompanying us southward, but we can't communicate with Germany."

"I have no idea."

"Oh, we've sent a ship back to the docks, so we have managed to get word back to them, and they've signaled us via airdropped buoy, but what's going on with the comm junctions?"

"Don't know."

"Where's your seacar?"

"No idea. Not on your screens?"

"Disappeared after we captured you."

I shrugged. "I have SCAV drive on that vessel. They've probably returned to Trieste."

"That's what I figured."

I scowled. "You don't have to torture us to figure that out."

"Perhaps. But punishment is necessary sometimes, don't you think?"

"Actually, I do."

"Good."

"Because that's why I'm here. To punish you."

She blinked. "The hit squad again?" A snort. "Had nothing to do with me."

"If you say. Last I looked, you're GSF, though."

"So we're all to blame for GSF HQ."

"Sure."

She shook her head. "Look, McClusky, you're in over your head. You're just the mayor of a tiny city in the Gulf of Mexico."

"With over 200,000 people. Not so tiny."

"In the grand scheme, you're insignificant. They are civilians. You have no power to speak of."

"If you say so. But you know my name, don't you?"

She offered a half smile. "Yes, of course. And my name is—"

"I don't care."

She choked back her words and stared at me in surprise. Then a look of absolute hatred spread across her features. "You're going to die on my boat. Do you know that?"

"Not really."

She continued to glare at me. "I can't see this going any other way."

"You could just drop us off at Trieste and promise not to send any more assassins."

"I can't speak for the GSF."

"Still, you could leave us—"

"And have you return to bother us?"

I shrugged. "If you left Heinrich with us, maybe I could make you a promise."

She burst out laughing. "Are you really trying to bargain? In your current situation?"

"I am. Because what happened to *Dark Winter* is surely going to happen to you, as well."

Her expression grew hard. "You can't do anything from here."

"Maybe not, but my people can. You left my seacar intact. Trieste might know we're coming. And if that's the case, and they see *Black Widow* on their sonar screens, they'll sink us."

"Then we'll all die on board this ship."

"Yes. And Heinrich, too."

She eyed me for a long moment. "You really came here for him. That's all?"

"Yes," I lied.

"Amazing." She looked away and exhaled. "We're on our way to rescue crew from *Dark Winter.* You had no right to sink that vessel."

"I had every right."

Her voice grew hard. "You had no right," she repeated. "And you will die for it. You fired on other GSF boats in the North Sea. You can't go free after that."

"So I'm going to die here?"

"As a message to Trieste, certainly."

"Where is Renée right now?"

The captain eyed me. I could see the thoughts churning through her head. She was wondering what Renée meant to me. "Why do you ask?"

"She's one of my team. Heinrich is not working his magic on her."

"Why is she with you?"

"She believes in our cause."

"But she's French."

"She believes in the underwater colonies. Where is she?"

The captain shrugged. "She's fine. Untouched. I don't torture women."

And it's okay to torture men? I wanted to ask. But I didn't. I didn't want to anger her and divert Heinrich's attention to Renée.

I finally settled on, "I appreciate that."

"But maybe if I want you to talk, I'll reconsider."

Shit. "But Heinrich isn't even asking questions. He's just inflicting pain. I've answered everything you want to know."

"I don't need any information from you."

"Then this makes little sense."

"I told you, it's about consequences."

"When will you kill us?"

"I'll let Heinrich work on you for a while longer. We're two days from Florida. So you have that long, I guess." She shrugged as she rose to her feet and slid the chair to the hatch. "People need to learn that they can't fuck with the German Submarine Fleet."

"You're nothing."

She laughed. "You're in no state to insult us."

"You can't stand up to our Navy. You have inferior technology."

"We have SCAV—"

"Torpedoes only. Not crewed vessels with the new drive. You wouldn't stand a chance against us, as I already proved. And your GSF is insignificant. You have only four classes of warsubs. Four. The USSF has twelve, as does the CSF. The RSF, thirteen."

"*Russia?* They're totally insignificant."

I barked a sharp laugh. "If you say so. But they currently have the largest warsubs in the oceans, with the deadliest weapon."

"You're referring to the dreadnought, destroyed weeks ago."

"Guess who destroyed it."

She stared at me. "Bullshit. The USSF did."

"Think what you want. But *I* did that."

She stepped toward me and put her finger in my face. "You are full of shit, McClusky, and you're going to die here."

She turned and stormed from the cabin.

And I smiled, for she had given me a very important piece of information.

Good job, Johnny.

He had kept pace ahead of the warsub and destroyed comm junctions as he did so, likely using the drones on board. And now there was a grouping of GSF subs sailing across the Atlantic toward the Gulf of Mexico.

The optics were perfect.

The USSF would only suspect one thing.

Attack.

I didn't have much time left to get moving on the plan.

Crawling to the toilet, I reached behind it and found the razor. Then I dragged myself back to the bulkhead, leaned against it, and gritted my teeth.

I knew what I had to do.

Interlude:
Meagan McClusky

```
Location:        Latitude:    28° 41' 24" N
Longitude:       94° 54' 5" W
                 The Gulf of Mexico, Seascape City,
                 USSF HQ
Depth:           30 meters
Date:            15 August 2130
Time:            Unknown
```

MEG'S EYES WERE BLANK.

Emotionless.

The bulkhead was a flat and featureless gray except for the columns of rivets every twelve inches apart. Her eyes had lost focus and her thoughts were confused and cloudy. She didn't even try to sleep anymore. Once her eyes closed, she knew what would happen. The two guards would crash into the cabin, haul her to her feet, drag her down the corridor, and she'd have to endure another session with Zyvinski. It was inevitable.

So she didn't sleep.

Her finger traced the raised and rough scars on her torso and legs. The bruising had discolored the majority of her skin; she couldn't stand to look at it.

So she stared at the bulkheads now.

Meagan had lost track of time. She no longer knew what was happening in the world outside. In the oceans. At Trieste. At Seascape for that matter. Troops moved about on occasion. She could hear the vibrations of large warsubs powering past. There was a construction project nearby, as well; sometimes she heard the distant sound of machinery.

The end of Oceania, she thought.

It couldn't happen now. Not with USSF HQ so damn close to Truman and Trieste, where they could monitor them closely, and make sure they weren't planning an uprising.

How long had she been at Seascape? How many days? Weeks? Months?

And where was Cliff? She hadn't heard about him in days. The last Zyvinski had said was that he was dead, but Meg hadn't believed her.

The gray bulkhead stared back at her.

The rivets were eyes.

She lost focus; the rivets grew fuzzy and melted together.

Her thoughts were so damn foggy. She couldn't keep a constant thought in her mind. She'd think about one thing and it would turn into something else, then something else, and so on. There was no point to thinking; her brain didn't seem to operate normally anymore. She was giving in. She knew it.

What were they building?

Docks? Umbilicals for warsubs?

They'd have to dredge the seafloor a bit. It was too shallow for the biggest ones.

Didn't someone already say that to her?

She was cold. The blanket was dirty. Crusted with blood.

The scars on her legs.

Her thumb traced the important one. It had healed more than the others, and there were signs of stitches on it, long since dissolved away, but their marks remained.

Meg's eyes closed.

The hatch slammed open.

Shit.

"Meg."

"Fuck you."

"Meg."

"I said—"

"I heard you, but it's Reggie."

"Fuck you."

"Reggie Quinn. The—" He choked back what he'd been about to say.

Meg turned to face him, her expression pained. Her vision was blurry and she had to blink several times to clear it. Reggie was beginning to look unkempt, as well. He usually kept a goatee, but now had stopped shaving the rest of his face. He was bald and wore glasses—those things hadn't changed—but his clothes were wrinkled and baggier than normal.

"The what?" she said in a soft voice.

"Mayor." He trailed off.

"Ah."

He stepped in and the guard outside closed the hatch behind him. Reggie crouched next to her. "Listen. I heard from Mac."

"Mac?" She didn't know what he was saying.

"Your brother. Well, not really from him, but from Johnny. But they're not together. Well—" He paused, then shook his head. "But not really. They are, kind of."

"You're not making any sense." She laid her head on her arms, which were crossed in front of her on her knees. "It's because I've lost control of what's happening. Can't think properly. I don't—"

"No, listen. Johnny is in *SC-1*. Mac is on board a GSF warsub. It's en route to the Gulf right now."

"To Trieste?"

"And Seascape." He lowered his voice. "They're coming. The plan is working. Johnny called me."

Meagan struggled to understand what he was saying, but her mind was in turmoil and she couldn't think clearly. "What for?"

"To tell me they're coming for you. They'll be here in two days. You just have to hold out for that long."

"Zyvinski won't let me. She's going to kill me."

"What does she want to know?"

"About Mac. About independence." She struggled to think. "I don't know, to be honest. I can't remember."

"You killed Benning."

"I had to."

"No, you didn't."

"He killed Dad."

Reggie exhaled harshly and shook his head. "We have forty-eight hours. They're coming."

She tried to process what he was saying.

She felt the scar on her thigh.

"When are they coming?"

"Forty-eight hours."

"You have to tell me when is a good time to go."

Reggie frowned. "I can do that, but I'm not sure how you're going to get out."

"You could do it for me. Right now."

He shook his head. "No. I can't break you out."

She snorted. "You don't want to get caught. You don't want to lose Seascape. But you know what? You already have."

"No, I—"

"You're nothing here now. Quintana is in charge. She's in your office. She's in control."

"I—I—"

"They've taken over. The tourists are gone. Now you have nothing." The thoughts were growing clearer, and she pressed on. "You have to help me. You have to get me out. Come to Trieste and fight with us for Oceania."

"There's a chance it'll all come back, Meg. I can't get caught. I can't—"

"I know." She tried to laugh but it hurt her ribs too much. A kick had either bruised or broken them. She had a hard time taking a deep breath. "Tell me when, then, and I'll make my break. You said there was a moonpool in this module, right?"

"On Deck One."

"Is it open?"

"There are no guards there, as far as I can tell. But there are troops everywhere. Walking in the corridors, moving around, living in the Staff Module as well as the hotels."

"Where am I, exactly?"

"In a smaller module connected by travel tube to four others. On the west is Staff Module A. North is the Repair Module. East is the Commerce Module, the largest one. And South is the Communication Module."

She tried to picture it in her head. She could get to the moonpool in her current module, and perhaps make it to water, but where would she go?

"Listen, Meg."

"What?"

"What is Mac's plan? Why is he in a GSF warsub?"

"I really have no idea. With him it's usually something no one could ever predict. It's how he's been so successful. It's why I joined up with him, despite hating what Dad had done." She sighed and thought about her life. She'd run away at eighteen. Gone to Blue Downs and started fresh. She hadn't wanted to hear about independence or think about how reckless Dad had been. But things had changed. Truman had brilliantly used the SCAV drive to attract other colonies to his quest, and he'd invested in further innovations in the oceans. He always seemed to be one step ahead of everyone else. Until the Russians launched their dreadnought, that is, but then he'd come up with an insane plan to take it down, and it had worked.

But they had destroyed Blue Downs. The Australians were rebuilding it, but most everyone she had known there was now dead.

And the USSF had trapped her in a cell.

She didn't think she'd make it out of this, but Mac always had a plan.

"When can I make my break?"

Reggie looked at the hatch behind him. "It's evening right now. I doubt troops will get you until after their dinner. But the next time they come for you, it'll be quieter outside."

"Aren't they on three shifts like at Trieste?"

"Yes, of course, that's standard, but it doesn't apply to this module. Nothing's happening here except . . . " He trailed off.

"Except torture."

"I was going to say interrogation."

"Same thing. When will Zyvinski call me again?"

"Her pattern is after her meal. Around twenty hundred hours."

Meagan nodded. So be it. She'd make her attempt that evening and try to evade the USSF sailors until Mac arrived in the GSF warsub. She shook her head. He was a conundrum.

She said, "Can you make sure there's a wetsuit and scuba gear for me by the moonpool tonight?"

His face flattened. "I—I guess. I'll have something there. I'll just leave it at the side."

"Something that doesn't stand out."

"The military wears black. That's what it'll be."

"Good." She took a deep breath, but the pain in her side lanced through her body and she winced.

"You sure about this?"

"I can't stand any more."

"It might be better to wait till tomorrow night. Till he's closer."

Meg thought it over. She just couldn't subject herself to any more. "No. This is it."

"Okay. I'll make sure it's there."

"Can you contact Johnny and tell him?"

"I'll do my best."

"Is he in touch with Mac?"

"For some reason, Mac isn't talking to him. Johnny thinks the GSF may have captured them, but the warsub is sailing toward us with five other GSF vessels."

"So six in total. Interesting."

"Yes." He rose to his feet. "I'll go take care of it. Good luck to you, Meg. I hope you make it."

"If you left a weapon I'd have a better chance."

He hesitated. "I'll see what I can do, but they'll know if I do."

"You have to pick a side, sooner or later."

"I already have."

"Really? Doesn't seem so. You won't do much for me. Do you think things are going to change for you here?"

He sighed. "I—I guess not."

"But you're scared."

"To say the least. The USSF is surrounding us. This is their HQ now."

"That's not going to change unless we do something."

"What?"

"Mac knows. He's got a plan."

Reggie snorted. "With a German warsub?"

Meg thought about it. Something was beginning to crystalize in her mind, and it was a scary thought. Something about what Mac had told the team back at Trieste during the meeting where she had confessed to them about killing Benning. He'd mentioned something then that might have something to do with this.

But if he did what she suspected, then all hell was going to break loose.

And it would probably start a war.

She could never survive it, though.

"Listen," she said suddenly. "Can you get me a vehicle? A seacar? Even a scooter?"

He backed away toward the hatch. "I said I'd help," he hissed. "Not break you out of here. The answer is no."

And he slammed his hand on the hatch.

"One more thing!" she snapped. "Is Cliff still alive?"

He nodded, and her heart nearly exploded.

"Barely," he whispered.

"Tell him what you told me!"

Then the hatch opened and with a last look at her, he marched into the corridor.

—••—

MEG KNEW IT WAS TIME to act.

No more delays.

No more hesitation.

She crawled to the toilet and, reaching behind it, grabbed the sharp clasp. She'd filed it down to a point now. She brought it to her eyes and stared at it for long minutes.

This was going to hurt like hell.

—••—

SITTING ONCE MORE AGAINST THE bulkhead, she pressed her back to it. She'd torn a strip of fabric from the blanket and tied it around her upper thigh. She gritted her teeth as she did so. She realized that if that hurt, then what she was about to do might be impossible.

She tore another strip of fabric from the blanket and crushed it into a ball. She shoved it in her mouth, gagging on the metallic and salty taste of dried blood and sweat.

Locating the old scar on her thigh, she placed the pointed clasp on it. Blood welled up at the point, and she tore it back toward her as she dug it in deeply.

She screamed into the makeshift gag, then clenched her teeth on it to stop from making noise.

She cut again.

And again.

Blood was spilling out now. She had to stop for a moment and tighten the tourniquet. She wished she had something to put under it to twist it tighter, but there was nothing in her cell.

She wiped the blood away but more spilled out.

She had to go deep.

Deeper still.

And even deeper.

She kept pulling the sharp piece of steel through the cut, slicing the fleshy part of her inner thigh.

It had been Truman's idea to bury it there.

Inside their bodies.

Meg's, Cliff's, and Truman's.

She cut again.

She'd keep working at it until she could see it.

But there was a lot of blood.

Part Seven: Endgame Begins

Chapter Thirty

I GRABBED THE RAZOR AND pressed it to the scar on my thigh.

This was going to hurt.

I'd come up with the idea during the investigation in Trieste. Despite our attempts at protecting Meg, I knew Quintana and Zyvinski would likely figure out what had happened.

This had been the backup plan.

I was in the GSF warsub *Black Widow*. The captain had just departed. I'd angered her with my insolence—which had been my plan—and hoped she would continue on course and not question why she was doing it. I wanted her to sail to the sunken *Dark Winter*, and the fact that she had brought five other vessels with her was icing on the cake.

But soon I'd be in control on this ship, and put my own plans into action.

I sliced along the scar.

The razor was thin enough that I could do that, and the scar tissue didn't have any feeling. But blood began pooling and it became difficult to make anything out. Soon I was cutting new flesh, and I had to clench my teeth against the agony.

I pictured Heinrich doing it. It was something I couldn't prevent or stop, so I just bore the pain and allowed it to happen.

I breathed deeply and tried not to cry out.

The razor sliced into my leg, deeper and deeper.

I felt around my inner thigh, searching for the hard object under the flesh. It was lengthwise along my femur, but not quite that deep. The muscles had held it in place—I'd been worried about it slipping down my leg, but the doctor had assured me that it could never happen—and soon I found it. Just a bit farther to go.

I stopped and leaned against the bulkhead, catching my breath.

The doctor had almost refused to do it. The weapons were TCI-issue, but we had never used them in such a manner before. When the USSF investigators had shown up, however, and looked like they were closing in on us, I'd told her it was either do it or three people were going to die.

So she'd done it, but had pressed her lips together during the procedure and hadn't spoken to me after.

I kept cutting, pushing deeper this time to get it over with quickly. Groaning inwardly, I thrust my chin in the air with the last slice.

Finally. I grabbed it with two slippery fingers and pulled it out.

It was ceramic so it wouldn't set off metal detectors. It was a tube about five inches long. It held three bullets with a trigger on one end; it worked by slamming your palm on it and firing from the other end. It was hard to aim, but with the tube under someone's chin, the bullet had nowhere else to go but up and into the brain. On the side with the trigger was a three-inch retractable blade. Once extended, you could spin the weapon in your hand and use it like a switchblade.

The blade was also ceramic. Not very durable—it could snap if it came up against body armor or even bone—but it wasn't meant for more than a few uses. Just to get us out of a cell should it come to that.

And I knew it would.

I hoped Cliff and Meg would be able to retrieve theirs.

—••—

THE PROBLEM NOW WAS THAT my leg was bleeding profusely. I should have ripped the blanket to make a tourniquet, but I hadn't thought to do that. Instead I pressed it to the incision and tried to staunch the blood that way.

With trembling fingers I opened the cylinder's side. There was a small pouch within, which fell to the deck. I wiped my fingers on the blanket and tried to open it. It was difficult but finally I had the contents out.

A needle and thread.

—••—

SOON THE JOB WAS DONE, and I stood before the hatch, testing the weapon in my hands. We called it *The Tube*. It had been slippery with blood, but I'd wiped it as clean as possible with the dirty fabric. It was now somewhat sticky, but that actually worked in my favor.

As soon as someone entered, I could either shoot them with one of three bullets, or use the blade to cut their throat.

Or, I could try to hide it to use on Heinrich later . . .

But I didn't have any clothes. No, I'd have to use it on the next person who entered the cell, then somehow find Rico and deal with Heinrich.

Or get Renée to make sure she was okay, and together try to take the ship again.

I swore. *Again*. It hadn't worked last time, because Rico had gone rogue and we hadn't worked as a team. This time would be even more difficult, because I didn't know where Renée was or who was watching her.

Ten stitches had sealed the incision. It was definitely not a great job, and it would have horrified the doctor, but the bleeding had stopped, and that's all that mattered.

I sat near the hatch, and waited.

—••—

RICO WAS LIKELY GOING THROUGH hell.

I thought hard about how I was going to do this.

There were twelve of them on this boat.

Footsteps approached outside, and I steeled myself. I had the tube gripped tightly in my hand.

The hatch opened.

A figure stepped in.

Then another.

I stood sideways to them, with the tube at my side, using my body to hide it.

They stared at me. It was the same set of guards who had dragged me here after the last session with Heinrich.

One of them smiled and said in a thick German accent, "Do you think you can handle us now after you've had a little rest?"

I turned and raised the tube to chest level. I held it in my right hand with my elbow bent at ninety degrees. They trained their eyes on it; confusion laced their features.

My left palm tapped the trigger end and there was a small noise. A red hole blossomed on the first one's chest. Then I switched aim and did the same to the second guard.

The noise wasn't like a typical gun. It was a loud *Pop!* and the guards, in sequence, took a step back and looked down at themselves.

One of them noticed the blood on his chest and opened his mouth to call for help—

Spinning the tube in my hand, I triggered the blade and leapt toward him.

It was easier said than done, for my body was aching and I just didn't have the same agility following the sessions with Heinrich. But I got there fast and rammed the blade into the guard's throat. He gurgled and gasped and fell back, clutching at his wound.

The other guard stumbled toward the hatch—silent—and attempted to lurch out into the hall. I caught him midway and pounded the blade down at the base of his skull. His body stiffened for an instant before going totally limp and thudding to the deck.

There was a snapping noise; the blade had broken in his spine.

The first guard was on the deck, bleeding from his chest and neck, and his eyes bulged as he stared at me. He tried to speak but only a choking gasp came out.

I watched him die.

—••—

I WAS IN MISSION MODE now. There was no time to feel guilt, no time for pity, no excuse to pause and reconsider my actions. It was now them or me, as had happened on so many TCI missions in the past. Sometimes I would wonder, *Why are they sending me to do this? What value is this to Trieste? Why do they want me to steal this for them?* Often I ended up in life-or-death situations, where some faceless guy was trying to kill me, and it always came down to self preservation.

The other person had to die.

There was no way around it. I needed to escape, return to Trieste, and continue to live.

And now I had to continue on my quest to save Meg and Cliff.

And these people were in my way.

I'd slid the hatch shut without locking it, and I removed both of their uniforms and pulled one on.

The guards had guns on their sides, and I took them. Two sets of holsters and weapons went around my waist. I strapped a knife to my left thigh. I smoothed my shirt and stared at the wet blood stains on the front. Hopefully no one would think twice about it, because I was going to use one of the guards to get me back to the clinic.

Hoisting the smaller of the two to his feet, I looped his arm around my shoulders and dragged him into the corridor. If anyone glanced at us, all they'd see was a GSF crewman dragging their naked American prisoner to the clinic for more interrogation.

I kept my eyes on the deck and stumbled toward the clinic.

This was tougher than it seemed; the man was dead, though thankfully much smaller than me. I found the clinic just up the corridor. Rico's screams were echoing down the warsub's arteries.

I took a deep breath just outside, then marched in, confident, and threw the corpse on the table. Heinrich was standing over Rico with a knife in hand and didn't pay any attention to me.

I strapped the body down, keeping my back to Rico and Heinrich.

"Der Schmerz fühlt sich gut an?" the German rasped.

"Fuck you," Rico muttered. He could barely speak he was in so much pain.

I spun on Heinrich and pulled the gun from the holster. Heinrich looked up at me, barely recognizing what was going on. He rose slowly and his face went blank. He glanced at the man on the table, and the realization in his features was clear.

I laughed inwardly. That man is dead. That man is not me, Heinrich.

"Back away from him," I snapped, gesturing with the pistol.

He raised his arms and stepped away from Rico.

I lowered my aim and fired.

His right kneecap exploded.

Heinrich opened his mouth and screamed.

And I saw his rotten teeth.

I smiled.

—••—

WITHIN MOMENTS I HAD UNSTRAPPED Rico. Together we hoisted Heinrich onto the table and he crashed onto the stainless steel. We weren't concerned about the noise; any passing crewman would just assume it was due to the torture.

He was groaning and clutching his knee, and I hit the side of his head with the gun, dazing him. The straps went on, I wrenched them tight, and he stared at us, dazed and not fully realizing what was happening.

"We have to gag him," I said. Screams were fine, but I had no doubt he'd start yelling in German soon.

He turned his gaze to me, realizing what I'd said.

He opened his mouth—

And I hit him again.

He grunted and gasped for air.

Rico found a leather strap. He fixed it around Heinrich's face, shoved a ball of cloth in his mouth, and wrenched it tight.

Rico, standing there naked, peered at Heinrich. His expression was one of pure madness. Sweat dripped from his face onto Heinrich's, and he growled,

"Now it's your turn, fucker."

Heinrich's eyes were wide. He shook his head.

Rico grabbed the electrodes from the floor and brandished them before the man's eyes. Then he tore the man's shirt open, buttons flying across the cabin, and clamped them to his nipples. "Get ready, Heinrich! After this I'm going to pull your rotten teeth out, one by one!"

—••—

I WATCHED, SOLEMN, AS RICO tore the man apart. Within minutes, sweat coated Heinrich's body and drenched his clothes, he'd arched his back and was screaming into the gag. Blood soaked his lower leg and covered the table, mixing with sweat and whatever Rico had left behind there—probably urine.

The smell of ionized air filled the cabin, along with charred meat. The skin around Heinrich's nipples had blackened.

After a while, I put my hand on Rico's shoulder. "Stop."

He looked at me, his eyes wild. "But Mac, after what he did to us—"

"We're better than this." I sighed. "I have no problem with revenge. But torture is . . . "

"What? It's not okay? It's okay to kill and sink warsubs and drown hundreds, but not inflict a little pain?"

Actually, it's probably thousands now.

I whispered, "No, it's not. Let's go finish the job here. We have to take control of the vessel. Every minute we waste here is dangerous. We can't let anyone find out until it's too late. If they signal their other vessels, then it's all over for Meg and Cliff."

His chest was heaving and his muscles tight. Fists clenched. He stared at me, then shot a glance at Heinrich. Then back to me.

He said, "He put me through hell, Mac."

"I know."

"He humiliated me."

"I know."

"And now I have to—"

"No." I said it forcefully, and it made Rico choke off what he'd been about to say. I continued, "I dealt with the same thing. And guess who performed some of the sessions? Johnny Chang."

His eyes widened. "Johnny? In TCI?"

"None other. He's currently on the mission with us, in *SC-1*. And he's my best friend and partner. I had to forgive him in order to move on with my life, Rico. It's the only way I could move forward. Because I'd shut down. I was through with everything. I couldn't function. Couldn't have relationships. I was farming kelp because it was the only job I could stand. My mind was just not capable of focusing on anything other than menial, hard labor. But once I recognized where the pain was coming from, and I forgave him, it gave me a path forward and helped me see things straight."

The concept horrified Rico. "You think I can forgive him?" He pointed at Heinrich, on the table and watching us warily.

"Yes." I shrugged. "Sure, he's a sadist. He enjoyed it. But he'll get what's coming to him eventually, and you'll end up with a heart soaked in hate and an inability to function in everyday life. Unable to forge relationships. Is that what you want?"

"Why'd you bring me on this mission, Mac?" His eyes were accusing.

"For this."

"To get revenge."

I shook my head. "More than that. To see what Heinrich is. To understand him more."

"He's a monster. What are you talking about?"

"In order to move forward in life, you need to put this to rest. I let you have some time with him. You've had your revenge. Now it's time to forgive and move on."

His jaw was on the deck. "You want me to just *forget*?"

I grabbed his shoulders, and he shrugged my hands off. I grabbed him again. "Rico, Benning murdered my father. I had to forgive him during the dreadnought mission to move on. But look what happened to Meg. Look at the situation we're in now."

Realization dawned on his features. "Because she couldn't get past it, she murdered him."

"And we're in the shit now because of it, and she's in prison at Seascape. They're probably torturing her, and on top of it, it's dragged Cliff into this." I shook my head. "Letting hate consume you doesn't work. I've come to see that."

He stared at me as heaving breaths continued to wrack his body. But soon they slowed, and his eyes lowered. "I think I see what you're saying."

I gestured at Heinrich. "Hell, Rico. He might not survive what's coming. None of us may. But we're above torture. I want independence for Trieste. I want to see Oceania. But I won't do it if it means sacrificing my values."

He continued to process my words. Then he took a deep breath and calmed himself. "But—"

"Rico." I put my hand on his shoulder. "It's over."

He stared at me for several more pained heartbeats. Then he deflated. "You're right. It's how I fucked up earlier. I wasn't thinking straight."

"You had good reason, after what you'd been through."

"No. I caused this. I'm the reason we got caught." He took another series of deep breaths and straightened. "Let's take the ship. Then we can deal with Heinrich."

"But we don't torture. No more."

He frowned as he eyed me. It was a weird contradiction, I knew. Death was okay, but not torture?

It was okay if it served my plans.

If it helped save Meg.

I motioned to Heinrich. "Make sure he's tied securely. Then we'll go get Renée."

I turned my back to him and prepared to move out into the hall.

Behind me, Rico adjusted Heinrich's restraints.

—••—

THERE WERE NINE OTHERS ON the warsub. Rico and I now both had weapons, although he was still naked. It was almost comical as we marched from cabin to cabin, me in my German uniform and him stark naked, but it actually fooled some of them into thinking I was the captor and he was my prisoner. They didn't question why we were out of the clinic and roaming the ship. Not at first, anyway.

We moved aftward from the clinic and cleared engineering first. Each GSF crewmember we encountered died from gunshot wounds. The puffs of air were quiet compared to the churning screws of the mighty engines, and we left the bodies lying on the deck in puddles of blood as we moved forward.

Soon we were at the cabin just aft of control.

Peering in, I found Renée staring back at me. At first she thought I was a member of the crew, then her brow furrowed and realization spilled across her features. She opened her mouth—

I put my finger to my lips. "Where's the captain?"

"I don't know."

"Are you okay?"

"Yes." Then she looked at me up and down. "I should be asking you that. I've heard you both screaming. For days and days now."

"I'll live." I almost laughed at that. It had been absolute hell.

"How'd you escape?"

"Tell you later," I muttered as I peered up the corridor, toward the control cabin. I handed her a gun, and she took up position beside us.

She peered at Rico. "You know you're naked, Rico?"

"Uh-huh."

"Are you hot or something?"

"Something like that."

She stared at the blood smeared across his skin, at the burn marks, and at the network of old scars covering his body. "What the hell did they do to you?"

"You don't want to know."

We crept toward the bridge.

Chapter Thirty-One

THE REMAINING CREW, INCLUDING THE captain, was there.

We stepped inside, brandishing our guns, and the captain stared at me. "What the—"

"It's over," I said. "Move into the center of the cabin. On your knees." Gesturing at the crewman at the communications panel, I made sure he did not touch an alarm button or send a signal to the other ships in the area.

My finger was tight on the trigger, and he noticed that I was paying attention to him and him alone. "Move."

He nodded and pushed away from the console.

The captain said, "You tried this before. It won't work."

"Except the only ones left on the boat this time are here, in this cabin. We've taken the rest of *Black Widow*."

"Bullshit."

"Think what you want, but it's true. It's all over for you."

—••—

HER FACE GREW PANICKED AS I tied her hands behind her back. "You can't do this," the captain snapped.

"You should have thought of that before you resorted to torturing a TCI agent."

"He was trying to corrupt a German underwater colony! He was—"

"There's no excuse for torture. I told you, when you attacked me and did those things to Rico, I was going to hit back. Now here it comes."

"What does that mean?"

"Get ready."

We had them restrained and together in one cabin—the officer's mess. There were four of them. The others were all dead, with the exception of Heinrich, still strapped to a table in the clinic.

Rico had found some clothes and we were in the control cabin. The ship was rounding the tip of Florida, near to where *Dark Winter* lay on the bottom, and I knew I'd have to decide on the next steps.

Sonar indicated the locations of the other GSF warsubs. They had taken up position behind us, had matched our speed and course, and were in perfect formation as we closed on the sunken vessel. We needed to mount a sizeable force toward Seascape, if possible, but I didn't want to do anything to make the other German captains suspicious.

"Renée, can you speak passable German?"

She sighed. "I can try. The language is similar, and I've heard it many times before. I do have some experience."

"Get on the comm. Order one of the vessels to stay at *Dark Winter* and search for survivors. The other four are to come with us."

"Which?" She was peering at the sonar and the labels there.

I wanted the largest, most powerful warsubs with us. "Tell the *Jäger* to stay here." The others were two *Attentäters*, one *Elite*, and one *Mörder*.

"Where to?"

"Don't tell them. Just say to match our course."

She processed what I was saying and began practising her speech. After a minute, she nodded. "I think I've got it."

"Try to sound like the captain of this vessel, if possible."

She put the headset on and clicked the mic. Her orders flowed out, sounding like fluent German. Then she stopped and leaned back, staring at me. "Done."

"You sounded like a natural."

"Only because I rehearsed. If I were to have a conversation, they'd figure out pretty damn—"

The comm beeped and her face froze. "Oh shit. They're asking . . ."

"What?"

She hesitated, listening. Then, "The *Jäger* is asking to use an active pulse to locate *Dark Winter*. I think."

I peered at the sonar. The vessel was slowing and falling from formation. "Give them the okay."

She nodded and said, "*Erlaubnis erteilt.*" Then she clicked off and looked at me. "Are you sure, Mac? Active searching will alert the USSF."

I smiled. "Precisely what I want. They already know we're here, anyway." I checked our speed. "We're not exactly running silent right now. I *want* the Fleet to know there are German warsubs en route to Seascape." I turned to Rico. "Take us around Florida and toward Seascape. Bring us close to Trieste, but not too close."

"What does that mean?"

"For the next stage of the plan." I turned back to Renée. "Can you raise Trieste?"

"Shouldn't be a problem, unless Johnny has destroyed all the junction boxes down here, too."

I snorted. I knew that was impossible. There were too many. He'd been able to do it up in the North Sea, but wouldn't have been able to keep it up for too long. Besides, he'd only had a few more drones.

She pushed some buttons on the comm and a second later waved me over. I put the headset on.

"Mac?" It was Zira Miller, at Trieste. "Is it really you?"

"It's me." I smiled, It was good to finally hear a familiar voice from home.

"Where the hell—"

"No time for that now. I need to know where Johnny is."

"He's still in *SC-1*. About 110 kilometers ahead of you. I can see you both on the map here."

She was referring to the large map of the Gulf and Caribbean in City Control. It had all vessels projected on it from the vast network of listening devices in the area. And Johnny was ahead of us, out of active sonar range, so the GSF subs wouldn't have known where he was. Clever.

"Thanks. I need to speak with Dr. Max Hyland."

"He's here, at Trieste?"

"In the Research Module, yes."

"One second."

I held my breath, waiting. I had given up on him following the destruction of our zircon mine in The Iron Plains, but if there was a chance . . .

"Hello, Mac? I haven't seen you in ages! Have you—"

I cut him off. "Max. I've been out of touch for a while. I'm sorry to tell you that we don't have a supply of the mineral you need. Someone destroyed our facility in the Pacific. We have to investigate to find out who did it."

"That's . . . unfortunate."

"Yes. But without giving away specifics, how is your work going?"

"Wonderful. I think I have a working device. We still have to test it, of course, but it seems—"

"Wait a minute." I paused, processing what he had said. Rico and Renée were both looking at me.

It felt odd, standing in the control cabin of that foreign submarine, in command of a German task force, forging into the Gulf of Mexico.

I said, "What did you just say?"

"I have one device, but not sure if it'll work."

"But how? I haven't given you any . . . *mineral*." I didn't want to say hafnium over the open comm.

"Well, I'm not saying it'll work, Mac. My experiments have gone well. But I did have some mineral from when I was in a proper lab on the mainland. I've been using it while waiting for your facility to provide more for me. What did you think I've been working on?"

"Well, I didn't know—"

"I have just a bit—a smear, really—but it'll be enough."

A grin spread across my face. "You're wonderful, Max."

"Why, thanks!" I could feel his excitement. "By the way, I did get out for a swim around the city. A woman I met in the entertainment district showed me around."

"How'd you like it?" I muttered. My mind was churning, not really paying attention. I was trying to figure out how to get him and his weapon on board *Black Widow*.

"It was fantastic! You were right. I love living underwater. I feel as though Trieste is my new home."

"You can bet on it," I mumbled. "Hold on a minute or two. I'm going to contact you with more instructions. Get the device ready."

"Are we going to test it now?"

"You could say that."

—••—

IN A MINUTE ZIRA HAD patched me through to Johnny. He sounded thrilled at my voice. I explained what had happened, and he said, "I figured as much. I stayed ahead of the warsub and took out as many comm junctions as I could, just to confuse them a bit. When they started on their way to Trieste, I figured you'd done it."

"I guess I kind of manipulated the captain. Angered her just enough to get her to sail south."

"Good job."

"I have something for you to do because *SC-1* is faster than us. You have to go to Trieste."

He listened to the instructions; I could feel his surprise through the comm line. Then he signed off, but not without a quick, "Good to have you back, Mac. I've been worried about you."

"Thanks, Johnny. See you soon."

Rico was staring at me. "I don't understand how you could forgive him after he tortured you."

I shrugged. "Life's too short."

Renée watched the exchange and seemed to understand immediately what was happening. She said to Rico, "I wanted to kill Mac for a whole year after what he did to me. Hunted him down, almost died trying to succeed. And you know what? I forgave him."

"Really? What did he do to you?" The notion shocked him.

"He fired on my warsub. I let him get too close. He killed a crewman, crippled my boat. I got demoted and blamed him for it."

"And you got past it?"

"I had to. It consumed me, Rico. Ruined my life."

He turned his back to us and marched to the VID screen where he could see the vessels around us. He wanted to be alone with his thoughts. But I noticed something interesting. His gun was not in its holster. His hand clenched it so hard his fingers were white.

Renée noticed, too. "Is he okay?" she whispered.

"I—" I trailed off. "Actually, I'm not sure. Heinrich has really affected him."

We both watched Rico for long moments, but he didn't turn around.

—••—

BLACK WIDOW FORGED THROUGH THE Atlantic just off the coast of Florida, rounding the southern tip and through the Straits of Florida, now much larger due to rising ocean levels. One of the GSF warsubs continued to veer off course; it had located *Dark Winter* and was en route to investigate.

The other four GSF warsubs stayed with us. We would pass within a hundred kilometers of Trieste, and continue toward Seascape.

And a massive confrontation.

I remembered how many USSF warsubs had gathered there.

It made me cringe with fear.

And they knew we were coming.

Something was prickling my scalp, and I continued to dwell on it. Rico was on my mind. He wouldn't speak with us, he was wound tightly, and he continued to hold the weapon as if he were ready to fire at a moment's notice.

As if he were expecting trouble.

As if he knew someone would—

The prickle on my scalp turned to a full-blown explosion of realization. My guts twisted and I stared at his back in fear.

"Renée," I hissed. "Watch him."

I darted out of the control cabin and sprinted toward the clinic. I opened the hatch. Inside, the smell hit me like a wall. It was a putrid mix of sweat, blood, urine, vomit, charred flesh, and ozone.

But that wasn't the worst.

I swore loudly as understanding hit.

Heinrich was gone.

Chapter Thirty-Two

RICO HAD *LOOSENED* HIS STRAPS, not tightened them as I'd asked.

He'd wanted Heinrich to escape.

And now we were in serious trouble. It put the entire mission in jeopardy.

I signaled Renée up forward and she answered in a split second. "Mac! Rico has gone aftward toward you. He wouldn't speak to—"

"Renée, check our prisoners in the officer's mess. Make sure they're still there."

"What's wrong? You don't think—"

"Heinrich is gone."

Silence met my statement. Then she swore. "Oh my god."

"Heinrich might try to release them. Go. Now. And be careful."

A voice behind me: "They're still there."

I whirled to see Rico, standing in the hatch. "What did you do?"

His face was hard. "I'm sorry, Mac. I can't do it. Can't get past it."

"You've put the whole mission in jeopardy. *Again.* Just to kill one man. We would have dealt with him later."

"I told you, I can't think about anything else."

I clenched my teeth. What Rico had done was unforgiveable. "You're a member of TCI. You're supposed to act for the good of the mission."

"This is my mission now. Once Heinrich is gone, then I'll—"

"That's not how this works!" I roared. "It's not to fulfill your needs. I know you went through hell, but I'm trying to see this mission through, dammit!"

"To save your sister, I get it. But maybe what I want is just as important."

My jaw dropped. "I've used the GSF involvement to bring two more ocean colonies into our alliance. The French cities. Soon New Berlin will join, as well. It's not just about Meg, but that's where we are now. It's about Seascape, too."

"My mission is important."

I clenched my fists at my side. "Rico, when this is over, you're out of TCI. You're done."

He stared at me, his face flat. "So be it, Mac. I can live with that."

I studied the determination in his expression. "He could be anywhere on the ship. He'll sabotage engineering most likely."

"Unless we stop him."

"What you've done is insane."

"If you say so." He checked the rounds in his gun and looked out into the hall. "Shall we?"

—••—

I WAS STUCK. THERE WAS no other choice but to follow his lead. We had to deal with Heinrich before anything else. If he somehow managed to stop our engines, the other GSF warsubs would realize something was going on. We wouldn't be able to explain it easily.

But why didn't Johnny just kill him? Why let him escape?

Maybe he had a conscience after all, and couldn't kill a defenceless man.

Whatever the case, Rico wasn't behaving rationally.

We moved into the corridor, and stealthily moved aftward, toward engineering. Soon we were at the ladder, and Rico gestured down.

I knew the layout of the ship, however; there was another ladder on the other side of engineering, closer to the stern. I pointed and Rico nodded. I continued toward it while Rico descended.

—••—

I CREPT DOWN THE LADDER into engineering. The sounds of the screws whistled in the air and the powerful electric motors—driven by a new generation of batteries that held a charge for weeks at a time and drove the screws with incredible force—buzzed with power as they drove the twin shafts. Each screw turned in opposite directions to maintain course, and both were still operating smoothly.

Thankfully.

Heinrich hadn't been able to stop us.

Yet.

But he was here, somewhere.

There was a haze of smoke in the air, though; thin wisps here rising up the ladderwell.

My stomach dropped.

Something had happened in engineering.

The ladder was steep, the rungs thin and, as I descended, thick hands reached out, grabbed my ankles, and pulled with tremendous force. My feet went out from under me and I fell forward, down the ladder and landed heavily onto the deck's steel grating. I barely got my arms out in front of me to protect my head and face. The gun skittered across the deck.

I scrambled to my feet but was moving slower than I was used to. The last few days had taken a lot out of me. A pair of arms wrapped around my neck and head.

I spun savagely to the side and struck an elbow behind me. It connected and I heard a grunt. Changing direction abruptly, I did the same on the other side, then ducked and slipped through his arms. Whirling, I swung my right foot up in an arc designed to knock teeth out.

But he'd ducked back, crouched, and faced me with a sick grin on his face.

We circled each other slowly. "You came to the wrong boat," he growled in his thick accent.

"Apparently. For you."

"We'll see."

Normally he'd be no match for me; I could have killed him quickly. I had the benefit of a lifetime of training for these exact conditions, and many cases of actually being in similar situations. But I was exhausted. My limbs ached. My body was weak and not behaving as it usually did. Pain seared through my thigh; I'd popped my stitches, and blood was pouring down my leg.

He moved in and I swung an elbow and stepped to the side. I connected with his jaw and it snapped his head back. But it didn't daze him; he countered and I didn't move fast enough. His fist crushed my nose and I fell back to the deck. He stood there, watching me, smiling once again.

"*Wie hat dir das gefallen?*"

I pushed myself back to my feet, exhausted and trembling with fatigue. Shit. I lowered my head and stood, deflated, as if I didn't want to fight.

He stepped in again, his face rigid with anger and pent-up rage, and swung—

I ducked under his fist and launched an uppercut at his chin. I jumped as I did so, putting every bit of energy I had into the strike. My knuckles connected and his head jerked back. He stumbled and fell, landing heavily on the deck.

I was gasping and could barely stand. My lungs heaved as I struggled to bring in enough air to keep me going.

Dimly, I realized the smell of smoke was growing thicker.

—••—

"WHAT DID YOU DO?" I gasped.

He only bared his teeth—now covered in thick, red, mucous-laden blood—and stared back at me. Some of them were broken and I felt strangely satisfied by that.

"Rico!" I yelled. "Back here!"

I heard his steps behind me; he'd been searching engineering and hadn't made it back this far toward the stern. He drew up next to me and stood, staring at Heinrich.

I glanced around. "There's a fire somewhere. Locate it. I'll deal with him."

"No."

I stared at him, stunned. "Rico, don't do this."

"I have to take care of this."

"He's done. I'll tie him up here. Give it a rest now. Find the fire."

"I said, no."

Rico Ruiz had lost all sense of what was going on around him. Nothing else mattered to him at that moment. Whatever he'd been through during his year on *Black Widow*, it had culminated in this, and he wasn't going to stop until Heinrich was dead.

A flurry of thoughts flooded my brain. I could protect Heinrich or I could save the ship. I didn't really have a choice.

I lowered my weapon and stepped back, staring at Rico's hard expression and his eyes, which were laser-focused on the man at our feet. His expression was grim.

I turned and bolted toward the smoke.

—••—

HEINRICH HAD DOUSED A BANK of batteries with an accelerant—kerosene?—and had set it on fire. He'd meant to start a chemical reaction that would put the engines out of commission, shut down our power, and cripple the entire vessel. Luckily the flames hadn't spread past the outer battery shield. I found an extinguisher and sprayed it across the flames. There was an alarm ringing in the ship, and it meant real trouble for us. The other GSF subs had likely heard it and would be wondering what was going on.

The smoke was thick now, and I was gasping and coughing. I vomited on the deck, but only bile came out. My stomach was otherwise empty. I stumbled to the bulkhead comm. I punched it and signaled the control cabin. It took a moment but Renée finally answered.

"Go ahead!" she yelled over the noise.

"Cut the alarm. I've stopped the fire."

"I'm searching the controls."

"Then contact the other warsubs. Tell them it was a minor fire and we've dealt with it. Tell them to stay on course."

"Got it."

I leaned against the bulkhead and took several ragged breaths. I was on the edge of consciousness. I needed sleep badly. Rest. My body was on fire.

Dimly, I grew aware of the sound of a struggle in engineering. I dragged myself over and stared at Rico standing over Heinrich, his arms around his neck, as he crushed the life out of the man.

Heinrich's body was twitching.

It was over.

"Rico," I said. No answer. He continued to squeeze the man's neck. Rico's face was a mask of effort and rage. Sweat beaded his forehead. I said again, "Rico."

Finally, he met my gaze and released the body. He rose slowly to his feet, smoke swirling around him.

"You put us all at risk."

"It's over now," he whispered, staring at the corpse at his feet.

I watched him, sad, understanding that he was wrong. It would never be over for him now.

He'd likely never get past this moment, and it would haunt him forever.

Chapter Thirty-Three

RICO SLUMPED AGAINST THE LADDER and stared at the body on the deck. He was breathing heavily.

I shook my head. Heinrich could have killed us all. Scuttled the ship. The fire could have prevented us from completing the mission. Hell, the alarms may have alerted the other GSF warsubs to severe problems on *Black Widow* and might still prevent us from finishing what we'd started.

I just couldn't believe what Rico had done.

Hate consumed him.

He couldn't be a part of TCI. I just couldn't trust the man anymore. I'd given him a chance at moving on, and he'd thrown it away and put everything at risk. Perhaps I'd made a mistake trusting him, but I'd have to live with what had happened.

"When this is all over, you're done."

"You already told me that. I have to accept it."

"Should I drop you off now? Make you swim to Trieste?"

He sighed. "I can understand if you want me gone. But no. I'll help with the mission."

"And I'm supposed to trust you?"

He exhaled. "Yes. Now you can. I couldn't think clearly before."

"And you think this will solve everything?" I snorted. "It's only just begun for you, Rico."

He frowned. "What do you mean by that?"

I waved his question away and marched up the ladder.

It was too late to explain.

—••—

RENÉE MET ME ON THE bridge. I'd stopped to grab some bandages and material for new stitches—the sight of the clinic sent waves of anxiety and rage coursing through my body, which I had to smother—and I was hoping Renée would help me take care of the open incision on my thigh. Worry painted her face, but I waved her concern aside. "It's okay. Heinrich is gone. The boat is ours."

"And Rico?"

I grunted. That was a different issue. "He's . . . " I trailed off, not knowing what to say. "He is not the person I'd hoped."

"What did he do?"

"Intentionally released him."

Her jaw dropped. "But why? That's—"

"Insane? Probably. He wanted an excuse to kill the man."

"But that put the whole mission at risk. Why not just leave him tied up for now?"

"Maybe he couldn't bring himself to kill a defenceless man. Maybe he needed an excuse to track him down on board and murder him." It made me pause, for the similarities with my family and Admiral Benning were clear. But Meg hadn't hunted her victim; she had *lured* him to her cubicle, where she had stabbed him to death.

And now here I was, trying to save her, while at the same time criticizing Rico for what he'd done.

I checked the sonar and our navigation charts. We were still rounding Florida's coast. Soon Johnny would be meeting us, and I had no idea what to tell the other GSF warsubs when the rendezvous occurred.

Renée sat at the communications console to process the news. It had stunned her. After a while, she looked up at me. "I can understand a thing or two about obsession."

"I remember."

"But I learned to get over it."

"Help stitch me up?" I held the first aid kit toward her. She grabbed the needle and thread and eyed my open incision. She poked the needle through my skin and began stitching.

I watched as she expertly knotted each stitch together. "But your whole life changed because of what I did."

She stopped and put a hand on my arm. "Truman, you made me rethink things. I identified with your struggle. I love living underwater, exploring the depths, making a new home for humanity. God knows the Earth needs it right now. The people topside need our help."

"And you saw that my way was better than what the superpowers were doing."

"Of course. It's why I'm here with you. Why I'm with Trieste."

I sensed something else in what she was saying. "But?" I added for her.

She sighed. "But, it's hard. I've left behind everyone I knew. My entire family lives topside, in France. They're suffering because but they think I'm dead. The FSF believes I died in the battle at The Ridge a few months ago."

I nodded. She was referring to The Third Battle of Trieste. "You haven't contacted them?"

"No. I've thought about it, but I don't want them to notify the Fleet that I'm still alive. They'll hunt me."

"Ah."

"But what's happening between us is something I want to explore. I want to continue."

"Me, too, Renée. I love being around you."

Her eyes grew harder and she stopped stitching. "I enjoy our physical relationship, Mac. But I don't want to be just a *fuck friend*, if that's the correct term."

I eyed the sonar, wondering if this was the correct time and place to be having the discussion. "I can live with that."

"But I do want more." Then she looked back at the wound and jabbed the needle through a ragged flap of skin.

I repositioned myself as she worked. Bruises, welts, cuts, and burns covered every inch of me. I ached everywhere. "I've had a hard time since Kat died. I've enjoyed your company. But—"

"But what?"

"I've realized something about myself recently, too. When dealing with traumatic situations, I tend to close myself off to relationships. I use sex as a means to avoid intimacy, if that makes sense."

She smiled. "It makes total sense. And I'm proud of you!"

I blinked. "For what? For realizing that I used you?"

"No, for realizing what's hurting you."

"I've been hurting for decades, Renée. Since the CIA killed my dad."

"Yes, but understanding where your pain comes from is the first step to recovery."

"You sound like I'm an alcoholic or something."

"In a way, maybe you are."

"Huh?"

"You're addicted to the quest, Mac. You're obsessed with Oceania. You can't think about anything else. It's all you want in the world."

"I'm doing it *for* the world. And for the people who live in the colonies."

"Perhaps. But your dad wanted it, too, and you're just following in his footsteps, aren't you?"

"His legacy. Yes, of course I am. I fought against it for years, then I realized that it's the only way we can survive as a species. We have to exist in the oceans to extract the resources without harming them. The superpowers don't care. But if the colonists do it, at least we'll be more careful."

"But you've killed countless people. Sunk submarines. Entire warsubs. Started wars."

"With a positive end in mind."

She stared at me. "Mac. Of course I agree with you. It's why I'm here. But you have to open yourself up to human relationships. Don't let your drive affect you so."

"The people expect it from me. They want me to achieve independence for Trieste."

"Sure they do. It means selling our products around the world, earning more money, making life a little bit easier. But don't kill yourself doing it. Don't sacrifice your happiness for it."

"I'll be happy once I achieve Oceania."

She grabbed my hands and stared directly into my eyes. "There's no reason why you can't be happy now. You already have eleven colonies in your alliance. That's something to be proud of. You've defeated major powers in battle. We're about to go attempt another crazy plan of yours. And still you're not happy."

"I was happy, until Kat died. Because of—" I choked off what I'd been about to say.

"Because of what?" Renée said. "You blame yourself?"

"I—I—" I couldn't answer, and suddenly my eyes grew blurry.

"Mac." Her voice was stern. "Katherine Wells is the one who wanted all of this. She invented the SCAV drive to lead Trieste in war. It was her intention all along. How can you possibly blame yourself for it? She's dragged you into it, not the other way around!"

"But I led the battle in the Mid-Atlantic Ridge. It was my plan."

"She knew what she was doing. There's no way she would ever blame you for what happened. Her control console exploded! A French torpedo did it! Not you."

I couldn't speak. Renée just held my hand and watched me. Then she said, "You really loved her."

"Yes, I did." She was the first and only person I'd loved in that way. I'd pushed my emotions aside when my dad died. But strangely, once I embraced his ideals and embarked on the same path, I'd found love.

But I stared at Renée now, and my heart was thudding. I felt the same with her now. And I knew one thing about myself above all else: I couldn't lose

Renée.

But her eyes were somber, accepting, and she pulled her hand away. "I understand."

"No, Renée, you don't. I've been obsessed—maybe *possessed*—by this struggle. That'll never stop. But I realized something during this episode with Rico. I can't be like him. I can't let my rage consume me. It happened after the Chinese released me, too."

"After the torture?"

"The emotional effects never end. They filled my life. It lasted for seven years! Then I found Johnny, and tried to kill him for it. But . . . but I just couldn't bring myself to do it. Instead I forgave him, Renée, and ever since I've been happier."

Her brow furrowed. "What are you saying?"

"I know that hiding your pain doesn't work. Pushing it down, concealing it, burying it. Whatever. It's still there. It still affects you. Affects everything you do. It's why I buried Kat's body in the Mid-Atlantic Ridge. I pushed her corpse into the airlock and flushed her out as deep as we could go." I remembered how my sister had looked at me during the funeral. She knew what I'd been doing. But Meg had done the same thing. She'd buried her anger at Admiral Benning, but it had boiled up and put us all in this situation, and now she was at Seascape, a prisoner, and it might derail all of our plans for Oceania.

I took a deep breath and continued, "I know I have to stop burying things. I have to just deal with them."

Renée eyed me again. "And how will you do that?"

I shook my head and stared at the deck. "I seriously don't know. But I do know this, I want you to be happy. You've sacrificed everything for our colony. For the movement. And I don't want you to feel alone."

"I have friends."

"But you don't have family."

"Maybe they're one in the same, Mac." And she smiled. Then she looked away and her face flattened. "But I can tell you're not ready for it. You need time to recover still. I need to leave you, to let you decide for yourself." And she drew in a breath and sighed.

I opened my mouth to speak and—

An alarm sounded.

The sonar screen indicated a vessel on a collision course with us. It had entered our passive range of thirty kilometers and the computer had recognized the danger.

Renée peered at the readout. "It's *SC-1*. Johnny and your prisoner, Franz."

I offered her a tight grin. "And one other person, with a surprise."

Interlude:
Meagan McClusky

```
Location:        Latitude:    28° 41' 24" N
Longitude:       94° 54' 5" W
                 The Gulf of Mexico, Seascape City,
                 USSF HQ
Depth:           30 meters
Date:            17 August 2130
Time:            2223 hours
```

MEG PACED THE CELL, RESTLESS. The incision on her thigh had been far from clean—the edges were torn and ragged—but she'd been able to stitch it closed. It wasn't pretty. Now she held the weapon in her right hand—*The Tube*—and practised how she would use it. Soon the guards would take her to see Zyvinski again, and Meg knew she'd have to act.

Mac was on his way in a GSF warsub—*how'd he arrange that?*—and there could only be one reason for the subterfuge: to deflect suspicion from himself and perhaps drag Germany into the conflict with the USSF. Meg would have to play into that plan here, and perhaps help it along, before she made her escape.

She hoped Reggie would come through for her.

She cut off the thought before it could go further. There was no use thinking about it. Mac was still hours from Seascape, and Meg needed a place to run before he made the attempt. If there was no place to go, then this would be the shortest prison break in history.

The Tube fit nicely against her inner thigh, and she'd used strips of her blanket to hold it in place. It was a makeshift holster. The problem was that the guards tied her to the chair in the interrogation cabin, which would make it impossible to grab the weapon and escape. She could only do it before they restrained her, or after the session when they released her.

She had to be ready.

—••—

THE GUARDS CAME HOURS LATER. As they dragged her through the corridor toward Zyvinski and the chamber, she got a glimpse through a viewport. It was dark outside. Probably close to midnight.

She took a deep breath and steeled herself for this. Her body was in agony. Every limb hurt. Her fingers were swollen and she had trouble moving them. Stitching herself up had been a *nightmare*. Her abdomen ached from previous strikes. She was starving and had lost a lot of weight in the past weeks.

She wondered absently if Reggie had relayed the message to Cliff.

"Tell him what you told me!" she'd said, meaning tell Cliff that Mac was on his way in a GSF warsub. It was time to remove the weapon, and get ready to make a run for it.

A *swim for it*, actually.

The guards opened the hatch and threw her inside. She barely kept her balance; she stumbled and almost fell, but the steel chair bolted to the deck kept her upright. She gasped; she'd collided with the chair and it had dug into her stomach. The guards shoved her down and tightened the restraints.

Zyvinski was there, flipping through a magazine nonchalantly. She didn't even look at Meg. She said, "Welcome back. I take it you don't have anything to say to me yet?"

"What do you want me to say?"

"You want to tell me about your secret facility, the deep-diving drive, the—"

"I don't know anything about all that. I don't even know what you're referring to, for the millionth time."

"Too bad, because Cliff told us all about it."

Meg snorted. "Funny. You told me he was dead."

Zyvinski sighed. "I thought he was. Turned out he'd just passed out."

"Sure."

"But he told us about your secret base in the Mid-Atlantic Ridge."

"Right."

"The French Submarine Fleet is searching the area right now."

"What are they looking for?"

"Apparently they lost a bunch of warsubs."

"Strange."

"We did, too, you know. Ninety-eight, to be precise."

"Really."

"Yes. We assumed the Russian dreadnought destroyed them, but Admiral Quintana is having second thoughts about that."

"I don't know anything."

Zyvinksi finally looked up from the magazine. "I'm not sure how much longer I can keep you alive. People want answers for these things. Your body might not be able to withstand many more sessions with me."

"Perhaps not."

"If only you'd answer my questions."

"It's hard when I don't know the answers. I can't make shit up."

"Why did you return to Trieste after living in Blue Downs?"

"I reconciled with my brother. Trieste is my home."

"Did it shake you up when Russia destroyed the Australian colony?"

"Of course. Almost everyone I knew there is dead."

"And you hate Russia for it."

"Yes."

"And what do you want to do to them because of it?"

Meg frowned. "I already did it. I was on the mission to the dreadnought. I helped take it down."

"With Admiral Benning's help."

"He was there, yes."

"Then you ended up killing him, only days after the mission."

"I admitted it."

"Do you have any other plans for Russia?"

"What do you mean?"

"Other vessels, other weapons?"

"Not that I know of."

"But we saw your deep-diving seacars during that battle. Where are they now?"

"Why don't you ask my brother? You left him at Trieste. I don't know anything about them."

"Yes, we will. No worries about that."

"What does that mean?"

"We intend to bring him here. Soon."

Meg laughed. "You left him there because you're scared what 200,000 Triestrians will do if you kidnap him."

"*Arrest* him, with good reason."

"Right."

"We could just occupy the city again."

"That would go over well."

"Why would I care, Meagan?" She sighed and leaned back.

Meg stared at her, wondering if she would get another chance. Probably not. She said, "I've heard there is a German Submarine Fleet attack force en route right now. Why is that?"

Zyvinski's reaction was immediate. Her expression went rigid. "How do you know about that?"

"Someone told me. Am I in danger here?"

"Why do you care? You're always in danger, regardless. Sooner or later the sessions will kill you."

"But why are the Germans coming here?"

"It's not really your business, but they're concerned about a vessel of theirs that sank off the coast of Florida. That's all."

"They think the USSF did it?"

Zyvinski chortled. "Right. Why would they think such a thing? We have no issue with them."

"Apparently they have one with you."

"Why would you say that?"

"Because the vessels are coming *here*. Not to their sunken boat."

Zyvinski frowned and looked away. "How could you possibly know that? I don't even know that."

Meg shrugged. "I just heard. A guard mentioned it, I think. I can't remember. It's hard to remember things here."

"Did one of you say this to her?" she snapped at the two guards.

"No, ma'am," both said in stereo.

Zyvinski stared at Meg. "I think we need to teach you a lesson about lying." She gestured at Meg, and both guards stepped toward her, brandishing their clubs.

Meg gritted her teeth. *This is the last session*, she reminded herself. Then it ends.

—••—

IT WENT ON FOR HOURS. Meg passed out several times from blows to the head or the pain lancing through her body.

But something interesting did happen: Zyvinski stepped out with her PCD in hand.

Who was she calling?

Meg smiled to herself tightly. She'd planted the seed. Now to see if it would grow.

—••—

MEG'S BODY WAS LIMP. THE guards grabbed her arms and hauled her to her feet, as had happened multiple times every day for weeks. They were used to this now. Meg would be limp all the way back to the cell, where they would throw her in until the next session.

But this time was different.

As they hauled her up, the restraining straps falling away, she pushed herself back and pretended to fall to the deck against the bulkhead with a heavy thud.

She dug her hand under her leg, as if she had twisted it in the fall.

She scrabbled at The Tube, pulling it out from the makeshift holster.

A guard grabbed her under the armpits and pulled her up—

She spun, placed The Tube under his chin, and hammered on the trigger with her other hand.

There was a sharp *pop!* and the top of his head exploded.

Blood sprayed behind him and splattered across the desk. His beating heart continued to pump, and an arterial gush spewed across the deck as his body fell in a heap.

The other guard watched, not quite understanding what he'd just witnessed. He hesitated—

And Meagan stepped toward him, turned The Tube, and pressed the trigger again.

A hole opened in his torso, and he glanced down, still not comprehending what was happening.

Blood poured down his sky-blue uniform, crimson streaks dripping down his pantlegs and onto his boots. Meg adjusted her aim and pressed the trigger with her left palm again. There was another pop and the bullet entered his brain through his right eye socket. His other eye dilated immediately, looked off into the distance over her shoulder, and his head snapped back and hit the bulkhead. He slumped down, a bloody streak mixed with gray brain on the steel behind him.

Meg turned to Zyvinski, who opened her mouth to scream.

Meg slowly turned the weapon around, triggering the blade. She stepped toward the other woman.

"Where did you get that?" she snapped, not fully understanding that she only had seconds of life remaining.

"Doesn't really matter, does it, bitch?"

"You wouldn't—"

"Don't even ask that question." Meg stepped toward the other, her face a mask of rage and hate. "I need your clothing. I don't want it covered in blood, though. Now take it off."

Zyvinski's hands trembled as she unhooked the clasps and removed it.

It bought her a bit of time.

But not much.

Meg didn't have a lot of experience with violence. She'd definitely had more since returning to Trieste and joining her brother—especially in naval battles—but killing someone you could see up close was another matter entirely. The ease with which she'd killed Benning had surprised her, but she'd had good reason to do so.

And now, she had another good reason. At that particular moment in time, she didn't really care about violence.

She'd kill everyone in her path to escape that city.

And at that moment, Zyvinksi was standing in her way.

Meg plunged the blade into her neck. Zyvinski stared back in disbelief, her eyes bulging in horrific realization.

Meg hissed, "These are the last moments of your life. My brother's on his way, and this place is going down. I wish I could drag this out the way you dragged it out for me, but sadly, I have to leave now. *Time for you to die.*"

Zyvinski tried to speak, but only bloody gurgles came out.

Meg twisted the knife, shredding the artery. Blood was spilling down Zyvinski's chest now, and Meg stepped back, watching her struggle to breathe. She collapsed on the table, blood pooling under her head.

Her body convulsed for two more minutes before it finally grew still.

—••—

MEAGAN KNEW THERE WASN'T MUCH time. The cabin was gruesome: three dead bodies and blood everywhere. She threw her clothes off and pulled Zyvinski's on. She'd lost so much weight that they hung off her, even though Zyvinski had been skinny. But appearances were everything here. She hoped people would just take a glance at her and then look away, not realizing that she was actually an escaping prisoner. She just had to make it down a few levels to the moonpool, then she'd strip them off and exchange with a wetsuit.

She peered out into the corridor.

There was no one there.

She took a deep breath and searched the guards to see if they had any weapons she could take. The Tube only held three bullets, and she'd used them all. Each guard had a gun in a holster, as well as a knife, and she took one of each. She also kept The Tube strapped to her thigh, once again using the strips of cloth to secure it in place.

She also found a set of keys on a clasp.

She stepped into the hall and walked with confidence toward her cell. She knew Cliff's was just a few hatches down from hers, and she needed to try to free him.

There was no one in the hallway. She peered into each cell until she found his.

She opened it.

Cliff was inside, sitting in a corner, staring at her. Realization dawned on his features, and his jaw dropped.

Then he stood, and Meagan saw the incision on his thigh.

He had a Tube in his hand.

"Ready to go?" she asked him.

He grinned through his swollen face. Teeth were missing.

—••—

THE CORRIDORS WERE BARREN. THEIR footsteps echoed around them as they marched toward the ladder leading down.

Cliff only had his prisoner's outfit, and he looked disastrous. Bruised, bloody, beaten . . . but despite that, he held himself with authority and any doubts she'd had about him being able to withstand the interrogation quickly disappeared.

He'd weathered the storm easily, and he'd been on the verge of making his own escape.

He, too, had spoken to Reggie, who had promised scuba gear at the moonpool.

They arrived on the lowest deck and approached the opening. Water lapped against the edges. It was an unguarded escape into the ocean.

Freedom.

She glanced around. There was no one else there.

An alarm began to hammer out.

"Oh, shit," she muttered.

She searched for the scuba gear.

There was nothing.

Reggie had betrayed them.

—••—

CLIFF AND MEG BOTH STOOD on the edge of the deck, looking into the water below. The alarm continued to blare, and now they could hear feet pounding from the corridor. Guards yelled to one another.

There was no other choice.

They dove into the water, without tanks, masks, wetsuits, or weight belts.

Part Eight:
Experiment's End

Chapter Thirty-Four

SC-1 APPROACHED *BLACK WIDOW* SLOWLY, silently. We didn't want to show our hand to the USSF, but we needed the rendezvous to set the final stage of the plan in motion. The other GSF subs would be able to watch the meeting happen, and no doubt wonder what was going on and why we were stopping to communicate with a mysterious civilian seacar.

We slowed to a full stop, made our depth thirty meters, and opened the war-sub's moonpool hatch. Renée and I stood over the water as a shadowy shape approached *Black Widow*.

Johnny Chang.

Following close behind was another figure, and he hauled himself over the lip, onto the steel deck, and he turned to face me. He pulled off his mask and grinned.

Dr. Max Hyland.

I shook his hand. "Welcome aboard."

He looked around him as he brushed his dark hair back and wiped seawater from his face. "Thanks, Mac. Good to be here."

"Tell me, how has your research progressed?"

"Wonderfully! Really, you've provided the most incredible lab with all the equipment I could have asked for. I've replicated my earlier experiments with ease."

As I recalled, his peers had, for the most part, been unable to do the same. Or, they had been unwilling to even try for fear of the scientific community blacklisting them. A few had indeed proven his concept, but had not published due to the same fears.

"And you have a working explosive?"

"I hope! Can't tell for sure until the test. We've equipped them in torpedoes. Two of them. They're over in the seacar right now, along with another man.

Your Deputy Mayor has restrained him for some reason."

That was Franz, the German special forces operative.

"He's part of the plan," I supplied. "He tried to kill me earlier."

"Ah." Hyland shook his head as he stared at the water below. "Weird life you live, Mac."

"Hazards of sea life, I guess." I smiled.

"What nation is he from?"

"Germany. They tried to assassinate us."

"Which is why you're now in a German warsub. I get it." He shook his head again and smiled to himself. "And the other subs?"

"They're just along for the ride." Then something he'd said clicked. "Wait a minute. You said *two torpedoes*. I thought you only had enough hafnium for one?"

His Isomer Bomb had intrigued me from the minute I'd first read the story. In some rare atoms, called *nearly stable*, nucleons existed at higher energy levels than their normal counterparts. Over time, these isomers slowly released that energy to return to their 'ground state.' But according to Hyland, a burst of X-rays could potentially trigger the release of energy all at once. It would be a nuclear-sized explosion, but in a non-nuclear package. Most scientists ridiculed the idea of an Isomer Bomb, but Max had proven his idea, and the scientific community just didn't want to believe it.

After today, they'd have to.

The fact that DARPA had invested funding for it told me that there had to be some truth to the concept, which is why I'd pursued the doctor, the originator behind the idea and the initial experiment.

The mineral Max had settled on was a hafnium isomer—178m2 Hf. Extremely rare and expensive to produce, our mine was supposed to have been the production facility for it, because hafnium existed in natural deposits of zircon. Mining zircon was a cover for the real purpose. The CSF—*maybe*—had destroyed our facility, but Max still had some hafnium left for one bomb.

But now he was telling me he had two.

"Actually, no," he said.

'But you just said—"

"Remember, the device needs a trigger. In this case an X-ray bomb."

Realization dawned. "Ah. So the first will send a burst of X-rays—"

"Which will then cause the real device to explode. The hafnium bomb."

"Got it."

"The torpedoes are tethered together. Electronically, that is. They'll stay in close proximity until the Primary detonates, and then—" he clapped his hands together "—*BOOM!* The Secondary goes up, and that'll be the big one."

"How does the X-ray Primary work?"

He shrugged. "Simple. Powerful batteries generate electrons from the cathode. They slam into a slab of tungsten and immediately slow. The process is called *Bremsstrahlung*, or 'braking radiation.'"

I frowned. "A German term?"

He glanced at the bulkheads surrounding us. "A fitting coincidence, wouldn't you say?"

"Definitely." I snorted. "So the electrons slow . . . ?"

"Rapidly slow, or brake. And as they do so, they release heat and X-rays. Ninety-nine percent of the energy is heat, which is why we use tungsten."

"Why?"

"Because it has a high melting point. The other 1% becomes X-rays."

"Which will penetrate your Isomer Bomb and trigger the hafnium."

He shrugged. "If my experiments are correct. I think I've planned for the right energy level."

"I don't understand."

"Of X-rays. There are varying levels. In this case, it depends on the wavelength, how far away the Secondary is, the density of the casing, the—"

"Next time, Max," I said. "Fill me in when it's all over."

"In the future I will try to make sure the torpedo contains both the Primary and the Secondary, but these prototypes were just too big to fit into one."

Johnny said, "And the weapons will originate from a GSF warsub, pulling all suspicion away from Trieste."

"That's the plan."

The others stared at me.

"It's incredible," Renée said, "but how do you intend to stay alive while rescuing your sister and security officer?"

"I'm hoping they'll get themselves out, actually. You see, I gave them a little advantage before Zyvinski arrested them." I told them about the weapons we'd surgically implanted, and their eyes grew wider. "There's also a tracking mechanism there."

"But it doesn't trigger any alarms?" Renée asked.

"The weapon is ceramic. Not durable, but also not detectable. The tracer activates only on a signal from us. Until then, it doesn't give off anything."

"So we'll be able to find them. If they've escaped," Johnny said.

"Exactly."

Silence descended over us as we stood around the moonpool. Hyland still had a grin on his dimpled face. For him, he was about to witness the culmination of his life's work. Topside, he'd been blacklisted. His career had stalled. The academic community had mocked him.

And then I had called.

Given him a second chance at life, so to speak.

He was going to find out if his theories could become reality.

We brought both devices into *Black Widow*, through the moonpool. We used cables and a winch to haul the torpedoes up through the opening and into the warsub. Then onto the system that moved torpedoes about the ship safely, and we transported them into the torpedo room at the boat's bow. Easier said than done; the entire operation took several hours.

We transported Franz over, too—also through the moonpool—and when he emerged dripping wet, rage cascaded across his features when he saw me standing there, in a German warsub.

"What the hell are you doing!?" he roared.

"It's almost time," I said in a soft tone. "You've been a good sport. Now it's almost over."

"A good sport? What the hell does that mean? You kidnapped me—"

"After you attacked Trieste and tried to kill me."

"—and held me, tied up, for nearly two weeks!"

"You're lucky you're not dead, Franz."

"And now you've hijacked a German vessel?"

I shrugged. "I admit to it all. But you're not dead, and you haven't really suffered, have you?"

"You tied me up!"

I lifted my shirt and showed him the network of scars and wounds across my torso. "Real torture looks like this. It's what your people did to me."

His face grew slack as he stared at the injuries. "They caught you?"

I shrugged. "For a bit. But I got away."

He didn't know what to say. He just stared at me. Then, "So what are we doing now?"

"We're going to attack USSF Headquarters."

His brow crinkled and he just kept staring.

I continued, "This is what you wanted, right? Revenge? Well, today you're going to get it."

"Not at the USSF. At Trieste."

I feigned ignorance. "Isn't it the same thing?"

"No. What about all your talk? About Oceania and fighting the superpowers?"

"What about it?"

"You told me about living peacefully in the oceans, not exploiting them for the good of topsiders."

"Sure. It's still my plan."

"So why attack the USSF?"

"They oppress us. Every superpower does. Germany, too. But today, this is my target."

He looked away. "I don't think the GSF would approve."

"They wanted you to send a message, right? Not to interfere with New Berlin."

"Yes. But that was you, Triestrian. Don't try to equate yourself with the USSF."

"But I'm American. You failed with me. Now we're going to try against my superiors."

My statements confused him. "What? I don't understand. Were you acting under American orders?"

"Of course we were," I lied.

"And your talk of independence?"

"This is a part of it."

He eyed me for a long moment. Then he squared his shoulders. "I want none of this. No part."

"I kept you alive for this."

"So now you'll kill me?"

"No. You're still coming with us. But I want you to know my motive."

He scowled. "You're not making any sense. Are you letting me go, then?"

I looked around. "I'll give you this GSF warsub back in a few hours. For now, you can wait in a cabin." Johnny took over and directed him down the corridor, toward the cabin where the warsub's crew had held Renée.

Then I turned and walked away. My insides were hollow, for I knew what it meant.

—••—

RICO WAS STILL WITH US, though he was now solemn and somber. He was not very communicative, he was keeping to himself, and he would only respond to questions in one- or two-word answers. I knew that he was suffering from the effects of his experience, and I decided to leave him alone for the time being. I was keeping an eye on him—to prevent him from disobeying orders again—but he really had nothing to do but sit around and wait, so that's what he did. I could tell he felt terrible for disobeying me, and now he had to deal with the guilt for that, as well as for what he'd done to Heinrich.

I'd tried to help him.

—••—

THE FOUR OTHER GSF WARSUBS had matched our course and velocity, which meant they'd stopped and waited while *SC-1* pulled up under us and we transferred personnel and the two weapons. To say the events confused them would be a massive understatement. Within minutes they were calling and asking just what the hell was going on.

I knew this was crucial. We needed them with us as we forged toward Seascape. If they broke off and returned to the *Dark Winter* wreck, my plan would still work, but it would appear less likely than an all-out GSF attack on Seascape. It would seem more of a rogue vessel with a vendetta.

Renée answered their calls and attempted to placate them. She told them we had an injury from the earlier fire and Trieste had offered to take the injured man in for treatment. It seemed like a believable story, and the communication officers on the other warsubs appeared to buy it. We had an open line between all five of the GSF warsubs, and Renée told the story as she'd rehearsed. I hoped they wouldn't detect her French accent or ask her questions for which we had no answer. Just in case, she'd rehearsed several paragraphs of German. One such example was:

"Command has ordered us to advance to the American colony Seascape, now USSF HQ. We're going to impress upon them never to attempt to interfere with a German undersea city again, as they did with New Berlin, or a GSF warsub, as they did with Dark Winter. *There will be no firing of any weapons. Our mission is to send a message only."*

Another was:

*"*Black Widow *is leading this group of ships to defend the GSF against American aggression in German waters. Their incursion at New Berlin and the firing on* Thorn Spider *and* Wolf Spider *are examples. But as per GSF orders, there will be no firing of any weapons. Our mission is to send a message only. Remember that these Americans also sank our vessel off the coast of Florida. Command does not want to sit back and do nothing. Make sure your crew is prepared for aggression should the USSF initiate hostilities."*

And:

"These USSF boats sank Dark Winter *and attacked us in the North Sea. They have also interfered with our colony, New Berlin. Command has ordered us to send a message to them never again interfere with us, and today we're going to do that. Remember to prepare for battle, though it is a last resort, and only if fired upon."*

A flurry of responses eventually returned, wondering why Trieste was not the target, and Renée answered each with her practiced response: "Wir folgen Bestellungen. Jetzt Funkstille einhalten."

We are following orders.

I knew the Germans as a culture respected, above all else, instructions from those in charge. It was a driving force for the people, and it was the right thing to say to the other warsubs. One by one their comms fell silent, and the warsubs continued with us, on course, for Seascape.

Toward the inevitable confrontation.

I swallowed past a lump in my throat.

Chapter Thirty-Five

IT WAS A 1,600 KILOMETER journey from the wreck of *Dark Winter* to Seascape. At sixty kph, it meant twenty-six hours. Stopping to take on Max Hyland, the prisoner Franz, and two torpedoes had delayed us by three hours, but we were back on course for USSF's HQ.

Within a few hours of resuming our mission, Seascape signaled for our intentions.

They knew there was a cluster of GSF warsubs on course for them. Johnny had also fed this information to Reggie Quinn, who I was sure had somehow relayed it to Admiral Quintana. They knew we were coming, and would search for logical explanations.

But there were none.

It was a suicide mission.

I recalled the collection of warsubs that had moved to the colony when they took over. Grant Bell in Sea Traffic Control back at Trieste had listed them.

Thirty *Houston* Class warsubs.

Twenty *Cyclones*.

Fifteen *Typhoons*.

Eleven *Matrixes*.

Also *Tritons*, *Neptunes*, *Tridents*, and *Reapers*.

Two hundred and fifty-two warsubs in total, not including surface vessels.

And USS *Blade*, Admiral Quintana's warsub.

And we were moving at a snail's pace toward them. I frowned when I checked our speed. Sixty. Compared to the SCAV drive, it was like warning the enemy a full day before a potential attack.

We were sailing into the storm, willingly.

I shivered.

"Attention, GSF warsubs in Gulf waters en route to Seascape. This is USSF

HQ and we are warning you off."

"Don't answer," I said to Renée. "We want to keep them guessing."

"I don't think they'll let us get *too* close," she whispered, staring at the display. We were still a few hours out, and tension was building.

They continued to order us away, but we ignored every call.

Eventually, they stopped.

They were preparing.

I'd managed to get a shower, some food, and some much-needed sleep. The crossing from the North Sea had been brutal to say the least. Rico had also collapsed for a spell, which was a good thing. He'd lost it for a while there and, now that he'd achieved his ultimate goals, had withdrawn into himself and was barely speaking.

It concerned me, because he was so likeable, and I couldn't ignore the fact that he had been through a horrible year-long ordeal and was likely suffering PTSD as a result.

We'd made sure the warsub crew was comfortable with food and water, and Renée had kept an eye on things while we'd slept.

But now we were approaching Seascape.

Johnny was nearby in *SC-1*, but I'd told him to move slowly. *Quietly hug the bottom*, I'd said. *We can't have anyone hear you.*

I was back in control, and Renée was there, looking tired but ready. She approached and held my hand for a moment as she stared into my eyes.

"You don't think it'll end here, do you?" I whispered.

"It's possible. But I didn't want to leave things the way we did."

I drew in a breath and exhaled. "I know. I have strong feelings for you. I don't want to lose you. Especially after what we've been through. It's not every day you fall in love with the woman who wanted to kill you."

She grinned. "They say opposites attract."

"True." I lowered myself to a chair and studied the sonar. The USSF was moving their ships into a steel wall before us.

A blockade.

"I'm sorry it felt like I was using you."

"It never felt like that." Her eyes flashed. "I was always willing."

"I know. But I want to take your feelings into account. I didn't consider what you gave up to be in Trieste."

A shrug. "I do love living underwater. It's given me so much, especially after my obsession of the previous year."

I offered a slight smile. "I have that affect on people, obviously."

"Obviously."

"My dad gave it to me. The drive."

"For Oceania."

"Yes. I sometimes don't think about much else."

"I understand."

I stared at her short dark hair, her dark eyes, and the wrinkles around them when she smiled. I came to a sudden decision. "Look. When this is over, let's start again."

"Start again?"

"Back at Trieste. Let's start over."

"How?" She frowned.

"A date maybe?"

She looked away as she processed what I was saying, then she turned back to me. "You mean, dinner?"

"Yes. In the entertainment district. I'll pick a nice place."

"But what are you expecting?"

"We'll see how the night goes, Renée!" I couldn't help but laugh. Then I reached out and held her hand again. "But it will be the start of a relationship. And not just physical."

A smile crawled across her face as she realized what I was proposing. "Are you sure?"

"I couldn't ever lose you. I don't want to."

"What about Kat?"

"I'll never forget her. But I have to move on." I took a deep breath. I needed to learn from the examples of Renée and Rico. I couldn't let things affect my mental state so. Couldn't continue to let trauma rule my life.

I needed to embrace what I had in front of me, and not dwell on the past.

I squeezed her hand, and she looked into my eyes. It was almost as if she were seeing into my soul, evaluating whether I truly was ready to move on.

A part of me knew it didn't really matter right then, anyway.

We were headed toward something bigger than the two of us.

There was a massive confrontation brewing, and there was a good chance that none of us would make it out alive.

—••—

WE PRESSED ON TOWARD SEASCAPE. The minutes ticked by quicker than I thought possible, like seconds on a clock, and we watched the sonar for signs of the USSF. When we hit their blockade, I knew we had to run through it.

Like a snail through a gauntlet.

We just had to push through and hope we made it close enough to fire our weapon.

The sonar began to scream at us, and we jerked our gazes to it. A bright light had appeared on it, along with a callout label, and it was moving quickly across the screen.

It was a vessel with a SCAV drive.

I nearly swore. I had given Johnny strict instructions. "I wonder why Johnny—" I choked the comment off with a startled gasp. It wasn't Johnny in *SC-1* at all.

But it *was* a SCAV vessel. A crewed ship, underwater, moving at over 400 kph.

It was a USSF warsub, equipped with Kat's invention. The USSF had finally done it. They'd put vessels to sea that had the superfast fusion drive.

It was a *Hunter-Killer*, also known as the *Fast Attack*. They had traditionally been the Fleet's fast and silent attack subs, small but heavily armed.

Now this one was screaming across our bow.

To send us a very clear message.

Turn back or die.

—••—

"OH MY GOD," RENÉE WHISPERED. "Mac, they've got—"

"We knew it had been coming. I just hadn't known when they'd make their appearance in the oceans." My stomach felt hollow. The USSF had adapted a micro fusion reactor to flash boil steam to propel a warsub into supercavitation. A bubble of air surrounded the vessel as it powered across our path. It left a tremendous wake hundreds of meters long, bubbles churning slowly to the surface.

The ship made a wide, curving arc and came back around.

"They're making a show of it," I murmured. It was the big reveal, I thought.

It could actually mean the end to our independence movement.

We'd been ahead in the oceans, technologically, for well over a year. And we still were, because we had the Acoustic Pulse Drive, which allowed our vessels to get to six kilometers or more underwater.

But when it came to speed, things were growing equal in the Second Cold War.

I gritted my teeth and stared at our course.

We didn't alter it.

Onward to Seascape.

—••—

MORE TIME PASSED, AND MORE ships started appearing. It was clear that the

USSF was putting on a display of force, but we hadn't actually communicated with them about our intentions.

And soon we were only an hour from Seascape.

They had formed a wall in front of us, but had kept pace with us on our course to USSF HQ.

My hands were sweaty on the yoke as I piloted the warsub toward the target.

Then our comm squawked. "Attention, GSF warsub *Black Widow.*"

I grunted at the voice. It was Admiral Quintana herself. The last time I'd dealt with her had been an interrogation about my sister and Benning's disappearance. Then she and Zyvinski had taken Meg, and had most likely been torturing her since.

Inside, tension built. I could feel it in my spine and my core. The anger swelled within me; I felt like a coiled animal ready to spring.

She continued, "You are approaching Seascape without permission. You've now officially entered US waters without permission. Unless you declare your intent, we'll be forced to fire on your vessel. This is your last warning. After this, we start firing, and we'll send all five of your warsubs to the bottom."

I shook my head at Renée. She'd been motioning to the comm.

Quintana said, "Your ships are no match for our SCAV drive."

And you're no match for our Isomer Bomb, I wanted to say.

I held my breath.

The blockade of ships was now only a few kilometers away. The seafloor was growing more shallow—it was currently at a hundred meters—and space was growing scarce. I stared at the VID to find a place to squeeze through the wall of steel. There were *hundreds* of them staring back at me.

Cold.

Emotionless.

Ready for war.

"Press on," I muttered. "Don't let them know what we're doing."

"Why's that?" she asked.

"If we declare our intentions, they'll just destroy us. Silence is better at this stage."

"We could make something up. We could say we're having mechanical issues. A fire, perhaps?"

"They'd see through it. We bypassed Trieste and Ballard. They'd know we were lying."

She nodded and stared at the image of the ships on the screen in front of us. Her hand was tight on the back of my chair. "Do you think they'd fire on us?"

"Not unless we fire first. I think they would be concerned about starting a war. They're likely trying to contact GSF admiralty, or high-ranking politicians, to determine our intentions."

"They'll know we're rogue then."

I shrugged. It was a game of shadows in this new Cold War. "Unless the German politicians were lying, and this really is a GSF attack on the USSF. Hell, look at it objectively: we're approaching their HQ, in their territorial waters, and won't respond to communications. We've ignored their warnings. And we are *five warsubs*."

"Seems aggressive to me."

"I just don't think they'd fire first. Not when there are so many of them and only—"

And then the sonar shrieked.

I stared at it, mouth agape.

Torpedo in the water.

—••—

IT WAS COMING RIGHT FOR us. A *Reaper* Class vessel had fired. Surely they meant to destroy us—

Then I realized that there was only *one* torpedo coming. Not fifty.

"They're testing us."

"Mac," Renée snapped. "It's closing the distance rapidly! What are you doing?"

"There's not much we can do."

She stared at me in horror. "Turn, dammit! Lead it away. Drop countermeasures."

"Then we'd be heading away from Seascape. We have to get closer."

"But the torpedo—"

"They want to see what we'll do. If we fire back or run, we're dead."

"You're crazy." Her eyes flashed. "We have to back off."

"No."

She shook her head as she stared at my features set like stone. "Don't do this. You can't do it."

"It's a test. I know it is." I studied the other warsubs. They weren't doing anything. No torpedo doors were open. No active pulses to calculate our exact distance. In a flash of realization I clicked the comm and signaled the other GSF warsubs. "Tell them to cut speed and come to a stop," I hissed.

She looked utterly confused, but she nodded after a heartbeat. She rattled the instructions in German, stumbling slightly, but it sounded good to my untrained ears.

Then we stared at the sonar, and both of us held our breath.

The torpedo was surging toward us.

Chapter Thirty-Six

THE GSF SHIPS ACCOMPANYING US—NOT even realizing that we were on a mission to save my sister and destroy the Fleet's HQ—slowed rapidly and came to a stop.

Meanwhile, the USSF torpedo continued to close on us.

Five hundred meters.

Three hundred.

Two.

One.

With a gigantic flash of white on the VID, it detonated directly in our path. It created a massive cavity of steam in the ocean, which immediately crashed in from all sides, creating secondary detonations that reverberated throughout the warsub. Pipes rattled and the boat groaned.

I looked around, worried.

I didn't know how reliable GSF warsubs were.

A few lights had winked out; the bulbs had blown in the concussion.

Red indicators had begun flashing on the control console, but I ignored them.

"It was a warning, and a test."

Realization dawned on Renée's features. "They wanted to see if we'd fire back. You were right."

"And they did it directly in front of us."

"Telling us not to go further."

The speed indicator hadn't changed. We were still forging ahead at sixty kph.

The USSF warsubs before us were growing larger, awfully fast.

Other torpedo doors now began to open on the vessels in the line before us.

The sonar was buzzing like crazy, trying to tell us.

Torpedo shutter open!

Torpedo shutter open!

Torpedo shutter open!

My stomach was in knots. I was risking a lot here, but my sister deserved it.

Max Hyland was in the control cabin with us. I'd forgotten about him. His face was tight and he was staring at the projection in front of us. He seemed pale, but to his credit, he had remained calm and collected.

Seascape was now in passive range. I could see it on the sonar. Her modules, travel tubes, and the water park stretched out serenely on the ocean floor south of the Texas coast.

Hyland was staring at it.

"What are you doing, Mac?" he finally asked.

"We're going to test your weapon."

"Where, exactly?" He looked to me, then back to the scope.

I pointed. "There."

He gasped. "But that's an underwater colony! The blast will kill everything in the area!"

"There are no tourists there anymore, doc. It's military."

He frowned as he processed that. "Military?"

"Yeah. The USSF. They've moved their HQ there. We have to stop them."

"But people will die."

I turned and faced him. Beneath our words, the sonar continued to shriek. "Max, what did you think your weapon was for?"

"I . . . I . . . our enemies, I guess."

I pointed. "There they are. They've been harassing us for years. They killed my dad. They exploit us. They occupied us last year."

"I thought you were concerned about the Russians. They're building more dreadnoughts."

"We are. We have to test the weapon, though. And this is where it's going to happen."

He remained tight-lipped and didn't say more, but his expression was taut.

He didn't realize the full impact the Second Cold War was having on the world. Battles were happening frequently.

And we always seemed to be in the middle of them.

I looked at the VID. The ships were still directly in front. "Make our depth eighty meters," I muttered. I pointed at the ocean underneath the *Reaper* Class sub. "We'll go under her. If they're smart, they'll go positive for a bit, avoid an impact."

"And if there's a collision?" Renée asked.

I shrugged. It didn't matter. *Black Widow* wasn't leaving the area intact, anyway. "Best to bring in some scuba gear just in case there's a breach," I said.

I felt reckless. Something had taken hold of me. I was doing things I'd never dreamed of in the past. They outgunned us. The technology on our warsub was inferior. The dangers were very real. Every warsub before us had flooded tubes with weapons ready to fire.

And still we pressed on.

"Reducing speed," I muttered. I pulled the throttle back and lowered our velocity to twenty-five kph. It would give them something to wonder about while I navigated through the blockade.

"They might fire," Max muttered from my side.

"It's possible." But it was also possible they would just watch as we neared to see exactly what we were going to do. Then if we made a move to fire, all hell would likely break loose.

I took a deep breath and glanced around me.

In just a few minutes, I had no doubt that the bulkheads of that GSF warsub were going to come crashing down around me.

— •• —

THE *REAPER* WAS JUST BEFORE us now. I reduced speed further and used the bow planes to bring us below it. There was barely enough room between the ocean floor and the vessel for *Black Widow*.

Alarms started to chime.

Proximity alert.

We were too close to the bottom.

A shearing, grinding, wrenching pierced the cabins and corridors of *Black Widow*. The noise set my hair on end. I squeezed the yoke unconsciously, as if it would prevent the hull from rupturing.

The tearing noise continued. I clenched my teeth. The *Reaper* was now just ahead of us, and more alarms were sounding.

Collison Alert. Collision Alert. Collision Alert!

Our hull was on the bottom and the boat was slowing. I pushed the throttle forward, and the vibrations grew worse. The sound of the engines filled the control cabin.

I blew ballast to try and lift us off the bottom slightly, but the *Reaper* was directly overhead.

"Mac, it's going to hit!" Renée blurted.

"I can't go deeper. They're trying to force us to a stop!"

I gripped the throttle tightly.

325

The *Reaper* loomed in our sonar now, and on the VID screen before us. The computer projection showed the hull directly over us. I'd never seen another warsub so close to one I'd piloted before.

I swallowed. "Hold on!"

The two vessels collided.

Chapter Thirty-Seven

THE IMPACT THREW US TO the deck. Alarms were *wailing* now. The bulkheads shuddered and everything loose on consoles crashed downward. Pipes ruptured. The ship continued to rumble and shake; it was so severe that I couldn't get back to my feet.

The lights winked out; flashing red strobes replaced them.

And abruptly blue lights began to pulse up and down the living spaces of *Black Widow.*

Blue lights.

Oh, shit!

Blue lights were the universal symbol underwater of pressure loss and flooding.

A rushing, roaring sound met my ears, from the rear of the vessel.

Water was pouring into the ship.

The sound of hatches slamming echoed through *Black Widow.* Automatic. Sealing cabins and areas of the vessel. *Compartmentalization* might contain the flooding, but too far back for anyone currently trapped in any of those areas.

I hoped the engines still functioned. We needed those.

The collision with the *Reaper* had opened our bulkhead aft of control, and closer to engineering. We were taking on water, making the ship heavier, and I had to compensate or we'd dig into the bottom and might never get moving again.

I hauled myself to my feet and stumbled toward the pilot's chair. Making ballast positive again, I made sure our engines were still roaring, and our screws still turning.

A schematic of the sub had several areas flashing blue.

Engineering had survived.

The *Reaper* was behind us. Sonar indicated that she had sustained damage, as well. Alarms were piercing that vessel; crew were likely scrambling to escape flooding.

If they were going to fire, now would be the time.

We'd just shown that we were not there to talk.

———••———

WE CONTINUED TOWARD SEASCAPE. THE Fleet was matching our pace and keeping a close eye on us. There were other warsubs arrayed near the city, and those were beginning to move closer to us to take up formation in another blockade.

I had no doubt that they would not let us get past that one.

This was it for us.

And, I noted dully, USS *Blade* was one of the warsubs.

I wondered if Admiral Quintana was on it.

———••———

I CUT BACK OUR SPEED. *Black Widow* was far heavier now, due to the water we'd taken on, and our ballast was set to full positive buoyancy. It was enough to keep us neutral in the water, but just barely.

We couldn't take on any more, or it'd bottom the boat.

The GSF warsubs were still with us, but they had fallen behind and were moving much slower. I'd given them the order to slow to present a more passive appearance, and it appeared to be working. The USSF had not fired any more torpedoes.

Soon we were five kilometers from the city and I pulled the throttle back to zero.

That would confuse them.

Max approached and checked the distance. He gasped. "But Mac, the explosion will surely crush us! We're way too close."

The explosion would be massive.

So be it.

"Don't worry, Doc," I muttered. "I've got this."

I glanced behind me and saw Renée standing there. On the deck at her feet was a variety of scuba gear, including flippers, masks, weight belts, and tanks.

Rico was standing nearby, watching events unfold quietly. I said, "Can you do this?"

His eyes moved to meet mine, but he was slow, uncaring. Eventually he nodded. "You trust me?"

I hesitated. "No. But I need you, Rico."

"I'm an Operative First Class, whether you let me continue or not. I'm here to help. I'm done with the . . . with the previous stuff."

He was saying that now that Heinrich was dead, he could move on. But I knew better.

I'd be wary.

"Then let's get wet," I said.

—••—

WE PULLED FRANZ INTO THE control cabin and he stared at the gear, horrified. Then he looked at me, then back to the gear. "What the hell are you doing? What happened to the boat? It felt like a collision with both the bottom and a—"

"We're going for a swim."

He glanced at the sonar and swore. "What the—"

"We really have no choice," I said. "This ship is minutes from destruction. If you stay here, you're going to die. You have to come with us." I pointed at the armada of USSF warsubs. "See?"

"But you said—"

"I was wrong."

He continued to stare at me, horror clear on his features.

Renée said, "Mac, what about the others? The captain and her crew?"

They were currently in the cabin just aft of control. I'd been debating with myself what to do with them.

"They're on their own," I whispered.

—••—

RENÉE STAYED ON BOARD THE GSF warsub. Rico, Franz, and I suited up to go outside. Franz was angry, and we kept our eyes on him, but he knew better than to stay on a doomed vessel. Perhaps the Fleet just outside was enough to convince him. Or, maybe he just wanted to see what the hell I was doing and take a chance on me. I hadn't killed him yet, after all. Maybe he trusted me.

The thought made me retch into my regulator as I tested it.

—••—

"ARE THE TORPEDOES READY TO fire?"

Renée said, "They're already in tubes one and two."

"Make sure they're set to impact detonation. I don't want countermeasures to trigger them early, or to move them off course. Aim at the nearest module."

She chewed her lower lip. "Mac, I don't really think it matters. We're so *damn* close to the city as it is."

She was right. The USSF, had they known we were threatening a nuclear-sized bomb, would have incinerated us hours ago.

But our actions had confused them.

And they were likely still talking to similarly confused politicians, who were trying to figure out exactly what was going on.

"And the remote controls?" I asked.

"I think they're set." She stared at the console before her. "I hope. Reading German isn't as easy as speaking it."

—••—

SOON WE WERE OUTSIDE. WE descended to the bottom, and began to swim toward Seascape. Above us, we passed warsub after warsub. Their shadows painted the seafloor like clouds on a summer day. We were quiet, barely making noise, and we soared only inches from the sandy bottom as we swam toward the colony.

The warsubs had no idea what we'd done.

They were monitoring *Black Widow* to see if she were going to fire torpedoes, not drop three people off to swim five kilometers.

It wasn't that far. We'd trained for far more. Rico and I kept Franz between us, and we churned our way through the warm Gulf waters toward Seascape.

The seafloor there was on an upward slope. As we swam toward the city, it acted as natural decompression for us. By the time we reached the outer modules, we'd already decompressed to four atms.

Infiltrating the colony would be easy; I'd done it a thousand times before.

Each module had a moonpool, open to the water. Entering was simply a matter of swimming under the module and moving upward into the pool.

Soon we had broken the surface and hauled ourselves onto the deck grating.

I peered around. There was no one. Red lights were flashing and a siren was howling.

They were on high alert, worried about the GSF warsub hovering only 5,000 meters away.

It was a nice distraction for us.

We were in the Communications Module.

Most undersea cities were similar in layout, design, and building materials.

Sometimes the only way you could tell where you were was from the signs on the bulkheads, or the language the citizens spoke. But Seascape was different. The lighting was unique, the transparent bulkheads different, even the smell was strange for an underwater colony. For so many years they'd serviced tourists—and *wealthy* tourists at that. It had left an indelible mark on the colony. It seemed clean. It smelled fresh inside.

And I recognized it instantly from the last time I'd visited to speak with Reggie, six months ago, when he'd turned down my offer of a partnership.

I gestured to Rico and Franz to ditch the tanks and weight belts, but to keep the masks on. We looked very much like the German hit squad that had attacked Trieste just a few weeks earlier.

Franz stared at his surroundings. The chamber was twenty by twenty meters. Lockers ringed the exterior. The sound of water lapping against the deck was pervasive—a constant white noise.

He said, "What the hell are you doing?"

"What do you think?" I whispered.

"I have no idea!" His voice was loud.

"We're here to rescue my sister. You're going to help me."

"Fuck you! I am German! I do what I want! You have no right to attack my vessel and take me prisoner!"

Good, I thought. *Say it louder.*

"What do you think about the USSF?" I said, my voice still low.

"I hate the USSF! They think they can control the oceans, but you're the worst! You tried to interfere with our colony. You tried to—"

"That's enough," I snapped. "Now shut up."

Rico and I were both holding needle guns, and Franz stared at them. "What do you want me to do? I won't be a willing prisoner anymore."

"Stay here. I don't care."

And then Rico and I marched off, leaving him standing alone by the moonpool. He watched us leave, his face laced with utter shock.

Chapter Thirty-Eight

RICO EYED ME. "WHAT THE hell was that? He tried to kill you back at Trieste. You've held him prisoner now for weeks. Are you trying to teach me about forgiveness again? If so, I think that's pretty—"

He had whispered, and I held my voice to a low hiss. "No."

"Then what?"

"Think about what he just said. He yelled."

Rico reviewed the last minute in his mind. "He was raging about how he was German, how you'd attacked his vessel—"

"Exactly. And when the USSF review these tapes, if they ever get them, what will they think?"

He gasped. "They'll see the German warsubs outside. There's a man with a German accent in here raging about Germany and an attack on his warsub. Meanwhile there's a sunken vessel—"

"*Dark Winter* off the coast of Florida."

"And then—"

"And then, a massive detonation takes out Fleet HQ." I shrugged. "Subterfuge at its finest, wouldn't you say?"

His face was ashen. "You kept that man around for this long just for this?"

"All part of the deception."

He shook his head. "My god. You could have just killed him after what he tried with you."

"They would have known his body had decomposed . . ." I mumbled, mostly to myself. My heart thudded.

Rico's jaw dropped inside his face mask. "You . . . you mean for them to find his body and recognize he's . . . he's not . . . "

"He's not Triestrian. Right."

"Planting evidence to frame another nation?"

"Things like this are done in war all the time." My voice was husky. I couldn't quite believe that I was saying it, though I had been thinking it for weeks. Ever since we'd caught the man trying to escape from Trieste after his attempt to kill me and Johnny. I'd decided then that I needed to use him.

I stared at Rico, wondering where the line between civilized and monster was, exactly. I'd criticized him for killing one man, while I had killed hundreds—no, *thousands*—during battle. Fired him from TCI for disobeying my orders. I'd called it *murder* then.

But here I was, framing an entire nation, sacrificing the remaining crew of their boat, and using one man to pin the crimes on a single nation to deflect suspicion from Trieste.

Was I any more innocent than Rico?

But torture was different, I screamed inwardly.

Death happens in wartime, and this Cold War was definitely no longer cold.

But I felt strongly that torture was not how civilized people conducted themselves. It had changed my life forever, and following my experience in Sheng City, I was a different person. Hate had consumed me, burned inside me, and played a role in nearly every decision I made. It was only when I found forgiveness in myself for what had happened that I was finally able to move on. And it was only then that I'd opened myself up to love and found Kat.

And now Renée.

Rico and I marched from the moonpool.

Renée.

She was out there, on a damaged boat, waiting for my signal.

I had put her in grave danger, and if something happened to her, too . . .

I thrust that thought away. I just couldn't handle it.

"But you criticized me for what I did to Heinrich," Rico practically exploded. "And you just—"

I spun on him. "I'm trying to protect you from the lifetime of guilt and torment that I've had to deal with! I'm lost, don't you see? I have no hope. I've killed thousands. Sunk whole warsubs. Killed in hand-to-hand combat. The GSF crew are likely going to die. *That's on me!* It's the only way to bring about a unified treaty between the undersea colonies. I have to fight for it. But you . . . I wanted to save you from this. Show you a better—" I choked off the thoughts as they bubbled to the surface. I swallowed and just stared at the man, preventing myself from saying more.

He eyed me, uncertainly, for the briefest of heartbeats. Then he turned away.

—••—

My PCD WAS IN MY thigh pocket, and I pulled it out. I was aware that we were now in enemy territory, and we had to be careful not to let a USSF sailor take note of us. We ducked into a side passage, more narrow than the main corridor, and waited while I signaled Reggie Quinn.

He answered a moment later.

"Hello?"

"Reggie, it's me."

"Truman? Mac? How is that possible? How are you—"

"I told you I'd be coming for her."

"But the GSF ships are still five—" Then he choked off his words. "You swam?"

I ignored him. "Where is Meg?" I didn't want to draw this out any further. I clutched a gun in my right hand.

He paused. I couldn't tell where he was, but I assumed he'd moved to where he could speak in private. He said in a softer voice, "She's in the module just west of the Commerce Module. Where are you?"

"Communications. The moonpool."

"Perfect. You're nearly there. It's the module just north of you."

"What kind of resistance will we see?"

"Everyone is on alert because of your odd approach. No one knows what to make of it. If those ships come closer, though, then—"

"They won't."

"What are you intending to do with them?"

"Rescue Meg. I told you that."

"Oh."

There was another long pause as we waited. Then there was the sound of footsteps, and a USSF sailor ran past in the main corridor, but he didn't look at us as he bolted by.

I waited until he was far enough away, then said to Reggie, "Where is she in the module? Where will I find her?"

"She's on Deck Three. In a cell. Cliff is there with her. Number 311."

"Got it. Thanks, Reggie."

"Glad to help."

I keyed off. Then I stared at my PCD for another long moment while Rico watched.

"What are you doing?" he hissed. He also had a weapon at his side, and he was ready to use it.

"One minute . . ." I muttered, manipulating the display.

Then I swore.

— •• —

"WE HAVE TO GO GET Meg now," I said, pulling him along with me.

"Careful!"

"Hide in plain sight."

We marched through the module, into the travel tube leading to where Reggie had indicated. We were in our black wetsuits with our masks still on. Strange to see in a civilian city, perhaps, but this was now a military outpost, and they were on alert. Lights were flashing on the bulkheads and there were shouted calls on the PA system, directing sailors to different locations. It was still a civilian colony, however, and most hatches did not lock automatically and require keycodes or security chips to open them. They slid aside at our command, and we moved freely.

In a few months, things would have likely changed there, as the military continued to alter the colony to more rigid security, but for now, this early in their occupation, it was easy to get from module to module.

The travel tubes were nearly entirely transparent. It was a beautiful scene outside, though there were shadows of warsubs very close.

Fish passed by, investigating us as we marched through.

Soon we were on Deck One of the prison module. The moonpool was next to us. There were numerous hatches leading into the chamber—one on each side—and a ladder leading to the decks above. I glanced at it. "Be careful now, Rico."

"Of course."

"Things are not as they seem."

He glanced at me, shocked. "What does that—"

As he said it, a number of troops emerged from the ladder. Their shouts echoed toward us, and I knelt and took aim.

"It means they know we're here."

I fired.

Chapter Thirty-Nine

THE FIRST SAILORS THROUGH THE opening fell, blood splattering from chest wounds, their mouths open in soundless cries. More steps thudded down the stairs, and Rico was firing, as well. The sailors could barely get their weapons up before our rounds hit them, center mass, shredding their lungs and hearts and putting them on the deck, motionless.

My ammo ran out and I reached for another clip—

But a USSF soldier launched himself off the ladder and was sprinting for me.

"Shoot!" I yelled.

"I'm out!" Rico was scrabbling at his pocket for another clip.

The sailor was raising his gun . . .

I made a decision and ran toward him to cut the distance before he could get the weapon aimed. The collision was momentous and it drove the breath from my lungs. The man was big, and well trained.

Dimly, I noticed that Rico had fallen to the deck and was searching for something.

I focused on the man before me. I threw an elbow, which he blocked, and he countered with his own. I ducked and tried an uppercut, but he stepped back and it missed. He grinned.

I feinted with a left hook and he moved to block it—

I swung a right and connected with his jaw. Then I kicked him in the gut, swept his leg out from under him, and he crashed to the deck on his back. As he went down, I grabbed him and pushed with everything I had.

He hit the steel and the sound was like a bag of wet kelp falling from a loader onto the deck back at Trieste. The air burst from his mouth and he groaned.

Rico was still reaching for his gun, and there were more sailors coming.

He'd been shot.

I was laying on the sailor's chest, and I grabbed his right hand. The gun was still in it, clutched tightly, but I twisted it backward, breaking his fingers as I did so. He tried to grunt in pain but was still gasping for air.

I brought the weapon up and aimed at the approaching USSF troops—
—and fired.

I was lying on the deck, using the man as a shield, as I put round after round into them. They fired, but each shot hit the sailor shielding me.

Eventually they stopped coming, but I knew it wasn't over yet.

"Rico! Are you okay?"

"I . . . I think so."

"Where are you hit?"

"Shoulder and . . . shoulder and thigh."

"Can you move?"

He laughed, but it sounded more like a bark. "Of course. I'm not staying here."

I fixed my gaze on the ladder leading to the prison levels, then I shot a quick glance to Rico. He was on his knees and loading his gun.

"How are we going to get up to Deck Three?" he said.

"We're not going to."

He snapped a look at me. "What? But we came all this way to—"

"Meg's not there."

"I don't understand."

A new voice sounded, and it was one that I recognized.

It had come from the ladder.

"I'm sorry, Mac, but it's all over for you."

It was Reggie Quinn, former mayor of Seascape.

—••—

HE SLOWLY DESCENDED THE LADDER and gingerly set foot on the deck. He stopped ten meters away. I aimed my gun at him, and he raised his hands in the air.

He said, "You can't escape."

"Why do you say that?"

"There are more sailors on their way." He glanced at the bodies on the floor, at the blood pooling around them. He grimaced. "I hate the USSF, and I'm not sad to see this, but it was the only way to get my city back."

I snorted. "You're crazy. You're never getting Seascape back."

"I think I can."

"Reggie, the USSF is here to stay. They've moved in. They took over City Control. Quintana took your office!"

"This might help, though, don't you think?" He shrugged and continued to stare at me, a blank, distant look on his face.

I remembered the first time I'd met him. He'd outright refused to listen to me about independence. He wanted to focus on his city and the tourists. But then they'd stopped coming, and he knew I'd been right all along, that Oceania was inevitable and he had to throw his hat in with us. But now he'd seen another opportunity, and was making a play for it.

"Reggie, they *hate* us. They only use the colonies for exports topside. They only used you as a place for wealthy tourists, but there are no such people anymore. You'll never get back what you had here. The surface destruction is escalating." I shook my head. "It's *gone*, Reggie. I thought you realized that."

"But then this opportunity presented itself, Mac."

I frowned, watching him. "Opportunity?"

He was slowly moving his hand. "To capture you. To present you to Admiral Quintana. She'll give me whatever I want."

I gestured with my gun. "Don't. I mean it. I'll kill you, Reggie."

"I don't doubt it." He glanced at the other bodies. "You have a habit of killing people around you." He tilted his head and eyed me. "How'd you know?"

"What?"

"How'd you know that Meg wasn't here?"

"I gave her a tracker. She's had it all along. She's not even in this module."

It took a moment for him to process the statement, then he chuckled. "I should have guessed. I wondered how she escaped."

"You didn't help her, I take it."

He sighed. "Sadly, no. I couldn't. I'm not sure where she went. We've been searching. But obviously you know." He stepped forward. "You have to tell me where she is. If I turn you both in, Quintana will really be grateful."

I stared at him, open mouthed. "Are you mad?"

"Why would you say that?"

"Because Seascape doesn't exist anymore! There is no tourist colony. It's gone."

"Don't say things like that, Mac. We're standing in it right now."

"We're standing in USSF HQ. You're a civilian. There's no place for you here."

His face flattened and a look of anger spread slowly across his features. "Don't say that."

"You're nothing to her. With me you would have had a job. I would have given you responsibility."

"Fighting for independence?"

"Yes. A real purpose in this world. It's falling to pieces topside, Reggie. People are struggling. The oceans are flooding coastal cities. Overwhelming the sea-walls. Croplands are dying." I exhaled. "I thought you saw that."

"I—I did." He'd stumbled slightly.

"It won't work for you."

"Why not?" The sound of pounding footsteps began filtering into the chamber from four directions—each from a travel tube entering the module—as well as from the ladderwell. They had surrounded us, and in seconds they'd be mobbing us. They were yelling and shoving ammo clips into high-calibre machine guns.

We had no other options.

I raised my PCD to my lips and he watched, not understanding. I said, "Renée, can you hear me?"

"Loud and clear," her voice came back.

"Fire the torpedoes."

"Torpedoes away."

The Isomer Bomb was heading for Seascape.

Chapter Forty

HIS FACE PALED. "WHAT DID you just do?"

"I told you Seascape was done, Reggie. The USSF are leaving, but not willingly."

I backed away, keeping my gun trained on the man. Beside me, Rico did the same.

The moonpool was behind us, and we inched closer to it. Reggie noticed, and now he frowned. "Mac, where are you going? You don't have a tank, a weight belt, nothing."

"I have a mask."

"The torpedo you fired won't make it here. Your ship is five kilometers away! You think it'll get through the blockade?"

"I guess we'll see." I started to suck in deep breaths, oxygenating my blood. Rico was doing the same, and Reggie just watched us, confused.

"You can't go anywhere," he said again.

"I'm sorry, Reggie. I truly am. You lied to me. You told me you'd help Meg. You told me you'd join us. It was all a lie."

"It wasn't a lie. I just found a better way."

"It didn't work. And now . . . " I trailed off. I couldn't bring myself to say it.

I turned and stared at the water. I glanced at Rico, and saw he was ready.

We dove in.

Leaving Reggie to his fate.

———••———

WE SWAM NORTH. THE REPAIR Module was that direction, but it was a long swim.

This was going to be tough.

We were in full face masks, and there was a tiny amount of air in there. Enough for one breath, perhaps.

I could see the module ahead. Tiny bubbles rose to the surface from its skin. Travel tubes led from the module and there were seacars, scooters, other divers, and warsubs in the distance.

I knew we could make it.

I knew, because Meg had.

This was the direction she had gone, and the tracker put her location in that module.

We didn't have weight belts, and our buoyancy kept trying to pull us upward. We had to fight it the whole way, and it made the journey far more difficult than it normally would have been.

Within thirty seconds my legs were aching.

Within forty-five they were burning.

At a minute, they were on fire.

We weren't wearing flippers, which made it all the more challenging.

Rico did a good job keeping up. He'd been shot twice, and still he was managing.

He impressed me, despite his other failings.

The module grew closer; we were making progress.

At two minutes I had nearly expended all my energy. Aerobically, I was done, and my muscles were now creating lactic acid.

My shoulders felt like they might lock up. I was pulling with every ounce of force I had.

My lungs were heaving and my vision began to grow dim. A ring of darkness encircled the view before me and I blinked to see if it would help, but it didn't.

I'd passed out before from holding my breath; I knew it was happening now.

Finally I'd had enough, and I took the only gasp of air I had in the mask.

It helped, but just a bit, and I think it saved my life. We passed under the lip of the Repair Module, looked up and saw a faint glow through the darkness threatening to overcome us.

The moonpool.

I pulled with everything I had left, and broke the surface. I pushed my mask up, took in several gasping breaths, and draped my arms across the edge with my face on the cold steel. Beside me, Rico was in a similar situation. He was coughing at the same time; he'd accidently sucked in some saltwater while surfacing.

We were a wreck. If there had been USSF troops there, they would have easily captured or killed us.

But there weren't, and I looked around while bringing in huge lungfuls of cool, damp, canned air.

It tasted sweet.

There were ships around us, floating at the repair docks, as well as scooters, and I searched for one that might be usable.

"How long will the torpedoes take to get here?" Rico said.

I did a quick calculation in my head. They traveled at eighty kilometers per hour, and had 5,000 meters to travel. "Three minutes and forty-five seconds."

His jaw dropped and he stared at me in horror. "My god. But it took us three minutes to swim here!"

I sighed. "Yes."

The torpedoes had been set to impact detonation and we'd targeted the nearest module to *Black Widow*: Supply. It was 300 meters to the south. According to Hyland, the explosion was going to be the size of a tactical nuke, measured in the megatons, and magnified by the surrounding water, which would increase the force substantially.

If the blast didn't destroy us, the concussion wave and water displacement surely would.

Seascape only had half a minute left.

Then an isomeric explosion would shatter bulkhead integrity, and the crushing water above would implode the city.

And the sea would smother us as if the colony had never existed.

We didn't have a chance.

There was nothing else I could do. I'd run out of options. They had been on the verge of capturing us. Reggie had betrayed me and given us up. I had hoped that Meg was still alive; perhaps I would get to see her before we died. That was my final wish.

But the independence movement on the ocean floors was my biggest regret.

It had been my father's life's work. It was all he'd wanted, all he ever talked about. He'd wanted the people who struggled on the ocean floors—who farmed the kelp and fish, dug minerals from the rock, risked constant death and injury under hundreds and thousands of meters of water looming above them—to one day be not only self-sufficient, but necessary for the topside nations and to have the ability to self-determine their fates.

To elect leaders.

To make choices.

To endure the colonization efforts, to survive, and to flourish.

He'd given his life for it, and his legacy had made a lasting impact on me and Meagan.

That was my largest regret.

I'd just sacrificed myself, as my dad had.

I'd followed his path, which I'd fought against for so long while growing up. Then I'd embraced it, and . . .

And, here I was.

About to die.

I could only hope that Johnny, somewhere out there in *SC-1*, would take up the mantle and lead the efforts when I was gone. Along with Richard, Jessica, Mayor Winton of Ballard, and our scientists Manesh Lazlow and Max Hyland, and the others who toiled away in TCI, helping the cause, going on missions for Trieste, and putting their lives in danger every day. Jackson Train, for instance, who had left the city for the isolated post at The Ridge, building our seacars and drones and living in a deadly location for the good of Oceania.

I remembered the songs his crew sang at dinner that day when Johnny, Rico, Renée, and I had stopped there on our way to Cousteau to recruit the French colonies to our cause:

For life and adventure . . .
For life annnndddd adventurrrrrre . . .
And enemies to kill!

Those people loved what they were doing. Each day they struggled with loneliness and isolation, but they did it because they believed in me and the cause.

If I allowed the enemy to take me, then there was a very real possibility that it would all end for us.

I wasn't sure if I could handle much more torture in my life.

And I had a lot of secrets that the world's superpowers could exploit to end the movement.

So I'd had no choice.

I checked the time.

Perhaps fifteen seconds remained.

I triggered my PCD. "Renée?" I whispered. "Do you read me?"

A few moments passed while my heart continued to pound. Then, "Got you, Mac. Can you get out of there?"

I glanced at the ships nearby. There was a chance, but the swim over had taken just too long. "I . . . I'm not sure. Where are the torpedoes now?"

Static filled the air. "A few seconds." Her voice was soft, sad.

"They made it through the blockade?"

"We steered them under the warsubs. Skimmed the seafloor, just like we did earlier."

"I love you, Renée. I'm sorry I didn't say it earlier."

"Don't give up, Mac." Her voice broke and she had to choke the sentence out.

"The USSF fired on *Black Widow*. She's gone. Sunk. Imploded. They're moving toward the other GSF warsubs now."

So the GSF crew was dead. Add them to the guilt that hung over my head every day. "I never do. It was my last play, though. Where are you?"

"*SC-1*. Johnny picked up me and Max. I fired the torpedoes remotely."

I smiled. "Great."

"Five seconds!"

"It's okay." I had accepted it. I laid my head on the deck, my body floating in the pool.

"I love you, too, Mac."

"I'm glad I met you."

"Two seconds!"

"I'm glad you tried to kill me, Renée. It pushed us closer. I know it sounds crazy but—"

Chapter Forty-One

I STOPPED SPEAKING AND LISTENED to the sounds around me. Alarms continued to clang out. The water was lapping at the deck. Ventilation fans. Warsub engines vibrated the hull as they passed by, likely moving toward the confrontation with the GSF vessels.

But there was no explosion.

No concussion wave, no water displacement.

Definitely not a nuclear-sized explosion.

—••—

"WHAT HAPPENED?" I WHISPERED.

"Nothing," Renée replied over the PCD.

"Did the—"

"The torpedoes collided with the Supply Module. They made it there all right. They hit, we heard it. But there was no blast."

"Did the Primary go?"

Max Hyland came over the air. "Mac, sonar is showing that the only sound was the collision of the two torpedoes with the module. There was no Primary detonation. No X-rays to trigger the isomer."

"So it didn't work."

"It works. But the trigger—"

"It didn't work."

"It *will* work. I've told you that."

"Dammit, Max, it didn't work."

Rico said from my side, "It's okay." He put his hand on my shoulder. "The ploy worked. The USSF thinks Germany attacked them. It'll draw the GSF into the conflict and we can pull New Berlin into Oceania."

"I was supposed to rescue Meg, and remove the USSF from the area."

Remove.

It was a funny euphemism for total destruction and the murder of thousands. I shook the thought aside. I'd deal with it later.

"You can still get Meg."

I looked around at the module. He was right. She was in there, somewhere, and I just had to find her.

She had escaped from the prison at Seascape, and had swum to the only place with which she was familiar: a Repair Module. It's where she had worked in Blue Downs. It's where she worked in Trieste. And it was a place where she likely had thought she'd be able to find a hiding place to avoid the USSF until I arrived.

I glanced at the PCD to find her tracking signal.

And while I did so, I noticed Rico drifting away from me.

He was out of arm's reach, and still moving away.

I looked up at him. "What are you doing?" A part of me wondered if he was going to disobey me again and go rogue, but I hadn't given him any instructions.

"Mac," he said. "I screwed up earlier. I'm sorry. I have to fix things now. Make them right."

He began to suck in huge gulps of air, and I knew immediately what he was planning.

"Don't do it," I snapped. "It's hopeless."

"I can make it. I made it here."

"But you won't be able to get to the Supply Module. Besides, the torpedoes are probably scrap metal by now. The collision destroyed them."

"You don't know that. There's still a chance. I just have to detonate the Primary, right? Then the Secondary will go."

"But it'll kill—"

"That's necessary. I did what I wanted to do. I took care of Heinrich. I tried to take care of my demons."

"But that doesn't mean you have to kill yourself!" I yelled. I began to move toward him, but he floated away.

"I'm not. I'll sacrifice myself, for your cause. I need to atone for what I did."

"You can't help what happened to you. The torture scarred you, but you can heal."

"I can never get over it."

I frowned. "You can try!"

He took another deep breath and said, "I still hate him."

And then he disappeared under the waves.

To make the long swim back the way we'd just come.

Interlude:
Meagan McClusky

Location: Latitude: 28° 41' 24" N
Longitude: 94° 54' 5" W
                   The Gulf of Mexico, Seascape City,
                   USSF HQ
                   The Mechanical/Repair Module
Depth: 30 meters
Date: 19 August 2130
Time: 1843 hours

MEAGAN AND CLIFF SIM HAD hunkered down inside a seacar that was down for repairs. It was a ratty-looking vessel, beat up, dented and old, floating at a dock in a far corner of the module. As soon as she and Cliff had surfaced in the moonpool, desperately trying to evade USSF troops searching for them, they'd picked it out of all the vessels there and decided to make their stand in it.

They swam slowly, trying their best not to ripple the water or alert anyone to their presence.

It had been hard. As soon as they'd surfaced, their lungs *bursting* from the intense swim from the Prison Module, they'd had to gulp massive lungfuls of air without making a noise.

There were sailors on the docks, repairing vessels, moving about the chamber.

The seacar was forty meters away.

Meg and Cliff did it quietly, slowly, delicately.

They barely rippled the water.

The module was the same size as the one at Trieste. The ceiling was fifteen meters over their heads. It was a large expanse, and there was a lot of other noise in there that helped mask their movements.

When they hit the dented seacar, Meg knew they'd have to climb in one at a time, enter through the hatch, then dog it securely behind them. But they couldn't *lock* it. If they did that, and someone checked, then it would give their hiding spot away. Instead, once they entered the seacar, they found a spot in which to hide—a cabinet in the engineering compartment. If someone started to open the top hatch, they had planned to bolt to engineering and lock themselves in the cabinet.

They entered the seacar without difficulty. Planned where to hide when the time came.

Sure enough, sailors did scour the module looking for them, searching the docks, under the water, in the offices and workshops along the perimeter. But before the search teams could begin looking in the many vessels in the module, alarms blared and lights started to flash.

Truman was nearby, Meg knew, and that meant they'd have to get ready.

The seacar was down for repairs, and she was the person who could get it up and running, *fast*.

—••—

THE EXPERIENCE HAD SEVERELY INJURED Cliff. Meg recognized this fact instantly. He'd had difficulty swimming. He probably had a broken leg. The guards had battered his body and had nearly beaten him to death. He needed to rest, to give his body time to heal.

So, he lay on the bench in the living area of the small seacar while Meg went to work on the engine.

Meg was also injured, but she knew how to repair seacars, and knew she had a job in front of her. It was a highly motivating factor. She was responsible for all of this. She'd murdered Benning out of rage, hoping it would make her feel better about her dad's death.

So far, it hadn't. She'd endured interrogations, torture, and guilt. She had dragged her brother Truman into this, and now he was putting his life, as well as the lives of others, on the line.

The guilt was enormous.

So she drowned the feeling and focused on work.

She set to repairing the vessel.

It didn't take her long to figure out that the batteries had shorted. Wires leading to them were old and frayed and corroded. She isolated the burned circuits and made quick work of them.

The engine was old and was desperate for some TLC. She dismantled large portions of it to see why the batteries wouldn't turn the screw. Hours passed as she pulled components, delicately organizing the nuts and bolts and access panels that she stripped, greased, and pounded back into shape on the tool bench in engineering before she put it all back together.

More hours passed.

She needed rubber seals for hydraulic filters to operate the dive planes. There were no extra seals in the seacar, so she fabricated her own out of the supplies she had on board. Every little repair she did was makeshift. A "bush fix," people in Blue Downs would often say. When you didn't have the right part in hand, you made your own. She wasn't sure where the term had come from. *Bush?*

More hours passed.

Eventually, she fell asleep on the deck, her body one huge, weeping, throbbing sore.

And when she awoke, she got right back to work.

More alarms were sounding now.

Cliff had noticed, as well, and he said, "Mac is close."

"He and his GSF attack group."

Cliff snorted. "I never put anything past the man. He's incredible."

"He does seem to get the job done, whatever it may be."

"How's this seacar? Seaworthy?"

Cliff was standing in the hatch to engineering, and Meg was lying under the engine, only her legs poking out. "The engine is turning the screw now. Not fast, but it's working."

"Great news. We should be able to use her to escape."

"Maybe."

Cliff detected the tone. "What?"

"I don't know anything about the ballast system or the hull integrity yet. It's an old seacar."

"It's why we picked it."

"Still." Meg frowned. "I guess we could submerge a bit, but stay moored to the dock. Hope that no one notices while we test the ballast system."

There was a loud bang on the top hatch.

Meg froze, but Cliff leapt into action. He grabbed the handle to the tool cabinet and yanked it open. They were going to hide in there.

The top hatch opened.

Meg swore softly and hauled herself out from under the engine. There were tools scattered across the deck, and she hoped no one would suspect two escaped prisoners had been attempting to repair an escape vehicle.

She climbed into the cabinet with Cliff, and began to pull the door shut.

"*Meg!?*" she heard.

She froze once more.

Her face tightened.

It sounded like—

"Meg?" the voice called again. The top hatch closed, and the sound of footsteps echoed down the ladder. "I know you're here! I've located the tracker."

"It's Mac!" Meg practically yelled. She bolted from the cabinet, raced out of engineering, and threw herself into her brother's arms.

He hugged her tight, but within seconds pushed her away.

Meg looked into his face. "What is it?"

"The reunion has to wait," he gasped. He looked toward the pilot's chairs. "We have to get moving."

"But why?"

"The explosion. It's only minutes away. And if it works, it'll kill us all."

Part Nine: The Bomb

Chapter Forty-Two

MEG LOOKED HORRENDOUS, BUT I didn't have time to comment or focus on her injuries. I did notice her two black eyes, swollen nose, and bruised face. Her eyes were sunken because she'd lost a great deal of weight. Her hair was pulled back, and it was dirty and unkempt. There were cuts on her forearms and neck. I was sure abrasions likely covered her entire body, but her coveralls hid them.

"What explosion?" she asked.

"Max Hyland. His—"

"His bomb?" she shouted. "The one you were telling us about before—before—"

"That's the one."

Cliff approached me from engineering and I looked him up and down. "How are you?" I winced at the question, for it was pretty stupid. The USSF guards had beaten him badly. He looked just like Meg. He'd lost weight, as well, though he was still heavily muscled. I did note that he was limping rather badly.

"Fine, Boss. You?"

That made me smile, at least. "The bomb. The torpedoes didn't detonate so Rico is swimming back to the module. He intends to find them and detonate them."

"Rico?"

I snapped a look at him, then realized. Rico had arrived only shortly before the USSF had arrested my sister and Cliff. They had no idea who he was. I said, "It's a long story. I'll tell you if we survive this."

"How big will it—"

"It'll destroy everything in the region. Crush us all. We need to get away fast. At SCAV drive if possible."

Meg snorted and gestured behind her, toward engineering. "All we have is a half-assed attempt at a twenty kph engine at best. I can barely get the screws turning."

I reflected on the other seacars I'd seen in the Repair Module. Most had been undergoing structural repairs. "Then this one will have to do. We have to get moving."

Meg sighed. "We won't get far."

"It'll have to do."

"I haven't tested the ballast system yet."

"We'll crawl along the bottom if we have to, but we have to get moving now."

It was enough. She winced for a moment, then spun on her heel and marched back to engineering. She called over her shoulder, "Start her up then. Descend and take us out of the module.

"And pray!"

—••—

I SAT IN THE PILOT chair on the left with Cliff to my right. It was an old model—at least thirty years—and the controls were simplistic. There was a lot of automation on the newer models; this one didn't even have computer-controlled trim tanks. The sonar screen was cracked and non-functional, and the pedals were rusty and difficult to move.

But I'd have to make it work, whatever the cost.

First I pushed ballast to negative, and listened to the pumps whine.

But they weren't just whining, they were *groaning*.

A creak and a shudder as the valves unlocked. Then a labored chugging as they allowed water into the tanks.

The sounds echoed in the cabin.

But it worked. The water lapped over the canopy a few seconds later, and I switched to neutral buoyancy.

We hovered near the bottom of the moonpool, and I slowly, gingerly, nudged the throttle forward.

Behind me, the engines began to shriek. The sound of metal grinding against metal pierced the seacar.

"Not so fast!" Meg screamed.

"Fast?" I muttered. I'd only pushed it to five percent power. I kept it as is, and aimed the bow toward the exit tube.

We were moving slowly, but at least we were going.

Cliff glanced at a blinking light and then turned to look behind him. "There's some leaking in the living space."

"Bad?"

"No. The pumps should be able to keep up."

Sure enough, I could hear a jet of water cutting through the space behind me.

"If they work," he added. Then he shook his head. "We've been through too much now to fail in this old rust bucket."

I pushed the throttle a tad higher.

Splashes broke the surface and several figures dove into the water.

They were USSF crew, armed, jumping into the moonpool to stop us.

"Shit," I said. I pushed the throttle higher.

The noise behind me grew in intensity. The controls were more for adjusting volume than anything else.

Meg yelled, "I said take it—"

"Sorry, Meg, I can't. We've got company."

There were several troops clinging to the hull now. They were crawling aftward, toward the airlock.

"Cliff," I started, but I didn't have to finish.

"I'm on it." He lifted his large bulk from the seat and limped backward, his steps loud on the bare steel. He pressed the LOCK button on the airlock controls.

I pushed the throttle more.

We were now out of the module and moving to the east. It was nighttime outside, dark except for the lights of the colony itself: the blue spotlight on the top of the Commerce Module, and the white lights outlining each module. Then we pierced the sphere of illumination, and entered darkness.

I wanted to keep us away from the blockade, which was to our south. The water was shallow here, and I knew it would magnify the explosion.

We were moving so damned slow.

The comm crackled to life. The voice was tinny and distant, and laced with static. The comm was just as old as the seacar.

"Attention, vessel departing Seascape to the east. Identify yourself."

I ignored it.

"Attention," the sea traffic controller bit out. "You do not have permission to depart. *Identify* yourself or we'll be forced to fire on you."

I glanced around, peering through the canopy. I didn't see any other warsubs about; I assumed they were all at the blockade, trying now to sink the GSF boats.

"How far do you think we have to get?" Cliff asked, crawling back into his chair.

"Hyland said five kilometers was in the kill area. He was shocked I'd sailed so close after announcing my intention to detonate the Isomer Bomb. I doubt ten would be much better."

"Twenty maybe?"

"Maybe. But I don't know for sure."

"Hug the bottom, perhaps. Maybe it'll keep them from seeing us."

"They know we just left."

"They know a seacar left. No necessarily us."

"Good point."

I angled down and skimmed the bottom. Our speed was twenty-seven kph. It was our max.

My PCD came to life and I jumped. I pulled it from my thigh pocket and checked the caller.

It was Rico.

Chapter Forty-Three

"Go ahead," I hissed into it.

"I'm at the Communications Module. The bodies are still all around the moonpool, but the troops have left."

"Be careful. Where are you—"

"I'm moving toward the south, toward the Supply Module."

That was where we had aimed the torpedoes.

"I'm in the travel tube." Rico was whispering now, and I could tell he was wearing his mask. He was likely moving fast, looking down, hoping no one noticed him. "The swim over was even harder, Mac. I almost drowned."

"You're a tough Triestrian," I muttered.

"Maybe. Not as tough as you, I guess."

"Don't say that."

"Why? I couldn't handle what I'd been through. Mentally, anyway."

"Physically you withstood far more than I did. You did one year. I only endured four months."

"But I couldn't handle the trauma, Mac."

I shifted in my chair. Cliff was watching me; he had no idea what we were talking about.

There was a long silence as we waited.

Then he came back on. "The hatch is shut, Mac. From the travel tube into the module."

"Security?"

"No." He paused and I heard a rustling noise. "There are blue lights flashing on the other side! Something has compromised the hull."

I frowned at that. How could that be possible? We hadn't—

And then a shiver coursed down my spine. "The torpedoes. They pierced the hull but didn't explode."

"And flooded the module? Yeah . . . yeah, it's full of water!"

"I'm guessing."

"I'll need a tank to get in there. To get at the weapons."

"Listen, Rico, it's okay. You don't have to do it. You can just hide. We'll come back for you."

"It's too late for me." His voice was soft. Accepting.

"Don't say that."

Cliff was still watching the exchange. I ignored him.

Rico was moving again. I could hear him rummaging through lockers, back in the Communications Module. "Locked. There's no scuba gear."

I grimaced, knowing what he was going to do. He would—

"I have to do it on a single breath, Mac. There's no other way."

—••—

I COULD HEAR HIM SUCKING in giant gulps of air. Getting ready to go out without a tank.

To detonate a bomb.

And kill himself.

If he didn't drown first.

My heart was pounding, and my throat was dry.

"Does he know how to trigger it?" Cliff asked.

I nodded. "TCI teaches that sort of thing. He'll have to open the casing and connect the correct wires. Hyland might also be able to help, if they can get in touch."

"Does he have a tool to open it up?"

"I suspect he'll search for something to use."

We heard a splash.

And then, nothing.

—••—

HE'D KEPT THE CHANNEL OPEN. I could hear a dim, rushing noise, as he pumped his legs and arms, pulling with everything he had. He'd have to swim to the Supply Module, and search to find the location of the weapons. If they were on the seafloor, he would go to work immediately. If they were sticking through the bulkhead, he might have to find the airlock in the Supply Module, open it, swim in, and get to the weapons that way.

Then open the torpedo, locate the wires, and short circuit them.

All on one breath.

—··—

A SOUND CAUGHT MY ATTENTION, and it was something that I hadn't expected. Our airlock ground open.

I snapped a look at Cliff. His eyes were hard, and he peered behind him for a moment before once again lifting himself from the chair.

The sailors outside, clinging to our seacar, had bypassed the lock. They had entered.

Cliff moved backward, his feet sloshing in water, and behind me, in our seacar, a struggle broke out.

He was fighting with three men.

—··—

I LET GO OF THE yoke to help my Chief of Security, but the seacar immediately yawed to the port. I grabbed it again to right it, and swore. To escape the blast, I had to hold it steady.

And Meg was in engineering.

There was no autopilot on this seacar.

—··—

THE SOUNDS OF THE STRUGGLE continued behind me. I could hear groaning, gasping, and one splash after another as a body hit the deck.

I hoped it wasn't Cliff.

Then he returned and sat beside me, as if nothing had transpired.

His face was set like stone.

And it made me chortle, but I suddenly remembered Rico, still trying to swim to the torpedoes.

I was holding my breath with him.

There was water around my feet. I stared at it, grim. My stomach dropped.

The pumps couldn't keep up.

A beep from the sonar console attracted my attention. The scope wasn't working, but the acoustics algorithms apparently were. Cliff stared at it. "A warsub just powered past Seascape. Headed for us."

"Distance?"

"We're eight kilometers from the colony now."

Surely it would catch us.

And then we'd be prisoners.

Again.

"It's USS *Blade*."

Admiral Quintana's warsub.

Did they know we were on board?

Probably not. At least not me. There was a chance they knew Cliff and Meg were, though.

"Come on, Rico," I mumbled. "You can do it."

There was a thumping noise over the PCD now. Then a voice floated to us, muffled by the ocean and the mask over the speaker's mouth.

Rico was holding the PCD to his full face mask, making his voice distant and ephemeral. "I found the weapons. Nearly out of breath. Opening the Primary with a piece of metal I found . . . "

I continued to hold my breath.

I didn't want to say anything. Didn't want to distract him.

"Eleven kilometers," Cliff said. "*Blade* is seven kilometers behind us."

Rico said, "Got it off. Searching for the cables now."

"*Blade* is six kilometers behind us," Cliff informed me. "She's now about five kilometers from the colony."

And the weapons, I thought.

"She's fired! *Blade* just fired two torpedoes!" Cliff was staring at the readout, studying the messages that were appearing in text format, for the display was not working. "Their speed is . . . " He trailed off, frowning at the readout. "My god, Mac, they're SCAV torpedoes. Speed is 1,063 kph! Time to impact is . . . *twenty-two seconds!*"

And our seacar was just a leaky bucket of bolts with a maximum speed of twenty-seven kph.

We didn't stand a chance.

Chapter Forty-Four

FINALLY, RICO STARTED GASPING. I could hear him sucking in air that just wasn't in his mask anymore. He was suffocating.

His choking was horrid. I could hear it echoing from the PCD I clutched in my hand. I stared at it, imagining what Rico was going through.

He'd been through so much pain already, and all for TCI.

It wasn't his fault that he'd wanted revenge so badly.

"*Ten seconds to impact,*" Cliff growled.

Rico didn't have the maturity or the wisdom to have been able to navigate through it.

Hell, neither had I! I had only made it through by sheer luck.

Then his voice, each word gasped through choking sobs, "*Sorry, Mac—you—were—*"

And then it stopped.

And the PCD squawked once—a *shriek*, really—and cut out.

—••—

I STARED AT THE SPEED readout, mentally straining to make the seacar go faster.

A vibration began to shake the hull.

I could feel it in the chair, at my feet on the pedals, on every surface around me.

The ocean outside the canopy suddenly lit, as if it were day.

"What the—" Meg said from over my shoulder.

The light grew in intensity until we were squinting to protect ourselves.

The vibration grew to a rumble, then to a violent shaking, then to a veritable earthquake underwater.

"We need scuba gear," I said in sudden realization. "The hull won't withstand this. We'll need tanks and regulators!" The shaking continued to build. There was a sudden wrenching and the seacar seemed to jerk in the water. "Hold on to something!" I screamed.

The Isomer Bomb had worked. Hyland's X-ray trigger had done it. It had released the energy stored in the hafnium all at once rather than over multiple half-lives of thirty-one years each. It was just a few grams of the stuff, and equivalent to Hiroshima.

A tactical nuclear bomb.

Like Bruce Lee, he'd said. *The one-inch punch.*

And we'd just detonated it next to USSF HQ.

The shock wave hit us, and it was a tidal wave underwater. A tsunami.

It picked our seacar up and in an instant turned it on its side. Meg landed on the bulkhead heavily and yelled at the pain lancing up her body.

The sound was like nothing I'd heard before underwater. It was as if a volcano had erupted next to us.

The scene outside the viewport was hellish. The bright white light had turned red, with sediment and sand and kelp and rocks and dead fish rushing by, propelled by the incredible explosion. Then bits of steel from the colony itself. And plexiglass, from the transparent water park module, shattered into trillions of pieces.

I realized that the explosion had vaporized a bubble of water the size of a city.

And now the surrounding water would have to crash back into it.

"Oh, *SHIT!*" I screamed. "Hold on!"

An unseen force seemed to grab the bow of the seacar and wrench it back, facing the source of the detonation to the west.

We started to move toward an immense reddish ball that was growing in size as we plunged toward it.

Precisely where Seascape had been a few seconds earlier.

The outside edges were blurry, indistinct. I had to blink to focus on it. It was a massive sphere of energy—an *island*—rapidly shifting intensely hot colors—reds and oranges and yellows—across its expanse. It also seemed to suck in the light around it; the edge of the island was as black as night, darker than anything I'd seen. I blinked over and over, but nothing helped, for my eyesight grew fuzzy and it was impossible to focus.

In an instant, a splitting headache cut through me, faster and more intense than anything I'd experienced.

The console speed readout now said fifty-nine kph, and it was climbing as the water surged back into the void, carrying us with it.

The wreck of *Blade* spun past us; pieces of its hull sheared away by the force of the underwater torrent. Cracks traced the side of the vessel and, as I watched, it broke into four large pieces, each hurled away as if from a giant's unseen hand.

Debris and people spilled from it, wrenched away instantly, torn to pieces as gargantuan forces took hold.

I clutched the armrests of the pilot's chair, willing it to end.

The world whipped by the viewport, carrying me with it.

Epilogue:
Trieste City

Epilogue

I WAS BACK IN TRIESTE.

The modules stretched out before me. It was daytime above, and the sun cut easily downward through the thirty meters. It shimmered in the Gulf waters, caressing the modules and travel tubes of the colony. Dark anechoic tile now covered as much of the city as possible, but there were plenty of viewports where I could see people moving about, conducting their daily business, going to work and play and volunteering duties. Behind the city, bubbles rose to the surface in endless streams—the fish farms. And next to them in the distance, huge kelp forests swayed in the currents. Our aquaculture sector managed them—harvesting was a daily activity because it grew so fast—and the department had laid out the farms in large rectangular blocks.

I was in my scuba gear following a morning swim, and was floating there silently, staring at the city.

It was beautiful.

Max Hyland was with me. He, Johnny, and Renée had rescued us from the flooding seacar following the detonation. Johnny had piloted away from Seascape in SCAV drive seconds before the detonation, and had returned to the aftermath to locate us, resting on the bottom, waiting to die. Meg had been unconscious, but Cliff and I had managed to get a tank and mask on her, get her into the water around the vessel—water significantly warmer than it had been minutes earlier—and into *SC-1*.

Now, back in Trieste days later, I had finally been able to free up some time to go outside with Max. He loved living in Trieste, and had set up a permanent lab in the Research Module, with quarters in a Living Module, and was enjoying this new chapter of his life. He was quite the socializer, had a huge network of friends now in the city, and from what I heard, also had quite a few female friends.

We were wearing full face masks, and I had enjoyed a conversation with him during the swim.

Now we floated together, resting on the bottom, and stared at the colony as the sun shone down on it.

"It's incredible, Mac," he whispered.

"It is. I came here over thirty years ago. It's really the only home I've ever had."

"You've fought hard for it."

"So have you, now."

He turned to look at me. The mask distorted his face, but I could see the distress in his eyes. "I have."

I studied him. "The bomb."

He sighed. "The bomb."

"It was your life's work. You got to achieve it, Max."

He didn't respond.

"You're concerned about the number of people killed?" I asked eventually.

He looked around and stared up at the surface. "I'm sure Einstein and Fermi and Oppenheimer had the same moral crises after their work resulted in Hiroshima. I don't think Teller ever had any doubts about his contributions, though."

"Teller?"

"The hydrogen bomb."

"Ah."

"The work those people did resulted in many deaths, and an escalation of the Cold War. Now my bomb will too."

I frowned. "People had blacklisted you, Max. They thought you were a crackpot."

"Hardly reason to detonate a bomb and kill thousands. We destroyed hundreds of USSF vessels."

It was true. After the battle in the Mid-Atlantic Ridge—where I had sunk a hundred USSF warsubs, and the conflict with the Russian dreadnought, which had resulted in the destruction of USSF HQ on both the Atlantic and Pacific coasts, and then the deadly battle in the Pacific—the Fleet was already suffering. And now this. Another HQ lost, another staggering defeat of over 200 more warsubs.

I wondered if another superpower would take advantage of the US struggle in the oceans.

I knew we surely would.

"It is good reason, Max."

"What do you mean?"

"You told me that DARPA was continuing funding on the bomb, despite their public condemnation of your work. Everyone said there was no such thing as a hafnium bomb. But they continued to fund it. Why?"

"In case another superpower developed it."

"Exactly. Which is why it was necessary for you to create it. Imagine if Russia did it first! Or China! You've *done* it, Max. And we proved it. And now the superpowers are quaking."

The news had ricocheted around the world in the days following the explosion.

It was immediately obvious to the media a massive detonation had taken place sixty-five kilometers south of Texas. News outlets broadcast that it had been nuclear, but had quickly retracted those statements when scientists noted that there was no lingering radiation evident. It had been nuclear-sized, with no lethal fallout. There had been a massive gamma burst in the first seconds of the explosion, but that was it. It was something of a mystery.

Then, hours later, came the first mention of hafnium.

And Max had been the man who had done it.

The First Cold War had revolved around atomic and hydrogen bombs. An escalating battle to build the most missiles, the best launch systems, and the best defensive strategies. The Atomic Age. Then came a period of cooling, while leaders fought to limit the number of weapons. Then, as the superpowers realized the best hope for survival amid the climate chaos lay in the oceans, the Second Cold War flared up. And the weapon this war would revolve around now became obvious: the Isomer Bomb.

And the world ushered in the Isomer Age.

"Max, how would you feel if China detonated this bomb on top of Trieste?"

He sighed. "I do understand both sides of the issue. Obviously I wanted to achieve my life's work, and now history will know my name. But I'm hoping not to be associated with death. There are so many other applications to this. In medicine, we can trigger nuclear isomers to release energy and burn tumors, for instance. The applications are endless. But . . . " he trailed off. "I killed so many."

"They were going to kill Meg and Cliff, Max. They've persecuted Trieste for decades. They took over a civilian city and were using it for military purposes. They were basically bringing a period of piracy and colonialism back to the oceans. You just stopped it."

"I know." He took in a huge breath, the bubbles from his regulator stopping for a moment, then he exhaled, and they resumed again. "It'll just take a while to process. I don't regret doing it, I'll tell you that. I just have to deal with the . . . the guilt."

I certainly understood that part of it. I lived with it every day.

"You'll be a target soon," I said. "Other nations need these secrets to trigger their own bomb. When they realize it wasn't Germany who did it, which they will one day, they'll come looking for you."

"Cliff told me. There are extra security details around me and my lab now." We floated there, staring at the city and the light shining down on it, for many more minutes before we finally swam back.

—••—

"Hiya, Doc," I said with a rap on the hatch.

Stacy Reynolds was inside the clinic, staring at a holographic display and tapping on a virtual keyboard on the desk before her. She answered without looking at me, "Mac. How are you doing." Her expression didn't change and her tone didn't waver. It hadn't sounded like a question; she was ambivalent about the answer.

"Feeling better, thanks."

"Did everything work out?"

"You could say that."

She sighed, finished the patient file she was working on, closed it, and turned to me.

We were alone in the cabin.

"The events at Seascape have been remarkable. Life changing."

"It's a new period in the Cold War, that's for sure."

She stared at me, and her eyes narrowed. "Did we play a part in that?"

It was why I was there. She had dealt with my injuries for many months now: needles through my leg, dislocated shoulders, and now burns and stitches and more. And, a few weeks previous, she had implanted The Tube and tracker into our thighs. She had protested, but had eventually gone ahead and done it. I now had to explain fully; I couldn't keep her in the dark any longer.

"Stacy, I'm sure you suspect what's been going on."

"I have a pretty good idea already." She stared at me, her face emotionless once more.

"You do?"

"Sure. You are fighting for independence for Trieste, just like your dad."

I blinked. "How did you know?"

"Come on, Mac. Your injuries aren't from farming kelp. I know something's going on."

"And yet you helped me."

"I certainly did."

"But I'm here to tell you more. I don't want to lie to you about it."

"Go ahead."

"I run an agency at Trieste. It's our intelligence agency. I send our operatives out on missions to protect our interests and improve our position in the oceans."

"We're a US colony, Mac."

"Yes. Each colony in the world has such an agency. We're always competing with them."

"And the USSF knows?"

I shrugged. "Maybe. They did at one point. It's why they arrested Shanks and Mayor Flint eighteen months ago, then occupied us."

"There's been a lot of turmoil since then, you're right."

She continued to stare at me, her face flat. Then she snorted. "Hell, Mac, if I seriously objected to it all, I wouldn't have treated you for these odd injuries all these months, and I wouldn't have implanted that bizarre weapon in your thigh. Or Meg's and Chief Sim's. Of course I'm okay with it. I love Trieste. I'll do anything to see her prosper in the oceans." Then she swore under her breath. "And I have dealt with too many injuries caused by foreign Fleet sailors who storm around the city on their leaves, harassing and assaulting our people. I've treated women following rapes too. Did you know that?"

"Of course."

"I'm fine with what you're doing."

"It's secret, Stacy."

"I'm fine with that, too. Count me in on anything you're planning."

I grinned. Her attitude was similar to so many other Triestrians. We'd been through so much since the 2090s. She was anxious to see us prosper in the colonization attempts. "Thanks, Stace."

"Now get out," she snapped. "I'm working on my charts."

---·••—

AN HOUR LATER, I WAS back at my desk in my office attached to City Control. The bulkheads seemed closer than normal. The metal desk smaller.

And the air stuffier.

But I was happy to be back. I inhaled deeply. It wasn't like the air at Seascape. There it was clean and fresh, even with the USSF presence . . . a holdover from its history of tourism.

Here it was canned and tinny. Processed.

I liked it at Trieste better.

I stared at the steel surrounding me. I had a small viewport, and outside the scene was wondrous.

Inside, however, there was a stack of paper on the corner—issues for me to deal with.

I sighed.

First I keyed the comm and signaled someone I'd been meaning to speak with for days.

He appeared on the screen and his eyes widened when he recognized me. "Mayor McClusky."

"Hello, Mister Gerhardt." It was the mayor of New Berlin. The last we'd heard of him had been in the Jade Bight, when I had contacted him to trigger the movement of GSF warsubs and expose their positions. We'd heard him struggling with someone before his comm shut off.

"Gunther, please." He smiled.

"Call me Mac."

"I'm not sure how much we can say here, over this line."

"I understand." I paused and eyed him. "I've had an interesting several weeks."

"Since you were in the North Sea."

"Yes. And are you . . . okay?"

He nodded. "Things are settling down here. Something else is occupying the GSF's attention. The US government is quite angry with Germany right now, it seems."

"It does indeed."

In fact, the US had been screaming at Germany about the Isomer Bomb in the Gulf. Politicians were hard at work, though the US was beating the war drum. The events had greatly weakened their ocean forces, but their topside military was as strong as ever. I didn't want a war to start on land, but I had been wanting a reason for New Berlin to join with us, and if the GSF was involved in a fight versus another superpower, it would free up their colony to join Oceania.

At least, that was my hope.

And their recent election had brought in a sympathetic ear for us.

"They're accusing us of attacking Seascape HQ for some reason."

"They are."

Gerhardt frowned. "Apparently there are GSF ships down there. Sunk. One off the coast of Florida, as well."

"Yes."

"And we've heard rumblings that there were German special forces troops inside Seascape minutes before the detonation."

"I've heard that, too."

Apparently USSF security at Seascape had contacted the Pentagon before the explosion, notifying them of a German intrusion. They'd heard Franz's comments and had sent a recording to the Joint Chiefs.

Franz, my prisoner, had effectively pinned the attack on Germany. There had been other evidence, as well—such as the GSF warsubs—but Franz had been the icing on the cake.

My gamble had worked.

He shook his head. "If it's true, then all blame points to us." He eyed me. "Mainland Germany, I mean."

"A GSF attack force sailed down here and straight for Seascape. Made quite a ruckus."

"Indeed." He continued to study me, but knew we could say no more because the GSF had compromised the lines.

"Perhaps a diplomatic visit between us soon would work?" I suggested.

His eyes brightened. "I would enjoy that! Can I come visit you at Trieste? I'd love to see your city."

"It would be my honor."

And below my desk, out of his sight, I clenched my fist in triumph.

It was one more city added to our alliance in the fight for Oceania.

—••—

CLIFF WAS IN CITY SECURITY. The effects of his experience were fading quickly, but these were just physical. His leg was now in a cast, and he'd begun to put some weight back on. He was grappling with security issues, since he'd been away for nearly two months.

I felt terrible about what had happened to him. Meg had drawn us all into this by killing the Admiral, and Cliff had followed my orders to try and cover for her. But it hadn't worked, and he'd ended up in a prison cell at Seascape.

He turned when I entered, and his severe features barely changed at my presence. But there was a hint of smile there, and I could tell that he held no ill will for the events.

"Quite a few weeks, wouldn't you say, Boss?"

"I wanted to say that I was sorry."

He frowned. "For what?"

I blinked. "For dragging you into this."

He sat down at his desk; behind him, a viewport showed the ocean. Fish, seacars, scuba divers, and more. He said, "But I am a part of this by my own choice, Mac."

"Covering for a murder is hardly a part of TCI's mandate."

"But he was an occupying force here. Meg did it, sure, but it's all part of the struggle."

"She murdered him. We'd worked together only days earlier, on the mission to defeat the dreadnought."

He shrugged. "Sure. But he did kill your dad. I was in the USSF back then. I remember the mission. I left shortly after and vowed never to take part in harassment of the colonies."

"I know."

"Then how can you think I wouldn't have helped you and Meg?"

"Because I ordered her not to kill the man."

He sighed. "Some things are inescapable, Mac. Like revenge."

I thought of Rico, and how he had killed Heinrich against my orders. "Revenge doesn't solve anything, Cliff."

"Maybe it does, for some people. And don't forget, we're at war."

"A war that some people don't even know exists."

"Still. War is war, Mac, whether they choose to accept it or not. Benning is a casualty of war, not a victim of murder."

"The same as my dad, I guess," I mumbled.

"Perhaps."

"I have to go speak with Meg now about all of this."

"How is she?"

"Recovering in her cubicle. The doctor has her on a variety of medications to speed the healing."

"Rico got his revenge, I heard," he said out of the blue.

It startled me. "I haven't told you much about him." He'd arrived at Trieste just before the USSF had taken Cliff, so he didn't yet know the whole story.

"I've heard from Renée about it. How he disobeyed you and compromised the takeover of the GSF warsub. All to kill one man."

"All to kill one man," I repeated. "It's amazing how the thirst for revenge can affect people."

"It affected you, as well."

"I got over it."

"You did. But some people just can't. The scars run too deep."

A choking gasp worked itself up my throat, and I buried my face in my hands. The raw emotion overtook me faster than I'd expected. I attempted to smother it, but failed. I could feel Cliff watching me. Eventually I managed, "Rico sacrificed himself for us. For Trieste. He thought I hated him for what he'd done."

I felt embarrassment for falling apart in front of a man I respected, but I couldn't control it.

He said, "For killing Heinrich?"

"Against my orders. Yes."

There was a long silence as I struggled to accept the reality of what had happened. I would have gotten past what Rico had done, I was sure of it. Eventually I would have. But I had fired him from TCI for opposing me, and it had resulted in his sacrifice.

"Mac," Cliff said, his voice stern. "Rico did it to save Trieste and the independence movement. The torture and his experience on the GSF warsub affected him deeply. It was a conscious choice he made. To save you."

"I know," I finally managed.

But it didn't help.

---•--

RENÉE WAS IN A LOUNGE in the entertainment district, having a coffee and watching the scene outside a deck-to-ceiling viewport. Families with children were there, enjoying the sights and having breakfast. She turned to me and smiled as I approached.

I sat before her, and she studied my features. "What's wrong?" she asked, worry lacing her features.

I waved away her concern. "It's not you. I've just been dwelling on Rico. We hardly knew him. He was an incredible person."

"I agree." A smile grew across her face. "He was a great Operative."

"I am feeling . . . morose, I guess."

She grabbed my hand in hers and squeezed it, but said nothing. We just sat there silently, staring outside.

I continued, "He sacrificed himself for all of us."

"I heard it all."

That shocked me. "What?"

"His broadcast over the PCD while he armed and triggered the Primary. Max talked him through a bit of it. We heard his final words to you. All encrypted of course, so the USSF doesn't know."

"It's . . . hard."

"I understand. But he sacrificed himself for all of us, Mac. A similar decision we might all face one day."

Another silence stretched out. Then she said, "What about us?"

"I've realized during these past weeks that following trauma in my past, I've isolated myself and pushed people away. Self-preservation. It's why I was alone for seven years after Sheng City. I know I can't do that now. I want to grow closer to the people around me this time. To draw from their strength. To lean on them. I don't want to feel all this guilt."

"Guilt for Rico?"

"For Rico." I nodded. "For all the warsubs I've sunk. For the sailors I've killed."

"It's natural, Mac." Her eyes were pleading, and she leaned toward me. "But think of all this." She gestured around us, at the children and their parents in the café. We were in the Commerce Module, and the terraces laced with vines and plants and the nine-level atrium with the transparent ceiling and the sun shining above. "We're underwater having a coffee at an outdoor café. There are 200,000 people here and you have protected them since you became mayor."

"I've put them in jeopardy."

She snorted at that and pulled back. Her face hardened. "Are you serious? You pushed away an occupation. You've kept them safe. Safe from harassment and abuse. They trust you. They love you. You've protected them, not put them in danger."

I sighed. "I guess you're right."

"I know I am."

"But there are two sides to it. The superpowers of the world would have another viewpoint."

"Which is why we're at war with them!"

I stared at her. She was vehemently arguing with me. "I like you like this."

"Like what?"

"Pushing me. Making me think and not dwell on things."

A smile returned slowly to her face. "And what about us, Mac?"

"I want to pursue a relationship. I was saying before that I was through pushing people away to avoid trauma. I need to draw closer to you. To rely on you, if you'll have me." It was against all my instincts, but when it came to relationships, those had proven faulty in the past. I needed to try something else, if I wanted to keep her in my life.

She made me happy. And together, we would see Trieste through to the formation of Oceania.

She was grinning now. "I wouldn't have it any other way."

"How about dinner tonight? Before you answer, though, you should know I've already made a reservation."

We kissed, and the people of Trieste around us were watching, and I dimly noted that they were smiling, too.

—••—

MEG WAS IN HER CUBICLE, and her eyes lit when I knocked and entered. "Howdy, brother."

I sat on her bunk and stared at her. She was looking better. Her eyes were brighter and the bruises were fading. Her legs were horribly scarred, and would remain so for the rest of her life, but she was still alive. Her ribs were healing and she'd spent most of her time in her cubicle after the incident.

She grabbed my hand and squeezed it. "I'm sorry about what I did," she said.

"It's okay. I've thought a lot about it. You did what you had to do."

"I caused a lot of pain for a lot of people."

"But it all worked out. The USSF is gone from the region. Quintana died in the detonation. Zyvinski—" I frowned. "I'm not sure what happened to her, actually."

"I killed her, too."

I blinked. "Really?"

"Yes. Stabbed her in the neck."

My jaw dropped. "You're serious." It was the same way she'd finished Benning.

"When I made my escape I did it. With the weapon the doctor hid in my thigh."

I considered the situation that faced her. "Are you feeling . . . better?"

"My wounds are healing up. My ribs are—"

"No, Meg. I mean, up here." I gestured at my head.

"Oh. Mentally." She took in a big breath of air and exhaled. "I have been thinking about Benning since I did it. After I killed him, it released a lot of pain. About Dad, and how he had died." She paused and then looked into my eyes. "It pulled a bunch of other people into it with me, and I regret that. I do feel guilt about it. And . . . and I still feel anger at Benning. It's weird. I killed the man hoping it would take care of things, but I'm still furious about what happened to our family. That pain isn't going away."

It was what I'd been trying to tell Rico.

Killing the source of the problem didn't solve the problem.

It just created another one, while the old one still simmered within.

"Cliff seems okay with it," she said.

"Yeah, I spoke with him already." I paused. "The bomb and the political fallout have kept the US government fixated on Germany. They haven't bothered us at all or even mentioned you to me. I don't think they even know Quintana took you to Seascape."

"So it's all over."

I studied her features. "As long as you can get over things. Over what happened to Dad."

"I know what you're saying. Trust me, I know. Revenge. It's so crude and animalistic."

"It is."

"But he destroyed our family, Tru. I had to pay him back."

"We have a new family now. Me, you, Johnny, Renée."

"Renée?" She smiled at me.

"Yes."

"I figured, you know. I'm glad you've straightened some things out, too." She sighed again. "I wasn't myself, Tru. I had withdrawn. My friendships and relationships were suffering. Now, I feel that I can get back to them. But I'm still simmering over what Benning did to Dad."

I frowned as I thought about that. I'd told Rico that revenge didn't work, that the feelings never went away just because you got rid of the person who had caused the damage. It would always be there.

Maybe, as Meg was saying, you could substitute the feelings of rage and hurt for ones of love and family.

After all, I thought with a jolt, that's what I was trying to do with Renée at Trieste.

I thought again of Rico. I was going to miss him.

—••—

THE NEXT DAY I MET with the entire team in a lounge in the central module. We had poured mugs of kelp beer and were celebrating the end of recent events. I searched the faces surrounding me. Manesh Lazlow and Max Hyland, our resident scientists who were innovating new technologies to fight the superpowers. Richard and Jessica, who continued to work on our city defences, and had just completed construction on a massive shelter under the city to protect the citizens in case of aggression. Cliff and Dr. Reynolds both of whom had been instrumental in defeating the USSF in the Gulf of Mexico. Johnny Chang, my best friend, partner in TCI, Deputy Mayor of Trieste, and the man whom I had forgiven for torturing me during my imprisonment in Sheng City years earlier. Renée Féroce, the French captain I'd convinced to join us in our fight for freedom from oppression, and my new love.

And there were others, who weren't there. The French mayors, in their undersea colonies. Grace Winton, Mayor of Ballard City. Gunther Gerhardt, our new German ally, Mayor of New Berlin. Jackson Train, working diligently at The Ridge, creating new ships and drones to continue the fight.

And more.

I raised a glass, and together we smiled. Even Stacy Reynolds, normally so serious and grim, sported a tilting half-smile.

"It's been a brutal year and a half since the USSF arrested Shanks and Flint and I took over as mayor and Director of TCI, but look how far we've come. We now have twelve cities involved in our alliance, and more on the way."

Cheers all around.

I continued, "We have a major problem facing us. There will always be issues to confront, but this one is . . . " I trailed off. They looked back at me, foreheads creased, but some were nodding. "Russia," I continued. "Soon they'll be putting three more dreadnoughts to sea, and we have to be prepared." It had taken everything we'd had to defeat just one—*Dragon*—a few weeks earlier.

"The new Isomer Bombs," Johnny said, and the rest cheered.

"The non-nuclear alternative. It worked for us, and didn't force anyone into launching nukes topside." If we had used a nuke, it just might have, I thought. The radiation, the psychological impact . . .

The isomer option was far better.

"But those dreadnoughts will be coming, and we have to prepare for them." Then I paused, and looked at my entire team. "To Trieste!" I said.

"To Trieste!"

I noticed Richard Lancombe, who had fought for independence with my father, and had helped us so much since he'd reappeared in my life, staring at Renée as he sipped his drink.

Outside the large viewport, a vessel passed by overhead, eclipsing the sun, and a shadow crossed over the city as we drank.

A Note from the Author

THANK YOU TO THE ENTIRE team at Fitzhenry & Whiteside. There's no way I can thank them enough for taking on Mac and Meg's story and publishing *The Rise of Oceania*.

Cheyney Steadman created the schematics for this novel. She is incredibly talented and she somehow brought my imagination to life before my eyes. Thank you, Cheyney.

Any errors in regards to the physics of cavitation and supercavitation, the effects of water pressure, nuclear isomers, hafnium, and SCUBA diving are mine alone.

I consulted with physicist Ian Martin about binding energy and nuclear isomers (not to be mistaken with molecular isomers). I am not a scientist and I freely admit that many of the details are beyond me. I so appreciate your help with the numbers.

The history behind the theorized Isomer Bomb is very real. I stumbled upon the story of Dr. Carl B. Collins, who worked at the University of Texas at Dallas, and immediately recognized the dramatic possibilities. It is a fascinating tale of drama, mystery, and wonder. Despite the numerous detractors (scientists and otherwise) there remain proponents of the hafnium bomb. The science of it discussed in this book is based on theory: nucleons within the 178m2 Hf atom contain energy that is slowly released as gamma rays over its thirty-one year half life. The isomer is called *nearly stable*. Collins's experiments demonstrated that the energy could be triggered (IGE, or *Induced Gamma Emission*) with X-rays and released all at once. It would result in nuclear levels of destruction in a non-nuclear package, meaning the energy release doesn't come from the splitting of atoms (fission), and nor does it come from fusing them (fusion). It would therefore skirt all existing nuclear non-proliferation treaties.

During his original experiments in 1998, his team did indeed employ a used dental X-ray machine, along with an audio amplifier to modulate the beam. His research was peer-reviewed and published, though later efforts to replicate the experiments failed. At that point, his science was criticized and he was more or less blacklisted from professional publications. It is now often equated with the cold fusion controversy. However, despite this, and most interestingly, DARPA has poured millions into researching the Isomer Bomb. The belief is that they need to continue development on it, if it is at all possible, in case another nation should succeed. The "I Believe in Isomers" poster featured in this book actually existed as pins that people at the Pentagon and other research facilities wore on their lapels back in the late 1990s.

Despite the naysayers and the experiments that have failed to replicate Dr. Collins's original experiment (such as two different experiments at the Argonne National Laboratory, boasting an X-ray source the size of a football field and 100,000 times more intense than what Dr. Collins and his students used for their original experiment), others claim to have succeeded at proving that energy can be coaxed from 178m2 Hf. Tests in 2001 at the Japanese Spring-8 facility successfully reproduced his work (according to Collins), and former student Pat McDaniel (present at the original experiment) apparently reproduced the results at Louisiana State University, though he never published. The Triggered Isomeric Proof experiment (TRIP) results have never been published as far as I can tell. Is it because they proved the concept and the Pentagon wants to quiet public speech about this new weapon? Or was it because of a total failure that might serve to embarrass proponents of the Isomer Bomb?

According to nuclear physicist Peter D. Zimmerman, when he was Chief Scientific Advisor of the Arms Control and Disarmament Agency, Ehsan Khan at the US Department of Energy (and now a Senior Advisor there) sent out a "strange letter" warning people not to speak with journalist Sharon Weinberger, who was researching the story of the Isomer Bomb. (Her Washington Post article is cited below and is freely available online.) In his letter, he apparently wrote that TRIP had been so successful, further research had been recommended. Additionally, according to Weinberger's article *Scary Things Come in Small Packages*, the State Department's Bureau of Non-Proliferation grew frustrated with players "discussing plans for a new super-bomb out in the open." They then sent out instructions to government scientists to encourage secrecy, otherwise "isomer technology could fall into the hands of terrorists or rogue states." These instructions frustrated opponents of IGE, who didn't understand why information about an 'impossible' weapon should be classified. Indeed, it has only made the mystery more profound, and the possibilities ever more interesting.

Most articles from legitimate sources were published pre-2010, and any published after that seem to be referencing the below articles.

People have indeed stopped publishing new information about the Isomer Bomb and IGE. The question that fascinates me is: *why?*

The Isomer Bomb is a truly interesting ongoing story in military research, though the medical applications mentioned in this book are very real, as well, as evidenced by Dr. Collins's championing of hafnium research for this purpose—the "Hafnium Seed" to burn tumors. But despite the critics, which include scientists, researchers, politicians, and others, DARPA has poured millions into IGE research.

Sharon Weinberger's article about Dr. Collins and the hafnium controversy provided great context for the Isomer Bomb in this novel. I want to credit her here. Her article, as well as two others I found interesting, are:

Alan, B. (2007, May 31). Half Science and Hafnium Bombs. Retrieved 1 May 2019, from https://www.damninteresting.com/half-science-and-hafnium-bombs/

Weinberger, S. (2004, March 28). Scary Things Come in Small Packages. *Washington Post*. Retrieved 1 May 2019 from https://www.washingtonpost.com/archive/lifestyle/magazine/2004/03/28/scary-things-come-in-small-packages/

Zimmerman, P. D. (2007, June). The Strange Tale of the Hafnium Bomb: A Personal Narrative. APS Physics, 16(6). Retrieved 1 May 2019 from https://www.aps.org/publications/apsnews/200706/backpage.cfm

The mention of waterboarding is from Jake Tapper's *The Outpost*. In the book, he cites soldiers in Afghanistan who experimented with its use. (At the time of the events in his book, there was a debate raging in the States about the use of torture to extract information in the post-911 era.) The American soldiers who volunteered only lasted four seconds; only one US soldier made it to eight seconds, and stated that it was indeed torture (Tapper, 2012, P. 450).

Tapper, J. (2012). *The Outpost: An Untold Story of American Valor*. New York, NY: Little, Brown and Company.

The Puerto Rico Trench is the deepest area of the Atlantic Ocean with a maximum depth of eight and a half kilometers (~8,500 meters).

There is a reason why I named the character Rico. The purpose was to mirror the Puerto Rico Trench, where Mac disposed of Admiral Benning's body. One of the themes in this book is that of trauma and how best to deal with it. Mac endured his trauma in the years before *The War Beneath*, and was hoping that he could 'coach' Rico to cope with his in the same way. The depths of the trench mirror the depths of Rico's emotions and the heartache that he faces during his journey. Mac attempts to hide a body (symbolic for his sister's rage and trauma) in the Trench. It doesn't work, and she ends up captured by the USSF. Rico attempts to also bury his rage and trauma in a trench (within himself). It doesn't work, either, and he ends up acting impulsively and endangering the mission and the independence movement. Earlier, in *Fatal Depth*, Mac also laid Katherine Wells to rest in a rift in the Mid-Atlantic Ridge. My message through this is that hiding pain doesn't work. It only makes things worse.

In fact, there are four characters in *An Island of Light* coping with trauma, paralleling one another, and each responds in a different manner. Some are more successful than others:

1. Truman has been dealing with the trauma of his dad's murder, torture during his capture by the Chinese, and Kat's death.
2. Renée has been dealing with the trauma Mac caused when he fired on her ship in *The War Beneath*, and her obsession with finding and killing him in *The Savage Deeps*.
3. Meagan has suffered from trauma due to the death of her dad, driving her to murder Benning at the beginning of this book.
4. Rico succumbed to the trauma caused by imprisonment and torture at the hands of the German, Heinrich.

Enrico Fermi and the story of prejudice based on ethnicity is yet another instance of 'Rico' in this story. Thankfully, Fermi continued to press the US military, resulting in the atomic bombs that ended WW2 in the Pacific, saving an estimated million lives.

In August 2019, during the writing of this book, I visited the Elgin War Museum's *Oberon* Class submarine HMCS *Ojibwa*, on display in Port Burwell, Ontario, Canada. The purpose was to draw inspiration for the events that take place on board GSF warsub *Black Widow*. The tour was fascinating and the sense of claustrophobia took me by storm. The boat housed seventy people in tight confines for months at a time, and it operated at the height of the Cold War. I wrote about the experience on my blog, and I encourage anyone in the region to visit and tour the submarine. Film crew from *Fast and the Furious 8 (The Fate of the Furious)* also toured it for their submarine sequences in the movie. *Ojibwa* is an incredible addition to the Elgin War Museum in Southern Ontario.

The mention in Chapter Twenty-Four of the ship's odors came from the visit to *Ojibwa*. You can still smell the diesel on board the boat. At the time I was writing this book, I was also reading *Shoot for the Moon*, about NASA's programs leading to Apollo 11 and the first manned moon landing. The story of the recovery team vomiting when opening *Gemini* 7 is true (Donovan, 2019, P. 176).

Donovan, James. (2019). *Shoot for the Moon: The Space Race and the Extraordinary Voyage of Apollo 11*. New York, NY: Little, Brown and Company.

During World War II there were many examples of subterfuge to confuse the enemy. One story involved the Allies planting evidence of an imminent attack at Calais on a dead German officer, then setting his body adrift in the Mediterranean, hoping that Nazi officials would discover it. Additionally, the Allies had constructed a false (or "ghost") army in England directly opposite Calais. Fake tanks, barracks, and so on. These were inflatable balloons or false structures. The subterfuge was highly successful. (In fact, senior officials, including Hitler, refused to believe that the attack was occurring at Normandy on 6 June 1944, even while Allied troops were landing there; Germany had prepared for an attack at Calais.) These historical examples contributed to this book.

Mac will be back in The Rise of Oceania Book Five: *The Shadow of War*.

Please visit me at Facebook @TSJAuthor and Twitter @TSJ_Author. Also visit www.timothysjohnston.com to receive updates and learn about new and upcoming thrillers, and also to register for news alerts.

My futuristic murder mysteries include *The Furnace* (2013), *The Freezer* (2014), and *The Void* (2015), all published by Carina Press.

Thanks again for investing your time in this novel. Do let me know what you think of my thrillers.

Timothy S. Johnston
tsj@timothysjohnston.com
1 May 2021

Coming soon from Timothy S. Johnston and Fitzhenry & Whiteside

THE SHADOW OF WAR

Book Five of The Rise of Oceania